The Worst Thing You Ever Did

KAREN PERRY

PENGUIN BOOKS

PENGUIN BOOKS

UK | USA | Canada | Ireland | Australia
India | New Zealand | South Africa

Penguin Books is part of the Penguin Random House group of companies
whose addresses can be found at global.penguinrandomhouse.com.

First published in Penguin Books 2023
002
Copyright © Karen Perry, 2023

The moral right of the author has been asserted

Set in 12.5/14.75pt Garamond MT Std
Typeset by Jouve (UK), Milton Keynes
Printed and bound in Great Britain by Clays Ltd, Elcograf S.p.A.

The authorized representative in the EEA is Penguin Random House Ireland,
Morrison Chambers, 32 Nassau Street, Dublin D02 YH68

A CIP catalogue record for this book is available from the British Library

ISBN: 978-1-405-94526-4

In spring 2010, the Icelandic volcano Eyjafjallajökull erupted. The cloud of ash from the eruption caused air travel chaos as flights across northern Europe were grounded. Thousands of travellers were left stranded as they waited for the ash cloud to disperse.

They're asleep when he enters the room. The soft rise and fall of breath, all that exhaled air – the staleness of it gathers between the bare floor and the stippled ceiling. His own breath is held fast in his chest. Important to make himself invisible, to maintain absolute silence as he moves through the darkness. But his heart is thumping so loudly it must surely give him away. At any moment they might wake and find him moving stealthily across the room towards the bassinet. He tries to swallow, but his mouth is dry, his whole body parched, wrung out. He needs to calm his ragged breathing, but time is running out.

A small swaddled shape lies in the basket, delicate wisps of hair on the sleeping head. A tiny fist has escaped from the confines of the blanket and is pressed against the infant's mouth.

If you love me, you'll do this, Faye had said.

Words like the sharp edge of a blade held to his throat. Words that continue to haunt him.

Rain patters evenly on the windowpanes like white noise. Something stirs on the ground beside him, the brush of an arm or a leg as a body rolls over, groaning in sleep. But the infant does not wake. Not even when he reaches down and takes the child, holds her close against his chest.

He backs out of the room the way he came, the soft bundle warm against his beating heart. The silence holds as he eases the door shut, then he turns the key in the lock.

PART ONE

I

Faye

It starts on the evening of Ed's book launch.

We're at home, both of us busy in our separate ways, bathing and grooming and readying ourselves for the night ahead. The house itself seems to have taken on a new energy, a fizz of excitement bubbling up through the domestic ease.

I'm standing in front of the hall mirror, putting in earrings – long gold dangly ones that were a gift from Ed on our first wedding anniversary – when he clatters down the stairs and pauses behind me, his hands on my hips, landing a kiss on the back of my neck.

'You look gorgeous,' he tells me, then continues down the hall into the kitchen, where copies of his book sit on the island in a neat stack. Scattered around them are cards of congratulations that had arrived in the post this morning; chilling in the fridge is a bottle of champagne sent by his publisher. Earlier in the day, I had heard the low drone of his voice coming from the attic bedroom he uses as a study, his warm melodious reading voice tentatively rehearsing the passage from the book he has chosen for tonight.

'We should eat something before we go,' I tell him, as I come into the kitchen and look around.

'I'm not sure I'll be able to,' he remarks, straightening up and putting his hands on his belly, and smiling haplessly. 'Nerves.'

He looks handsome, my husband, in his charcoal-grey suit, a crisp white shirt open at the collar to reveal a triangle of lightly tanned skin. He is that rare being: a red-head with sallow skin. It's the brown eyes, I suppose. My own hair is brownish in colour, tending to auburn, and my skin is pale and prone to freckling, hopelessly Irish. Back when I was a student, I wore my hair long – I can still remember the heavy swing of it, a chestnut shine from its natural hue. But after college – after everything that happened to me in Barcelona – I cut it short, and it's been short ever since. These days I wear it in a neat bob with blonde highlights. Catching a glimpse of myself in the reflective glass door of the oven, I see a carefully put-together look: neat eyebrows, subtle make-up, a linen dress with a square-cut neckline. Anyone who knew me back in those distant university days would scarcely recognize me now.

'You have to eat something,' I insist. 'All that wine on an empty stomach. We'll have cheese on toast, and then we'll go.'

He acquiesces, and I start pulling out ingredients from the fridge and the breadbin while he opens the grill.

'Christ, it's gotten in here too,' he exclaims. 'Look at this!'

He holds up the grill tray so I can see the fine layer of white dust coating it.

Six weeks have passed since we moved into our new home, and still, when I wake in the mornings, the roof of my mouth is coated with a thin powder, my tongue

6

parched. The plaster dust gets everywhere – on furniture, in cupboards; it clouds the windowpanes. In the bath this evening, I'd felt the grit of it between my skin and the enamel.

Ed says: 'It's like living in an ash cloud, don't you think?'

They're just words – a throwaway remark – but they come at me sideways, unexpectedly. Immediately the feeling surfaces: a tightening, as if I am bracing myself against a sudden blow. I try to keep my features calm and inexpressive, but he catches it nonetheless.

'What is it? What's wrong?' he asks, the grill pan still in his hand but his focus entirely on me now, the warmth of his brown eyes misting with curiosity and concern.

I could tell him. It is the opening I have needed. Almost as if by uttering the words 'ash cloud' he's given me licence to tell him everything – about Barcelona, about Michael, about the thing we did . . .

But the clenching inside me has reached my throat, cutting off the opening and sealing those words deep inside. Instead, I force a smile and step briskly forward, taking the grill pan from his hand, saying, 'Nothing. I'm just famished, that's all!' and busy myself rinsing the dust from the pan into the sink, while he turns his attention to slicing the cheese.

It worries me, though – how quickly it had awakened. An old pain that I thought was buried. A nerve touched to life that easily. I watch the ash sluicing down the drain and remind myself to be more careful.

It's a beautiful late-spring evening, the laburnum trees planted at the edge of our estate drop with bursts of golden-yellow flowers as I guide the car past them out on to the road. Ed is too nervous to drive. I'm feeling a little nervous myself. So much rests on how this event goes, and I can't help but feel responsible. He flips through his book, thumbing open to the pages marked with neon-pink Post-its, as well as reading through some words he has jotted down on a flashcard, silently rehearsing his lines while I navigate the traffic.

'Relax,' I tell him. 'You're going to be amazing.'

He exhales and grins. 'If you say so.'

'Grab a glass of wine when you get there to calm the nerves, and then enjoy the evening. This is your night, love. Soak up every bit of it.'

He reaches across and squeezes my knee. 'Thanks.'

'For what?'

'I dunno. For knowing what to say. How to calm me.' Adding, as an afterthought: 'Unlike my dad.'

'Oh? Did something happen?'

'He sent me a text earlier when you were in the bath.' Picking up his phone, he reads from the screen: *Faber est quisque fortunae suae.*

'Translation?'

'*Each man is the maker of his own fortune.*'

I feel the prickliness emanating from him, and think, not for the first time, that he needs to be less sensitive about these things. His father, in particular, gets under his skin. 'I think he means well, Ed.'

'You don't think it's some kind of a dig? You know, like he's telling me to go and paddle my own canoe, instead of hijacking his?'

'You've been talking about writing this book ever since

8

I've known you. If anything, the reason it's taken you so long to do it is your father and his career.'

It's a sore point, this. The shadow of his father's success looms large over this new writing enterprise, and Ed has confided in me on occasion about his fear of being judged in comparison with his father's considerable body of work.

'I asked him if he would introduce me this evening,' he tells me, adding that it was his publisher's suggestion.

'And?'

'The old man turned me down. Said that he *didn't want to draw the attention away from me on what should be my night.*' These last words he utters in his father's characteristic stiff and gruff delivery.

'He was probably trying to be considerate.'

'You think?' he asks sceptically.

'Of course. He is sensitive to the fact that comparisons will be made between the two of you. If he's trying to distance himself, it's only so that you can stand on your own rather than in his shadow.'

'I suppose so,' he admits quietly.

I look across and see the tightness of his jaw, the pinch of anxiety in the furrow of his brow, and I feel a corresponding squeeze of uncertainty within myself and wonder, not for the first time, whether we've made a mistake. And, if we have, then it's all my fault.

Neither one of us had ever intended returning to Ireland – not to live, anyway. Even our trips home at Christmas were always brief – a bare forty-eight hours before jumping back on a plane and taking off for some far-flung destination, our 'real' holiday. Ireland was a duty, a burden that we had both long ago shrugged off. Our lives were in London, Ed working in the theatre, me with my role at the UK branch of Enterprise Ireland. We had our flat in Fulham, a good circle of friends with whom we shared a busy social life, weekends away, foreign holidays. We were happy. And then, one afternoon, at a lunch organized by the British-Irish Council, I found myself sitting next to Jess Power, a businesswoman from home that I had dealt with frequently over the years. Jess was in town raising finance for her latest venture – a small tech company focusing on data analytics for the consumer market. I'd set up meetings for her with some investors, and we'd ended up spending much of the week together. She was forthright, sparky with ideas, a straight-talker – the kind of person who might be intimidating, but I enjoyed her company.

'I've been thinking,' she told me as our entrées were cleared away, 'I need someone to help me to scale up the business. Someone efficient, practical, an organizer who can act on her own initiative. Someone just like you, in fact.'

'Are you offering me a job?' I asked, joking, surprised, then, when she replied: 'Yes.'

My first instinct was to refuse, uttering platitudes about being flattered by her offer, but she waved them away with impatience.

'I'm not talking about some office manager Girl Friday role,' she insisted, 'but a senior role. It might not be permanent and pensionable like the job you have here – but you'd be an independent consultant on a generous daily rate, as well as being a member of our board. And we could work something into the package about share options, the chance for you to have some equity in the company. Just think about it, Faye – an opportunity to be involved in something new and innovative and exciting. Instead of sitting on the sidelines, you'd have a chance to actually get your hands dirty, to be involved from within, building a company from the ground up!'

Her enthusiasm was infectious, and, despite my misgivings, I found myself getting drawn in to the exclusion of all other conversation around me. Jess and I spent the rest of the lunch discussing her plans and how I could be involved, what my role would entail. An ember of excitement fanned by her passion was kindled into a small fire. I came away from that lunch with a new spring in my step, temporarily carried along on a wave of ambition. It was only when I got home that evening and raised the matter with Ed that my excitement made contact with reality.

'Leave London?' he said, his forehead creased into a frown. 'You'd actually consider that?'

'Maybe. For the right job.'

'And you think this is it?'

'I think it's worth giving it some thought.'

'Well. By all means think about it.' He turned away from me then, glanced down at his phone. 'There's a Kurosawa movie showing at the Picture House shortly,' he remarked. 'Do you want to go?'

We went to the cinema that evening, both of us quietly simmering in the darkness, and on the walk home the row erupted. He didn't want to leave London, he argued, and it was selfish of me to assume he would up sticks and go back to Ireland just so I could indulge some entrepreneurial fantasy. I accused him of hypocrisy, all his talk of being an enlightened modern man who believed in equal rights for women just meaningless bullshit. When it came down to it, he deemed my career to be second to his, even though I easily out-earned him. It was an ugly argument, shaking free the resentments we had each quietly harboured and unleashing words from within us that should never have been spoken. Ed slept on the sofa that night, and I made no attempt to dissuade him. It was not an auspicious start.

We made up the next morning, both of us weary and contrite and needful of regaining our usual balance. I rang Jess on the way to work, thanked her for the offer but explained that I was not yet ready to give up my life in London and return to Ireland.

'When you're ready, come and talk to me,' she said, and I promised that I would, while thinking that it was never going to happen.

We went back to the way things were, but something was different. While I had been aware for some time that I had been coasting at work, now I felt actively bored. I began putting out feelers for potential job offers, but nothing really captured my imagination. My unhappiness at work seeped into our home. Our flat felt too small and cramped. I was aware of being unsettled and tense. Weekends away were an escape, but, as soon as darkness fell on Sunday evening, the sense of restlessness drifted in once more. I told myself that these feelings would pass. That things would change. But still it kept needling away at me, so that when the first lockdown was announced weeks later, and Ed's work in the theatre dried up overnight, the possibility of returning home to Ireland felt like a kind of solution. Ed began working on the novel he'd always talked about writing, and, quietly, I'd contacted Jess to see whether the job prospect was still a live one. This time, when I raised the idea with Ed, he did not seem so averse, and as the weeks passed slowly I worked away at him, persuading him that it made sense. We had both felt the worrying distance between us and our elderly parents back home over the long months when we couldn't travel, the constant spectre of the virus and their vulnerability to it hanging over us. Eventually, he acquiesced. We sold our flat and made the move back to Dublin, purchasing a new-build in Blackrock, a suburb of South Dublin, straight off the plans. Ed finished his book and found a publisher, while I threw myself into my new job, exhilarated by the challenges and the rewards. For all my doubts and anxieties, it has turned out better than I had hoped.

And now there is to be a new change to our lives, more vast and profound than all that has gone before. Earlier in the week, the two us had sat huddled side by side at the edge of our bed, staring as two pink lines appeared on the wand in my hand. Another pregnancy test yesterday had yielded the same result, and it seems miraculous to both of us: that we should receive this blessing on top of everything else we are fortunate enough to possess.

Sitting up a bit in his seat, Ed brightens with a new idea. 'Hey, do you think we should tell them this evening?' he asks. 'Mum and Dad? About the baby.'

'You're kidding, right?' My voice rises with incredulity, and he laughs.

'I know what you're going to say: that it's early days —'

'It's far too soon!'

'But I'm dying to tell someone! And just think how happy they'd be!'

'No —'

'I could announce it from the lectern, when I get up to make my speech.'

'Don't you dare!' I cry, and he laughs.

'Don't worry. I wouldn't go that far.'

'Let's just try and get through the first trimester,' I plead. 'I know you're not superstitious, but I really don't want to risk telling people and then something going wrong.'

'Fair enough,' he concedes, giving a mock sigh of disappointment, and I can't help thinking how boyish and handsome he looks.

'Besides,' I add, flicking my indicator as I pull the car into a space, 'don't you think it's sort of special, that this is just between you and me? Our own little secret?'

My husband, with his open face, his warm brown eyes and clear gaze, takes his eyes off the road for just an instant and looks at me. 'I've never much liked secrets,' he declares.

The launch is being held on the upper floor of a bookshop; its large windows give on to a sideview of Trinity College, the cricket pitches glowing green in the evening sunlight. Sounds of the bell and soft acceleration of a tram are carried up from the street below. Almost immediately,

Ed is handed a glass of wine and ushered away to sign books, while members of staff create a little fuss around him. Soon guests start arriving and the room quickly fills. I edge my way around, greeting friends of Ed as well as some of his parents' set who have come along to celebrate. Some of my work colleagues have turned up, and I detach myself from the group I am in and go to join them. Jess, my boss, puts an arm around my shoulders and gives me a warm squeeze.

'Look at this!' she cries, waving the glass in her hand in a sweep of the room.

'It's a great turnout,' I remark.

Conversation is at a roar, and we have to lean in towards each other, shouting to be heard, but the arrival of my parents-in-law heralds a temporary hush. Regina – small and stout with a permanent expression of merriment on her face that belies a steely resolve – leads the way, Desmond's hand tucked under her elbow. By far the taller of the pair, even with the stoop that has entered his frame this last year, Desmond looks distinguished, urbane, his thinning hair blazing white beneath the overhead lights.

'The great man himself,' Jess says, observing the customary awe his presence generates.

'I can't believe Desmond Sharpe is your father-in-law!' Kelly exclaims. 'I've read nearly everything he's ever written!'

This is no surprise to me. Kelly, our receptionist, always has a book on the go. Her literary tastes are pretty catholic, judging by the various paperbacks she keeps discreetly tucked away behind the front desk: from potboilers to science fiction to the latest Booker Prize winner, her reading matter seems indiscriminate. She's already purchased Ed's book and examines the cover now.

'Look at it. Just gorgeous,' she remarks, and it's true, the cover image of verdant green foliage with the title tooled in gold is a thing of beauty. 'You must be so proud of him!'

From across the room, I see Ed being drawn towards the lectern. Dan, Ed's publisher, is clearing his throat and testing the microphone, before casting his gaze around the crowd expectantly. Ed catches my eye and flashes me a nervous look, and I raise my hands to mime hands on a steering-wheel and mouth the words: 'Drive it like you stole it,' and his mouth widens into a smile that catches at my heart, a smile charged with the warmth and charisma that first floored me all those years ago.

Later, I will look back on this moment – the clarity of light falling through the window, the cheery cacophony of voices, the swelling tide of goodwill – and recognize it as my last moment of pure happiness. My heart full and unfettered, joyful at the sudden and profound realization that this is my life. This man, this family. All of these people are gathered here together because of us. Yes, it's Ed's night, but I am intimately part of it. And it feels, somehow, miraculous. Barely any time at all, it seems, has passed since I was a student, working four nights a week in a bar on Leeson Street, struggling to pay my rent on a shared room in digs to the west of the city. But, now, here I am surrounded by all these people imbibing wine on a warm spring evening and swapping book chat, while my husband holds court at the centre of it all. And he and I have started something. A secret that lies deep within the fibres of my body, where cells divide and multiply, threading together to create a new piece in the jigsaw of our life together.

'Ladies and gentlemen,' Dan begins, pausing to allow the crowd to hush, and it is at that moment that Kelly whispers: 'Oh, Faye. I almost forgot! This came for you.' She slides a blue envelope from her handbag. 'It was dropped into the office just after you left. I'd have waited until Monday to give it to you, only it looked personal.'

I take it from her and glance down. There's a floral motif in one corner of the envelope, and my name is written in a shaky scrawl – *Faye Sadlier*.

'That is you, isn't it?' Kelly asks. 'I wasn't sure because of Sadlier –'

'It's my maiden name,' I tell her. 'I don't use it much any more.'

It starts then, the rumble at the edge of my thoughts. A feeling of familiarity, like déjà vu. As if I've seen this someplace before.

'Aren't you going to open it?' she asks.

The noise around is suddenly too loud, voices like a swarm of bees.

'Christ, it's hot in here,' Jess says, fanning herself with a copy of Ed's book as she looks around the room.

With my index finger, I slit open the envelope. Inside there's a single sheet of paper, and I see at once that it is a newspaper cutting, an old one, judging by the yellowed paper, the smudged print, the creases along the folds worn away to tearing point. I unfold it quickly, and stare at it, cold pooling in the pit of my stomach. The headline reads:

IRISH FLIGHTS GROUNDED AS ICELANDIC ASH
SHUTS AIRSPACE

I don't read the article underneath. I don't need to. Instead, my eyes pass quickly over the word that has been scrawled over the text in red marker, the ink bleeding through the page.

'Why do they always overheat these rooms?' Jess demands.

The cold moves upwards from my stomach. It wraps around my heart. I stuff the clipping back in the envelope quickly before either Jess or Kelly can snatch a glimpse.

At that moment, my husband steps towards the podium, and the audience begin to applaud. The sound of it echoes loudly in my head. I feel the long reach of the past, and all the assurances I'd given myself – that it was behind me, that nobody would ever find out – evaporate. The envelope in my hand throbs with its own imagined pulse, the poisonous word flashing across my mind's eye:

Murderer.

2

Faye

It does something to you, this kind of fear. Outwardly, you can appear normal. You can smile and clap and even laugh in the right places throughout your husband's speech whenever he cracks a joke. But, on the inside, there's paralysis. Not the inward jangling of nerves but a total stillness, almost like calm, in which you become hyper-vigilant, alive to everything around you.

He could be in the room. Now, at this very moment. He could be here, watching me. The thought is shocking to me. It makes me want to crane my neck, to swing around and survey the gathered faces, but I'm positioned awkwardly near the front of the crowd; curious glances steal in my direction – me, the wife Ed lovingly credits with being his support and his inspiration.

'When the pandemic hit, and my work in theatre dried up overnight,' he says, 'it was Faye who encouraged me to write. Thankfully, I was on furlough at the time, so I suppose you could say that I have not just Faye to thank but also Rishi Sunak.'

The crowd laughs, and I have to force my face into an expression of mirth, but my skin prickles, nerves communicating from my hairline all the way to the base of my spine. I keep still and absorb the soft timbre of my husband's reading voice as he shares a passage of his novel, sentences that he has painstakingly crafted, phrases he has agonized over, loved. But as soon as it is over and a ripple of applause moves through the crowd, I turn around, my eyes searching the faces assembled there, combing the room for a glimpse of a tall thin youth, floppy blond hair, a pale blue gaze.

'Didn't he read well?' Kelly says, snapping my attention back. 'And an amazing turnout.'

Jess agrees. 'Hard to believe that this wouldn't have been possible a year or two ago, right?'

'Right,' I say. 'Umm, Kelly? That letter you gave me – you didn't happen to see who delivered it, did you?'

She thinks for a moment, then shakes her head. 'Sorry, Faye. It was so busy this afternoon. Why? Is everything okay?'

'Yes, fine. It doesn't matter,' I tell her, a sweep of embarrassment coming over me at having drawn her attention to it.

I'm grateful when the PR girl interrupts us. 'Do you mind if I steal you away for just a sec?' she asks.

There's a photographer waiting with his Nikon; he groups us together amid the shelves, Ed holding his book in front of his chest, flanked by me and his parents, his sister, Martha, on my other side. Martha has brought along both of her children; the youngest, at five months old, is strapped to her chest. I look down at his bare pudgy feet, his little kicking heels, and think of the tiny being sprouting deep inside me, the size of a blueberry according to what I've gleaned from the Internet. There is something growing inside me that already has tooth-buds and kidneys. It's a vertiginous sensation, and, in the light of the letter burning a hole in my bag, it makes me feel a jolt of panic.

'Perhaps we could get one of father and son together?' the photographer suggests.

Martha turns to me and murmurs: 'We know when we're not wanted.' Then she smiles to show no harm is meant, and Regina adds with a tinkle of knowing laughter: 'Oh, you'll get used to it, Faye! Trust me.'

I have always liked Regina – her easy warmth, her tremendous ability to set people at their ease, a contrast with her husband, whose military bearing and gruff manner has earned him the family nickname of The Major.

'How're you holding up?' she enquires. 'Not always easy, being the one in the background. Acting as the scaffold to these creative types.'

Her warmth calms my anxiety, helps me to push down on the fear that has risen out of the blue.

'I'm just glad that the book is out there now,' I tell her. 'Despite all reassurances, Ed's been nervous.'

'I can imagine. He's always been a bit of a worrier. A wee bit insecure. He's like his father in that way.'

I cannot imagine the gruff imperious Major being anything other than solidly confident and say as much.

She laughs. 'Age and success have abraded much of his insecurity, of course, and I'm sure the same will be true of my son.'

We talk some more about the book, the launch, the people who are there.

'I didn't see Maggie and Leonard,' she remarks delicately, referring to my mother and her boyfriend. 'They couldn't make it?'

'I'm afraid not,' I lie. I didn't invite them.

It's hard to explain, even to someone as empathetic and understanding as Regina, how difficult I find it to be in the same room as my mother. How nervous she makes me. I know that if I had invited her, she would have come this evening, shown up wearing something festive and glittering, her confidence bolstered beforehand with a glass of wine or two. She would have showered Ed with praise and me with affection; she would have been delightful and charming to those around her. And, all the while, I would have been watching her. Watching her accept another glass of wine when it was offered, her stories getting a little more adventurous, a bit more risqué. I'd have been tense, waiting for the strain to appear in her face, the telltale pull of muscles in her neck as she looked around for whatever young man or woman was carrying the bottle, refilling the drinks. And soon enough it would have happened. Someone around her would have laughed too loudly, or said something stupid, and she would have snapped like an elastic band, mimicking the person's laughter, or openly deriding the silly thing that had been said.

I've lost count of the ugly scenes over the years, the humiliations, the tempers lost, the offences given. Even at my own wedding, when she'd drunk too much and openly derided my new in-laws.

'Oh, Faye,' she'd sighed with a growl of exasperation. 'Those people – how can you bear them?'

'Stop it. They'll hear you.'

'God forbid!' she'd laughed. 'That Regina – holier-than-thou and so judgy. I can almost hear her saying: "Look, there she is, the woman who abandoned her daughter."'

Regina was standing nearby, pretending not to listen, but I could tell from the way her neck stiffened that she could hear every cruel word.

'And as for him, *The Major*,' Maggie drawled in mockery. 'The way we all have to bow down and kiss his ring. Disgusting!'

'They're nice people.'

'*They're nice people!*' She'd turned on me then, making an ugly parody of my politeness to Ed's parents, deriding my respect for them as sycophancy, demanding to know how any daughter of hers could demean herself by bowing down to the patriarchy in that way, going on and on until I burst into tears and Ed intervened with a few home truths about how Maggie was hardly a paragon of parenting, having practically abandoned me once I hit my teens, throwing her own words back at her, words that she had spat at me on a particularly low point in my childhood: 'God, I wish I'd never had you!'

The words hit their mark. She'd recoiled, wounded, and, despite the miasma of drink that engulfed her, I saw the sharp pain in her eyes. The worst thing she had ever said to me, and I had told him. I had snitched. To her, there was no lower sin. Loyalty was everything.

She had drawn herself in, tilted her chin a little higher with defiance. 'It wasn't easy, being a single mother. I made mistakes, but God knows I did my best.'

There was no point in fighting; our positions were too

entrenched, and the argument always spiralled off in the same direction. She railed at what she saw as my refusal to accept the difficulties involved in single-parenting, whereas I maintained that she didn't raise me at all, dumping me on my grandparents at every available opportunity.

The day after the wedding she was all apologies. But a new distance had come between us – a coldness. It's been there ever since.

Perhaps it would have been different if there had been a father on the scene, if she hadn't had to do it alone. A voice shimmers up from the darkness: '*Poor fatherless child.*' Michael's soft voice, blue eyes glinting with humour, but there was tenderness too. More than anyone, he had understood what it was like to feel the keen absence of a father. He too had had a difficult relationship with his mother.

'Well, we'd best be getting on,' Regina says, breaking my train of thought.

She glances across at Desmond, who looks tired and cross, and then reaches out to hug me. I inhale her scent, floral and powdery, and feel the firmness of her embrace and it calms me. During the course of our conversation, I have given no thought to the letter in my bag and this, somehow, lessens its power. If I were to show it to Regina now, she would dismiss it as rubbish. 'Just some idiot with too much time on their hands,' she would reassure me before urging me to get rid of it.

And, as we leave the bookshop and spill out on to the street, I take the envelope from my bag, crumple it in my hand and drop it in the nearest bin.

*

24

We head to Grand Canal Square, where Dan, the publisher, has arranged some post-launch celebratory drinks. My heels click on the paving stones, the red lighting poles of the square sizzling against a turquoise sky as people move in groups towards the theatre and restaurants, a distinctive end-of-week vibe in the air. I've regained my optimism, having shaken off my earlier fright, and I squeeze my husband's hand, as the chequerboard frontage of the Marker Hotel rises up before us. He pulls open the door for me.

'Shall we?' he grins.

Inside, it is a storm of noise. Styled like the underground lair of a Bond villain, the vaulted ceiling is all geometric shapes and gold up-lighting, a Modernist cavern where the denizens of the surrounding offices congregate on a Friday evening. A few grey-haired theatregoers are digging into their pre-show plates of chicken masala, their cod and chips, but in reality this is the realm of the young executive type – well dressed, well groomed, with money to spend.

Dan's fiancée has arranged to meet us there, and, across the sea of people, a woman with a black angular haircut and a slash of purple lipstick rises and waves us over. She greets Ed with a kiss on the cheek, congratulating him on his book, and, as she turns to me for an introduction, I notice her smile slip, a frown of confusion clouding her face.

'Faye? Faye Sadlier?' she asks in a low voice, and a jolt of alarm goes through me. The second time this evening my maiden name has been used. 'Oh my God, is it really you?' she says, her voice rising. 'Don't you remember me? It's Suzi. Suzi Moore.'

Memory comes in a rush: the Spiegeltent, a brass band playing jazz, the sticky taste of sambuca in my mouth, Michael's hand in mine, and a skinny girl in a crop-top that showed off her pierced navel, her eyes widening with wicked delight, saying: 'Michael, you dark horse. You never told us you were bringing *a girl*!'

She's reaching for me now, and I'm surprised at the strength of feeling in her hug, the rush of familiarity that comes over me as her sharp bony frame crushes against mine. When we draw back from each other, she's still holding my arms, shaking her head and smiling with amazement. 'Faye Sadlier. Jesus, I can't believe it.'

'I haven't been called by that name in a long time,' I tell her, laughing with the surprise. It's so strange being back in her company again – the force of her attention, the familiar fruity strains in her voice.

'Old friends?' Ed guesses.

'We knew each other at university,' I explain.

'God, UCD seems like a million years ago now,' Suzi says. 'I almost didn't recognize you. And your hair! It used to be so long and thick! You look so sleek and put-together now. Whatever happened to the Doc Martens and baggy jumpers?'

'Wait. Let's get some drinks,' Dan says. 'Then let's hear all about Faye's fashion crimes.'

We laugh and a waiter comes to take our order, Suzi's amazement still evident, her eyes passing over my clothes, my hair, my figure. Nothing unfriendly in her gaze, but I can see her absorbing all the changes that I have carefully and meticulously applied to myself. She shakes her head in amazement. 'I always wondered what happened to you.

After you and Michael broke up, it was as if each of you vanished into thin air.'

'Who's this?' Ed asks.

'No one. Just a guy I went out with for a while.'

Suzi shakes her head in disbelief, and says to Ed: 'I can't believe you've never heard about him.'

'That serious, eh?' he grins, but I can tell beneath his humour there's a question.

'You remember the way it was back in college,' she explains to the men. 'There was always one couple who got together early on, and then remained a constant. While the rest of us were flitting from one break-up to the next and snogging anything with a pulse, still there was this one couple who remained rock steady. Like we were the kids and they were the grown-ups, you know? That was Faye and Michael.'

I laugh to make light of it, trying to disavow her words.

'He was a sweet guy,' I say, 'but we were both young. At that stage of life, things appear to be more serious than they actually are.'

'Didn't you live with him for a while?' Suzi asks.

Ed's gaze sharpens.

'No –'

'In that weird creepy house out in Monkstown. Or was it Dalkey? I forget. Oh, and that old crone he used to live with. Moll, or Maisie, or something. God, what was her name?'

Min. Her name was Min.

'I don't remember,' I answer, my voice level.

'She was about ninety,' Suzi tells the men, 'and pickled in gin. She smoked these disgusting black cigarettes and flirted like mad with all the boys while fixing her gimlet eye on any girl that happened to wander across her threshold. I wonder if she's still alive?'

'So what happened?' Ed asks pointedly. 'With you and what's-his-name?'

I give a casual shrug. 'He went away to Germany for his Erasmus year and we broke up.'

'Just like that, eh?'

I catch his eye. 'Yes. Pretty much. As I say, we were young. Once he went away, we both realized it had run its course. I sat my Finals, and by the time he came back from Erasmus I had moved to London.'

'And you never heard from him again?' he asks.

I think of all the unread letters, the unanswered phone calls, all the emails directed straight to trash.

'Are you telling me you stay in touch with all your exes?' I laugh.

'Fair enough,' Ed concedes, holding up his hands in surrender.

'But what about you two?' Suzi interjects. 'How did you guys meet?'

I'm grateful for her interruption, steering us back into safer waters. Ed and I look at each other and smile.

'I stole her away from another man,' he jokes, and I laugh.

'Hardly!'

I tell them the story – a first date with a guy I'd met at a party. At my suggestion we'd gone to see a play in a small theatre off the West End. During the first act, my date had closed his eyes and was soon snoring gently. At the interval, he excused himself to use the gents but didn't return.

I'd spent the second act next to an empty seat, reconciling myself to the rejection.

'It was only when the curtain fell and the lights came up that I looked beyond the empty seat and saw this handsome guy smiling at me.'

Ed takes up the story. 'I leaned over and asked if she'd been abandoned. When she said yes, I said one man's loss is another man's gain, and asked her if I could buy her a drink.'

'And that was it,' I finish, warmed by the memory of that night, that first meeting, which still has the power to evoke such feeling within me.

I have heard Ed telling people that when we met it was love at first sight. A small exaggeration, but there's no denying how swiftly things got serious between us. Privately, Ed admitted to me that I was a lifeline for him. That I helped to draw him out of darkness and back into a normal life. In the two years before we met, he'd gone off the rails, lost his way. It began one night when, walking home from a party, he'd been jumped on by a gang of teenagers who'd stolen his wallet and left him bleeding out on the pavement, a stab wound in his belly. The alarm was raised by someone in one of the neighbouring houses, and Ed was rushed to hospital. He'd lost a lot of blood, but his injuries were not life-threatening and within a week he was patched up and discharged. But, while his physical wounds healed, the psychological ones festered. He felt scared all the time. He couldn't sleep, couldn't eat. He tried to drown it all out with booze and then drugs, but nothing worked. For about a year, he just slipped off the grid. When his parents finally tracked him down, he was living on a barge with six other people and three dogs. It took a lot of hard conversations and much persuasion, but they got him out of there and helped him to find his way. Through friends of his parents, he found work in a London theatre. Administrative work, but he'd enjoyed the proximity to the creative arts and was grateful for the regularity of employment. I came along shortly afterwards, providing the support – the scaffolding – that he needed.

Neither of us mentions this to either Suzi or Dan. It's a private matter, and I know how sensitive Ed is about his struggles with mental health. And, while I didn't know him during that dark and difficult time, I have glimpsed his vulnerability on the rare occasion he opens up about it. Each time he does, it breaks my heart a little. I can't bear to think of him in such pain.

Our conversation splits then. Dan and Ed turn to each other and talk about next steps for the book. Suzi pulls her chair closer to mine. She sips her cocktail and leans in, her voice lowered so the men won't hear.

'I hope I didn't stir up any trouble for you? All that talk of Michael –'

'No! God. Ancient history.'

'You're sure?' Her eyes watchful, confidential.

'Honestly.'

'And you really didn't keep in touch with him?'

'Really! Sometimes you just need a clean break, you know?'

'Hmm. But, you did hear about what happened, how he dropped out? You did know about that, right?' she asks.

I shake my head no, a teetering feeling inside. She sees the look on my face and her own expression changes, grows gentle but serious.

'Look, I don't know the full details. All I heard was that he was in the library one day and he just lost it. One minute he's sitting quietly at a desk, the next thing he's tearing the place apart. One of the librarians tried to intervene and she was knocked unconscious.'

I can feel her eyes on me, but cannot meet her gaze, too stunned by this information, eviscerated by old feelings. 'What happened to him?' I ask.

'I'm not sure. I'd broken up with JP at that stage, so I wasn't hanging around with Michael's group any more. But I did hear that after the incident in the library he never went back to university. As far as I know, he never even sat his Finals.'

Our drinks arrive, and I'm grateful for the diversion. My mouth is dry, the room is too hot, all these memories clamouring in my head. I gulp my Virgin Mojito, wishing there was a dash of something stronger in it. The room is full now, cacophonous. A heated conversation between a couple at the bar is climbing to a crescendo, until the woman – pink-cheeked with rage, the wings of her hair swinging – tosses her drink into his face, and stalks out. We watch with a guilty amusement as the man dabs at his dripping face with paper napkins, before resuming our conversation.

'I met him once,' Suzi tells me, 'a few years back – Michael. I was coming out of Fallon & Byrne and bumped into him, right there on Exchequer Street. We stopped and talked for a few minutes.'

'Oh?'

'Just small talk. He'd gone back to Wexford, he told me, and was living with his mother.'

This piece of information pierces me in a way I find unexpected. Theirs had been a difficult relationship. In all our time together, I met her only once. I remember a small, well-put-together woman – cashmere jumper, corduroy skirt, lipstick of a subtle shade – an air of quiet perfection about her. She smiled throughout our introduction, while her eyes roamed busily over my clothing as if hunting for a stray bit of lint to pick off.

'I can't imagine him going back there. They never really got on.'

'Maybe he had no other option,' she says, adding: 'To be honest, Faye, I was fairly shocked by his appearance. He looked dreadful. Overweight, pasty skin, hair unkempt. His clothes were dishevelled and dirty. And he used to be so good-looking. Remember how the boys used to tease him in college about how metrosexual he was? Although he always seemed sort of neutered to me. Sexless. But that's what made it so disturbing.' She casts a sideways glance at the men, then lowers her voice. 'The bang off him.' Her nose wrinkles with distaste.

I don't respond. The thread is there – the twitching sensation of a thin skein of fibre running behind my navel, rousing a wave of nausea. And I think once more of the note I'd received, the newspaper clipping about the ash cloud, and wonder: why is he doing this? What does he want from me?

'You know, it's funny,' she says, 'seeing you this evening – how different you are to how I remember you – well, it's almost the same as how I felt when I bumped into Michael on the street. Both of you have changed – changed considerably.' She picks up her glass, still looking at me, and I feel the question in her stare. 'It hardly seems fair, though,' she adds.

'What do you mean?'

Her eyes narrow as she takes in my hair, my make-up, the diamond pendant that hangs off the delicate gold chain circling my neck.

'You and Michael. Where he has declined, you have thrived.'

Lying awake in bed that night, I briefly conjure this new image of Michael that Suzi has described: dishevelled, dirty. It hovers greyly in the shadows of my bedroom, wraith-like. I am bothered by Suzi's words – her doom-ridden account. It threatens to tap into the deep well of guilt inside me. Michael – my beautiful boy – has he really become this wretched creature?

In the darkness, my mind returns to that one occasion when he took me back home to Wexford. I can't remember the details of the occasion – a cousin's birthday, or an anniversary – some family gathering he was required to attend. I had bought a present to give to his mother, Nuala – a milk jug patterned with jaunty-looking bluebells beneath the glazed surface. She had accepted it with warmth and politeness. It was not until later in the evening, when I was returning from the bathroom, that I passed the open kitchen door and overheard a snippet of conversation between Michael's mother and his stepfather as they cleared away the dishes.

'Where do you want this to go?' Jeff asked.

'That ugly thing? Just shove it to the back of the cabinet,' she answered, her voice tired, drained of energy.

'It was sweet of her to bring it, though,' he remarked, and I realized they were talking about me, about the little jug I'd brought.

'Yes, I know. It's just a shame, that's all,' Nuala went on. 'It's clear she hasn't any taste.'

The burn of that remark travels back up through the years, coming for me once more as I lie in my bed, hot-cheeked and furious.

The silence in the room is punctuated by the distant shrieks of foxes mating in the strip of wasteland beyond the perimeter of our estate. The only other sound is the undulating rhythm of my husband's breathing. He has gone to bed tired, happy, a little drunk, and fallen asleep quickly. I turn my face to look at him, and imagine reaching out to grip his shoulder, to shake him awake gently and say: 'There's something I need to tell you . . .'

My hand hovers briefly in the air, poised above him, but the moment passes and I draw it back under the covers, turning over on to my other side. How could I even begin to tell him? The thought of his reaction, the expression of shock that would fill his face – how appalled he would be – makes me shrink back under the covers.

3

Michael

April 2010

They were in Barcelona when the volcano erupted.

Michael learned of it first. He had woken early, thirsty, with a hankering for something sweet, and, leaving Faye asleep under the low eaves of their hotel bedroom, he had dressed quietly, then slipped from the room. Passing through the windowless Reception area, the darkness broken only by the bluish light of the vending machine and the flickering illumination of the TV behind the desk, his eye was caught by an image on the screen: a plume of smoke rising from the low curve of a mountain, forming a cloud in the pale blue sky above. Beneath the image, a line of text moved along the news ticker. Michael didn't stop to read it. He nodded in the direction of the man behind the desk, who barely glanced at him, and then walked out into the warm spring sunshine.

The hotel where they were staying was to the north of the Ramblas – a grotty little place near the train station. It was cheap and as close to central as they could afford, but at this early hour, with the sun just starting to warm the air, the streets seemed less seedy, less threatening than they had appeared to him when he had arrived the day before. He had landed in Barcelona first, his flight from Dusseldorf touching down just after 10 a.m. Faye's flight from Dublin wasn't scheduled to touch down until late in the afternoon, and rather than waiting for her at the airport he'd made his way to their hotel. With his backpack heavy on his shoulders, he'd hurried through the streets radiating out from the station, chaotic with traffic and noise; and, consulting his map, he'd navigated roads and lanes which grew cramped and filthy as he neared the hotel. A stink rose from the drains, and neon signs suggesting cheap booze and prostitution flashed in the windows of dodgy-looking establishments.

The guy behind the desk who'd checked him in had been terse and scowling, and when Michael finally reached his room, up five narrow flights of stairs, he'd found to his disbelief that he was unable to stand to his full six feet of height and was forced to crouch a little to avoid his head hitting the ceiling. The room contained a bed and a tiny wardrobe. The window wouldn't open and gave on to a view of a water-tank blackened with grime, and from the tiny adjacent shower room came a lingering smell of disinfectant and urine. Michael had sat on the bed, deflated, and felt an agitation stirring in his stomach.

His nerves had stemmed from the prospect of their reunion. It was almost three months since they'd last seen each other; the longest they'd been apart since that first sunny evening on the West Pier over two years previously. He'd gone for an evening swim, and was sitting on the grass reading, when he looked up from his book and saw a girl he recognized from his class at university. A small girl in a red T-shirt, with heavy reddish-brown hair – she was pushing a bike along the path when their eyes met. He was struck dumb by the force of the green gaze coming from her elfin face. A thunderbolt, he'd called it later, and she too had described how all the noise and clamour of the evening crowd on the busy walkway by the sea had fallen away, so that there was only her and him. They spoke these words aloud to each other, not caring how prosaic it sounded. Passion, like a struck match that had lasted through first and second year, weathering the storms of parental disapproval, flickering beneath the bemused teasing of their peers. And when Michael had been accepted on the Erasmus programme and packed his bags for a year in Germany, they both believed their love would endure the time and distance apart.

But, as Michael sat in that cramped bedroom, the bedspread a depressing brown chenille, he felt the doubt pressing in. Would they still feel the same way about each other? All had been well between them the last time he'd come home – an unexpected trip necessitated by his mother's sudden illness. It was a common theme, these bouts of ill health in his mother. Whenever she was feeling a little down, a little ignored, Nuala would discover a lump or develop some worrying symptom that led to blood tests, scans, a period of anxious waiting. His mother was a hypochondriac, Michael had explained, although Faye seemed to think the woman was spoiled, an attention-seeker. Perhaps she was right. The illness – whatever it was – seemed to clear up quickly once Michael returned. A day or two of sitting by her bedside, drinking tea and swapping stories, and she seemed to rally.

It was when Michael was preparing to leave again that

he suggested they break the long separation between then and the summer with a weekend in Barcelona in April. Faye had met the idea with the wide-eyed delight and exuberance that he loved her for. He had booked and paid for the tickets, found accommodation online, made all the arrangements. But lately, in her letters and emails, he had noticed a new vagueness; the outlines of her days became blurry and distant to him. In their weekly phone conversations, he sensed hesitation and reluctance whenever he raised the subject of their forthcoming reunion. When he tried to tackle her about it, she was lightly dismissive of his concerns. She was just tired, she said, and anxious about her forthcoming exams. Faye had not applied for Erasmus, as he had done, choosing instead to go straight into her final year. This was partly down to the brute reality of her financial situation – unlike Michael, she simply could not afford to take a year out – but also because she was eager to graduate and then begin a research Master's degree, for which she had already received a tentative offer.

'You are sure you want to come?' he'd asked in their last phone conversation, after they'd hammered out the details of when and where they'd meet.

'Of course I want to,' she'd replied. 'It's just –'

'Just what?'

'I just wish it wasn't so close to my exams,' she'd admitted. 'I want to be able to be with you and not have the shadow of them looming over me.'

'It's just one weekend,' he'd said, hoping he didn't sound whiny and petulant.

'I know.'

'Come on, you deserve a break! If anyone has earned it, you have.'

She thought about this for a moment, then conceded: 'You're right. Fuck it. A couple of days is not going to make a difference.'

'Absolutely! And I'm going to spoil you this weekend –'

'Oh, Michael.'

He had heard the peal of her warm laughter and felt encouraged.

He walked the quiet streets of Barcelona that morning while Faye slept, a bitter taste filling his mouth – the previous night's beer coating his tongue with staleness, his hangover gnawing away at his stomach. He needed to clear his head, get something to eat, so he ducked inside a café and loaded his tray with cans of Coke and bottles of Orangina, ham-and-cheese croissants packaged in plastic wrap, bars of Nestlé Crunch and packets of crisps. While waiting to pay, he noticed a group gathered to one side of the café, clustering around the television. Another news channel, the same imagery of the cloud, interspersed with footage of aircraft sitting on a landing strip, and, inside the airport, passengers staring up at Departures boards or sprawling on terminal benches, their baggage scattered at their feet. The café was a tourist hub, and those gathered beneath the screen had the air of worried travellers, their faces staring gravely at the screen, murmuring to each other in their own languages. After paying, Michael took the plastic bag containing his items and approached the group.

'What's going on?' he asked a blonde girl wearing a Northwestern sweatshirt above denim cut-offs and Keds.

She turned and looked at him. 'You haven't heard?' her accent confirming her as American. 'A volcano has erupted in Iceland. All the flights into and out of northern Europe have been cancelled.'

'What? But how come?'

'They said the smoke from the volcano has filled the air with particles of dust. If it gets in the engine of a plane, it can damage it, cause it to crash or something.'

He felt a wingbeat of anxiety in his chest. 'But for how long?'

The girl shrugged. 'Could be a few days, a few weeks. Fuck knows when we'll get out of here.' Then she turned away from him, her concentration fixed again on the screen.

It seemed unreal, far-fetched, almost ridiculous. As he walked back towards the hotel, the sun shining through a bright blue sky that was completely clear, not a wisp of cloud in sight, he felt there had to be some kind of mistake. The hollowness inside him was competing with a new anxiety, and he stopped at an Internet café. Sitting at a terminal, logging on to news sites, both Irish and international, he found that one after the other confirmed what the American girl had said. All air travel over Europe had been suspended until further notice. Their flights home to Dublin and Dusseldorf the following evening had already been cancelled, the airline's website advising passengers to keep checking for further details but implying that it was at the whim of the weather. In the lap of the gods.

Back in their hotel room, he found the blanket smoothed over the mattress, the pillows restored to their place. From the little bathroom came sounds of running water, and when Faye emerged a moment later, holding her bag of toiletries, her features drawn and tired, he told her what he had learned about the volcano, about the grounded flights.

'What will we do?' she asked, a frown of concern puckering the skin above her nose.

He shrugged. 'There's nothing much we can do except wait for it to pass.'

He tried to sound relaxed, casual, but the tension in the room remained.

'Hopefully it'll just be twenty-four hours,' he added, and she nodded but said nothing.

'I mean it's a cloud,' he went on. 'They pass over quickly, right? They disperse.'

He emptied his bag's contents on to the bed and reached for the crisps. Her silence was starting to annoy him. 'A couple of nights maybe and then it'll blow over. And hey, it's not the worst place in the world to be stranded, is it?'

She zipped her toilet bag and set it down on the bed; then, carefully, she said: 'Michael . . .'

All the doubts he had felt on his arrival yesterday seemed to crowd back into the little room. What had been a mild lapping of uncertainty now seemed to calcify. The way she was looking at him . . . he felt it in his stomach – a cool hard stone of panic.

'There's something I have to tell you,' she said.

4

Faye

A week passes before the second letter arrives.

I'm breezing into the office, carrying the freshness of early morning with me, when Kelly looks up from behind her desk at Reception and remarks: 'You've a spring in your step this morning, Faye,' and I smile in acknowledgement.

'It's the good weather,' I tell her, glancing towards the window where the arm of a red crane slowly swings into position against a crisp blue sky.

It's not just that. For weeks I've been working hard to raise the company's profile and finally my persistence has begun to pay off. An early-morning phone call with the business editor of the *Irish Times* confirmed a feature piece in that newspaper, including an in-depth interview with Jess. There have been various snippets in the press so far but mostly just the odd photograph in the social pages of magazines; this will be our first big spread. I tell Kelly about it now, informing her that they'll be sending a photographer into the office later in the day to take some pictures of Jess and the whole team. We chat about it for a few minutes, both of us excited at the news.

'I'd better get to my desk,' I tell her, and she reaches behind her to the cubbyhole where my post is stored. Straight away I spot it: a blue letter, the little posy of flowers in the corner semaphoring the poison that I know instinctively it conceals. The sunshine outside, the pleasantness of our conversation – all of it falls away.

'Everything okay?' Kelly asks, noticing the smile vanishing from my face.

'Yes, fine.'

'Another one of those funny letters,' she remarks.

'Yes. So it appears.'

'Kind of quaint, really,' she goes on. 'You don't really see stationery like that any more, do you? It reminds me of something my granny might have sent.'

'You're right,' I say, forcing a breeziness back into my voice. 'Thanks, Kelly. I'd better get to work.'

Briskly, I make my way to my desk, dropping on to my chair and tearing open the blue envelope. Unlike the previous newspaper clipping, this one is fresh, new, and I recognize it immediately. A photograph published in one of the Sundays – it was taken at Ed's book launch. The two writers flanked by their wives. The same picture that Regina has framed and that now occupies a space on the wall in her kitchen. But in this new cutting, someone has taken a red sharpie to the image and defaced it, circling my head in a noose-like ring. In spidery lettering above, the same red ink marks out the words: *Do they know what you've done?*

Nerves jump in my throat. An inward clutching. I stare at it, paralysed by a wave of silent alarm, a voice in my head saying: *Oh no, oh no.*

My paralysis is only momentary, and then, moved to anger, I cross the room quickly to the shredder and am just about to feed it to the blades when I pause, raise the envelope to my face and smell it. Old paper and dust, and, beneath it, the faintest odour of something sweet and cloying. It calls to mind ancient dusty rooms, the creak of old furniture, a pall of cigarette smoke, and I remember Kelly's remark about how the envelope reminded her of her grandmother. An image wafts up from the past of a small spry woman, stick-thin with a dowager's hump: Min. Standing in the hallway in her tweed trousers and roll-neck jumper, the first time Michael brought me home. Large square glasses, the lenses tinted brown, and behind them her eyes narrowed and dry as she drawled: 'And who do we have here?'

'This is Faye,' Michael had said, holding on to my hand, and I could feel the pulse of excitement where his skin met mine, both of us giddy with anticipation. We were halfway up the stairs and I waved down at her from the step, a sloppy grin still on my face, my hair plastered to my head from the sudden downpour we'd gotten caught in on the way home.

She'd looked up at me with a wry expression on her wizened face, a thin ribbon of smoke rising from the cigarette held in her left hand. 'Fey, meaning able to see the future? Or doomed?' she'd demanded in that bored regal tone. I'd giggled with nerves, the two of us swaying on the step, caught sneaking up the stairs to his bedroom. Michael grinned and told me, 'Don't mind Minnie. She just loves showing off her erudition,' then pulled me by the hand, our feet tripping over the stairs.

Once inside his room, my eyes travelled over the polished surfaces of the wardrobe, the chest of drawers, the chair tucked neatly into the desk where a binder of notes lay open, stacks of library books lined up against the wall. I briefly thought of my own study space – one corner of a shared bedroom in a grim housing estate out beyond the city limits, the only digs I could afford. By comparison, Michael's bedroom, with its airy ceiling, its blackened fireplace, held a delicious masculine opulence.

'Nice house,' I remarked. 'How long have you been living here?'

'A few years now.'

'A few *years*?' It didn't make sense. We were only in our first year of university.

He smiled shyly. 'I moved in here when I was fifteen. My mother had remarried a couple of years before that, and things were a bit tricky at home.'

From downstairs came the sudden loud thump and crackle of a needle meeting a record before the voice of some Rat Pack crooner filled the air. That the volume was turned up loud seemed deliberately pointed, and I looked at Michael to say as much, but he was used to Min's ways.

'Didn't you mind?' I asked. 'Moving out of your own home? Coming to live with an elderly aunt?'

He grinned and shrugged. 'Actually, it was kind of a relief moving in here with Min. Back home, with my mother, it was so stifling, you know? Even before she married Jeff. She has such high expectations – standards, she calls them – but it can be unrelenting, you know? I just find it claustrophobic living under her constant scrutiny. It almost tempts me to fuck up!' he laughs, adding: 'Min's cool. You'll like her once you get to know her.'

'Am I going to get to know her?' I asked, teasing him,

while part of me thrilled at the implication – this was not going to be a one-night stand.

'Oh, I think so,' Michael whispered and pulled me down on to the bed.

More than a decade has passed since I last set foot in that house. Rarely in those years have my thoughts turned to Min. I had presumed her dead. Her health had never been good – the cigarettes, the booze, the paucity of food she allowed to pass her lips. But now, with that envelope in my hand, I consider the possibility that she is still alive. Remembering all over again the way she used to dote on him – how she adored him! – and, conversely, how her coldness towards me had persisted, the suspicions, the barely concealed doubts, all the way up until the end. Until the volcano erupted. Not for the first time, I wonder whether he had told her? They had always been close. Closer than he was to his own mother. Min worshipped him. 'The son I should have had,' Min used to declare of Michael, tenderly running her fingers through the sweep of his sandy hair. And, if he had told her, how she might have twisted the facts he gave her. With that envelope in my hand, I catch once more the vinegary whiff of her dislike, and my suspicion deepens.

My hands are shaking, the room around me suddenly cold. Quickly, I feed the envelope and its contents into the shredder as if that might obliterate the poison. But instead it lingers in my thoughts, malodorous, threatening. I can't tell Ed – he's already on edge waiting for the reviews of his book; he's been promised that they'll appear in the papers this weekend. And, besides, I can't tell him anyway.

*

On Saturday morning, I wake to an empty bed. Ed's gone out early to buy the papers, so I get up and go downstairs. I'm putting on the coffee when he comes in and kisses me hello, leaving a bag of pastries on the kitchen island, before busying himself taking apart the newspaper.

'Is it there?' I ask, putting out plates, knives, jam, and glancing over at him.

'Should be,' he murmurs.

Having found the correct supplement, he begins parsing the pages until he alights on the article, his eyes flickering over the words. I pour the coffee and wait, the silence surrounding him taking on a tense quality. Then, under his breath, he utters an astonished '*What the fuck?*'

When he glances up at me, there is fury in his eyes, before he reads aloud in a cold voice:

'The debut novel by Ed Sharpe owes a debt of gratitude to the author's father, the award-winning writer Desmond F. Sharpe. It goes without saying that Sharpe Junior is well versed in the distinctive narrative voice of the elder. Indeed, it is not a stretch to imagine that he kept close to hand copies of his father's novels as his own frothy but entertaining *The Thief of Happiness* took shape.'

The paper slips from his hands. It lands spreadeagled on the floor as he drops his weight on to one of the barstools and exhales: 'Christ.'

I round the corner of the island and slip my arms about his neck. He holds himself stiffly in my embrace, not yet ready to be comforted, too absorbed in his disbelief and rage.

'Those fuckers,' he says, his voice icy and controlled. 'They actually think that I plagiarized my own father?'

I pull back from him, bending to pick the offending newspaper from the floor.

'They didn't say that,' I offer in a gently reasonable tone, but inside I feel the swell of anxiety.

'Aped his style, then,' he counters. 'And, I'm sorry, but *frothy*?'

'To hell with them. One bad review among all the great ones you've received.' There's a strain in my voice that sounds like desperation. But I want so badly for him to be happy.

'Not great. Good or middling. But at least they were polite. This is a hatchet job.' He shakes his head, and I can see that some of his anger is seeping away, replaced by raw hurt. 'But to make comparisons with Dad . . .'

This time he reaches up to touch my arms when they go around him.

'You are your own man,' I tell him, 'not some beta version of your dad. You've written a beautiful, eloquent book, and I'm so proud of you.'

Regina says the same when she calls later that morning. We're in the car at the time, and her voice coming through the speakerphone sounds unusually strident.

'What a ridiculous thing to write. Absolute blithering nonsense. You do know that, don't you, darling?'

'Yes, Mum,' Ed replies with a patient sigh.

'Your father agrees with me.'

In the background we can hear The Major threatening to contact the editor of the newspaper. 'Tantamount to slander!' he barks.

Ed and I exchange a look.

'Why don't you come over?' Regina pleads. 'Call in for a chat. It will make you feel better.'

It's a good suggestion, and, when we arrive at their house a short time later, his mother wraps Ed in a warm hug of reassurance, and his father slaps him on the back and commiserates, even bringing out some examples of bad reviews that he's been on the receiving end of in his career. Ed's sister, Martha, arrives with her two small children, and the house instantly fills with noise as her little girl dashes around the furniture until a vase is knocked over, the smash waking the baby, who begins to howl in his pram. Martha sighs and lifts the infant, affecting an exhausted despair, saying: 'Think twice before you two choose to procreate, that's all I'm saying.'

'A bit late for that,' Ed remarks.

The words are out of his mouth before I have a chance to shoot him a glance of warning. He grins at me as his family reacts – Martha squealing with delight, Regina bursting into tears and Desmond clearing his throat, his face breaking into a rare beam of pleasure.

I can't be angry with Ed, not when faced with such a thrilled reaction. The bad review is forgotten, banished by the bright optimism of our baby news. There are questions then about an early scan which is due to take place in a couple of weeks' time, about whether we intend to find out the gender or if we prefer to keep it a surprise. Martha plonks her baby on to my lap, saying: 'There you go, Faye. Get a little practice in.'

Instinctively, my hands go around the child's soft middle, feeling the give of his flesh. Little hands flail briefly, and his head wobbles, turning on the narrow stem of his neck to look at me, his cries briefly subsiding with shock.

I can feel them all staring, especially Ed, who leans back in his chair, his arms crossed in satisfaction, and says: 'Do you know, I think this might be the first time I've ever seen you with a baby in your arms?'

'Really?' The infant shifts on my lap, his little legs kicking out with sudden violence, and my heartbeat quickens. Ed's gaze is too heavy – I feel myself start to sweat beneath the weight.

'So any ideas about names?' Martha asks.

'I don't know,' Ed says. 'Perhaps we should revive an old name. Something that's fallen out of fashion.'

'Give us an example,' Martha says.

He thinks about that for a minute, a mischievous air coming over him. 'Algernon,' he says, 'or Octavius?'

His sister laughs. 'Can you imagine, Faye?'

I offer a wobbly smile, but my heart is pounding.

Regina doesn't approve. 'You can't pick the baby's name before he or she is born. It's bad luck,' she asserts, which elicits groans from both her children.

Aware of the drum of blood in my chest, or perhaps just recovering from his shock, the baby whimpers, and makes a sudden alarming gurgling noise, like mucus has caught in his throat. His body feels hot in my grip, my hands sweating into the cotton of his Babygro. None of the others seem to notice.

'Don't be so superstitious,' Martha chides her mother, before returning to their conversation. 'What about naming this child after a fruit or a vegetable?'

'Hmm. Like Persimmon or Kumquat.'

'Romanesco?' Martha suggests. 'Roman for short?'

'If it's a boy. Jicama if it's a girl.'

'What the hell's a jicama?' she asks.

'I think it's some kind of turnip,' he says, and Martha snorts with laughter.

The baby jumps. I feel the leap of his flesh in my hands, and think: If I drop him . . .

I stand up quickly, thrust the baby towards his mother. 'You should probably take him,' I say, struggling to keep my voice level.

Martha reaches for the child and Ed's brow creases into a frown. 'You all right?'

'Yes, fine,' I say, glancing at my watch and explaining that I have a dental appointment that I'm going to be late for. 'Do you mind if I take the car?'

'Sure,' he says, his expression still mildly perplexed, and Martha offers to drop him home.

With smiles and apologies, I back out of the room, out of the house and into the car, waving goodbye to Regina, who has come outside to see me off. It is only when I get around the corner out of sight that the shaking starts.

I grip the steering wheel, trying to bring the pounding of blood in my temples under control.

'Get a grip,' I say aloud. What the hell is wrong with me?

But I know the answer to that. It's there all the time now, ever since that first note arrived: *Murderer*. The feeling of someone watching me, willing something bad to happen.

As I drive through roads that are lazy with Saturday traffic, I think of the notes that have been sent, and imagine the steps taken: the finding of the relevant articles, the sharp incision of a cutting blade as each one is carved out. There is malice channelled down into the red pen making its vicious slanders, its threats. And care is taken, folding it all into an envelope that's then sealed, addressed, stamped and sent. This act is not done impetuously or by accident. Oh, no, this is a meticulous enterprise involving calculation, discipline, intent. My hands grip the steering wheel a little tighter and I sit up straight, a steeliness taking hold.

Years have passed since I've taken this route, and I feel the push of familiarity, slowing as I pass a row of low-rise shops: a bookies, the off-licence, the newsagent with grimy windows where Min went to pick up the *Irish Times*. Gripping the wheel, my limbs no longer shaking, taken by a new determination, I turn the car off the main road and on to a quieter street. Here the houses are clumped together in narrow uniform rows, tiny strips of gardens delineated by gravel-stippled walls. Social housing – or anti-social housing, as Min scornfully referred to them – though, judging by the Volvo estates parked in the driveways instead of the rusting vans and the souped-up hatchbacks I remember, the street has been undergoing gentrification in the years since I left.

I pull the car into the side by the kerb and park, switching off the engine. Little kids on bicycles come streaming towards me. They circle the vehicle, peering in with unguarded curiosity. After a few moments, they peel away and, left alone, unobserved, I roll down the window and stare up at the house.

St Jude's. A bay-windowed Victorian with red-brick walls long blackened to a dull sheen, it appears stranded here among the sea of modern semi-d's like some last outpost of Victoriana, stubbornly clinging to the past. It's so strange coming back here to a place that stands like a pillar in my memory. I had once thought it so grand! But, now, I look at the paint peeling from the window frames, the dull panes, the stained and crumbling pointing between the bricks, and I see a house that has long ago tipped over into neglect. Meagre scrubs of grey lavender line the path to the door, the rest of the garden a tumble of briars and nettles. There is a light on beyond the hall door, but the rest of the house is in shadow. Parked in the driveway is a small white van and a mint-green Citroën that has seen better days. I don't remember this car any more than I can imagine Michael – or Min, for that matter – driving it.

What am I doing here? Did I think that I was going to march up to the front door, come face to face with Min after all these years and fling an accusation at her? Anonymous notes, crude threats scrawled on scraps of old newspaper – is this what I had in mind? Now that I am here and I see the forlorn state of the place, sadness rolls over me – the heavy weight of regret. I spent two years of my life in this house, give or take. Me, Michael and Min – an unusual triumvirate. And Foyle, the dog – a yappy little German shepherd pup when I arrived, a shaggy muscled hound by the time I left. I look up at the house and think: *I was happy here once.*

'Have you moved in?' Min asked me one morning.

I was in the kitchen at the time, making tea to bring upstairs to Michael, who was still sleeping. He'd been working on his essay until well after midnight. Min was leaning against the worktop, tapping ash from her cigarette into the sink.

'No. Not really.'

'You seem to be spending a lot of time here.'

'Do you mind?' I asked, and she tilted her eyebrows. I hadn't intended it to come out so harshly.

'No, I don't mind.'

'Good.'

I put the milk back in the fridge, and took hold of the two mugs of tea. I was just turning to leave the room when she said, her voice dry yet without its usual confidence: 'Be careful with him, won't you? He's more fragile than you think.'

Sitting here in my car, all these years later, I remember again her dislike and how it persisted. She disliked most people – women especially – as if the whole of humanity were a massive disappointment to her. Except for Michael, whom she adored. And, even though I became accustomed to her wry observations, her pithy disaffection, I was never entirely easy with her. And after Spain, after the volcano, when I left Michael overseas and fled back home, I came here one last time to clear out my things, and Min had hissed at me like a viper: 'What did you do to him? What did you do?'

Even now, as I remember, my hands on the steering wheel shake.

The front door opens and from the shadows of the porch a tall Black woman steps out of the house. She's dressed casually in jeans and a loose-fitting jacket, a tomato-red scarf wound tightly around her head. Slim and attractive, at this distance I guess her to be in her early thirties, about my own age. Calling back into the house through the door that stands open, she shouts: 'Come on! We don't want to be late.' A child runs out, a little girl, four, maybe five years old, her hair pulled into two fat bunches. The child moves past her mother to the mint-green car, but the woman's still standing there. She's looking straight at me.

'Can I help you?' she asks.

It comes at me in a rush. Min is gone. And Michael. This house has new occupants, new life.

'Sorry,' I tell her. 'I just thought . . . Never mind.'

I shake my head and fumble with the key in the ignition. I can feel the woman still looking at me, but there's a lump in my throat, a wave of unexpected emotion. Everything that happened in this house – how much it once meant to me, how much he meant to me . . .

It was a mistake coming here. I had sworn to put that part of my life behind me. Now, as I swing the car into reverse, I glance back. The woman is still staring after me, one hand raised to shield her eyes from the glare of the sun. And then the front door of the house opens once again and a man hurries out, raising aloft a forgotten schoolbag. I pause. I can't help myself. With a painful leap of the heart, I realize that it is Michael. He has come to the end of the driveway and is standing there, his hands on his hips, staring across at me, his mouth open in amazement.

The engine roars to life and the car takes off, swinging out on to the main road, a horn sounding angrily behind me, my heart thumping. Seconds later, my phone sounds with an incoming message. Stopped at the lights, I look at it and the wash of fear comes over me again. The same number from all those years ago, deleted from my contacts but surfacing once more.

You came back to me. I knew one day you would.

And I cannot believe how foolish I have been. Stupid, stupid. Returning to this place when I should have known to keep away – it is my first real mistake.

5

Faye

That night, Ed and I go to the theatre – a performance of *Constellations* at the Gate. In the darkened hush of the auditorium, I look up at the actors on the stage – a man and a woman, circling each other, the repetition of various scenarios in search of a different outcome each time. It's a romantic comedy of sorts, and yet, as the performance progresses, I become aware of a low hum beneath the actors' voices. I can feel it rumbling up through the floor beneath my seat. It's probably the sound design, but nevertheless it unnerves me, makes me think of shifting plates beneath the ground, the pulsing energy at the earth's molten core. Glancing around at the rows of pale faces held by the performance, there are none that I recognize. It's silly, this sense of unease, as if some malign presence is lurking in the dark. But still, I feel it like a breath passing lightly over the skin, a disturbance in the air, a shapeless threat.

At the interval, we go to the bar, and I check my phone while Ed queues for service.

> So unexpected to see you today. Why did you drive away? It would be good to meet up after all these years. M

I read the message quickly, heat coming into my face,

my throat. Then hastily I put the phone on to flight mode and slot it back in my bag as Ed turns around with our drinks.

'Everything all right?'

'Fine,' I say, pushing a smile on to my face, pressing my voice with a cheer I don't feel. 'Just work – nothing important.'

We find a corner where we can perch to the side of the bar area. Ed takes a sip from his pint, then says: 'So I was talking to Martha earlier. She gave me the details of the antenatal class she went to – said it was brilliant. We should get in touch with them, put our names down.'

'Isn't it a bit early for that? Those classes are for when you're in the third trimester.'

'Yeah, I know. But no harm in putting our names down now. Martha also recommended a yoga class she went to when she was expecting each of hers.'

'Sounds like Martha is trying to project manage my pregnancy,' I remark, not sharply, but I feel a little crowded.

'She's excited, that's all. Everyone is.' He checks his watch, takes another swig from his pint before putting it down on the ledge and turning to me abruptly, as if he's finally arriving at the question he's been wanting to ask. 'So have you spoken to your mother yet?'

It's been a constant refrain of his lately, and instinctively I draw in a deep breath.

'Not yet –'

'You have to tell her.'

'I know –'

'Now that everyone in my family knows – and you know what Martha's like, pretty soon everyone will find out – she's going to hear about it from someone,' Ed warns. 'This is a small town.'

'I'll call her – I will. I just have to find the right time.'

He nods, his eyes flickering briefly over the crowd at the bar, the polite jostle as they queue to be served.

'Have you thought about how involved you want her to be with the baby?' he asks.

The question takes me by surprise. The truth is, I haven't given it much thought.

'I'm not sure she'll even want to be involved. She's never been much of a one for babies, even little kids – they're accompanied by too much mess. I've heard her myself, complaining about nappies to change, noses to wipe, sticky fingers on everything.'

'That's other people's kids,' he points out. 'She might turn out to be a doting grandmother.'

I have to laugh at the notion. 'Really? Maggie, a doting grandmother?' I shake my head, and a drop of bitterness enters my voice. 'She was a crap mother, even during her sober intervals. Always distracted, and then resentful when some demand was made on her, and I mean simple demands, like had she washed my school uniform over the weekend or was there any food for my school lunch. She showed more interest in the various boyfriends that trooped in and out of her life than she showed in me, and, when the responsibility of having a kid got too much for her, she dumped me on my grandparents, or my auntie Jean, and then hightailed it off to wherever the party was happening.'

He listens to all of this calmly, patiently, without interruption, even though he's heard it plenty of times before.

'So I'm sorry, but I just can't see her suddenly develop-ing a soft cuddly side.'

'You never know. People change,' he says affably.

'I don't think she's had her Road to Damascus moment yet. I mean, would you even trust her with our baby? Can you imagine an evening like this, you and I going out to the theatre and leaving Maggie to babysit?'

He doesn't answer but I know what he's thinking. The very idea of it is ludicrous. We both know she'd be at the booze as soon as the car had pulled out of the driveway.

'I know I have to tell her about the baby,' I say, soften-ing now. 'And I will. It's just part of me wants a new start for us, free from any of the things that dragged us down in the past.'

'Like your mother?'

'Yes,' I answer, but thinking too of Michael. Of all the danger he holds.

'But, as for her having any kind of active part in this child's life,' I go on, 'that is just not going to happen.'

The interval ends, and we take our seats, the lights dimming and the auditorium growing hushed as the play resumes. But the words swish past me, the perform-ance a blur. I try to concentrate, but I'm on edge now – all that talk about Maggie and motherhood has unearthed deep-buried thoughts and feelings that I don't want to relive. That, and the text message on my phone – a differ-ent tone to the notes I've received, less overtly threatening – but still giving off its own peculiar danger-ous energy. Why did I go back there today? After years of careful avoidance, of discipline and distance, to give in to a moment of weakness, and risk what I have so carefully guarded? Stupid. Reckless.

A quick glimpse of him was all I got – enough to be sure that it was actually Michael; enough to register shock at the alterations within him. The beard was new, and the weight. Something lumbering and ursine about him, unkempt, but it was the contrast that so upset me. The Michael I had known was always careful with his appearance, slim, shaven, neatly dressed. His T-shirts were always so brightly white, pristine, and I remember now, with a sudden and shocking drill of old longing, the smooth, lightly tanned skin of his back emerging as I peeled away that white cotton T-shirt from his body.

'He looks like he's been raised by maiden aunts,' my mother had drily observed on the first of the very few occasions she had met him. A comment meant to deride not only Michael but me as well, because I had chosen him, because I loved him. My mother with her weakness and insecurities, for all her negligence, couldn't bear the thought of my loving anyone but her, least of all a bright-eyed boy with a sensitive face and eager manner, immaculately dressed. Even the last time I saw him, in the airport at Barcelona, after everything that had happened, he still retained that quality of neatness and cleanliness, whereas I was wretched, grimy with cooling sweat and half crazed as I willed the minutes to pass so I could get on board that plane and escape the place. The ash had cleared, the sky a brilliant blue, and we had stood facing each other as my flight was called, both of us shaking as much from our imminent parting as from the thought of what we had done.

'It's over,' I told him, my voice a whisper, half afraid someone might overhear. 'We have to put it behind us,' I went on, while a crease appeared in his forehead and his eyes brimmed with tears.

'How can we?' he asked, bewildered.

'Because we have to. What choice do we have?'

'We could tell them. We could go to the police. We could –'

'No.'

'But –'

'Michael, no.' My voice had risen sharply, grown insistent, and the sudden urgency drew glances from others around us in the Departures lounge.

Stepping closer to him, I took his hands in mine and fixed him with a long steady gaze. 'We need to put these past few days out of our minds. We must forget.'

'But how?'

'By not speaking about it – not even thinking about it. By putting it in a box and then burying that box in the deepest corner of your mind. By building a thick wall around it and pretending it never happened.'

The troubled crease was still there on his brow, but I could tell that he was listening to me carefully.

'Eventually, if we keep doing that – if we keep pretending – it will come to seem like it never happened at all.'

'It doesn't feel right. It doesn't seem fair . . . for us to leave like this. To get away with it –'

'Would you rather go to prison?' I'd asked, and he'd looked at the ground, profoundly unhappy.

The exhaustion was making my eyes scratchy and my limbs weak. I wasn't well; the pain in my belly had increased and that morning I had noticed a thread of fresh red blood. I needed to lie down, to rest. It felt like days had passed since I'd slept.

'If you love me, you'll do this. Please, Michael – we can't ever speak of this. Not to anyone. Not even to each other. Please?'

He heard the note of terror in my voice, and after a pause he nodded his assent and the wave of panic in me fell back a little, the tightness in my chest easing fractionally.

Over the tannoy, a voice in Spanish was announcing the last call for my flight.

'I've got to go,' I told him, hating that we were parting like this. So much between us remained unresolved.

Before I left, I leaned in and kissed him. We had hardly touched during the previous forty-eight hours – as if each of us had been contaminated by the run of events, and wary of comforting each other. Even as I felt his lips against mine, I mourned the loss of them, as if I had an inkling that our parting would be final. I think I knew, even then, that it was over between us. There would be no way I could forget what we had done, no chance of putting it in the past, when his very presence served as a reminder. Later, I would tell him. In a long and painful phone conversation, I would lay bare to him the decision I had reached: that he and I would never see or speak to each other again, and that I would be leaving Ireland. But that day, in the airport, I knew that he was too shattered to hear it. That speaking those words would break him. So I kissed him and it was a long bittersweet kiss, full of unspoken words and broken hopes, and, although I was desperate to leave, I did not want that kiss to end.

The room around me erupts, sudden applause startling me. I turn and see my husband beaming up at the stage, vigorously clapping. Stunned, I drag my attention back to the room as the audience around me whistle and stamp their feet, their volume raised with rapturous applause. The play is over and I've hardly listened to a word. In a daze, I get to my feet along with everyone else, and join in the applause.

'Wasn't that amazing?' Ed shouts above the noise, shaking his head in marvel, and I nod my agreement, my hands tingling as the actors bow low, graciously receiving the rapture.

We file outside, and Ed says he'll bring the car around. So I wait on the front steps of the theatre, and dig my phone out of my bag. I switch off flight mode, and instantly there are alerts for three new text messages. I scan them quickly.

The first says:

Please let me know when and where it would suit you to meet. Think it would be really good for us to talk. M

The second was sent a half-hour later.

Just so you understand, I'm not angry about anything. I just want to see you. Text me. M

64

The third says:

> Can't stop thinking about everything. You're back in my head again.
> Wish you weren't, but there you are. Need to talk. Soon. M

There's an urgency to the messages that stirs up my alarm, a desperation in the frequency with which they've been sent. A fourth text appears on the screen even as I'm reading the others.

> Look, you came to my home, right? That can only mean you want
> to see me too. Better if we talk in person, don't you think?? M

I don't like those double question marks, their insistence, the self-righteousness they suggest, the implied threat. I don't like the feeling of obligation, the lingering pressure of a debt that needs to be repaid.

The car pulls up by the kerb, Ed ducking his head a little, trying to catch my eye.

I feel the weight of his unspoken enquiry as I take my place in the passenger seat and draw the door closed.

'What?' I ask, laughing, but still some nerves enter my voice.

'You seem a bit out of sorts this evening. Kind of jumpy.'

'Am I? I'm just tired. It's been a long week.' I smile at him and he seems happy with my response. As he pulls the car out into the stream of slow-moving traffic, I feel my bag resting in my lap. My phone remains silent for the duration of our journey home. While I waited on the theatre steps, I'd taken care to block Michael's number.

I rest a little easier after that.

Still, the nerves don't entirely disappear. I've blocked

his number, but I'm aware that there are ways of getting around that. For the first time in years I check my old Yahoo account, curiosity getting the better of me. But there are no emails from Michael, either to that account or to my Gmail. On a whim, I Google his name, trying to whittle down my search to those Michael Jamesons that are in Ireland, but, after a fruitless trawl through pages of results, most of them linked to Irish whiskey, the only evidence I can find online for him relates to various UCD clubs that he was once a member of: the L&H, the mountaineering club, Dramsoc. I find a photograph of Michael with the other backstage crew at a performance of *A Clockwork Orange*, another of him smiling through a misty rain on a club hike in Kerry, his lime-green rain jacket tugging at my memory and his frank open face pulling at something deeper, more intimate. The paucity of these results is frustrating. How can someone live in this age without leaving a greater Internet footprint? It's almost as if his life had stopped the moment we said goodbye.

I give up on my search, but, just before I log out, an idea occurs to me, and, before I realize the foolishness of acting on it, I'm typing in another name, and then another. For we were not alone that week of the ash cloud. There were others. Sheena, Adriana, Mateo ... One by one, I find them online. One by one, these faces from the past come back to me. My fingers are poised over the keys, ready to type in one more name, but something holds me back. A slow cold trickle of shame. Shame at my own cowardice. This is chased by a feeling of disgust at my lack of self-discipline. In conjuring up those names, all these years later, I am breaking one of the key rules I live by: the past is a sleeping dog. Let it lie.

A week later, the feature piece in the *Irish Times* is published. Jess takes me out for lunch to celebrate. Over bowls of chowder, we discuss the feedback on the article. Invitations to participate in various tech conferences and summits have already begun flowing in. Jess gratefully acknowledges my role in all of this, and, even though I hadn't planned to, it feels like the right time to tell her about the baby. She expresses delight at my news, waving away my assertions that I will work right up until my due date and return to the office as soon as my statutory leave ends. She reassures me that she's happy for me to take whatever time I need.

'Your first baby,' she beams. 'It's something really special. You must take the time to enjoy it.'

'You're right,' I say, even though a small part of me tenses with anxiety when I think of all the hours and days spent at home alone with a small baby. I wonder whether I'll be able to cope.

After lunch, we go back to the office, and I leave work late but happy, riding the wave of excitement that I'm achieving something in my career. That I'm making something of myself.

When I get home, I find Ed in the kitchen making dinner. A plume of steam rises from the rice-cooker; next to it is a plastic tub from Avoca emptied of its contents – curry, judging from the spices lingering in the air as the saucepan heats on the stove.

'Hey, you,' I say, kissing my husband hello.

He asks after my day and I show him the feature in the paper, kicking off my sandals and throwing my bag on to the sofa as he scans the article and nods appreciatively.

'That's fantastic,' he says. 'Great picture too.'

The photograph shows Jess in the middle, flanked by me on one side and Frank, our product-development manager, on the other, the rest of the team fanning out behind us. I'm flattered by the prominence it gives to my position.

'Well done,' Ed tells me, and I sense a slight flatness in his tone.

The doors to the garden are thrown wide and a warm breeze wafts through the room.

A bottle of wine is open and he picks it up and sloshes some into his glass. I can see that it's not his first and I raise an eyebrow questioningly. It's Wednesday and we have a rule about mid-week drinking.

'I know, I know,' he says, raising his hands in mock-surrender. 'But I feel like I need it.'

'Oh?'

He sees the concern entering my gaze and tries to shrug it off. 'Ah, it's nothing really. Just an interview that pissed me off a little.'

I remember then how he had mentioned a call with a journalist from a magazine. Several weeks have passed since Ed's book was published, and, while there had been an initial flurry of interest from the press, that has all but died down now. The request for an interview had come out of the blue, and it had given Ed a new shot of vigour.

'Who was it again?'

'Steve Meagher. I mean, he's a nice enough guy. That's not the issue.'

'Then what? Did he ask tough questions?'

'It's not that they were tough, they just weren't . . .' He stops and shakes his head, then takes a swallow of wine.

'Weren't what?'

'They weren't really about the book. Or me. They were mainly about my dad.'

I inhale deeply, and it makes sense then: the wine, the tension in his shoulders, the silent fuming.

'It's just a bit tedious,' he goes on. 'Every interviewer asks the same questions: *What's it like, following in the footsteps of a famous father? What does Dad make of my foray into writing?*

'Foray?'

'He actually used that word, I'm not kidding. But I was polite. I answered with a smile on my face – I didn't get touchy. Still, he kept banging on about it. *Did I show the book to Dad while I was writing it? Did he give me any advice? How influenced was I by my father's writing style?* It almost felt like he was questioning whether I had written the damn thing myself or had gotten my daddy to do it for me.'

He takes a swift gulp from his glass and reaches for the bottle. Behind him, the rice-cooker has flicked to OFF but Ed doesn't seem to notice.

'It's like I only exist as an extension of The Great Man. Like I'm some kind of literary spawn.'

'I know it's annoying,' I say gently, trying to calm his mood. 'But it's only natural that they'd ask – people are curious about that sort of stuff. It will be different the second time around.'

'Yeah. If I ever get this book written.'

He turns now and switches off the hob, reaches up to the shelf for the bowls that are stacked there. Steam rises from the rice-cooker when he takes the lid off.

'How's it coming along?' I ask. A delicate subject, but I haven't asked in a couple of weeks and this seems like an opportunity to check in.

He shrugs. 'Up and down. Some days I fly through it, but then other days – like today – I look back over what I've done and think it's utter shit.'

'You were probably distracted by that interview.'

'Or maybe I only have the one book in me.'

'Don't be silly.'

He spoons curry on to the rice and passes me a bowl before sliding the naan bread from the oven on to a plate. We take our seats at the kitchen island and he tops up his glass again. Seeing the pointed look I give him, he lets out a heavy sigh.

'Just spare me the guilt trip, Faye, okay? It's been a rough day.'

'Okay.'

We eat in silence for a few minutes. It worries me, seeing him like this – the doughy pallor of his face, discontent lingering in the silence.

'Did you get out at all today?' I ask.

'Just down to the shops to pick up dinner.'

'You didn't meet anyone?'

'No. Why?' His eyes flick up from his plate, and I see the suspicion entering them.

'No reason. It must get a bit lonely for you, sitting up in the office by yourself all day, not speaking to anyone.'

'I spoke to that journalist.'

'You know what I mean.'

'You're worried I'm brooding?'

I shrug. 'It just doesn't seem healthy.'

He passes a forkful of curry into his mouth, and doesn't answer.

We sit in silence for a moment. I think about the earlier excitement in the day, the lunch with Jess, the buzz in the office that afternoon – all of it seems so different from the quiet dullness of this room. Somewhere along the way our paths have managed to diverge. While I have been building relationships at work, which spill over into lunches outside the office, drinks in the evening, invitations to events, Ed seems to have withdrawn further into himself, his days empty of company. It worries me, the thought of his spending so much time alone.

'What about meeting up with some of your friends? What about Alex? Didn't he mention some five-a-side football?'

'Faye –'

'Sorry.' I see the weary irritation dragging down his features, and bite my lip.

Ed closes his eyes briefly, then he reaches forward and takes my hand. His voice has thawed when he says: 'Please don't try to organize me, love. I know you mean well, but I'm a grown-up. This is the life I have chosen. Writing is a solitary endeavour. But it's what I want to do. And I can figure out how to make it work.'

'I know you can,' I tell him.

But the worry remains. And I think of how happy he was in his old job, before the pandemic. How he thrived in the theatre atmosphere, feeding off the collegiate energy, humming with happiness at the end of a working day. Circumstances forced a change in direction, and I supported his choice. I also know that, in this instance, silence is best.

'And if it makes you feel any better,' he continues, 'I'll be getting out of the house on Friday. There's a panel discussion in the Lexicon in the evening – me and a couple of other debut authors.'

'Oh, that's great!' I say, unable to disguise my relief, and he smiles at my optimism.

'And there's tomorrow,' he adds.

'Tomorrow?'

'The scan,' he explains, laughing because I've forgotten. 'So you can stop worrying,' he tells me.

I promise him that I will.

'First baby?' the sonographer asks.

I nod and watch as she reads through my details on the computer screen.

The corners of her examination room are occupied by giant pot-plants – ficus and monstera and a feathery asparagus fern.

The jelly is cold on my belly, and the paddle presses hard into my flesh, causing discomfort as it moves back and forth. From the street below, traffic noises rise up and filter through the tall sash windows. Ed sits beside me and I can feel his nerves and excitement communicated through the hand that grips mine, the heat and pressure of his flesh, all his focus now on the medical professional. She's a woman in her forties with a brisk air of professionalism thinly veiled with warmth. The monitor is turned away from us so we are left trying to read from her expression whether there's cause for concern. She frowns with concentration. The silence stretches agonizingly.

'Is everything all right?' Ed asks, and I can hear his voice tight with nerves.

Her frown deepens.

'There,' she says, and that one word punctures the tension.

She turns the screen and I crane my neck, astonished to see the little form, so tiny but already so infant-like. I had expected a misshapen blob hunched around a rapid flicker, but there are hands and feet, knees and elbows, a face with eyes that seem to be looking right out at me. The limbs twitch suddenly and Ed gasps.

'Oh my God!' he exclaims, squeezing my hand hard, and laughing. 'Did you see that?'

'This little one's putting on quite the performance,' she says, pointing to the tiny hand going to the mouth, a minuscule thumb being sucked.

Her finger indicates the spine and the various organs, the pitch and tone of her voice reassuring as she takes measurements, calculates weights and dates.

'So is everything . . . normal?' I ask hesitantly.

'I don't see anything to cause concern,' she asserts.

I open my mouth to speak and to my surprise tears come in a rush of emotion. I gulp in air, and, as Ed leans down and kisses my forehead, stroking my hair, he says: 'It's okay. Everything's okay.' And I can see that his eyes are also watering, but he's laughing too.

'Tears of joy,' the sonographer remarks, her professional veneer cracking to allow a warm smile.

'Tears of relief,' Ed corrects, laughing as he swipes at his eyes.

I look at the little shape on the screen, the greyscale image, and I think of how wanted this child is, already loved and cherished, and am nudged by a deep and private guilt.

Perhaps she sees it. She rests her hand on my shoulder. 'Your baby looks healthy, Faye.'

I nod, calmed by her assurance.

We leave the clinic and sit for a while on a park bench under the shade of the trees in Merrion Square. The day is hot, sun beating down on the grass as seagulls and pigeons descend, eyeing us curiously for food as they strut carefully around. Ed stares at the image on his phone – the ultrasound picture we have been emailed fills the screen. I also have a paper copy folded and tucked safely inside my handbag. We don't say much to each other, but we cannot stop grinning. This is way bigger than lines on a stick. We have glimpsed the little being we have created together; we have seen it move. Now it is real.

'This is actually happening,' Ed says.

'Yes.'

'New Year's Eve.' He squeezes my hand.

'Everything will be different,' I tell him, and he agrees, our voices full of wonder.

It stays with me, this feeling of joy and awe, after we kiss each other goodbye on the corner of Merrion Square, the statue of Oscar Wilde lounging on a rock behind us. I float back to the office, weightless with all these thoughts and feelings, climbing the stairs in a daze. I push open the glass doors and smile hello to Kelly as I walk through Reception. No sooner have I reached my desk than the phone rings. I pick it up and hear Kelly's voice.

'A call for you, Faye. He won't give his name.'

I am still in the cloud of my happiness, the residue of wonder and joy clinging to me like a protective skin, which is why I don't think anything of this. Blithely, I tell her to put the caller through.

'Hello?' I say, reaching for the mouse of my computer and calling the screen to life, as the voice at the other end of the line says: 'Faye?'

It strikes me in the gut. His voice, once so familiar, coming down the line, corroding my joy like acid.

'Are you there?' Michael asks the silence.

I think of putting down the phone, but anger prompts me to speak. 'What is it you want?'

'You know you can't keep avoiding me,' he says.

6

Faye

We arrange to meet in the café of the National Gallery. Leaving the office shortly before eleven, I make sure that I am there first, arranging myself at a table near the back, so that I have a full view of the entrance and can watch for his arrival. Already, I'm feeling twitchy and defensive, wary of getting caught out by any surprises. It's noisy in here, the acoustics bouncing the sounds around as the tables fill up with a morning-coffee crowd. I might have chosen some small tucked-away-in-a-corner café, soft furnishings absorbing the sounds, our knees pressed close together beneath the table. The thought turns my stomach. I have chosen this place because it is bright and airy and loud. Because there will be witnesses. I realize that I am nervous of being alone with him.

A group of women and their children are at the next table – two of them are breastfeeding their babies. One of the mothers is grappling with her toddler, trying to get him to sit in the baby-chair. He's resisting strongly, arching his back and shrieking while she attempts to grab hold of his feet and yank them into the slots. It's clear she's in danger of losing it with this kid, and the other mums are politely pretending not to notice as her handling of the child grows rough and insistent. The toddler's mouth

76

opens wide, a rusk-filled maw of indignant refusal, his mother's eyes two black beads of fury. *That's going to be me*, I think, with a jolt of panic, the thread in my belly twanging in a minor key. And then someone moves to interrupt my view, and I hear a familiar voice saying: 'Hello, Faye.'

Despite all my preparations, he still manages to startle me.

'Michael –'

'God, it's good to see you!' he exclaims, making a sudden darting movement towards me. Realizing he's going to kiss my cheek, I give a swift shake of my head, a gesture that signifies a clear no. He draws back and the smile that has lit up his face falls a little, replaced by a brief confused expression.

'I don't have long,' I say, my tone neutral, a little cold. 'We should make this quick.'

My arms are folded on the table. There's a stiffness to my posture, a formality that is studied and deliberate. There's a decaf latte by my right elbow, alongside it the leatherbound notebook I use for work, my iPhone sitting on top of it. Anyone looking might assume this to be a work meeting. I need him to understand that this is not some friendly catch-up. There'll be no teary-eyed nostalgia, no wistful reminiscences. My single intention is to put a stop to his harassment and I want there to be no ambiguity.

'You've already got a coffee, I see,' he remarks, then inclines his head back towards the serving counters: 'Mind if I grab one?'

'Go ahead.'

I keep my gaze on him, watching as he walks head

down towards the coffee station and takes his place in the small queue. What I'd observed from the distance of my car the other day is now confirmed. He's older and heavier, and there's a slump to his posture that wasn't there before. The unfamiliar beard looks scraggly and unkempt – it doesn't suit him, blurring the definition of his face. 'You could slice apples on those cheekbones,' I had told him once, running my fingers along the high ridges of his face. Teasing him and yet marvelling at his beauty too – a handsomeness made striking by the vividness of his bone structure. All of that has disappeared now, swallowed up by the beard and the flesh.

I don't feel afraid. Even the nerves that had played on my stomach have diminished. Watching him at the till, parsing the coins on his palm, what I feel is closer to embarrassment. There's something cringing about him. Is this really the same youth that I had loved? With a jolt of memory, I'm struck by the image of the two of us lying on a bed, the sheets bunched around us, our bodies naked and spent. It almost makes me shudder to think of it, to acknowledge that there was once intimacy between me and this man lumbering back across the room, his gaze held by the tray he carries. Impossible to believe that under those clothes lies the same flesh, the same skin, the same beating heart I had listened to through the wall of his chest. Despite the summer day, he's wearing a brown suede jacket. I remember this jacket, although the suede looks worn to a shine in places and one of the buttons is dangling loose on its thread. By contrast, I am wearing one of my more formal summer suits – coral linen, with a white sleeveless blouse underneath. On the floor by my feet is a handbag in stiff black leather – Ed calls it my Thatcher bag – it's expensive, as are my high-heeled shoes. Everything I'm wearing today was chosen to semaphore the changes in me. I want Michael, when he looks at me, to see a woman he doesn't know. All traces of the girl he once loved obliterated. Nothing familiar at all.

He takes the seat opposite, puts his tray down. On it there's a pot of tea, a scone, little plastic containers of jam and butter sliding around the plate, and he spends a moment moving each item from the tray on to the table; then, tucking his chair in close, he picks up a knife and cuts the scone in two, takes the foil from the butter. Something fussy about all this arranging, even though his hands are larger than I remember. I notice that his fingers have swelled, the nails are torn-looking, and there's a graze across the knuckles of his right hand which makes me think he must work as some kind of labourer.

'You can have half,' he tells me, spreading jam on the scone. 'I won't eat all of this.'

'I'm fine. Really.'

'We always shared a scone with our coffees, do you remember? We'd meet at eleven in Hilpers and we'd always get a scone.' He beams at me unselfconsciously and I see the sliver of a gap between his front teeth. It does something to me.

'I don't any more.'

His eyes pass quickly over me, taking in my hair, my clothes. Even though the weather is hot, I've kept my jacket buttoned to conceal the new thickening around my waist.

'I knew one day you'd come back,' he tells me. 'I knew

79

it.' His eyes return to the plate in front of him, but he makes no attempt to pick up the scone. His fingers reach under the cuff of his sleeve to scratch at the skin there, and he continues: 'All those things you told me in that phone conversation, when you rang me a few days after leaving Barcelona – about how we couldn't see each other again, about the need to keep away – I always knew that one day you'd change your mind. That one day you'd see the sense of it. That you'd feel –'

'Michael,' I say firmly, interrupting him, 'I agreed to meet you today so that I could tell you to your face that this must stop.'

'What?'

'All of this. The text messages, the letters, the phone calls – I want you to stop. I want you to leave me alone.'

'Leave you alone?' He laughs, but it feels forced, a jittery energy emanating from him.

'I want you to stop contacting me. This meeting today is so that I can make it clear to you that I have no interest in pursuing any kind of friendship with you. Whatever we once shared, it's in the past. I have no wish to revive –'

'But you're the one who came to me. You're the one who came to my house.'

I draw back for a moment, feeling the colour coming into the skin on my neck. 'That was a mistake.'

'You came to me,' he repeats, louder this time, the insistence in his voice drawing the attention of some of the mums at the next table. His hands are on the table resting on either side of his plate, palms facing up. He scratches at his wrist again, and this time I notice the welts there, raised and reddened. They look like hives.

'What did you think? That you could just turn up at my home like that and drive away and not expect me to contact you?' He laughs again, but it dies quickly. 'How could I not when you were clearly sending me a message?'

'I wasn't,' I countered. 'I shouldn't have gone there that day –'

'So why did you?'

'I don't know. Curiosity, I suppose. But also . . . also to tell you that I want you to stop what you've been doing. Stop this harassment.'

'Harassment?'

'What else would you call it?' I respond, trying to keep my voice calm and steady. 'The newspaper clippings, those awful threats –'

'What newspaper clippings?'

'Oh, please, don't deny it. I know that it was you. It can't have been anyone else. Although I have to say that I'm shocked at the meanness of the gestures – the bitterness. I didn't think you'd stoop to something like that. And I'm also pretty sure that sending threatening messages like that is verging on criminal.'

His brow has furrowed, and he's watching my face avidly.

'I have literally no idea what you're talking about. What messages?'

The blank expression on his face goads something in me. I'm tired of this. Tired of the shadow he's cast over my life in these past few weeks, tired now of his obfuscation.

Leaning closer to him, my voice lowered so that the other diners can't overhear, I say: 'Clippings about the ash cloud. About what happened. Ugly messages scrawled across them, an implicit threat.'

'What threat?'

'Oh, come on. You know what I mean –'

'Why did you come back?'

His question catches me off guard.

'That phone call,' he goes on, 'all those years ago, when you told me that you were leaving Ireland. That we would never see each other again. You insisted that you would never come back here. So why did you?'

Flustered, I answer: 'I was offered a job. And Ed's father was in poor health –'

'Ed?' The name drops from his mouth with disdain.

'My husband –'

'Ed what?'

'Sharpe,' I admit.

Michael nods at that, like he's squirrelling the information away in some corner of his brain. I have the uncomfortable feeling that I've already told him too much, given him too much detail about my life as it is now, when what I want is to shut him out completely, seal the doors and windows against him.

'So where are they?' he asks.

'What?'

'These clippings. Show them to me.'

'I can't.'

'Why not?'

'I got rid of them. I threw them away.'

He makes a small huffing sound, and it angers me.

'What did you think I would do? Hold on to them? They were poisonous!' It comes to me again – the garish red ink hooping my throat in one picture – and I can almost feel the tightening about my own neck. 'Look, I don't have time for this, so you can drop the act. I just want it to stop, okay? All of it – the texts, the phone calls, those fucking notes. You're to stop. Okay?'

I glance across at the table of mums, and at the elderly couple seated just behind Michael to see if they are looking. When I bring my gaze back to him, his face is blandly mild, the only betrayal of his feelings the flaring of his eyes.

'You know, Faye,' he says quietly, 'you turn up at my house out of the blue after years and years, uninvited. Then you come here today and accuse me of sending you threatening notes and yet you can't provide a single one. For all I know, they don't exist. You've made them up.'

'Why would I do such a thing?'

'As a ruse. To make contact with me again. To meet.'

'Don't be ridiculous!'

He shrugs, his smile quietly self-satisfied, almost smug.

'I know it was you,' I insist. 'It has to be. No one else knows.'

'Are you sure about that?' he asks.

'Yes.'

'You never told anyone? About what happened, what we did?'

'Of course not!'

'Not even your husband?'

The question feels pointed, and I lower my eyes, shamed by my own deception. 'We both promised, remember? That we'd never tell a soul.'

He absorbs that information, looks down at his coffee, something shifty entering his manner.

'Did you?' I ask. 'Tell someone? Your mother or –'

'Of course not!'

'Did you tell Min –'

'Min didn't send you any threats. She's old now, bedridden. She can't even make it to the bathroom without help.'

'What about your wife?'

His frown of confusion is back. 'What wife? I don't have a wife.'

'Girlfriend. Partner, then.' Seeing the frown persist, I explain quickly: 'The woman I saw outside your house. The woman and child. I assumed that they –'

He laughs – a quick blurt of amusement – and shakes his head. 'Verona? You thought she was my wife?'

'Why is that funny?'

He bites his lip, brings his laughter under control. 'Sorry,' he says. 'You're right, it's not funny. And Verona is a good person. A good friend. It's just . . .'

He stops, grows suddenly serious. Leaning in slightly, he pushes his plate aside, his eyes sweeping the surface of the table, and in a low voice says: 'There's only ever been you, Faye. Always has been. Always will be.'

The words shock me into silence. The simplicity of the message, the gentle but forthright way he's stated it.

'Things have been hard for me, these past few years,' he says. 'I just can't seem to get my act together.' He laughs briefly, embarrassed more than amused. 'But whenever things get really bad, do you know what I do?'

I shake my head, uncomfortable as he holds me with his gaze, his face open and guileless, his eyes clear, the vivid blue I so well remember.

'I turn my mind to an evening in October – years back,

84

but it's still vivid. There'd been a run of hot days – an Indian summer – and I'd headed out towards Dún Laoghaire for a swim. Afterwards I'd taken my book to the West Pier and was sitting up on the grass reading, when a girl appeared on her bicycle – a girl with long chestnut hair. We hardly knew each other, but I recognized you from class. It was pure serendipity, both of us being there together. I remember everything from that afternoon. The red T-shirt you were wearing with your jeans, the little silver decals on your bike. I even remember the book I was reading – *The Corrections* – it weighed a tonne. We walked along the pier together, the evening sun throwing orange light on the rocks. And by the time we reached the end of the pier, I knew that I loved you. When things get bad for me, I go back there, to the end of the pier. It holds a special place in my heart. It was the first place we kissed –'

'Stop it,' I say, alarmed at how far he has gone into this, how far I have let him go, allowing myself to get pulled into his web of nostalgia, momentarily forgetting how dangerous he is to me.

'Faye –'

'Enough!' I stand up quickly, picking up my phone and dropping it into my bag. I'm reaching for the notebook when his hand shoots out and grabs my arm. His fingers circling my wrist are hot and clammy, his grip tight. My heart is beating faster now. 'Let go of me,' I tell him, keeping my voice very calm and very cold.

The mothers at the next table have fallen silent and are openly staring at us.

'You're the love of my life,' he tells me, the statement

uttered earnestly, without guile or embarrassment. Part of me knows that I should feel a rising anxiety, that I should be repelled, and I am. But I'm fascinated too. Despite the vague sense of threat, I am held by the strength of his feeling.

'The love of your life? You don't even know me.'

'How can you say that? After everything we've been through together?'

'What is it you want from me? Some sort of closure? Some peace of mind? I don't know how I can help you. What happened between us happened a long time ago. We're both different people now.'

'You really believe that?'

'I believe it's best to leave the past in the past. Move on.'

'All I've ever wanted,' he continues, 'is to hear the knock on my door, to see your outline behind the glass and to know that finally you had come back to me. That you had realized it too.'

'Realized what?' I ask, knowing that it's foolish to ask the question but I can't help myself.

'That we can't live without each other.'

Enough. I wrench my hand free and lean in quickly, lowering my voice: 'Whatever it is you think, whatever thoughts are spinning around in your head – it's a distortion. It's not real. I've moved on with my life – I'm married now – and it's time you moved on too.'

'And you love him, do you? You're happy together? Fulfilled?' Scorn leaks into his voice, and it's a relief from the relentless pull of his emotional pleading. Scorn I can handle.

'My marriage is none of your business. In fact, nothing

in my life is any of your concern. I want you to leave me alone, do you understand, Michael? You're to stay away from me –'

'Or what? You'll call the police?' The corner of his mouth pulls up fractionally – a shadow of a smirk. 'Aren't you afraid of what questions they might ask? Who knows what they might find out?'

It's disconcerting, the way his manner leaps about from adoration to implicit threat.

It's an effort to keep my voice calm. 'You can't threaten me.'

He holds my gaze. 'Sometimes, in the night, I think I can hear crying –'

'Right. That's it.' I reach again for my notebook, my hand accidentally brushing against the tall glass that holds my barely touched latte. It topples off the saucer, coffee splashing everywhere, and, as I fumble to right the glass, my notebook slips from the table and falls to the ground, a flutter of loose pages landing around it.

'Shit!' I put down my bag and bend to the floor.

Michael moves on to one knee, hurriedly retrieving the scraps of paper that have scattered. He hands them to me and I mutter a thanks, then straighten up, fixing the handle of my bag over the crook of my arm. I've stayed long enough, and now I just want to get away from him.

I turn back to say my goodbye, but it dies in my throat. His hand is outstretched. Caught between his index and middle fingers is the grainy greyscale image of the curled-up child that I am carrying.

'You forgot this one,' he says quietly.

The air in the room seems to inflate and then collapse.

I reach and take it from him, stuffing it into my bag, my heart pounding. *It's just a picture. It doesn't matter*, I tell myself, but my inner voice sounds weak and unsure.

'Goodbye, Michael,' I say, turning from him quickly, but, as I do, my hip knocks forcefully against the back of a plastic chair, threatening to topple it. He reaches forward quickly, rights the chair, setting it back on its four legs, and as I look back to mutter my thanks I see that he is staring at me. All traces of his earlier affection have gone.

'Does he know?' he asks me now. 'Your husband?'

'I don't know what you mean,' I answer, flustered.

'Yes, you do. You know exactly what I mean.'

And what he says next makes my blood run cold.

'I mean *our* baby. Have you told him about that? Or have you led him to believe that this baby is your first?'

7

Michael

April 2010

'Are you sure?' Michael asked.

Faye nodded quickly. 'Positive.'

Triply positive, in fact. Over the course of ten days, she told him, she had done three pregnancy tests, her heart sinking a little more with each one.

His hands went to his cheeks, which felt suddenly hot, fingers pulling downwards.

'I just can't believe it,' he remarked, shock in his voice. He couldn't feel his face, as if all the nerve endings had suddenly died. Confusion swept through his brain, thoughts clambering one over the other. She had been on the Pill for two years – they had been careful. It just didn't seem possible.

'How?' he asked, and a rushed explanation came tumbling out – an incident of food-poisoning, she said, some undercooked chicken.

'It must have interfered with the pill,' she told him, as he stared at the food he had bought, spread out on the chenille bedspread – ham-and-cheese croissants, bars of Nestlé Crunch, a bag of crisps he had opened – but the smell rising from them seemed to overpower the little room, making him feel sick.

'Why didn't you tell me? I mean, that was months ago. It's April.'

'I didn't know until last week. I didn't realize –'

'How could you not know? I mean, didn't your periods stop?'

'Not really.'

'What do you mean?'

'I was still getting them at first, but they were lighter. A lot lighter.'

'And you didn't question that?'

'I just figured it was because I've been studying so hard and maybe not eating as well as I should have. Lots of women stop getting periods when they're stressed – it happens. I figured it was that.' Her cheeks burned, and he felt how excruciating this was for her, but the shock held him apart.

He stared hard at the floor, the cogs of his brain working through the problem, but the solution seemed distant and opaque. A silence fell over them, taut with unspoken things. He didn't see the emotion building inside her until she blurted out: 'You can't even look at me!'

Immediately, his gaze lifted and met hers, and he saw that she was frightened and confused and crying out for comfort. He reached across the bed and pulled her to him.

'I'm sorry!' he said, kissing her hair, her face, which streamed with tears. He wiped them away with his thumb. 'Forgive me, please. I should never have acted like that – this is so much worse for you. I'm a selfish prick, okay? You have every right to be mad at me.'

He kept on hugging her and offering reassurance, but still she held herself stiffly in his arms. A patch of blue sky was visible through the closed window, and he stared out at it, searching for traces of the ash cloud casting its shadow as it amassed silently and stealthily overhead. He felt the ceiling lowering on them, the room suddenly too small and cramped, the walls beginning to narrow and close in.

'Let's get out of here,' he said.

It was good to be outside in the fresh air. The oppression of her news lifted as they walked side by side, his arm around her shoulders, the sun warming their limbs.

'The way I see it, we have two options,' he told her. 'Either we terminate the pregnancy, or we get married, have this baby and live happily ever after.'

She managed a small smile. 'Be serious,' she said quietly.

'I am being serious,' he claimed, and was surprised by how much he meant it. Right in that moment, he would have committed his life to her with the whole of his heart.

'We can't get married.'

'Why not? *Mrs Faye Jameson*. It has a nice ring to it, don't you think?'

She shook her head and laughed briefly – the notion was ridiculous to her. Of the two of them, she was the more pragmatic. Life had made her that way. With a mother who was flaky at best and negligent at worst, and no father ever on the scene, Faye had spent her childhood being parcelled out from one relative to another. She had learned early that she had to be resilient and resourceful to survive. Like Faye, Michael had also grown up without his father. The age difference between his parents had been significant, and his father had died before Michael had even started school. His memories of the man were dim and untrustworthy. Shortly before Michael's tenth birthday his mother had remarried. A man called Jeff who drove a Jaguar and wore a moustache and lived and breathed golf. They didn't get on, and it was a relief to everyone when Michael was shipped off to Dublin to live with Min and attend the local school, then later university, where he'd met Faye. They'd bonded over many things but this was one of them: that they were both fatherless children, both carrying the scars of their unstable upbringings. It had been worse for her, and so he could understand her reluctance now about the baby. The uncertainty of her own early years hovered in the background as she listed all the reasons why they couldn't have the child.

'We're too young, we've no money, we're both still in college –'

'You'll be finished in a few months, and I've only one more year.'

'And how could I get a job with a newborn baby to look after? I was hoping to do a Master's.'

'You still could. Lots of people have babies and continue their studies.'

But Faye wasn't buying it. Those single mothers trying to work towards their degrees while juggling childcare – they always seemed hassled, frustrated, exhausted. She didn't want to be pulled apart in that manner, unable to give her full attention either to study or to motherhood.

'I wish I'd realized earlier,' she told him. 'Straight away. If I'd only taken the morning-after pill . . . I feel so fucking stupid.'

'It was an honest mistake. Neither of us thought of it. And, anyway,' he went on, his mood lifting, 'this might turn out to be a good thing. Maybe even the best thing that's ever happened to either of us.'

'Be realistic. It's a disaster. What was I even thinking – coming to Barcelona? I should've gone to the UK or the Netherlands. Found a clinic in the middle of nowhere and just gotten it sorted out. Instead, I'm here, wasting time.'

He heard the rising panic in her voice and said: 'Listen, we can still do that if it's what you want. We can get on the Internet first thing in the morning and make an appointment. We could be on a plane in a few days –'

'If this ash ever clears –'

'And this whole thing could be over in a week. But, for now, instead of freaking out, let's just calmly consider our options. When we've had a chance to sleep on it, let's make a decision.'

She seemed grateful for his calm sense of reason.

'Whatever happens, I'll be there for you, okay? You're not going to have to go through this alone.'

Their most immediate concern that afternoon was accommodation. Originally, they had booked to stay for two nights at the little hotel north of the Ramblas, but, with flights across Europe grounded indefinitely, neither of them could be sure how long they might expect to spend in Barcelona. After half an hour of haggling at the Reception desk, with the desk clerk's limited English and Michael's even worse Spanish hampering progress, they secured the room for an extra night but at a higher rate. Michael knew he was being fleeced, but, with so many tourists trapped in the city, unable to fly out, there was pressure on hotels and guesthouses, and what limited availability remained would be snapped up quickly. He didn't like to think about the cost of it all, about the dwindling funds in his bank account, and, given Faye's anxiety about the pregnancy, he judged it best to keep his concerns hidden.

Faye seemed to perk up a little once they'd eaten and their accommodation was sorted out, but she remained subdued for most of the day, not saying much as they drifted around Barcelona, occasionally stopping at Internet cafés to check for updates, or dipping into bars to scan the news on the TV.

At his suggestion, they went to visit the Basílica de la Sagrada Família. Michael took the view that they might as well check out the sights while they were stuck there, and he was drawn to the Gothic angles and Art Nouveau flourishes within Gaudí's design. The unexpected drama of Subirachs' sculptures was a bonus, but while he stood marvelling at them Faye touched his sleeve.

'I'm going inside to sit down,' she said.

'Are you okay?' There was a pasty sheen to her face, and her mouth seemed tight.

'Fine. Just tired. All this walking around . . .' Her voice trailed off and she turned away.

He watched her disappear into the vault of the basilica, her dress a pale shimmer, before she was swallowed by the darkness, and felt a wave of tenderness towards her, and regret at his initial reaction. It was natural to be shocked, but now, in the warm spring sunlight, on a leisurely afternoon, he felt an unexpected uprush of excitement. All day he had found himself snatching glances at her when he thought she wasn't aware. She appeared different to him: the news had attached a new importance to her, so that, while there was no visible appearance of her pregnancy yet, she seemed weightier. He imagined that her curves had taken on a new roundness, and she seemed to hold herself more carefully. Within the folds of her body, she was carrying his child. He was going to be a father, a thought that ought to have scared him but oddly didn't. It seemed miraculous to him that the love they shared had come together to create a tiny being.

'You're here too?'

The voice dragged him out of the spiral of his thoughts. He looked down and saw blonde hair in two plaits, the Northwestern sweatshirt. It was the girl he'd met that morning in the coffee shop, the one who'd told him about the ash cloud.

'Seems like we're all on the tourist trail now,' the American girl said, smiling to reveal dimples, a set of white teeth.

'Yeah, I guess,' he laughed, reaching up to rub at the back of his neck.

'I'm Sheena,' she said, thrusting out her hand to shake and repeating his name back to him, the introductions made.

'So did you manage to find somewhere to stay?' she asked.

'Yes, for now. The hotel are letting us stay on for a couple of extra nights. It's costing an arm and a leg, but what choice do we have?'

'I guess.'

'How about you?'

'We're still at the hostel, but there's talk of leaving the city tomorrow. Friends of ours have a house in the mountains. There's room there if we want it.'

'That's lucky.'

'You could join us if you like? I'm sure there's space, so long as you don't mind sleeping on the floor.'

She was still smiling up at him with her open face, while her light green eyes with their coronas of blonde lashes remained fixed on his in a way that went beyond friendliness. Interest was there; he could feel it; and it made him nervous and bashful.

'Well, I'm not sure . . .' he said, looking around him for Faye, for this girl's group.

'It'd be fun,' she told him, giggling and adding meaningfully: 'I guarantee we'd have lots of fun.'

'Right, but . . . it's just that I'd need to check with my girlfriend, what she wants to do . . .'

He saw her registering that new information, processing it, and then deciding to press on regardless.

'Some of us are going out later to a bar down by the waterfront. Why don't you swing by? We could have a beer together, talk about what you want to do, make a plan.' She kept smiling at him, and he found her confidence compelling.

'I'm not sure what we're doing later . . .' he mumbled, uncertain. Striving then to redeem himself, he added: 'But, yeah. That sounds cool.'

Sheena told him the name of the bar, gave some loose directions, but Michael knew he would not go there; and later that evening, after a supper of spaghetti with clams which they ate in a small restaurant near the marina, Faye

96

declared she was tired and they began making their way slowly back to the hotel.

The quarrel began over the cost of their supper, which had surprised them both in its exorbitance. They had checked the menu beforehand, but some mistake had been made – a misunderstanding over additional costs, taxes, an extra charge for the bread, an error in the wine they'd ordered, the more expensive house white being brought to the table – and they'd ended up paying far more than anticipated.

'We'll have to be more careful tomorrow,' Faye said. She had her arms crossed over her chest, her eyes fixed on the pavement as Michael walked alongside her, his hands in his pockets.

'Don't worry. It'll be fine.'

'You keep saying that,' she muttered beneath her breath, and he felt a spike of annoyance within himself to match her own.

'Are you okay?' he asked. He deliberately slowed his pace so that she would too, and, as they walked alongside each other, she said: 'I'm worried we'll run out of money; we've barely enough to pay for the hotel, and God knows how long we'll be here. We ought to be economizing, not eating out like this.'

He felt the barb. The restaurant had been his suggestion.

'We'll wear the hairshirts tomorrow,' he suggested, trying to make a joke of it to lighten her mood. 'Nil by mouth for twenty-four hours, huh?'

'I'm serious, Michael. We need to be careful. We're going to need money – not just for food and our hotel, but for later, after all this is over . . .' Her voice drifted, but

97

he felt the nub of something there – the root of her silence over dinner. They'd been together long enough for him to be able to read her cues.

He stopped in the street and she turned to look at him. 'What is it?' he asked her. 'I know this is not about the restaurant, so why don't you just tell me.'

She chewed her lip and looked anxious. Not meeting his eye, she said: 'I've made a decision,' and he felt his stomach plunge, as if his insides understood first where this was going, his brain lagging behind.

'I can't keep it,' she went on. 'No matter which way I turn it over in my mind, it doesn't work.'

'Wait –'

'I'm not interested in being talked out of this, Michael. I've made my decision.'

Her chin jutted up a little as she said this, a defiant tilt, and he felt a lurch of sudden anger. 'Don't I get any say in this?' He kept his voice calm and low, but his hands were on his hips, his shoulders squared. A couple walked past, both of them turning their heads to observe the clear and obvious hostility.

Faye met his anger with her own dry-eyed coolness. 'No, you don't.'

He shook his head and laughed – a brief, mirthless bark.

'What?' she asked.

'I just . . . I can't believe you. You come all this way to meet me, you break this news to me only this morning when you could have told me at any stage over the phone, and then, after all that, you make this decision? I mean, why did you even come here?'

98

'You think I should have just kept this to myself? Not bothered you with it?' Her voice tipped upwards into a sharp squeak of hysteria.

'No! For fuck's sake –'

'Well, I'm sorry to trouble your conscience with all this. It must be so difficult for you.' Tears had sprung in her eyes, and she turned from him now and began striding quickly away. He had to half run to catch up with her.

'I'm not suggesting for one moment that this is harder for me than it is for you –'

'Aren't you?' she snapped, without slowing her pace.

'Don't be absurd. All I'm saying is that you could at least share your thought process with me – talk to me about this. I'm not saying that I'm going to object to whatever it is you choose, but I feel that, for something this big, we should at least have a reason.'

'A reason?' This time, she did slow down, long enough to cast a glance of disbelief at him. 'I'm twenty years old and I don't want to be a mother,' she said quietly. 'That's my reason.'

A silence fell between them, unbroken until they neared the Internet café they'd taken to frequenting, lit within by fluorescent-tube lighting. When Faye stopped outside and checked her wallet for cash, Michael said: 'Again? Really? We've been in there like four times already today.' He couldn't explain it, but the thought of once more sitting at one of those terminals, his fingertips skating over keyboards grimy from hundreds, maybe even thousands, of strangers' touch, made his skin crawl.

'I need to do some research,' she said, sliding her wallet back inside her bag, fixing the strap over her shoulder.

'Research?'

'I don't even know if abortion is legal in Spain,' she answered quietly. 'My hunch is that it's not, or else it's very restrictive. I'll need to look into flights, clinics.'

'Can't you do that in the morning?'

She shook her head. 'I don't want to wait. It already feels like I've waited too long. I don't even know how easy it will be to organize.' She shrugged, and then, seeing the expression on his face, she added, in a cool voice: 'You don't have to come in, you know. I can check it out myself.'

'Right. So I'll just loiter here in the street while I wait for you.'

Her features darkened. 'You don't have to wait for me, Michael. You can go back to the hotel, or go for a walk, or do whatever you want. You're a free agent.'

'What? I'm just going to let you walk back to the hotel on your own?'

'I'm a big girl. I don't need you to protect me,' she told him, suddenly angry. 'And right now, frankly, I'd welcome the space.'

'Suit yourself,' he said, turning on his heel, and he walked away from her briskly, purposefully, into the night.

The bar was a small establishment on a side street near Port Vell, busy with tourists and locals, the pitch of noise hitting him as soon as he walked inside. He'd found the place easily enough, and moved through the crowd until he saw her white-blonde hair.

'You came!' she cried, touching his arm and grinning. The college sweatshirt was gone, replaced by a halter-neck dress in a shiny fabric, striped in various blues, reds and gold.

He knew it was wrong, that his motives for doing it were impure and largely driven by an anger that had whipped to life inside him. But Sheena's smile, her blithe relaxed manner, the small pert breasts in her colourful dress pressing up against his arm, all seemed to push him inevitably onwards. Someone put a beer into his hand and he felt the coolness of it, the welcome relief as it filled his mouth and travelled down his throat.

'So this house in the mountains,' he began, and Sheena's mouth broadened into a slow smile, the dimples reappearing. 'You reckon there's room for a couple more?'

8

Faye

Summer unfurls, bright and hot and arid. Across the country, temperatures soar, reaching record heights. In the park across the road from the office, the grass dries out to tawny patches that crackle underfoot when I walk there during my lunch-breaks. On the ruined lawns, people stretch out under the sun, men with their shirts off and girls in bikinis, limbs and torsos broiling in the heat. My own body swells as the weeks pass, the baby growing to the size of a lime, then a lemon, then an apple. Bemused, I mark the progress of my pregnancy in terms of fruit. When it becomes an avocado, the ticklish sensation that at first I'd mistaken for indigestion grows more frequent and insistent as the baby turns inside me, making his or her presence felt.

The office empties out over the summer weeks as colleagues disappear to Italy, France, Spain, the Greek islands. Ed and I spend a week in south Kerry, where we swim every day in water that is clear and blissfully cool, temporary relief from the relentless and unusual heat. A brief holiday that is over all too soon, but, with the fatigue of the first trimester well behind me, I am taken with a new energy that sparks my ambition, absorbing me in my work. I have secured an exhibit space at TechConnect

Live in September, an opportunity to promote the company and make valuable contacts, so Jess and I spend long hours locked in brainstorming sessions with Frank, our product-development manager, and Sophie, our communications manager, and when I leave the office late in the evening my mind is buzzing, alive to all the possibilities within our reach.

From time to time, in unguarded moments, I will suddenly remember the look Michael gave me after bending to pick up the greyscale scanned image from the floor, one loaded with accusation, and then a shiver of nerves goes through me like ice-cold water cascading over my neck and shoulders. These memories are free-floating and sharp-edged; they come at me with unnerving clarity, recalling the fury that had lit up his eyes. But when these moments happen, I simply breathe deeply and wait for them to pass, and, as July unfolds into August, there are no more letters or phone calls or texts, the silence from Michael lengthens, and I begin to relax. I stop glancing around me every time I'm on the Dart or walking towards the office. I don't tense whenever my phone sounds with an alert. I convince myself that what happened between us is in the past, and all thoughts of promises made and broken, secrets shared then buried, begin to fade.

Towards the end of August, Ed packs his bags to leave. I sit on our bed on the eve of his departure, watching him throw some clothes into a holdall, a tower of books and notes piled on the floor waiting to be stowed away into his rucksack along with his laptop and chargers.

'You're sure you'll be all right?' he asks me for the umpteenth time.

'Of course! I'll be fine.'

'You'd tell me if you wanted me to stay?'

'Seriously! It's just for ten days. I can manage on my own for that long. And you're looking forward to it, right?'

'Yes. I really am,' he nods, his eyes lighting up with excitement. A week at a writers' and artists' retreat in a remote part of the country to work on his book, and, at the end of it, two days at a Literary Festival in Clare, where he's booked to do a reading. 'It's just what I need,' he admits. 'Some time carved out to focus, try to break the back of this draft. Did I tell you some of my writers' group might be coming down?'

'Really?'

'Yeah. Jamesie's on for it, maybe Hugh.'

It's good to see him enthused, fired up about his work and making friends. Recently I'd noticed some despondency creeping in about his writing, mention made of difficulties with the plot of the new book he's working on. Often in the evenings when I got home from work, he seemed quiet, brooding, which made me worry that he's unsuited to the solitary lifestyle. On more than one occasion, he's intimated that perhaps he'd made a mistake. I've tried my best to keep him upbeat, to remind him of all the positives about the new direction he's taken, but still I know that he feels disappointed that the book did not turn out to be the breakout hit he'd hoped for.

He zips up his holdall and throws himself on the bed beside me, pulling me to him so that his nose is nuzzling my hair, his mouth close to my ear.

'So will you miss me?' he asks, and I pull his arms tightly around me.

'Maybe,' I answer coyly. 'But I may be too busy to miss you, between work and organizing a certain fortieth birthday party.'

He groans and pulls me in closer. 'No! Don't remind me.'

'The attainment of middle age ought to be celebrated,' I tease him.

'I'm in my prime,' he insists. 'Promise me you won't go too mad, okay? No DJs or novelty entertainers. No T-shirts with my face on them or slide shows of my childhood pictures –'

'Don't worry. It'll just be a few friends and family members over for a get-together. A glass of bubbly and some cake. Nothing fancy.'

'Hmm,' he grunts, unconvinced. 'I know you, Faye. The whole place will be decked out in flowers and bunting, a circus tent on the patio, camels grazing on the lawn . . .'

The baby kicks inside me, and his hand travels under the folds of my top to press gently against my skin. It smooths and caresses.

'I know something we can do before I go,' he whispers, and I hear the seductive smile in his voice, and turn in his arms to embrace him.

The week that Ed is away is a hot one, so hot in fact that temperature records around the country are broken. I sleep with the windows open, yet when I wake the sheets are damp with sweat, bunched and mussed as if there are two people still occupying the bed. In the office, there are fans set up at intervals between workstations to encourage the movement of air, but still a desultory atmosphere lingers. My desk by the window, once coveted for the view, becomes a furnace under the glare of the sun. Even with the blinds down, the heat still seeps through. It's difficult to concentrate.

'Got a sec, Faye?'

I look up and see Jess beckoning for me to join her in her office. I grab my notebook and phone, and when I reach her door she nods and says: 'Close that, will you?'

I'm surprised because her door is always open, and, as I take a seat, I feel a sense of unease, my brain quickly running over the possible avenues this conversation might take.

'This is a bit delicate,' Jess begins, 'so I'm just going to come right out with it. I received this in my post this morning.'

She reaches into her desk drawer and pulls out an envelope. I recognize it instantly – blue with a posy of flowers. The whispered warning inside me rises to a scream. It's all I can do to maintain my composure as Jess hands it to me, although I can feel the blood rush to my cheeks.

'Open it,' she tells me.

A quick glance at the envelope reveals that it has been addressed to her, and, when I draw out yet another newspaper clipping marked with red ink, I feel an upsurge of nausea, the taste of vomit in my throat. The photograph is of me, Jess, the whole team – all of us assembled in the foyer of the office, arms crossed and smiling with confidence – the picture accompanying the article in the *Irish Times* that I was so proud of. Now I look at the red ring marked around my head in the image, and the word scrawled above it: *Criminal*.

'Oh my God,' I breathe, dropping the clipping on the

desk and leaning my elbows on the armrests of the chair, my hands going up to cover my face. In the tented darkness of my hands, I feel the whoosh of blood in my veins, and, beyond that, the silence as Jess waits for me to explain.

'I'm so sorry,' I begin, taking away my hands and raising my eyes to look at her. 'I can't believe you've been dragged into this.'

'Dragged into this?' she repeats, incredulous. 'What is going on?'

'Look, I can explain –'

'Who would send something like this?'

'It's complicated, Jess. And it's a private matter that you should never have been involved in.'

'Do you know who sent this?'

'Yes. At least, I think I do.'

'Who?'

I think about this for a split-second, and then I lie and say: 'A family member.' Even now, I know it's not safe to disclose my true suspicion. I can't talk to Jess about Michael, about the grudge he's carrying – nothing that might risk being traced back to Barcelona, the volcano, what we did . . .

She's staring at me, nonplussed, awaiting an explanation, and so I mumble something about a cousin harbouring resentments, a cousin with emotional and psychological problems.

'Am I right in thinking that this is not the first poison-pen letter he's sent?' Jess asks, and I admit that there have been a couple of others but that this is the first time he's tried to involve someone else.

'And what have you done about it?' she asks. 'Have you confronted this person?'

'Yes.'

'And?'

I shrug. 'He denies it, of course, but I know that it's him.'

'Have you spoken to the police?'

'No –'

'Why the hell not?'

'It would only antagonize him. I prefer to deal with it in my own way –'

'By ignoring it?' She sits forward, draws the clipping towards her, casting her gaze over it once more, her expression one of horror. 'This is frightening, Faye. This level of harassment, of threat. It seems to me that ignoring it is just going to make things worse. I mean, now that he's started sending these notes to other people, it's an escalation, right?'

The truth of this rocks me a little, giving me pause.

'What does Ed think?' she asks, and my eyes flicker away from her.

'I haven't told him.'

'Jesus Christ. Why not?' she demands sharply, and I feel the colour rushing to my cheeks again.

'I didn't want to worry him.'

'But he's your husband!'

'I know! But it's just . . . it hasn't been easy, Jess. This move back to Ireland, the change in his career – it's been unsettling for him. He's been stressed about the book and he's found it difficult to meet people, make new friends – I didn't want to add another layer of worry to the situation.'

'Don't you think he deserves to know?'

'I'm just trying to protect him.'

She shakes her head, then holds her hands up in a gesture of surrender. 'Look, it's your marriage, I'm not going to get involved. All I'll say to you is that in these situations it's best to be upfront and truthful. Full disclosure. No good comes of keeping secrets in a marriage, trust me.'

And I think then of Ed's words to me: *I don't much like secrets.* A wave of guilt washes over me.

'In the meantime, what are we going to do about this?' Jess asks, fingering the clipping with distaste.

I get to my feet and reach across, taking the clipping from her hand.

'I'll talk to the police,' I tell her.

'See that you do. Because, Faye, you might be hoping that whoever is sending these things to you may grow bored and it'll all just peter out. But what if he's only getting started? What if he decides that notes are not enough?'

The suggestion of violence shimmers in the air between us.

I keep my voice steady. 'I'll take care of it.'

I leave the office early, and, true to my word, I call into the local garda station on my way home. When I show the clipping to the guard behind the front desk, his reaction is a mixture of scepticism and boredom, like he's already seen a dozen of these that day. He takes down my details and asks some questions about when the note was received, what other communications had there been. I explain to him that all the letters have been sent to my workplace, none to my home. I have that at least, the comfort that Michael doesn't know where I live. When I explain to the guard that I had destroyed the previous notes, he sighs, a small huff of impatience, then delivers a mini-lecture on the importance of keeping all future correspondence and making a careful record of dates, notes received, any form of communication tagged so that a case can be built based on the evidence, if it comes to that.

'And you've really got no idea who might be behind all this?' he asks, and I shake my head and lie.

'No idea at all.'

The last thing I want is the guards going around to Michael, questioning him on his motivation, poking around in the past.

He gives me his card and tells me to call if anything further happens, and I walk out into the sunshine with the vague feeling of having evaded scrutiny, as if I'm the guilty one who has somehow escaped justice.

That evening, I call Jess and tell her that I've spoken to the guards.

'And Ed?' she asks.

'He's away until the weekend. But once he's home I'll sit him down and tell him what's been happening.'

He had rung me earlier in the day, just to say hello, and I had detected uneasiness in his voice. When I pressed him gently, he admitted things weren't going great at the writers' retreat. He was stuck on a critical part of the book, trying to untangle the plot, which had grown convoluted. His voice sounded agitated, nervy, and, from what I gathered from his conversation, he seemed to be spending a lot of time alone in his room. The last thing he needed was an account from me of the complicated weave of threats and coercion that I've experienced over the past few months.

Jess, however, seems content with my response.

'Listen, why don't you work from home tomorrow?' she suggests. 'You've no meetings, and it can't be easy being pregnant in this heat, traipsing in and out of town.'

I take her up on it, appreciating the unexpected lie-in the next morning, and then the coolness of my kitchen, where my laptop sits on the island, my notes spread out on the worktop, bare feet on the tiled floor. In a lull during the morning, I make some phone calls about glassware and equipment hire for the birthday party, getting quotes on catering services and organizing wine deliveries. For Ed's present, I have bought a watch – a TAG Heuer, expensive. I shy away from any thoughts that the extravagance of the gift is to appease my own conscience. Instead, I justify the cost with the thought that it might be the last opportunity for splashing out before the baby comes. I want to spoil him a little.

I've arranged for the watch to be engraved at a jeweller's in Blackrock village, and at lunchtime I walk down to collect it. I have to wait a little while the work is completed, and, by the time I leave the shop, the watch stowed carefully in my handbag, the sun is at full tilt. A heat-haze quivers above the road, and I can feel the footpath blazing through the soles of my sandals as I begin the walk home. I have brought an umbrella with me, not in anticipation of any rain – although it would be welcome – but to provide some shelter from the sun. And it is thanks to that umbrella that I see Michael but he doesn't see me.

It happens as I'm walking up the main road towards home. Our estate is the second turn-off to the left after the pedestrian lights, and I'm paused there, waiting for the lights to change so I can cross, when I turn my head to the right, checking for traffic, and see him emerging from our estate. He has his head down, hands in his pockets, and is walking quickly, but it's definitely Michael. The stooped posture, the curve of his shoulders, the sandy sweep of hair – I'm sure of it.

Panic snatches at my stomach, a sudden uprush of bile. He is walking in the direction of the village, where I have just come from. If I cross the road now, I will be directly in his path – there's no way he won't see me. The lights change, the insistent beeping alert startling me, but I don't cross. Instead, I remain on my side of the road and turn to walk uphill, pulling my umbrella down low and tilting it so that my face is shielded from his view. I keep walking, past the junction where the road from our estate links to the main road, continuing until there is some distance between us before I risk looking back. I scan the pavement on both sides of the road, but I can't see him. Perhaps his pace had quickened and he's already reached the village. A bus hurtles along towards the main drag and I wonder if he might have jumped on. Still, it puzzles me, how quickly he's disappeared, as if he's vanished into thin air. Only when I'm sure he's no longer within sight do I cross the road and track back towards home.

Once inside, I pull the door shut and dump the umbrella on the ground, holding on to the wall for support, the blood rushing to my head. I feel my way along the hall and into the kitchen, where I fill a glass of water from the tap and drink it quickly, then another.

The walk, the heat, the fright he's given me, combine to make me exhausted. I take the watch from my bag and climb the stairs. In my bedroom, I draw the curtains in swift tugs to block out the light. And then I sit and wait for the blood to stop pounding in my ears, for the tingling in my hands to fade. Perhaps it wasn't him. Perhaps I imagined it. And, even if it was him, can I be sure he knows which one is my house? It might be pure coincidence that he was walking past – these things happen.

But even after my body calms, and I shake myself off, even after I've stowed the watch in the drawer of my bedside locker and stretched out on the bed, turning the side of my face to the cool pillow, still it remains – the one thought that keeps racing through my head, slowly solidifying into conviction: *He knows where I live.*

That night, the weather breaks. I lie awake listening to the lash of rain against the window, curtains of it falling from the sky. After the sultry stillness of the last few days, the noise of the downpour is startling, and while my mind whirrs in different directions, I try hard to bring discipline to my thoughts, corral them into some kind of order. With forensic detail, I trace back over all the contacts I've had with Michael over the past few months: the notes, the texts that night at the theatre, our meeting in the National Gallery – every instance balled up tightly in memory, but a fine thin thread of danger running through each case. What does he want from me? Why is he hounding me like this? I can't work out if it's an apology he seeks or some form of retribution? The newspaper clippings marked with red ink seem to vibrate with fury, with vengeful anger. Their purpose seems to be to frighten, not to woo. And yet, on the occasion of our meeting, it was not anger that I felt from him but a strange calm, a blandness that I found infuriating, even a sort of joy. He seemed so happy to finally see me again, after all those years. 'There's only ever been you, Faye. Always has been. Always will.'

I squirm at the memory, my legs getting knotted in the sheets, which I kick away angrily.

'We can't live without each other,' he'd told me at that same meeting, and I wonder again at his strategy. Does he hope to rekindle some romance between us? The prospect is ludicrous, but, if he does, why is he trying to frighten me with these notes? He'd denied them, of course, tried to act as if he'd had no part in sending them. It was a convincing performance: 'I've literally no idea what you're talking about' – his expression blank. But what if I'm wrong and it's not Michael who's sending these notes? What if there's someone else out there with a malign intent towards me? What if there's another living soul who knows what I've done?

Through a gap in the curtains, I catch a flicker of light from the garden. It only lasts a second or two, but I sit up quickly, then move to the window. Rain lashes the glass, and when I peer down through the darkness there's only the blackened mass of shrubs and the gleam of puddles on the patio. But I'm convinced I saw something: torch-light, the brief flare from the screen of a mobile phone. I grab my own phone and go downstairs quickly, pulling my dressing gown on as I hurry towards the kitchen. It's dark in here, but as I cross the room the security light outside comes on suddenly, the sensor sparked by movement in the garden. A gasp escapes my lips and instinctively I raise a hand to my mouth to stifle any noise. I stand perfectly still, all of my senses alert to any movement beyond the glass.

Rain falls, catching the light, bouncing off the paving slabs in brisk splashes. And then, beyond on the grass, the flick of a white-tipped tail. A fox. It jumps up on to the fence and disappears into the garden next door. My hand goes to my chest, feels the galloping of my heartbeat as it starts to calm.

After a minute, the light in the garden goes off. The rain has started to ease, and I fill a glass of water and go back upstairs, shaken by the incident. Michael's presence so close to my home this afternoon has taken my fear into new territory and I realize now that I should have picked up the phone and contacted the guard I'd spoken to, informing him that I hadn't been entirely truthful – that there is someone I suspect, and that I'd caught sight of my tormentor that afternoon close to my home. I resolve to make the call first thing in the morning, and in the meantime I call Ed, just to hear his voice and take comfort from it, knowing that talking to him will help make me calm. But his phone rings out and I don't leave a message, knowing that my voice will sound tense and uncertain.

Finally, I sleep, waking the next morning to the clearness of light filtered through a thin layer of cloud. I get up, shower and dress, and then downstairs I turn on the kettle and pull the curtains back. Steam rises outside the window as last night's rain evaporates.

I pull open the sliding door and take my tea outside, smelling the air – so green and fresh this morning. My phone rings and it's Ed calling to see if I'm all right. He'd just seen my missed call and was worried something was wrong.

'I'm fine,' I tell him.

'You were up pretty late last night,' he remarks. 'Everything okay?'

'I just couldn't sleep. I . . . I kept imagining I was hearing things.'

'What kind of things?'

'Noises outside in the garden.'

'Do you think there was someone there?' A new sharpness enters his tone and I move quickly to dispel his worry.

'No, it was just a fox.'

'Are you sure?'

'Positive. I saw it jumping over the fence.'

'Listen, if you're nervous about being in the house on your own, why don't you go over to my parents' house? They'd love to have you to stay.'

'I'm fine, honestly. But how about you?' I ask, changing the direction of conversation. 'How are you getting on?'

'Yeah, good. I think I've turned a corner with the book. Oh, and Jamesie is coming down.'

'Who?'

'One of the writers' group in Dublin. You've heard me talking about him, haven't you?'

Jamesie. I try to locate the name in my memory, but I can't recall him.

'We met at the reading in the Lexicon a few months ago,' Ed explains. 'He's a nice guy.'

'That's great. You guys will get to hang out for a day or two.'

'And he's giving me a lift to the festival on Friday.'

The animation in his voice as he talks about his plans for the next few days is a balm to me after my restless night. I try to picture these people he's telling me about. Jamesie, and Gerry, an older writer, both of whom are acting as sounding boards for the ideas he has for the new book. I feel a sense of gratitude towards these people I haven't yet met, relieved that Ed has found this group.

With the phone to my ear, I walk around the garden. Parched from the long dry summer, it has perked up a little with the night's rain. The leaves on the bamboo shoots flutter in a gentle breeze, and the waxy foliage of the camelia bushes shines with dew. And, as I listen to Ed, my eye is caught by a mark on one corner of the patio. A muddy smear – about the size of a man's boot – on one of the paving stones beneath the kitchen window. I see it and my hands go cold.

Could someone have come over the wall in the night? Could they have crept up to the house and paused here beneath the kitchen window to peer in? For a brief moment, I see myself as I was the night before, staring out from behind the glass sliding doors as the fox slipped over the fence — could Michael have been crouched beneath the kitchen window at the time? And, if he was, he'll know that Ed is away. That I'm all alone here.

'Hey? Are you still there?'

'Yes, sorry,' I say, the shudder passing quickly through me. 'You know, maybe I will give your parents a call.'

'Do,' he agrees, his voice lowering with concern as he asks: 'Do you want me to come home?'

It's tempting to say yes. If I were to tell him about the footprint beneath the window, about seeing Michael on the street, the letters I've been receiving — everything — he'd return home immediately. I wouldn't be able to stop him. But I know how important these few days are to him. I can't drag him away now, not when he's just getting into his stride. So, instead, I laugh it off, telling him I'm just being silly. But once inside the house I make sure the doors and windows are locked, double-checking before I leave the house.

After that, I go back to the office. I need to have people around me, the buzz of conversation, the protection of the herd. Several times that day, I take out Garda Bourke's card with the intention of calling him, but on each occasion I waver. As the day wears on, I start to question myself — was it really a muddy footprint I saw on the patio? Or was it just a bit of earth that had spilled from a plant pot disturbed by a passing cat or even that fox I had glimpsed in the night? Nonetheless, I stay with my parents-in-law that night, and the following evening I join Martha, Will and the kids for an outdoor cinema screening of *The*

Princess Bride. Thursday comes and I call Suzi and arrange to meet her for a drink after work.

'I've been meaning to reach out to you for ages,' I tell her. 'I should really have done it before now.'

I don't tell her that I'm frightened of being in my own home alone.

Friday swings around, and I'm excited and relieved in equal measure, as Ed will be home this evening. I'm planning something celebratory to welcome him, and finish up early so that I can swing by Fallon & Byrne on the way home. The afternoon is warm and humid, good barbecue weather, so I buy some marinated lamb to throw on the grill, then pick up some fresh salad ingredients and a slab of soft focaccia, along with a bottle of rosé.

I'm on the Dart home when he calls to tell me he's been delayed.

'Are you on the train?' I ask, hearing voices in the background.

'No, actually I'm still in Clare. Jamesie wants to hang on for a couple more nights – there's a reading he's keen to attend. So I thought I'd stay on, then get a lift back with him on Sunday.'

'I thought you'd be home tonight. I bought something special for dinner.'

'I know, and I'm sorry, really. But I felt I had to say yes. He's a mate, and he did come all this way after all.'

Once more I think of the muddy footprint on the patio. The quiver of fear is still there, and I can't help but feel a stirring of annoyance at the delay to Ed's return. Yet I can't deny how happy Ed seems, and I'm glad that he's found a friend who shares his interests and seems to pep him up. So I keep my feelings to myself.

'When do I get to meet this guy?'

He laughs. 'We'll arrange something when I'm back. You'll like him – I know you will. Listen, love, I'd better go –'

'Wait, what time will you be back?'

But my Dart enters a tunnel at that moment and the connection is lost.

I walk home, mulling over our brief phone conversation; dissatisfied at being cut short, I continue the conversation in my head, the thread of it becoming an argument. But I'm tired, and a little cross now, worn out from work, from staying out each evening, from being unable to relax. By the time I reach the estate, I'm exhausted. The shopping bags I'm carrying are cutting lines into my hands, and as I approach my house I switch the bag in my right hand to my left, looping it over my wrist, then feel in my handbag for my keys. It's quiet at this end of the street. Even though most of the buildings are fully occupied now, a lot of the cars are absent, the windows with blinds and curtains drawn, signalling a holiday exodus. I'm putting the key in the lock when a shadow crosses my peripheral vision – a shape stepping out from behind a tree. My heart pops. I drop the keys and take a step backwards towards the door, the shopping bag slipping off my wrist and crashing to the ground, contents spilling over the doorstep.

The figure moves towards me quickly, resolving into a recognizable shape, and I put my hand to my chest where my heart is madly beating, and say: 'Jesus Christ! You scared the shit out of me!'

'Oh, Faye,' she says in that voice I know so well – crabbed and wheedling, hoarse from too many cigarettes, too many late nights. 'My darling –'

'What are you doing here?'

'Can't a mother call to see her daughter?'

She's a small woman, my mother, even in her heeled sandals, thin and slight. Her frame has grown more stooped in the three years since I've last seen her, and I'm surprised by the sudden push of tenderness I feel at the sight of that dowager's hump rising beneath the grey silk of her blouse.

Maggie laughs, her hand fluttering nervously to her neck, touching the amber brooch that pins her collar. 'Aren't you going to invite me in?'

Reluctantly, I turn and pick up my keys, my shopping, and open the front door, switching off the alarm and leading her into the kitchen.

'This is nice,' she remarks, her eyes travelling the room. It's only now that I notice the wheelie suitcase she's dragging behind her.

'What's going on, Maggie?'

'What do you mean? Nothing's going on,' she laughs, her eyes sliding away from me.

She has large eyes, pale and hooded; the lids are coated in a dusky pink powder, sparse lashes mascaraed into spiky little thorns. I can see that she's made an effort with her appearance – the clothes, the make-up, the neat bob of hair. At first glance, she appears glamorous, well-put-together, but on closer inspection you see the cracks: the chipped nail polish, the band of grey along her hairline where her roots have been neglected.

I press a little harder, asking: 'Where's Leonard?' and she gives an angry little huff.

'Leonard's gone!' she announces. 'I've finished with him. No, really, I have! We are *finito benito* this time, I swear it.'

I pull out a chair and sink into it, already tired by this conversation. It's the endless repetition that gets to me – the same mistakes made over and over, throughout the years, the different boyfriends flitting in and falling out, although Leonard has stuck around longer than most. A small, yellowish sort of man: dirty-blond hair fading to white, teeth and fingers stained yellow from years of smoking, a sun-worshipper, his sallow skin marked with lines carved into his face in deep grooves. I have never liked him, distrusting his exaggerated charm, the way he splashes his money around, the way his eyes constantly slipped away from your gaze – it lent a shiftiness to him. He didn't just enable my mother's addictions, he encouraged them to match his own.

'What happened this time?' I ask drily.

'You don't believe me, do you? But I mean it, darling! I've had it with that snake of a man! Do you know what he did?'

'Surprise me.'

'We were supposed to be going away to Majorca! We had the money all put by, the flights booked, a deposit put down on a nice little apartment –'

'Don't tell me. He gambled away the money, right?'

Her mouth snaps shut and her outrage gives way to

some other tighter inner fury that she directs at me through her narrowed gaze.

'Would it be so hard for you to muster a little sympathy for your mother? Or am I totally beyond that?'

I shake my head, answering in a voice that I am keeping very calm: 'You turn up here, out of the blue – not a word from you in months – how do you expect me to react?'

'You're right,' she says, her voice going up a notch. 'I know you're right. I'm a terrible mother –'

'Don't –'

'Neglectful, selfish, infantile, demanding . . .' She grows shrill as she lists off her faults, repeating back to me the very labels I have pinned to her in previous arguments. They all come rushing back. 'Unreliable, embarrassing –'

'Stop it, please.'

'Why? It's true, isn't it?' She sniffs loudly, her eyes filling up with tears. 'It's only what I deserve.'

Her handbag is on the floor, and, with the back of one hand pressed against her nose, she moves forward to search for a tissue within. The heel of her shoe goes from beneath her and she staggers forward, clutching at the chair, and it confirms what I'd suspected from the minute she stepped forward out of the gloom: she's drunk.

'For God's sake, it's barely six o'clock,' I mutter.

'Don't be angry with me,' she wheedles. 'If you knew how upset I've been, you wouldn't judge me.' She presses a balled-up tissue to her nose, fixes me with her watery gaze. 'I know I've let you down, and I know you're angry with me, but I don't know where else to turn.' Her voice dissolves in tears, and it pulls at something inside me – the thin thread that binds me to her.

'What about Jean?' I ask calmly. My aunt Jean – her sister – is always the one she falls back on any time she and Leonard have one of their spats.

'Jeanie's got her own troubles. She's been in hospital again – did you know?'

I shake my head, shamed by how little contact I have with my own blood relatives.

'I can't be a burden to her, not while she's recovering.' She sniffs loudly, and, when she speaks, her voice wobbles with emotion: 'Do you think there's any chance I could stay with you?'

'Oh, Maggie –'

'It would just be for a few days,' she continues in a rush. 'I need somewhere to stay for a little while so I can sort myself out?'

I think of the times I've let her stay and how all of them ended in calamity. In drunken rows and accusations, wounding words that have left scars. I know better than to give in to her. And yet an image floats to the surface: the muddy footprint beneath my kitchen window. I'm still wary of being home alone.

'All right,' I say. 'But just for a few days.'

'Oh, darling, thank you. I won't be any trouble, I promise.'

The baby gives a sudden kick and instinctively I put a hand to my bump. My mother's eyes follow the movement, flaring then with the realization.

'My God, you're pregnant,' she declares, breathy with shock.

I don't try to deny it, and the room fills with a silence that is both heavy and tense.

'How far gone are you?'

'Nearly five months –'

'Five months?' she repeats. 'Why didn't you tell me?'

'You weren't around.'

I don't admit my reluctance to tell her at all. How what I want more than anything is a clean break with the past, and that includes her.

There is something going on now behind her expression. I have the sense that she is thinking furiously. Up until this point, she has been fidgety with nerves, fingering the brooch at her neck, or touching the ends of her hair. But now a stillness enters her posture and her gaze on me is fixed, eyes slightly round as if amazed.

'What?'

'It's just . . .' she begins, then stops herself.

'Just what?'

'I never pictured you with a baby. I always thought you sort of looked down on motherhood, thought it beneath you.'

'I never said that.'

'I thought you didn't want children and I think I know you pretty well.'

There is heat now prickling over my neck. 'Well. People change. I've changed.'

'I see.' Again the small voice, coolness there, judgement.

'Look,' I tell her. 'We have to have a few ground rules if you're staying. I have to ask you not to drink while you're here.'

'Of course.'

'I really mean it, Maggie.'

I hate laying down this rule, but I know from experience that it's necessary.

She comes towards me, her arms held out for me, and for the first time in almost three years I feel the warmth of my mother's embrace. She leans against me, small, bird-like, and I feel how insubstantial she is.

'Thank you, darling,' she says. And then the clutch of her hands around me tightens suddenly, and her voice rasps close to my ear: 'Be careful.'

9
Faye

'For how long?' Ed demands.

'Shh, keep your voice down,' I whisper. 'She'll hear you.'

It's almost midnight on Sunday, and I'm still blinking in the light, dragging myself up from a deep sleep. Ed stands by the bed dressed in jeans and a black hoodie, the smell of beer and cigarettes brought into the room with him along with the brisk suggestion of the grassy outdoors. His holdall is a weight on the bed where he dropped it next to me.

'Seriously, Faye – how long will she be here?'

'I don't know. Just a few days, she said.'

'And you're okay with this?'

'I didn't have much choice. I could hardly say no, could I?'

'You could. You'd be perfectly justified.' There's a hardness in his voice that sparks to life the burning memory of the last time my mother stayed with us. London, not long after we were married, three days during which her drinking steadily grew worse and the barbed comments became nastier, her behaviour ever more outlandish and threatening, until it all culminated in a furious row and terrible recriminations. Ed was shocked by the things she said to me, the accusations made, the deeply hurtful epithets. Afterwards, he vowed that she would never spend another night under our roof, which is why I know the hardness in his voice is not anger directed at me. It's an anxiety borne of a need to protect me, coupled with sheer surprise that I have let her back in.

'The first sign of trouble and she's out of here, I promise.'

'All right,' he remarks, mellowing. 'It's you I'm concerned about. I just don't want her upsetting you.'

'I know.'

I listen to him in the bathroom, the squeak of taps, water hitting the basin, the buzz of an electric toothbrush. I know that he's annoyed, and bewildered at my decision. I can't tell him how my mother's presence here these past couple of days, regardless of her ropy history, has helped keep at bay those fears that dog me – the footprint on the patio, the sense that Michael is lurking nearby, watching me. She has made me feel safe.

Upstairs, my mother is asleep in the bed I have made up for her in the spare room – the room that will become the baby's nursery but that, at the moment, is still full of boxes and stuffed black refuse sacks, the last remnants of our move having drifted up to the top of the house. I wonder if she's awake and listening to us but find the thought unlikely. She'd barely touched her dinner, picking away at the bowl of tuna pasta I'd served up. The lamb and rosé I'd bought in Fallon & Byrne on Friday remained stashed in the back of the fridge once I knew that Ed would not be home for dinner. In a way I was glad he wasn't there for that first evening with my mother in the house. Her mood was brittle. I could see her eyes flashing around the rooms, taking everything in, making little purring noises about how nice it all was – 'modern' was the word she kept using – and I could feel my own defences rising, hearing judgement in each remark she made, the unspoken undercurrent of jealousy and resentment.

She'd picked away at her pasta for a bit and then seemed to slump forward with exhaustion. After showing her to her room and wishing her goodnight, I'd gone back downstairs, scraped the crockery, put on the dishwasher. Then I emptied the contents of our drinks press, the bottles clustering along the kitchen worktop, bagging them up along with the wine from the wine rack and some cans of beer under the sink. I was just about to head upstairs to my bedroom, thinking I'd stash them away in the wardrobe, when I turned to the kitchen door and saw her standing there, ghostly and pale, watching me, taking it all in. Her eyes gleamed with sudden hurt and I said: 'It's just a precaution.'

She held me there with her silence throbbing with unexpressed emotion, and I thought: *Damn you, anyway.* Why should I feel guilty when I've learned the hard way that these precautions are necessary?

She'd slipped past me and wordlessly filled a glass with water for herself before wafting back out of the room. The bags of booze pulled heavily on my arms. I heard each painful clink of the bottles as I climbed the steps upstairs and hid them in my room.

Ed gets into bed beside me, his body warm, his breath minty with toothpaste, and he pulls me against him and sighs with tiredness.

'Do you think she'll still be here next Saturday?' he asks.

His fortieth birthday party – a casual lunch here in the house. I've ordered food from the Butler's Pantry, and wine from Mitchell's. Crockery and glassware are to be collected on Friday from Caterhire, along with extra seating and a cocktail bar. Martha's husband, Will, has promised to play bartender for the afternoon, and I've spent several evenings making up playlists of Ed's favourite tunes. I want it all to be perfect.

'I doubt it. She'll have moved on by then. Definitely.'

'I wish I shared your optimism,' he murmurs.

'I think she's making an effort. She's really trying to change.' I can feel the heaviness of his body sinking into the mattress, and can tell from the drift of his breathing that sleep is taking him. Just before he drops off, he says: 'How is it you described her to me once? A virus.'

I expected my mother to be crabby and irritable, defensive, rude, but on the Monday evening, when I arrive home after a crazy day in the office, I find her and Ed outside in the garden, my mother's tinkling laughter rising up into the soft warm air. Lamb is sizzling on the barbecue; the patio table boasts a spread of salads, cubes of focaccia, some crudités and dips.

'Darling!' my mother greets me from her deckchair. 'Look what I'm reading.' She holds up Ed's book with a flourish. 'It's marvellous! I had no idea he was so talented.'

Ed is on a stepladder hooking up a string of lights that swings from one fence to the other; he looks down at me and grins. 'Another adoring fan,' he jokes, and my mother laughs.

'Don't be so self-deprecating – it's true!'

He climbs down the ladder, and kisses me hello. His hand automatically slips over my belly and he leans down and says an exaggerated 'hello' to my bump. I squirm away from his touch, laughing uncomfortably. 'Don't!'

'What's the matter?' he asks. 'I'm just saying hello to the little one.'

I can't articulate it – certainly not in front of my mother – this discomfort I feel when he does this. I understand that he's excited and affectionate, but something in me recoils from it.

'You two seem in good form,' I remark, and my mother uncrosses her legs and leans forward. Her eyes are covered by the large square lenses of her sunglasses, and she has brightened her thin lips with cerise lipstick to match the chiffon scarf entwined round her neck.

'We've been doing some catching up,' she tells me. 'Long overdue.'

Ed flips the meat on the grill, and steps back indoors.

'He's been telling me all about this party you have planned,' my mother goes on in her bright voice. 'It sounds like the world and his mother are invited.'

Her smile is open but I can't see her eyes behind the shades, and I'm nudged by a new guilt.

'You are of course welcome too,' I say.

'Oh, well, thank you.'

'Although I'm not sure if it's really your cup of tea. There'll be a lot of kids running around. And all of Ed's family are coming, and I know how much you dislike them –'

'Darling! Whatever gave you that idea? I adore Des and Regina!'

I stare at her. 'Seriously, Maggie? Have you forgotten the last time?'

She gives her head a little twitch.

'You called Des a pompous old bore?' I remind her. 'And Regina an interfering cow?'

Beneath her make-up my mother blushes, then gives her shoulders a shake. 'That was years ago. And I was upset that day –'

'Drunk, you mean.'

'All right, Faye. I admit it. I behaved terribly that day, and I felt awful afterwards.'

'Did you?'

'Oh, yes, I did,' she says, her voice growing indignant. 'I know you have this view of me that I sail through life unconcerned – worse, completely unaware of the harm I visit on other people – but you're wrong. If anything, I'm plagued by guilt. That is my penance – being forced to constantly remember, to relive these awful events in my past and wish I had acted differently. Have you any idea what that is like? To live with the constant wash of guilt coming over you?'

Her voice trembles with emotion, and I can see the shake in her hand as she reaches down for her glass and takes a quick swig of wine; there's a bottle open and sitting in an ice bucket on the patio beside her chair. It's the rosé I'd bought in Fallon & Byrne. In my haste to clear out all the alcohol, I'd forgotten that I'd stashed it in the fridge.

She sees the glance I give her and says: 'I'm all right on rosé. Even white wine, I'm fine. It's the rouge that slays me. As for spirits . . .' She makes a slicing motion across

132

her throat and giggles. She doesn't once meet my gaze because she knows I don't trust a word of this.

'Maggie –'

'All right, darling. You don't need to say it.' Abruptly, the levity collapses, and she leans forward, upending her glass so the contents spill into a potted geranium. 'There now. Happy?'

'I just need you to understand that while you're staying here you cannot drink.'

Her back stiffens. 'If that's the rule, who am I to argue? I'm here at your pleasure.' She swings her legs off the lounger and gets swiftly to her feet, but I can see how unsteady she is, not from alcohol but from the uprise of sudden emotion.

'It gets too messy otherwise,' I continue. 'I don't want to fight –'

'And nor do I.' She smooths down her skirt with a swift flick of one hand. 'Now, if you'll excuse me, I think I'll lie down.'

She passes Ed as he re-emerges from the house, handing him her empty glass.

'Night, night, darling,' she coos.

'Off already?' he asks. 'But what about dinner?'

'I'm very tired. And you two need your time alone.'

She withdraws with forced graciousness and he turns to me. I'm sitting with my head in my hands, already drained.

'Did something happen?' he whispers.

I take my hands away from my face and hiss: 'Why did you give her wine?'

'She helped herself. What was I supposed to do, wrench the glass from her hand?'

133

'You could at least have taken the bottle away.'

'I didn't want to make a thing of it,' he says, reaching for it now and refilling Maggie's empty glass. He takes a sip and sits down in the vacated seat. 'Come on. It was just one glass.'

I sigh, and lean back against my sun lounger, eyes closed.

'Hey, I'm sorry,' he says, and I feel the warmth and weight of his hand on my leg, the squeeze of reassurance.

'It just makes me nervous,' I tell him. 'You know what she's like – one glass becomes two and then –'

'I know, you're right,' he soothes. After a minute, he adds: 'She does seem to be trying to make an effort, though. She and I were talking before you got home about the baby, and it seems she really wants to be involved.'

'You think?'

'I got the impression that she sees it as an opportunity to rebuild some bridges. A chance to repair some of the damage.'

The warm evening air hardly moves. Overhead, the contrails of two airplanes criss-cross in the haze of blue, their thin trails fattening and puffing out as the crafts disappear from view.

'Second chances,' I murmur.

'Something like that.'

At the bottom of the garden, beyond the wall, the bushes shiver with sudden movement; there is a snap of twigs underfoot; branches shift, then fall still. I sit up quickly, the hair rising at the back of my neck.

'Maybe it's your fox,' he suggests teasingly, but he still gets to his feet, goes down to the wall.

I watch him, my pulse quickening at the thought of Michael crouching there. What if Ed discovers him? What if it all comes rushing out? I've been fighting for so long just to control this thing, to keep it tucked away in the darkness where no one can see it. The growing sense that it's being pulled out into the open, that Michael is forcing its discovery, fills me with panic.

I sit still and alert while Ed peers over the wall. He calls out, but there is no response, and he turns back, smiles at me, shrugging, and I feel a faint sense of relief nudging past the twitching unease.

He takes his seat once more, picks up his glass and relaxes. But I can't relax. My eye strays briefly to the kitchen window. Beneath it there's a terracotta pot planted with pelargoniums, vibrant flower clusters on long stalks hiding the footprint beneath.

IO

Faye

Friday evening, and it's warm, noisy with gulls, the pathway splattered with their droppings as Ed and I stroll along the promenade. 'Nesting season', according to a piece on the radio that day. My mother has shooed us out of the house after hours spent cleaning and tidying in advance of the party tomorrow. I'd taken the afternoon off work, and she and I had spent the time setting up tables and chairs, arranging the bar, cleaning and hoovering. The food was delivered from Butler's Pantry, and the wine from Mitchell's arrived shortly afterwards. We laid it all out in the kitchen while Ed drove over to Caterhire and loaded up the car with glassware and crockery, napkins and serving-ware. It was hot, tiring work. Eventually, my mother plucked the tea towel from my hand and said: 'Go. Have some time to yourselves. Get something to eat. It's a beautiful evening.'

'What about you?' I'd protested, but she'd swatted away my concerns.

'I'll make myself a sandwich and watch some TV, try not to spill crumbs. Go on. Get out of here.'

Ed needed no encouragement.

'She'll be fine,' he'd remarked, unconcerned, and eager to embrace the warmth of the summer evening. He'd taken my hand and suggested we stroll towards Monks-town. There were plenty of restaurants along the Crescent – we could grab a bite there.

'Are you looking forward to tomorrow?' I ask him as we walk, and he smiles awkwardly and shrugs.

'Yeah, of course. It'll be great to have people over. I just don't want too much of a fuss.'

'Don't worry. You won't have to make a speech or anything.'

'Phew!'

'Did you invite your writers' group?'

'Yep. Hugo can't make it, but Gerry's going to try to swing by, and Jamesie said he'll definitely be there.'

'I'll finally get to meet them.'

A couple walk past in the opposite direction, the man with a baby strapped to his chest in a papoose, tiny bare feet exposed to the warm evening air. Ed squeezes my hand.

'That'll be us soon,' he says, and I feel the vertiginous slide of my thoughts at the prospect.

'Twenty-week scan on Monday,' he goes on. 'Have you decided yet?'

'I don't know. I can't make up my mind.'

'Come on,' Ed teases me. 'If we find out the gender, we'll know what colour to paint the baby's room.'

'You can find out if you like, but I'd rather wait until the birth.'

'No! That's no fun! And I'd never be able to keep it to myself. Come on, why are you so reluctant? Is it some weird superstition?'

I can't articulate what it is that's holding me back. Not

superstition exactly. The closest descriptor is a kind of queasiness that comes over me whenever I think about the reality of the baby. It's not something I can admit to Ed. It's not something I can admit to anyone. How, when I imagine holding my baby in my arms, feeling the soft skin, the fleshy limbs, the tiny face, what I experience is not just love or excitement or hope but a fleeting stab of terror. Which is probably why I'm so hesitant about discovering the baby's gender. It will make it all so much more real and I'm just not ready yet.

'And if we know, we can pick a name –'

'Oh, just drop it, please!' I try to say this jokingly, but it comes out more aggressively than I'd intended. 'I'm sorry, I'm just –'

'Tired. I know. We both are.'

We're still holding hands, but the air between us has cooled. We walk on in silence.

A crowd has gathered by the Martello Tower, the sea flecked with evening swimmers. All along the narrow strip of beach, children are playing, running in and out of the water. A group of teenagers are playing music loudly from their phones; along the promenade different sizes and breeds of dog are being walked; while the Dart rushes past beyond the wire-fencing, the windows catching the evening light and reflecting back the tranquil sea. I'm caught by the sudden memory of sailing along this path on my bicycle, heading towards the West Pier, so long ago now it feels like a different lifetime. Another sunny evening, orange light on the rocks . . .

It was pure serendipity, both of us being there together. I remember everything from that afternoon.

Michael's voice in my head again, summoned by the setting, this the very place where my memory was imprinted – but it's the wrong memory. I don't want it in my head. In recent days, I've been plagued by memories. And then yesterday my mother asked me about Michael out of the blue.

'That boy you used to be mad about. Michael. Do you ever see him any more?'

I'd thought about the shiver of leaves behind the garden wall. In the morning, I'd gone out there and found a sandwich wrapper on the ground, the weeds flattened where someone may have crouched.

'Him? No. Haven't seen him in years,' I'd said lightly.

'Good,' she pronounced. 'Never trusted that boy. Something about him . . .'

'Slow down,' Ed says now. 'What's your hurry?'

I realize that I have increased my pace, as if I wanted to outrun my own thoughts. An old trick – motion is everything. A woman zips past us dragged by a cocker spaniel whose claws scrabble on the tarmac, and I think of Michael's dog Foyle when he was a puppy, his delirium whenever we took him for a walk. I'm struck by the realization that Foyle is probably dead by now.

'We should get a dog,' I say. 'It'd make us walk faster.'

'We'll have a pram to push soon,' Ed says, adding quietly: 'Or have you forgotten?'

'What's that supposed to mean?'

'Remember, when we first started talking about trying for a baby, you actually suggested that we get a puppy instead?'

'I was joking!'

'Were you?'

'Even if I wasn't, you can't surely think that's what I'd prefer now?'

He relents. 'No, I don't, but . . . I just wish you could get a bit more excited about it. It feels like I'm the one who's driving all of this. Most of the time all I get from you is this sense of . . . not regret but reluctance. And it makes me feel bad, like I somehow forced you into this, and it's not what you really want.'

'You didn't force me into it. I'm just nervous, that's all.'

'About what?'

'I don't know – everything. What if something happens, what if there's something wrong with the baby?'

'Then we'll deal with it. But this is supposed to be a special time – that's what everyone keeps telling me anyway. Why ruin your pregnancy worrying about something that may never happen?'

'I'm not trying to ruin it –'

'I know you're not. And I know that lots of people harbour superstitions, particularly around pregnancy,' he continues, adopting a reasonable tone. 'Not wanting to paint the baby's room or bring any baby clothes into the house until the child is born. Not wanting to discover the baby's gender. But for most people it's because they want to savour the anticipation, they want the surprise. This doesn't feel like that. It feels more like denial. Like the first scan we had – I had to book it, because any time I brought it up with you, you just kept putting it off. I'm not sure you even realize it but whenever I try to engage you in conversation about anything to do with the baby – what kind of birth you want, what kind of childcare plan we should look into, even down to picking out a pram – you just clam up like you're trying to avoid the issue.'

His voice has become raised, pushed with frustration. We're not holding hands any more – his are shoved into his pockets, while mine are wrapped defensively around the satchel strap that criss-crosses my chest.

'I wish you could focus a little more on the joy of it. This amazing experience, and I just feel like –' He stops abruptly. Having glanced at me, he's seen that I'm biting down hard on my lower lip. Instantly, he's remorseful. 'Faye, I'm sorry. I went too far. Hey, please just stop.'

He grabs my elbow, draws me to one side. There are people walking past, some of them looking.

'What if I'm a bad mother?' I ask, choking on the lump that rises in my throat. 'What if I hurt the baby, damage it in some way?'

'You won't –'

'What if I don't deserve this child?'

His arms are around me, pulling me into him, and I hold on, feeling the warmth and solidity of his body against me. The fear that I have expressed hovers in the air around us, giving off a little electrical pulse. It's the closest I've come to telling him the truth.

He kisses the top of my head, pulls me a little closer. 'You're going to be a fantastic mum,' he tells me. And then he adds: 'You're nothing like your mother. You've got to realize that. You've got nothing to be afraid of.'

He says this with conviction and I take in his words, a little stunned. This is what he thinks? That I'm frightened of turning into my mother, of inflicting the same precarious upbringing on my unborn child? I nod my acceptance, because it's easier this way – a more palatable fear – and, when he draws back to look at my face, I make myself smile. I want so badly for us to be happy. For nothing to get in the way of that – not Michael, not my own fear or guilt. I refuse to let it spoil what I've worked so hard for.

'All right,' I tell him. 'We'll find out.'

'Boy or girl?' His face breaks into a smile. 'Are you serious?'

'Yes. Why not?' I say, and then he pulls me in for another hug, tighter than the last.

It doesn't feel like defeat or even much of a concession, not when I can feel the thrum of excitement through his chest. And it helps a little to dispel my own fear, pushing down hard on the dark thing that rises inside me.

It's late when we get home. After dinner in Lobstar, we bump into a couple of neighbours enjoying drinks on the street outside, and we decide to linger a while, soaking up the summer-evening atmosphere. By the time we emerge from the taxi outside our house, it is past midnight. All the lights are on, music blaring from open windows, but there is no sign of Maggie. The house is entirely empty.

'Jesus,' Ed breathes, staring at the mess.

In the living room, it looks like a giant packet of crisps has exploded, shards scattered everywhere. There's a heavy pall of smoke in the air despite the open windows, and on one of the side tables a cereal bowl holds the fag ends of a dozen cigarettes as well as the thickened stub of a cigar. Leonard, of course. I can almost catch a whiff of Rive Gauche and Guinness sweat, his distinctive odour. On the mantelpiece, a couple of empty bottles of Rioja stand like sentries, and I recognize the label – the wine we'd bought for the party tomorrow. In the kitchen, further evidence of the party that has swept through in our absence. More empty bottles, more broken glass on the floor around the sink. Food has been pulled out of the fridge, the foil covering the lasagne discarded, a fork sticking out of the centre where someone has already made serious inroads. The door on to the patio is open, curtains wafting in the breeze, and, as I cross the floor, something crunches underfoot – peanuts scattered everywhere. Outside in the garden, more detritus – glasses and bottles, further evidence of breakages, crisp packets blowing over the lawn like tumbleweed. The bar-counter which we'd hired for the event has also been dragged out here and a couple of chairs lie on their sides as if they toppled over as the revellers fled.

'You don't want to go into the bathroom,' Ed tells me when I step back indoors. 'Someone's been sick there.'

'Christ.'

A feeling is boiling up inside me – an old rage. At my mother, yes, but also at myself. Why do I never learn that it always ends this way? I am furious at my own naivety, my own willingness to trust her. I snatch my phone from my bag and dial, but there's no answer.

'Faye?' Ed asks carefully, wary of my mood. He can tell how close I am to the edge; I am trembling with emotion.

A thought occurs to me and, without speaking, I cross the room and climb the stairs, hastening to my bedroom. The drawer in my nightstand lies open. I reach inside and feel for the hard corners of the leatherbound box that contains Ed's watch, but there is nothing there. It's gone. And then I see the scrawled note propped up against my reading lamp, the writing barely legible. *Don't be angry, darling. Len needs me. XXX*

I tear it in two, then four, then eight, shredding it with such fury that I don't hear Ed come into the room until he puts his hands on my shoulders and I turn around and bury my face in his chest and howl. This pain is so old and familiar, yet each time it returns with renewed force, the seams of the open wound biting and raw.

'It's okay,' Ed murmurs, rocking me. 'It's okay.'

For a long time, I lie awake listening to him cleaning up the mess downstairs before finally he comes to bed. The next morning, we air the rooms, and, while I set about readying the house for our guests, Ed goes out to replenish the food and booze that has been consumed or stolen – it's amazing how much they were able to carry with them, Leonard and his friends, passing through like some kind of war party bent on pillage and destruction, carrying my mother along with them.

I feel an ache of sadness for what has happened. The anger has fizzled away leaving me deflated. 'Please don't tell anyone,' I ask Ed. 'I'm so embarrassed.'

He takes my hand. 'You've nothing to be embarrassed about. You've done nothing wrong.'

'I should have known not to trust her. I should have –' I break off suddenly, the tears rising up without warning. 'It's your birthday, and I don't even have anything to give you.'

'Fuck it,' he says, attempting to lighten things. 'Who needs a watch, anyway? Why be a slave to time?'

I'm grateful for his efforts, yet I can't escape the sense that his birthday has hardly begun and already it's ruined.

At noon, our guests begin to arrive, and, while the house shows no evidence of the previous night's events, I feel tense, my mood brittle, nerves running close to the skin. I'm exhausted, but I try to bury it beneath a show of good cheer as the house fills up, growing crowded and loud. I accept help when it's offered, issuing instructions to Martha and Regina about heating up the lasagne and garlic bread, laying out the salads, putting out plates.

'Where is your mother, Faye?' Regina asks, scanning the room for her.

'Oh, she's gone, I'm afraid,' I tell her. 'Left last night.'

'Really?' I feel her concerned gaze, and, while I try to force the brightest, most confident smile on my face, I feel the effort it costs me.

'She'll be so sorry she missed all of this,' I say, 'but still. There'll be another time.' Then I ask her to chivvy the guests through to the kitchen to help themselves to food.

We've sung 'Happy Birthday' and cut the cake; my brother-in-law, who's in charge of the music, has just put on 'Let It Go' for his four-year-old daughter while the adults all protest. The fine weather has held, and those who are not already in the garden go out there now to escape the *Frozen* soundtrack. I'm clearing away the dishes and go to stash the empty serving trays in the utility room. As soon as I approach the door, I hear crying. Inside, Martha's baby is in his pram, left here to sleep while the rest of his family party. A blanket lies on the floor where he's kicked it off. Legs and fists wave angrily in the air, and from the blotchy colour of his face, the sheer rage in his screaming, I can tell he's been crying for some time.

A gale of laughter sweeps in from the garden where the others are amassed.

I put my head out the back door and call: 'Martha? The baby's awake. He's crying.'

But Martha is bending low over her older child, holding a tissue steeped in blood to her nose. There has been some kind of accident, and there is fussing around the child. Martha, harassed, throws a response in my direction: 'Just pick him up, would you?' a note of irritation in her tone.

I scoop the baby up into my arms, clasp him quickly to my shoulder. Perhaps my own irritation makes me rough, but his scream grows loud and shrill, as if my very touch burns him. He smells of soured milk and talcum powder; his screams are loud in my ear. I jiggle him up and down, trying to hush him, picking up toys from his pram, which he bats away with some force. When I attempt to put his soother in his mouth, he thrashes his head from side to side, a furious refusal. My own blood rises. Sweat oozes from my pores, it runs in rivulets between my breasts, I taste the salt of it on my upper lip. The doorbell rings, and I shout for Ed to answer it, but he doesn't emerge from the garden. I hear his loud guffaw.

Holding the child, I stomp down the hall and fling wide the door. The earth tilts. Blood beats in my skull.

'Hello again,' he says.

The beard has been trimmed in the days since I saw him in the street, but his eyes are the same: pale and watery. I stare at him in disbelief. His hair has been wet-combed – it clings to the contours of his scalp. The shirt he's wearing is buttoned to the collar, pristine and white. A glowing presence in the shade of the porch. He looks like a bible salesman, a spreader of the Gospel, a Witness. The observation is fleeting, knocked over by the tidal wave of my anger.

'What are you doing here?' I whisper.

I'm aghast at his presence – worse than that, I'm incensed. A part of me has known all along that he would betray me – part of me has been waiting for it – but that he would come here to my house, in front of all our family and friends, on the occasion of Ed's birthday, and unleash the full horrors of our history –

'You made it!'

Ed sweeps past me and throws his arms around this man. I stare at them, confused, as they embrace like they're old friends, slapping each other on the back and laughing. When they draw back from each other, Ed's arm remains slung around Michael's neck and he grins at me and jabs a finger into the white-shirted chest and says: 'Babe, this is my mate Jamesie, from the writers' group.'

I almost drop the child from my arms.

'Jamesie, meet Faye, my wife.'

He nods his head, and beams.

'I've heard such a lot about you, Faye. It's nice to meet you at last.'

PART TWO

11

Faye

For a moment, I don't move. The breath in my throat is hot. I draw it into my lungs with quick sharp bursts. The baby moves in my arms, and I see Michael's smile falter, his eyes flickering over the infant, and it is unbelievable to me that he is here. My mind bends to try to comprehend it: *this* is the man whose friendship has consumed my husband for these past few weeks?

'Come on, let's get you a drink,' Ed tells him, and they brush past me, heading down the hall and into the kitchen, from where I can hear the lively hum of conversation, the sound of the fridge door being pulled open, the clink of beer bottles, voices raised as introductions are made.

The front door is still open, and I realize that I cannot do this. I cannot be in the same room as that man, not even in the same house. The thought of it is unbearable. I step outside and close the door softly behind me, and then I start to walk. Down the path that meanders around the houses of my neighbours, past the neatly clipped box hedges, the sprouting agapanthus, the sprays of catmint and salvia, all of it a blur as my pace quickens, rushing now until I'm out on to the street. Traffic moves alongside me as I head down Carysfort Avenue. For the second time in less than a week I find myself scurrying along this road because of Michael, my heart banging wildly as if trying to escape my chest.

But Jamesie? Where did that name come from? I'd never heard him called by that name ... Of course – Michael Jameson. The piece fits into place, and it pushes another button inside me – the lengths he has gone to in order to conceal himself from me, all the while accelerating the insidious creep of his presence into my life.

I walk swiftly and purposefully but also aimlessly. Driven only by my need to get away, I don't know where I'm going but I keep going anyway, not really thinking about the direction I'm taking. I find myself in a park, kids playing on the grass, people jogging. I sit down on a bench under the shade of a giant sycamore. A sunny Saturday afternoon in early September, and I'm shaking with fear on this park bench, my mind dragged unwillingly back over the past. The whole nightmare of it dredged up, the house in the hills beyond Barcelona, the dusty rooms, the rusting chunks of metal that littered the yard. And they are there with me too, the ghosts of the past – Mateo, Sheena and Adriana, Amaya, the little girl with the blue glasses – all of them slipping around me like shades. I can almost feel them moving behind the trees.

I don't know how long I sit there, rewinding the past, the reel of old images flickering against my inner eye. The shadow of the sycamore is cast on to the sunlit lawn, and I watch it lengthen, until it's stretching all the way across the green – and then a voice, rushed and breathy, pulls me from my thoughts, saying: 'Jesus Christ, Faye! What the fuck?'

Startled, I look up and find Will, red-faced, furious.

Before I can speak, he has snatched the baby from my arms. The sudden violence of the movement wakes the child and sets him off bawling once more.

'Did you not think to tell anyone where you were going?' Will demands. 'Not even to bring your fucking phone?'

I stammer an apology, but I'm stunned by his fury. Will is normally so mild-mannered, so affable. We like each other, we enjoy a camaraderie being married to these quirky siblings. It's shocking to have his rage levelled at me in this way.

'I just . . . I needed some air,' I try to explain. 'I was only taking him for a little walk.'

'A little walk?' he splutters. 'You've been gone hours! We were about to call the fucking guards! Martha's going out of her mind!'

He jiggles the baby on his hip, tries to hush him, kissing the top of his head and whispering soft words of comfort. Then he shoots me another look: still furious and baffled, but there's concern there too.

'What the hell were you thinking?' he asks.

It's late, and the last guest has gone. All the plates and glasses have been cleared away; the dishwasher is humming through another cycle. When I finally returned to the house, trailing Will and the baby, shame-faced, exhausted, I'd gone into the kitchen and found Regina removing the apron she was wearing, then folding it and putting it on the worktop. She saw me taking it all in – the clean floors, the spotless worktops, the whole party tidied up and neatly put away. 'I had to do something while the others were out looking,' she explained gently, 'to keep my mind off it.'

Martha and Will had swept up their children and taken off, their SUV screeching out of the driveway, as if they couldn't get away quick enough. Martha hadn't even looked at me, let alone spoken a word. She didn't need to. I felt the waves of distress and fury coming off her.

And Regina as she left, her hand resting on my forearm, fixing me with an anxious gaze: 'Are you all right, dear?'

Warmth and concern in her voice, but there was suspicion there too.

'So you kind of freaked out there,' Ed states, straight off the bat as soon as the last guest has left. He's thrown himself on the sofa, exhausted and wrung out, a half-empty glass of Rioja balanced on his chest. I'm not sure he's really up for this conversation. I'm not sure either of us is. In contrast with his barely concealed hostility, there's an agitation building inside me. I perch on the edge of an armchair, feeling the disquiet crawling around my body like ants beneath my skin.

'I know. I'm sorry. I don't know what came over me.'

'Well, it was one way to wrap things up.'

'Don't say that, please. I already feel guilty. Not to mention mortified.' Even as I say it, I'm assailed by the memory of all those people staring at me as I returned, indignation mixed in with their relief that the child was safe.

'I don't understand how you could do something like that. You were gone for so long, I thought something had happened to you.'

'I was tired. And overwhelmed. He kept crying and it

seemed like a good idea to take him out for some air. I didn't notice the time.'

'It's just so unlike you, Faye. You're normally the calm one.'

'I know –'

'Stable, unflappable –'

'I just flipped out, okay?' I say, becoming defensive.

'Is that what that was? You flipping out?'

'I don't know – maybe. It just all got on top of me.'

'You could have asked me for help.'

'You were too busy entertaining your new friend.' This comes out more pointedly than I'd intended. He notices and frowns.

'Jamesie?'

'Yes.'

'Didn't you like him?' he asks, confused, and I shake my head, flustered at the turn this conversation has taken.

'He was fine, I just –'

'What?'

I drop my head into my hands. 'Nothing. He seemed nice enough.'

When I look up, he's sipping his wine, gazing pensively into the middle distance.

'So how do you know him?' I ask tentatively, adopting a conversational tone so as not to arouse his suspicion.

'I told you. He's in my writers' group.'

'Right. And this group – how did it come about?'

'I told you this already. It was back in June, when I did a reading in the Lexicon. Afterwards, a few of us went for pints nearby, and some readers joined us. Jamesie was one of them.'

My mind runs through the dates, busily calculating. June – that was when I met Michael in the National Gallery, when I warned him to stay away. I'm not certain, but the conviction takes hold nonetheless that the reading in the Lexicon was shortly after this – perhaps only a day or two later. Was it possible that Michael had contrived to be there? That he had somehow sought out a meeting with my husband and used this as a way to forge a connection?

'So does he write too?' I probe.

'Not really. But he's a big reader. And I get the feeling that he's a bit lonely, you know? Kind of looking for his tribe.'

'And you? Are you his tribe?'

His gaze narrows. 'Why all the questions about him?'

I shrug. 'No reason. Just curious.'

It shocks me to realize that in all this time, during all the conversations I had with my husband after my return from the office in the evenings, not once had I picked up on Michael's presence in his life. He has hidden himself so carefully from my view – the name change! All this time, his poison has been slowly seeping into my home, my marriage – it frightens me to realize just how successful he has been at infiltrating these private spaces.

'I'll call Martha tomorrow to apologize,' I offer meekly. 'I realize now how worried she must have been. It was stupid and thoughtless of me. God, they must think I'm mad.'

'I told them about your mother, about what happened here last night.'

'You did?'

'I know you asked me not to, but, under the circumstances, I thought they deserved an explanation.' His voice is calm, but there's an edge to it, as if he's holding something back, some unspoken suspicion. 'Was I wrong?'

'No, you were absolutely right, they deserved an explanation –'

'No, I mean was I wrong that that was the reason? Or is there something else?'

'Of course not –'

'Because, if there is, you should just tell me.'

He holds me there with his stare, and I see the worry, the suspicion, and the words shrivel inside me. 'There's nothing,' I croak.

He shakes his head. 'You haven't been yourself lately. I can't put my finger on it, but you've just been sort of off. Moody, distracted, a bit down. And then today, going off like that – it's just so out of character. Look,' he continues, getting up off the sofa and coming over so that he's perched on the armrest of my chair, his hand on my back, gentle, supportive, 'I've been doing some reading on the Internet, in some of the chatrooms – it seems like a lot of women find the hormonal changes during pregnancy can be challenging. That for some women the baby blues actually occur during pregnancy, not after.'

'I'm not depressed.'

'Are you sure?'

I can see how easy it would be for him to believe this, and, in an odd way, he's closer to the truth than he thinks. Something is going on in my head. There are rooms of memory that have long been shut up, left to sleep in the darkness for years. But now the locks have been picked, the doors flung open, and all the ghosts have come slithering out.

'Honestly, I'm fine,' I tell him. 'Just tired, that's all.'

'Promise?'

'Promise.'

It amazes me how easily the lie slips off my tongue.

Ed goes to bed early; the dramas of the past twenty-four hours have taken their toll, although he tries to blame it on the wine.

'All that early drinking has me beat,' he claims. 'Are you coming up?'

At that moment, the dishwasher beeps and we hear the clunk of the door opening, the hiss of steam released.

'In a minute,' I tell him. 'I'll just empty that first.'

'Leave it till morning,' he urges, but I insist I don't mind, and he shakes his head and disappears upstairs.

I spend a few minutes putting away dishes still scalding to the touch. And then, when enough time has passed so that I'm sure Ed won't reappear, I take out my phone and dial the number.

Blood hammers in my throat, my temples, as I wait for him to pick up.

His voice, when it comes on the line, sounds distant and groggy, like he's been pulled from sleep. 'Somehow I knew you'd call.'

'What were you thinking?' I hiss.

Down the line comes a sigh of resignation. 'Faye —'

'Coming to my house like that . . . And Ed? You've been meeting him for weeks. Months! Befriending him like that — what the hell are you playing at?'

'Look, I didn't know he was your husband –'

'Oh, come off it!'

'It's true. I'm telling you, I was as surprised as you were when you opened the door to me this afternoon.'

'Do you really expect me to believe that, Michael? Or should I call you "Jamesie"?'

He sighs again, but this one feels more defensive than resigned. 'It is my surname, Faye – Jameson – remember?'

'I never heard you called anything but Michael. Not even "Mike".'

'But that was a long time ago. A lot has happened since. Some people call me "Jamesie" now, it's not a big deal! Really, I wasn't trying to hide anything.'

'So it was just coincidence, you meeting Ed, striking up a friendship?'

'Yes –'

'Like hell it was. He told me he met you at a reading in the Lexicon. That reading took place just days after you and I met in the National Gallery.'

'Honestly, I didn't know. I didn't make the connection.'

'You specifically asked me what my husband's name was –'

'I'm telling you – I just happened to be at the reading, that's all. A group of us ended up in the pub afterwards – I never realized he was your husband.'

'Never once? When he talked about his family, his wife, did you never say to yourself: "Hmm. Faye. That's an unusual name. I wonder if, by any chance . . . ?"'

'He never mentioned you by name,' he tells me quietly. 'It was always "my wife". I didn't know.'

'Why is it that I don't believe you?'

I can hear him breathing. The space around him sounds echoey and cold – a bathroom, perhaps.

'He doesn't know, does he?' Michael says. 'About us. About what we did – about the baby.'

'Why are you doing this? I thought I made it clear to you – I don't want to see you. I don't want any kind of friendship with you. I don't want you anywhere near me. How could you possibly imagine that I would when you keep trying to hurt me?'

'I'm not trying to hurt you –'

'Yes, you are! These stupid threats you keep sending me! Even after I made it clear to you how I feel about them –'

'God, not this again –'

'Sending one to my boss, for Christ's sake!'

'Your boss?'

'Oh, don't give me that! Don't try to pretend it wasn't you who –'

'Look, I haven't sent you anything!' he says sharply, raising his voice as I try to interrupt. 'No, please just listen to me. I want to try and explain . . . to apologize. The day you showed up outside my house – it was so unexpected, so out of the blue – and I'm afraid I reacted badly. I can see now what it must have felt like for you, being bombarded with all those text messages from me. And then, when I called your office and we arranged to meet – I understand you might have felt a bit pressured. But I want you to know that I'm sorry if I upset you. Things that I said on the day that we met. Things I said about the past – about how I loved you –'

'Don't! Please just –'

'But I tell you solemnly, I never sent you any threats. Why would I?'

The sincerity in his voice, the conviction – for a moment I am thrown. I scramble about for a reason. 'I feel like you want something from me but I don't know what. And I'm sick and tired of it . . . I really am . . .'

My voice catches. Exhaustion, all the emotion of the day taking its toll. At the other end of the line, there is silence, and I sense a genuine pity there.

When he speaks, his voice is tender. 'It's hard, isn't it? Living with this thing, day after day.'

'I don't know what you're talking about –'

'Yes, you do. I've struggled with it too, over the years, and I know now that I'm not alone. That you too have felt it. Do you sometimes wake up in the night and think that you're back there in that house in the mountains?'

'No.' But the word trembles in the air, uncertain, unconvincing.

Tentatively, he continues: 'I do. Sometimes I dream about it. It's like that night again, and I'm coming down from the mountains, down from the milk lake, the others following, and then I'm back inside the house, coming down the corridor, opening the door into that bedroom –'

'Stop it!'

He draws in his breath. When he speaks again, his voice sounds steady, but it's changed. Something new has crept into it.

'Earlier today, when you went missing, when the hours went by and you still hadn't returned, your sister-in-law became very upset, and Ed kept telling her: "Don't worry. Nothing's going to happen. Faye wouldn't do anything to harm that child." And I thought to myself: *He doesn't know.* I couldn't help thinking: *What would happen if I were to tell him all I knew?*

'You wouldn't dare,' I say in a low, shocked voice.

He doesn't answer.

'I want you to listen to me carefully, Michael. You're not to contact me or come to my house again. You're to stay away, do you hear? And you're to leave Ed alone.'

'Why? It seems clear that he needs a friend. Just like we all do.'

'Stay away from him, do you hear me?'

'Friends. Facebook friends. It's amazing how you can find people, how you can reunite. People that live far away, people you haven't seen for years and years.'

A sly edge has come into his voice that makes me pay attention.

'You'd be amazed at who you can find.'

'What are you talking about?'

'I found Adriana first – that part was easy. Facebook, of course. Through Adriana, I found Sheena, and then Mateo. All the pictures on his feed! It was quite the trip down memory lane. All the familiar faces. Efrain, Amaya. A little girl with blue glasses –'

'Stop it!'

'Remember what you said to me that night? *If you love me, you'll do this.* Remember? Well, I did what you asked of me, and now you want to pretend like it never happened. I've got blood on my hands because of you –'

Quickly, I hang up the phone.

12

Michael

April 2010

The bus from Barcelona dropped them at a village at the foot of the mountain. There were six of them in the group, and they waited under the shelter until an open-backed truck pulled up in a cloud of dust, a tanned arm slung from the driver's window raised in salute. Sheena and her friend Adriana took their places in the cab alongside the driver, a swarthy-looking guy in dirty Levis and a white vest who introduced himself as Mateo. Michael and Faye climbed up into the tray at the back along with another couple – Greg and Bree were their names – whose white-blond hair made them look more like siblings than lovers. Michael chatted with them as the truck careered along the winding road up into the hills, but Faye, he noticed, remained silent.

They reached the house as the sun started to dip down behind the hills, the sky bruised with lilac clouds. A low, long, ranch-like dwelling with dirty yellow walls and a terracotta roof sat in the clearing. Some of the roof tiles were missing in places like gaps in the mouth where the odd tooth had come loose. The yard surrounding it was pocked with scrubby bushes, and a clutch of tall eucalyptus trees off to one side seemed to loom over the house itself. He felt Faye's silent disapproval, and his own heart sank a little at the carcasses of various cars rusting in the dust, weeds growing up through the cavities where the upholstered seats should have been. A couple of picnic tables nearby sported scalloped parasols, Orangina logos fading in the fabric that fluttered in the occasional breeze that blew through the hills.

Mateo cupped his hand around the flame of his lighter and lit a cigarette; squinting through the smoke and tilting his head towards the house, he said: 'Go. Find rooms. Make yourselves at home.'

Sheena asked: 'Which rooms should we take?' but Mateo just shrugged like he wasn't interested in the particulars.

Michael picked up their bags. 'Shall we?' he asked Faye, mock-gallant. Her mouth was a tight line as she followed him inside.

After the glare of the sun, the interior of the house seemed very dark. A long corridor stretched through the house like a central artery, rooms radiating off on each side. A stale smell hung in the air: marijuana mingling with a dank bathroomy odour. They followed the giddy laughter of the girls down the corridor, glancing into rooms as they went: tatty curtains hung over windows grimy with dirt, sleeping bags ruched and unzipped, thrown over mattresses, windowsills lined with toiletries and empty beer bottles. Something crunched underfoot, and Michael looked down and saw a line of buttons from the eucalyptus trees outside. Someone had left them lying in a row along the tiled floor of the corridor, like Hansel and Gretel, he thought.

They found an empty room near the end. It was devoid of furniture, but there were a couple of camping mats and an old Navajo blanket sitting neatly against one wall, and Michael put down the bags and looked around at the space, saying: 'This is okay, isn't it?' One window gave on to the yard, and he went to it now and drew back the curtain, rubbing some of the dust off the panes with the flat of his hand. 'I mean, it'll do for the short term, right?' he went on. 'And it's free.'

He needed her to relax and fall in with the others, to make the best of it as he was doing. But the spring inside her seemed tightly coiled, her shoulders high and stiff, hands clutching her elbows like she didn't want to touch anything.

'What is this place, do you think?' Faye asked.

Michael shrugged. 'It's just a house.'

'Don't you think it's a bit weird? I mean, who are all these people? Is it some kind of commune or what?'

He laughed, affecting an ease he didn't yet feel. 'Of course not!'

'Then what are they all doing here?'

'Same as us. Looking for someplace temporary to stay until all of this blows over.'

He knew what she was getting at. It didn't have the feel of a house that had suddenly been thrown open in response to the ash cloud and the crisis it had created. There was a listlessness to the place, a settled air of staleness and drift, that suggested this was something other.

'Hey, listen. If they start preaching or trying to brainwash us, we'll get out of here, okay? If they turn out to be Scientologists or, I dunno' – he scrambled for an example – 'Branch Davidians or whatever the fuck, then we'll leave immediately. Okay?' He was laughing again, genuinely this time, tickled by the idea of the two of them stumbling accidentally into some Doomsday cult.

He could hear the others outside now, amassing in the space beneath the trees.

'We should go and join the gang,' he suggested, and she acquiesced, although he could tell she'd already had enough of them. Sheena and Adriana grated on her nerves – their constant giggling, and the way Sheena kept flirting with Michael, a point he didn't try to refute. It was obvious to everyone, and, besides, he was doing his best to discourage it.

They walked back down the corridor, Faye pausing outside one of the doors, her attention caught by something in the room. Michael looked past her into the dim space and saw a little girl staring up at them through small blue-framed glasses, a large flesh-coloured plaster covering one eye, her hair in bunches. She looked to be no older than four or five, the expression on her round face grave and dignified. Michael could make out a shape on the bed behind her, a woman's dark hair falling over a pillow, the rounded hump of her hip. The little girl put her index finger to her pursed lips, her one small dark eye flaring with warning. They heard a grunt and a sort of snuffling noise, but the woman didn't stir. Over the hump of her hip, Michael saw a tiny bunched fist briefly flailing. An infant, suckling at the woman's breast while she slept.

'*Mi hermano*,' the little girl whispered, her voice surprisingly deep and husky for such a small child.

'Come on,' Michael whispered, stepping away from the door.

But Faye continued to stand there, transfixed.

'Faye,' he hissed, and finally she moved away.

Later that evening, when they were all outside, gathered around a campfire that had been set and lit at a distance from the house, he saw the woman again. Through the blue smoke of the fire, he observed the long curl of her black hair falling over one shoulder as she came down along the track towards the others, the hem of her skirt catching at the grass as she passed. The baby's equally black hair was visible above the crook of her elbow where his head rested. The little girl held on to her mother's free hand, stepping carefully, her one good eye behind the glasses fixed on the uneven ground.

The woman moved like water, a slow ripple of ease, the gentle sway of her hips, the placid smile on her face. She wasn't beautiful, but she was striking – regal with her square-set shoulders, her self-possession. She seemed at once so much older than the rest of them gathered there. She had a worldly air, a sort of condescension as she took her seat among them on a sun lounger that had been vacated by one of the others at her arrival.

As the night wore on and the sky above them darkened to show a smattering of stars, his gaze kept getting drawn back to her. She was called Amaya and the little girl was Amalia. The baby was never called by his name, but always referred to as *bebito*. He was handed around like a parcel from one to the other, each of the adults taking turns to hold and placate him, to rock him back to sleep whenever he became fractious. He was tiny – perhaps no more than eight or ten weeks old – wisps of black hair curling in a whorl about his crown. Michael noticed Faye tracking him with her eyes, her attention drawn back again and again to the fat little legs, the bleats and cries that he emitted.

Later, in their room, huddling under the heavy blanket that smelled of dust and mouse droppings, Michael said to her: 'Who do you suppose the father is? Of Amaya's baby.'

His arms were around her, his body tense against the cold which had come down quickly with the night. It was spring and the real heat had not arrived yet, and up there in the mountains the temperature plummeted during the hours of night and early morning.

'I don't know. I had assumed Mateo,' she answered. 'Why do you ask?'

'I just wondered. It hadn't been clear to me which of them was the father.' He didn't need to say Mateo or Efrain. They were older than everyone else by a good ten years, and both men held a casual authority. Efrain rolled joint after joint, then passed them around.

'He's a cute baby,' Michael remarked, tentatively. 'I saw you looking at him.'

'Was I?'

'All evening. Your eyes kept going back to him.'

She said nothing, and after a minute his hand moved and came to rest on her tummy, his fingers spreading there.

'Don't,' she said, pushing his hand away, the uprush of her irritation so strong it stung him.

They didn't speak further, the two of them withdrawing

to their individual mats, suffering the cold and the silence apart.

Michael watched them over the next few days: Amaya and the coterie that swarmed around her. She seemed to be at the centre of things without ever really involving herself with the others. There was something magnetic about her – the calmness she exuded, the dreamy indifference, the sinuous way she moved through doorways and around furniture, like a cat. Once or twice, he tried to speak with her, and she stared at him through her large hooded eyes, blinking slowly, then offered him her trippy smile. She had bad teeth – the one chink in her overall beauty. They were large and unevenly spaced, each tooth outlined with a brown rim at the edges – a smoker's teeth. Evidence grew that Efrain was her partner, while Mateo acted as some kind of uncle to the children. Their bedroom was a constant hub of activity. Noise drifted from the room – music playing from tinny speakers, indie rock mostly, the occasional pop songs that Amalia sang along to in her sweet husky voice. Sometimes, he could hear the accomplished plucking of a guitar, the plaintive notes of some vaguely familiar tune.

It was driving Faye crazy, she told him. The constant noise.

'How am I supposed to study,' she demanded of him, 'with that racket?'

'Look on the bright side,' he pointed out. 'At least you'll get some notes now. Something to work with.'

One of her lecturers – the course coordinator whom she'd emailed in a panic to explain her predicament – had rung her that morning, informing her that he had emailed some PDFs of articles that were pertinent to his course. There were also scanned copies of lecture notes one of her friends had attached to an email. Michael had arranged for Mateo to drive them to the nearest town, where Faye could print them off at an Internet café.

While they waited for her, Mateo and Michael leaned against the truck, Mateo smoking one of his little rollies. He was a lean man, with an angular face, stringy sinewy limbs that moved slowly.

'We thought it would be just a couple of days,' Mateo said. 'But now? This cloud is going nowhere, man.'

'What are you saying?' Michael asked.

Mateo grinned and scratched at the stubble along his jaw.

'Lots of people are stuck here. Everyone's looking for some place to stay.' He shrugged, his grin widening, taking on a wolfish air. 'I got bills to pay, man. Mouths to feed.'

Michael understood. He asked how much and when Mateo named the price, Michael baulked.

'For a week?'

'Hey. You got the first few days free, didn't you?'

'Even still. That's more than they charge at the hostel.'

'In the hostel you have to share a room. And they don't pick you up and drop you to the Internet café, do they?'

It was a lot of money, but Michael felt his bargaining power was limited. Mateo was right about a growth in demand, and, besides, Michael didn't want to start looking for alternative accommodation. It would be only one more week, surely, and then normality would resume.

He acquiesced, and, taking the wallet from his jeans pocket, he removed the agreed sum and watched as Mateo counted the notes, then slapped him amiably on the shoulder, saying: 'Appreciate it, dude,' before sauntering around the truck and climbing into the front seat just as Faye exited the café.

Michael waited until they were back at the house and alone in their room. He watched her expression changing as he told her in a hushed voice about the exchange with Mateo.

'I know, I know,' he said, before she even had a chance to utter a word, but he could see the indignation in the way her mouth fell open, and already anticipated her concern. 'But it's not like we have much choice.'

'Three hundred euro?' she repeated, then threw her pen down on to her notes in a display of petulance. 'But that's most of the money we have!'

'We can get more –'

'When? And where from?'

'We'll go back to the city in a few days. I'll go to the ATM –'

'Michael –'

'You don't need to worry –'

'But I am worried!' she countered.

A snort of laughter came from the next room and Faye heard it, a frown coming over her face. She beckoned him to come closer and he joined her on the sleeping mat. She lowered her voice to a whisper, but her anxiety and indignation were still there.

'We need to start saving some money,' she told him.

'Okay. But, come on, this was an unforeseen event, right?'

'And what about the other unforeseen event?' she asked pointedly. He noticed now that she had one arm wrapped protectively around her tummy and his eyes settled there, as if trying to see beneath the layers of clothing and skin and fat and membranes the curled form suspended like a white silken cocoon.

'We'll figure something out,' he told her.

'I looked it up online. Do you realize how much an abortion costs? Five hundred euro,' she said gravely. 'I don't have that much money, do you?'

He shook his head.

'We'll have to get it from somewhere,' Faye went on, and he put his hand out to steady her.

His mother would have it. She would give it to him if he asked for it, but he couldn't stand to think of the look on her face when he told her what he needed it for – her unmasked disappointment, yet another grave error to add to the long catalogue of sorrows he had caused her over the years. Also, he knew that Nuala disliked Faye, a fact that just compounded his aversion to asking her for the money.

'Let me talk to Min,' he suggested instead, kneading her wrist, the tenderness of bone there, the striation of blood vessels where the skin thinned.

The thought seemed to pain her, and she winced. 'Christ, she's going to love that. It will confirm everything she ever thought about me.'

'I wouldn't jump to that conclusion. I think she'll want to help us. Once we tell her what's happened and what our plans are – she'll want to be involved, to be a part of it.'

Her eyes narrowed with suspicion. 'What do you mean – she'll want to be a part of it?'

It was risky territory, but he'd seen the way she'd been watching Amaya and her baby. He'd noticed how her eyes had feasted on the infant, alive to every wave of his fist, every gurgle from his mouth. Michael had felt it in himself when Amaya had given him the baby to hold while she saw to Amalia's dinner. Without warning, she had wordlessly dumped the little bundle into his arms and turned away to stir the spaghetti, and Michael had felt like she'd given him something precious but frightening, like being handed a jewel-encrusted grenade. He'd felt the soft weight in his arms, the infant instinctively turning his head inward towards Michael's chest, and it amazed him, the squirrelly movements of the child, the sheer delight that bubbled up inside him in response. For the last few days, the feeling had wormed around inside him, and, whenever he caught Faye looking at the baby, he suspected she was experiencing the same thing. It was natural that she should feel afraid, but he began to understand that she needed reassurance from him that it was possible. That there was another path they could take.

So he ploughed on: 'A part of the baby's life.'

Instantly, she snatched her hand out of his grasp. 'No –'

'Just listen a moment –'

'No, I won't listen! Don't tell me to listen, when you refuse to hear a single word I've said. I've made up my mind – don't you understand that? Why can't you just accept my decision and support it instead of putting up obstacles?'

'But there is another way! Surely, if we've learned anything this week, it's that we can make this work. If they can make it work, why can't we?'

'You can't be serious?' She looked shocked, and then an ugly smile came over her face that looked more like a sneer. He felt himself draw back from it. She tossed her head in the direction of the room where the others were gathered – Amaya, Efrain, their little family – and said: 'You call that making it work? Open your eyes, Michael. They're living in poverty. Amaya is stoned half the time, and I'm not entirely sure what the situation is between her and Efrain and Mateo, some twisted threesome. Those kids are neglected. And that's what you aspire to? Jesus Christ, wake up.'

'Keep your voice down, will you?' he hissed. 'They'll hear you.'

He glanced up quickly at the walls, which were paper-thin. But she had already turned her attention back to her notes and he felt shut out from her. There was little else he could do, so he pushed himself up off the floor and moved to the door. Their argument made him uneasy – not the outcome, not even the seriousness of the subject matter. It was the new sense of anguish that had material-ized within him – that she didn't really need him any more, and that by heedlessly starting a baby together, they had somehow heralded the ending of their own heartfelt love.

13

Faye

The weather changes, September giving way to a cold and blustery October. The mornings are chilly now, an autumnal bite is in the air. The nights too are drawing in. Mindful of the diminishing amount of time before my maternity leave begins, I stay later in the office. The need to prove myself is still there. I've been successful at securing slots for us at various tech and start-up conferences as well as doing a big marketing push, but there is increasing pressure to convert all this publicity into real investments in the business. While we have a tentative lead with a couple of angel investors, Jess has made clear that we need to hook a serious industry partner if the company is to scale up. With this in mind, I have booked some conference space in Citywest for a morning in early October, inviting all our potential investors. Our aim is to present the complete showcase of our business with individual presentations as well as one-on-one meetings, break-out talks and a lavish lunch, at the end of which we aim to secure the investment we need. I feel how much is hanging on this one event, and so I remain at my desk late into the evenings, planning and preparing, often not realizing the time until my stomach starts to rumble and I look up to find that all my colleagues have left for the night.

Sometimes, when I'm turning out the lights, I feel the empty stillness of the office space and an inkling of my own vulnerability seeps in. One night, as I'm locking up, I hear a noise behind me – movement, like a sudden swish of air – and when I turn and catch sight of a face staring back at me, a loud gasp of fright escapes my throat. But it's just my own reflection in the glass door. 'Stupid,' I mutter aloud, needing to break the emptiness with my own voice, but I fumble with the keys, my hands trembling, and hurry down the stairs, an irrational gratitude coming over me when I reach the street.

It's not really fear but more a sort of vigilance. I'm alert to strange noises, to sudden movements. Walking towards the Dart station, if footsteps behind me get too close, I turn my head quickly, expecting it to be him. Waiting on the platform, if someone brushes against me, I tense for confrontation, poised for a challenge. I see Michael everywhere: he's there in the rush of commuters in the mornings; I see him in the flash of faces crowded on the platform as my train goes rushing past. Pushing my trolley of groceries around the supermarket, I round a corner and see a bearded man in a suede jacket and my heart skips a beat. He's everywhere and nowhere. Ethereal and ghostly, the whisper of a presence. But worse than all of these imaginings is the one constant: he's in my home.

I get back late one evening, and find the house quiet as I step in through the front door. The walk up the hill from the station had been arduous, leaning into the wind, and I'm tired as I shrug off my coat in the hallway and hang it in the closet, feeling the weight in my belly. The baby, I am given to understand, is now the size of a cauliflower, and I feel every ounce of it, an ache communicating all the way from the small of my back down to the soles of my feet.

The kitchen is empty, but the patio door is open, cold air gusting through the gap.

Ed is outside leaning on the fence that separates our garden from next door. Our neighbours, Adrian and Clare, are retired teachers, and I can hear the constricted nasal sounds of Adrian's voice rising up from his garden.

'I think it's worth considering. It's a small investment in return for some peace of mind, don't you think?'

Hunger growls in my stomach, and I look for evidence of dinner preparation under way, feel a pinch of annoyance when I find the worktops and cooker bare. I fill a glass of water, gulp it down.

'What's that all about?' I ask, when Ed comes back inside, sliding the patio door shut.

'Oh, just some nonsense – Clare getting her knickers in a twist about strangers loitering beyond the back wall.' He kisses me in greeting, then adds: 'Adrian wants to put up a CCTV camera. I told him I haven't noticed anything and I'm home all day. How about you?'

He goes to the fridge and takes out some salmon fillets, then puts a skillet to heat on the hob. My eyes are drawn to the dark shapes of bushes and trees rising up above the back wall. I remember the flattened patch of grass, the footprint in the summer, the eerie sense of someone watching us, and the hunger dissipates, replaced by a cold hollow.

'I wouldn't worry about it,' Ed adds, seeing my

distraction. 'It's just teenagers messing. God love them – they need somewhere to go and drink their tinnies, do their snogging, right?'

'I suppose so.'

I fill my glass again and notice two cups in the sink, the dregs of coffee hardening into rings at the bottom.

'Did you have a visitor?' I ask, and Ed glances over.

'Jamesie called in.'

I try to keep my manner light, casual. 'Oh?'

'We were supposed to go for a walk, but it was fucking freezing. So I picked him up in the car and brought him back here. I wanted to show him part of the hotel.'

'The hotel?'

He laughs at my confusion. 'It's the working title for my new book. *The Hotel.* What do you think?'

'I like it. When did you come up with it?'

'I didn't actually. The title was Jamesie's suggestion.'

I feel myself bristling but do my best to hide it.

'It's the term he uses to describe the hospital he was in for a while,' Ed explains, adding: 'All the inmates called it that, apparently.'

'Inmates?' I say, cold needling my stomach.

He corrects himself. 'Patients, I mean.'

'What kind of hospital was he in?'

He glances up at me, catching the note of disquiet in my tone. 'Well, it was a psychiatric facility.'

Both of us are standing on opposite sides of the kitchen island. The air between us seems to tighten and cool. I remember Suzi's words to me all those months ago: *All I heard was that he was in the library one day and he just lost it. One minute he's sitting quietly at a desk, the next thing he's tearing*

178

the place apart. One of the librarians tried to intervene and she was knocked unconscious. I'd questioned her on it, and she'd been vague on the details other than to say that Michael had never gone back to university and didn't sit his Finals. Was it possible that he didn't return because he'd been committed to a psychiatric hospital? The shock of this new possibility catches me off guard. I lean against the island, steadying myself.

'Why was he there?' I ask Ed carefully.

'He was suffering a bit of depression. Some PTSD. There's no shame in it, you know? Lots of people seek help for mental health issues these days.'

'I know that,' I reply testily. Nerves are rattling inside me, making me irritable and tense.

'Really? Because you're acting like I'd just told you he's psychotic or something.'

He turns away from me, sliding the salmon fillets on to the skillet, where the fat hisses on contact. I drop my weight on to one of the bar-stools. My mind is working quickly. I think back to the day I met Michael for coffee in the National Gallery, and remember the way he kept scraping at his wrists – raised red marks on his skin like hives – something manic about the constant scratching.

'So how long was he there for?' I ask tentatively.

'I'm not sure exactly. A few months here and there.'

'Here and there? He's been admitted more than once?'

'That's right.' He has his back to me, tending to the fish, but I can see the tension running the taut stretch between his shoulders. Still I press on.

'Did he tell you why?'

'I already said –'

'Yes, but do you know if he went into these institutions voluntarily or was it because of something he'd done –'

There's a loud clatter as Ed drops the spatula he's been using to tease the fish around the skillet. He turns to me now, his face fixed into a frown.

'Why are you being like this? All judgemental.'

'You're spending a lot of time with this guy. How much do you really know about him?'

'You don't think I'm a good judge of character?'

'I didn't say that. But let's be honest here. Someone reveals they've been in and out of mental institutions and that doesn't raise alarm bells for you?'

'He had the blues, Faye, and sought help for it, which seems to me like the sensible option. You're making out like he was manacled and dragged off by the guards.'

'Now you're the one being overly dramatic.'

'Whatever.' He turns back to the fish, which has started to burn, and takes the skillet off the heat.

'I'm sorry,' I tell him. 'I don't want to fight.'

'Neither do I.' His voice drops, and I see him shake his head quickly, turning as if to say something, but then stop, held back by a reluctance that sounds a warning inside me.

'What?' I ask him.

'It's just something that Jamesie mentioned.'

'What did he say?'

'How often it seems like those who are closest to you – the ones who should be the most supportive, the most understanding – are actually the hardest people to talk to about what it's like to have a mental illness.'

'He said that?' I keep my voice quiet and controlled, masking the turmoil of my thoughts.

Ed sighs and takes a step closer to the island so that we're facing each other.

'You seem to forget that I've been in his situation myself.'

I've been so consumed with my thoughts of Michael, his mental illness, that I had not stopped to consider why Ed would feel an affinity, a connection.

'I'm sorry,' I tell him, and his eyes when they meet mine seem guarded, unsure.

'We never talk about it, you and I,' he says. 'About the time I was, to use my mother's euphemism, "a bit lost".'

'I didn't think it was something you wanted to dwell on.'

'Well, it's not like I want to chat about it all the time,' he says with a rare burst of impatience. 'But there have been times – particularly lately – I don't know, maybe it's because of the move, but I've been thinking about it a lot. Not dwelling on it but . . . It's just been ticking away in the background. I'm actually mining some of those experiences for this new book.'

'I had no idea,' I admit.

He shrugs. 'Sometimes it's easier to talk about this stuff with someone who's more removed – there's less pressure.'

'What do you mean, pressure?'

He glances up quickly, hearing the defensive note in my voice. 'You're always checking to make sure I'm okay, if I'm keeping busy, making friends, that I'm happy.'

'That's because I'm your wife and I care about your happiness –'

'Yes, but you're not responsible for it.' He makes a gesture of muted exasperation. 'It can be a bit much sometimes. You come in the door from work and straight away you're quizzing me about my day, trying to assess my mood. I feel under pressure to always be upbeat, to hide it from you if I had a bad day because otherwise you'll just fuss over me and push me to get out more, meet people, take up some exercise, whatever!' He laughs to take the sting out of it, but his frustration with me is evident. 'It can feel a bit stifling.'

I don't answer, too busy questioning myself. All along, I've felt a degree of guilt because I'm the one who pushed for us to move home to Ireland. But have I really been smothering him the way he describes?

'I'm not saying it's all your fault,' he adds, drawing back a little. 'Part of it's mine. I guess it's just easier to talk about all that stuff I went through after the breakdown with someone who's been through it himself.'

'Jamesie? You've talked to him about it?'

This comes out laced with hostility – I can't help it – and the muscles around his jaw tighten.

'Yeah, I've talked to him about it. He's a friend, and he's been through something similar.'

'I see. And what exactly has he been through?'

'I don't know the full details, but something to do with an old girlfriend, a baby that was lost. He's sort of evasive about it, like the wound's still tender.'

'So what do you talk about?' I ask, the warning note still sounding in my head.

'We compare notes on things –'

'What things?'

'Well, like the different medications we've been on.'

'Okay . . .'

'He has more experience than me, of course. I've taken Valium and Xanax, but he's tried a whole range of psychopharmaceuticals,' he continues, warming to his subject now. 'Actually, his experiences have been really interesting. Some of the stories he's told me . . . You know, he met a guy once who'd had a cingulotomy?'

'What is that?' I ask, trying to mask my growing horror as he explains a procedure that sounds frighteningly similar to a lobotomy. Ed, on the other hand, seems enlivened by the account, momentarily forgetting the coldness that has sprung up between us. 'The guy just lifted up his fringe one day to show Jamesie the tiny round dot of a scar on his forehead where the surgeon had drilled through his skull and inserted the laser.'

'That's horrible.'

'But a great detail. I had to put it into the book. Jamesie didn't mind. In fact he said that part read particularly well.'

'You've let him read the new book?'

'Sure. Most of it is set in a psychiatric facility, so it's helpful to have someone to check for accuracy.'

'But you never let anyone read an early draft. Not even me.'

The words fly out of my mouth like an accusation. His eyes narrow.

'Are you jealous?'

'Of course not! It's just –'

'Because I'll print off a draft for you if that's the case –'

'No! I mean, yes, I want to read it, but that's not the issue here –'

'Then what is?' he snaps with exasperation.

I shrug, not able to formulate the words, not able to communicate the warning I feel in my heart that Michael is trying to drive a wedge between us, that this friendship with Ed is just a ruse to get to me.

Ed's had enough. He pushes himself away from the island, turns back to the hob and takes up the skillet.

'We should eat,' he remarks without enthusiasm, dishing out the salmon on to two plates.

We eat in silence, neither of us hungry.

14

Faye

The day of our conference finally arrives. I'm feeling nervous and excited as I drive to the office in the early morning. Kelly is waiting, and together we fill the boot of my car with presentation packs and merchandise that we plan to distribute among the various investors who have committed to attend. In the end, there have been fewer acceptances of invitations than we'd hoped for, but Jess remains confident that we should emerge at the end of the day with a major investor in place. She'd had dinner earlier in the week with Alan Wright, a retired property developer who'd made a fortune in the Middle East. Alan is well known for his finicky ways, his mild eccentricities – he's a man who likes to create a little fuss around him, which Jess was happy to do in order to secure his backing. Her feeling, at the end of the meal, was that his support was almost guaranteed. He had as good as said as much. Still, the pressure is on, and as we drive through the city streets I run through my presentation in my head. Despite all the preparations, all the late nights, the rehearsals, the fact-checking and role-playing, I still feel a pinch of anxiety as if there's something I've forgotten.

'What's this?' Kelly asks, her legs brushing against the ring binder in its tote bag sitting in the footwell.

'It's a draft of Ed's new book,' I tell her. 'You're not to look at it. He'd kill me if he thought I'd let anyone sneak a peek.'

'*Guard it with your life*,' he had intoned as he'd handed me the ring binder containing a copy of his latest draft. Despite his jokey manner, I knew that he was entrusting me with something dear to him. 'Seriously, Faye. Don't lose it or anything. It's still a rough draft and I'd die if anyone else were to read it and pass judgement.'

My sensitive husband.

'Don't worry,' I'd told him. 'I'll keep it safe.'

All week, I've been schlepping it around with me in a cloth tote, reading snippets of it on my morning commute, parsing the text in quick snatches on my lunch-break. I read hungrily, scouring the text for Michael, knowing the influence he's had over the writing. Reading the description of the psychiatric facility: the yellow walls, beige tiles on the floors, the twin odours of gingivitis and disinfectant fighting against one another, one of the characters remarking: 'All of us had bad breath from the Lithium.' And I wonder if this character is Michael? Is it his own lived experience when the character's mouth grows dry and ulcerous, his gums bleed, when the weight starts piling on? I think of the Michael I had known – that lean and vital youth – and, when I compare him with the overweight bloated creature he has become, I cannot help but believe that the account in these pages is his own bitter truth.

The traffic is light enough, and the car moves quickly, Kelly chattering animatedly beside me, which helps stave off my nerves.

'Jess has just arrived,' she tells me, reading the screen of her phone. 'She's gone up to the conference hall but says to call her when we get there, and she'll come down to help us carry all the gear up.'

'Okay. Great,' I breathe.

My phone is clipped on to the dashboard and it pings, drawing our attention. It's a notification of some sort but not one I recognize. I put out my hand and touch the screen, and straight away a map appears showing the grid of streets through which we're travelling along with a trail of red dots.

Kelly leans forward to get a closer look. 'That's weird,' she says.

'What is it?'

'I don't know, but it's showing the route we've just travelled.'

When the car stops at the traffic lights, I glance down and see that she is right. Even after the lights change, and I put the car in gear again, turning left at the next corner, the trail of red dots on the map follows me.

'It's like we're being tracked,' Kelly remarks.

By the time we reach our destination, I'm feeling a little uneasy. I pull the car into a parking space and turn off the engine, reaching for my phone. Scrolling through, I find the notification and read it.

'It says something about an AirTag,' I tell Kelly. 'What is that?'

'Oh, I know what that is. It's like a little Bluetooth gadget for finding your keys or your phone – it's a little disk you stick on and then you can monitor the where-abouts from your phone.'

'But . . . I don't have one of those.'

Kelly is already busy looking around the car, opening the glove box, searching in the well behind the gearshift. 'It must be here somewhere.'

Together, we look for it, scanning the back seats, looking under the carpet mats, until finally Kelly finds it tucked beneath the passenger seat. A small disk no bigger than a one-euro coin, bearing the familiar Apple logo. 'It's probably Ed's,' she says, handing it to me. 'Either that, or you've got a stalker.'

A throwaway remark said flippantly, but it catches me off guard.

There's no time to think about it, and, once I reach the conference space and start setting up the room, I manage to push away any negative thoughts, welcoming the investors with a smile and a firm handshake. We have coffee and chat for a while, before everyone takes their seat and the presentations begin. Jess kicks things off, welcoming everyone and giving an account of how she came up with the idea for the company. Frank picks up the baton and talks through the product design, how it's being developed, the various features, clicking through his slide presentation with confidence and fluidity. A bank of laptops has been set up along a row of tables with the software installed, and he invites the investors to spend some time exploring the programs.

There's a good buzz in the room, and I'm standing to one side, observing, when Kelly gestures for me to join her. She's chatting with Josh, one of our software developers, and, as I approach, she leans forward and says:

'I was just telling Josh about that thing we found in your car, Faye,' she begins.

'Oh, that.' I'd put it out of my mind during the presentations, but now the uneasiness is back.

Kelly elbows Josh. 'Tell her what you told me.'

Josh pushes his glasses a little higher up the bridge of his nose and says: 'Well, they're used mainly as key-finders. They're relatively cheap – you can pick one up for less than fifty euro – and they're easy to use.'

'How do they work?'

'So you attach the disk to your keys or whatever, and then whenever you want to find them you just check the Find My app on your phone and it'll bring up a map to show you where they are.'

'Wait, though. The AirTag that I found in my car doesn't belong to me. I don't even have the Find My app. So why did it show up on my phone?'

'Ah. Well, that would be an alert to notify you to the presence of the device. You see, Apple have designed it so that if an AirTag not registered to you is seen to be moving with you over time, then you get an alert.'

'A warning,' Kelly adds, and Josh nods.

'Tell her about the surveillance stuff,' Kelly prompts, and the tightness in my chest squeezes up a notch.

'Yeah, so there've been some concerns expressed about these devices being used to track people, rather than keys.'

'Didn't I tell you?' Kelly says to me, a small note of triumph in her voice. 'A stalker!'

'I don't have a stalker,' I answer quickly, but my heart is beating fast.

There's no time to think about it. At that moment, Jess calls me up to the podium. It's my turn to present to the investors.

For weeks, I've been preparing for this moment, practising my speech over and over again, but now, unnerved by the conversation with Josh and Kelly, I find myself rushing through my slides, stumbling a little over my words, making small mistakes. When taking questions from the floor, I get flustered over my answers and am embarrassed when one of the investors corrects my facts and Jess has to step in, smoothly taking over, but I can tell she is furious.

Afterwards, she corners me.

'What happened to you?' she hisses.

'I'm sorry. It's nerves, I guess.'

Her eyes flash. 'Well, get them under control. Now is not the time, okay?'

After that, I pull myself together. Any thoughts I have about Michael, or AirTags, or stalkers are pushed firmly aside. I focus ruthlessly on working the room, answering questions competently and professionally. It takes all of my energy, and by the time we sit down to lunch I feel the creep of exhaustion.

Jess and I have planned the seating arrangement so that each of the senior members of our team is next to a major potential investor. I've been appointed to sit alongside Alan Wright. He's interesting company, regaling me with tales of deals done in Saudi and Qatar, and I'm grateful for his chattiness, his ease of conversation, although his fussiness grates a little. The starters are served, and immediately he begins quizzing the waiter on the provenance of all the ingredients.

'I only eat organic,' he explains to me, and I tell him that I'll speak with the chef, which seems to reassure him.

I return from the kitchen, armed with guarantees as to the nature of the food, to find my uneaten starter has been cleared away. But when the main course arrives, Alan complains that the salmon is undercooked and sends his dish back, advising me to do the same.

'Especially in your condition,' he adds, nodding to my bump.

I'm tired now, and my hunger has been blunted by the strain of the morning. I just want this meal to end so I can go home and collapse on the sofa. In the lull between our main course and dessert, unwelcome thoughts begin trickling through. I catch sight of Josh across the room, and think again of what he'd said about the AirTag. Was it possible that Michael had planted it in our car so that he could track my movements? I run through all the various possibilities, the different occasions when he might have had an opportunity. Might Ed have given him a lift at some point? I seem to recall a wet afternoon when they'd returned to the house instead of going for a walk. Might it have occurred then?

'Don't eat that,' Alan says, interrupting my thoughts with a jolt. He's taken hold of my wrist, restraining me from putting a piece of Brie in my mouth. 'You might want to check because I'm pretty sure that's unpasteurized.'

Something in me snaps. 'It's just a piece of fucking cheese,' I say with a quick laugh that doesn't go far enough to mask my irritation. I see the look that comes over his face, the shuttering of his eyes, the small moue his mouth makes.

'Sorry,' he says coldly. 'I was just trying to be considerate.'

'I know you were, and I'm sorry if I seemed rude,' I tell him, hastily backtracking, but it's too late.

He turns away, making polite conversation with the guest flanking his other side. I try to draw his attention back to me, but he pointedly ignores my attempt. Shortly afterwards, he excuses himself from the table. I see him saying a quick goodbye to Jess and then he's gone. She shoots me a quizzical look that communicates an anxious surprise at his hasty exit, and all I can do is shrug in return.

It's a relief when the lunch ends, the guests leave, and I can pack up the leftover materials into the boot of my car. It's late afternoon, the sky already darkening, street lamps coming on as I drive back to the office with Kelly. Together we unload the boot, returning the materials to Reception. There's a message from Ed on my phone: he's got tickets for Verdi's *Requiem* in the National Concert Hall – a last-minute thing. When I call him, his voice sounds rushed, and there's background noise like he's in a station.

'Oh, come on!' he urges when I tell him how tired I am, how I've had a shitty day and I just want to curl up on the sofa. 'We're going to have months and months of being stuck at home after the baby is born.'

'I know, but –'

'No buts! Just put your shitty day behind you and come. The music will relax you, I promise!'

I don't want to go but I'm aware of how strained things have been between us lately. Ever since our conversation about Ed's new friendship with Michael, there has been a simmering tension in our home. Perhaps a night out together with some beautiful music in a comfortable setting will help us to ease back to the way we were. And so, as soon as I've finished following up on various actions arising from our presentations that day, I leave the office and hurry past Leinster House, which is lit up tonight in blue and yellow, and make my way around Stephen's Green. The concert begins at 7.30, and I am already at risk of being late. Breathless, I arrive in the foyer of the Concert Hall to find the crowd drifting towards the open doors of the auditorium. I cast about, looking for Ed, while simultaneously unwinding the scarf from about my neck. It's hot in here, and the swift walk from the office while carrying my bags has left me feeling sweaty and drained. Already, my feet are aching and I'm looking forward to slipping off my shoes and slumping in a comfortable seat, while soothing choral music fills the auditorium, my husband at my side.

I see him then, across the room by the bar, chatting to a woman in a red dress, a patterned orange scarf wrapped around her hair. As I weave my way through the crowd, Ed catches sight of me and waves and the woman turns and smiles. I don't know this woman, and yet there's something familiar about her.

'You made it!' Ed says, leaning in to kiss me, then takes a step back and turns to the other woman. 'Verona, this is my wife, Faye. Honey, meet Verona.'

I shake her outstretched hand, and see a flicker of curiosity in her eyes, a pleat in the smooth dark skin of her brow as the introductions are made. She's trying to place me, but I get there first. A beat of panic in my chest, and then she says: 'Didn't I see you before? Outside the house –'

'What's this?' Ed asks, leaning into the conversation, but at that moment Michael arrives, wiping his hands on his jeans.

'Faye. So good to see you again.'

The breath quickens in my throat, as he leans forward and kisses my cheek. The ticklish brush of his beard makes me recoil, his lips against my skin a violation. It is all I can do to maintain some semblance of poise, of calm.

His arms rise briefly as he beams at me. 'Look at all of us here. Isn't this great? I'm just so glad you guys could make it.'

I shoot a glance at Ed, who explains: 'Jamesie here had the tickets. There were a couple going spare so when he rang and offered them to us, I jumped at the chance.' Turning to the others, he explains: 'Faye loves choral music.'

'Really?' Michael says, his eyes lighting on me.

'It's how she relaxes,' Ed explains. 'A hot bath and Rachmaninov's *Vespers*, isn't that right honey?'

'Ed.' I flash him a quick glance, alarmed at the words pouring out of him, details which seem too intimate a revelation.

'What? It's true. You're always saying as much.'

'*The Vespers*, huh?' Michael remarks, his gaze still locked on mine.

It frightens me, this charade we are playing. And it shames me too, my husband looking on smilingly, unaware of the great lie that is unfolding around him. But somehow the moment for owning up to the past, admitting to an old intimacy, a relationship that had been deep and important, has slipped by. Time and events have moved too quickly, and now any attempt to explain it, to rationalize the deceit, just seems too difficult, too dangerous.

'When are you due?' Verona asks.

'The end of the year,' I tell her.

'New Year's Eve,' Ed clarifies.

'Oh, that's exciting! Perhaps your baby might be the first child of the New Year! It's always the picture on the front of the paper, isn't it? A woman holding a tiny baby. I love those shots!'

There's a musical lilt to her laughter. I look at her, this woman – the fine dusting of gold powder high on her cheeks, short lashes curled and frosted with mascara that is an electric shade of blue – and I wonder at her relationship with Michael. Is she a girlfriend or is this an early date? The latter, I suspect, given the lack of physical touch between them, a certain unease in the way they stand together that suggests they are not used to being paired in this way. But then I remember her coming out of his house that day and getting into a little green car.

'Is this your first baby?' she asks.

'Yes,' I say, avoiding Michael's stare, which I know has tightened, grown focused and intense.

'Shall we go in?' Ed suggests.

In the darkness of the auditorium, I cannot relax. I try to concentrate on the music, or on the warm pressure of Ed's hand in mine, but I am too aware of Michael's presence. I keep thinking of the AirTag found in my car, the footprint in the garden, this feeling I have of being under his constant surveillance. Separated from him by Ed and Verona, I am alive to his every movement. Every shift in his seat, each turn of his head – I follow it all with my peripheral vision, like an animal grazing nervously, alert for a predator.

When the lights go up for the interval, and the room thunders with applause, it feels like I've been holding my breath for the past hour. Ed lets go of my hand and suggests a drink to the others, and we are all filing out of our seats when it happens.

Michael, who has the aisle seat, stands aside to allow Verona out first and then Ed, each of whom slips into the stream of people making a beeline out of the auditorium and towards the bar. And so it is that I am the last to make my way out of the row. Michael waits in the aisle. I avoid eye contact with him and am edging past when he thrusts out his hand and grabs my belly.

'What are you doing?' I ask, breathy with shock and confusion – he *grabbed* me – but he doesn't answer, and, when I look at his face, I see his features have darkened, his mouth set in a grim line of determination.

'Stop it!' I hiss, alarm jumping in my throat. His grip is hard, insistent; the baby turns over inside me.

I push away from him and stumble into the aisle, forcing my way through the crowd, not caring how brusque I appear, desperate to get away.

The foyer is buzzing with noise, people milling about and clotting around the bar, but I head straight for the ladies, pushing the door through into the nearest available cubicle. I slam the door behind me and flip the lock, before I bend over double, leaning into the closed door, the blood pounding in my temples, my limbs trembling.

From outside the cubicle come sounds of taps turning and toilets flushing, hand-dryers loudly humming, alongside the murmurs and shuffles of those waiting. Minutes pass, but still I don't leave. Occasionally, someone pushes against the door, testing to see if it's occupied, but I remain where I am. I can still feel the imprint of his hand on my belly, the current of need that channelled through his fingers right into my womb – a dark want, the feeling of a debt owed to him, a debt he was going to call in.

When the buzzer goes at the end of the interval, I emerge from my cubicle and see Verona waiting by the sinks.

'Are you all right?' she asks.

'Yes. Just . . . you know,' I answer, flustered.

'Ed asked me to come and check on you. He was worried –'

'Of course. Thank you. Just tired. But I'm fine, really.'

I move past her to the sink. Turning the tap, I catch sight of myself in the mirror. Two spots of high colour have appeared on my cheeks; the rest of my face is wan and drained.

'No wonder you're tired. Uncomfortable too, I imagine. Trying to sit in those seats with that little one resting heavily on your lap.'

She tugs a paper towel from the roll and passes it to me so I can dry my hands. I remember the day I saw her outside Michael's house, the child clambering into the back seat of the car.

'Do you have children?' I ask, and she smiles and shakes her head.

'No. But I have a niece – my sister's little girl. I was

her birth partner – she was doing it alone, you see. So I kind of lived it vicariously. Which is not the same, I realize.'

'And you and Jamesie,' I say tentatively, that name sounding artificial coming from my mouth. 'How long have you been –'

She laughs suddenly, a rich burst of sound, the skin above her nose wrinkling with amusement. 'No, no. It's not like that. I mean, we're friends, I suppose. I was in the house when he offered the tickets, so I said yes.' She tilts her head to one side and says: 'It's funny the way you and Ed call him "Jamesie". Everyone else – me, his mother, even Min – we all call him Michael.'

I take in this piece of information and it prods the suspicion within me – that this friendship between Michael and my husband is just a ruse to get to me. He has taken care to hide his identity from me. Why else would he use this nickname? Verona sees the expression on my face and misreads it as confusion.

'Min is Michael's aunt,' she explains. 'Or great-aunt, actually. I'm her carer. I look after her several days in every week.'

'How long have you been her carer?'

'Just over a year. She'd had a series of falls, you see, and Nuala – Michael's mother – wanted her to go into a nursing home. But Min was having none of it. Her body's frail, but there's nothing wrong with her mind. Sharp as a tack, she is, and pretty feisty too.'

She tells me then about the closeness that has developed between them, about how Min's health has been failing recently, and I remember what Michael had told me: *She's old now, bedridden. She can't even make it to the bathroom with-out help.*

Perhaps this is true, but, then again, I've only his word for it – that, and Verona's vague testimony. This version of Min – frail, helpless – doesn't tally with my memory of her. There was a side to her that was waspish and vindictive. I could never be entirely sure whether she liked me. Of all the people he might have told our secret to, Min remains the most likely. And what would she do with that knowledge, I wonder. That spidery handwriting – could it be Min's scrawl? Michael had dismissed the notion, but he'd always thought the best of her, naive to what she was capable of. But the Min I knew was shrewd and calculating. If she wanted something done, she would find a way of doing it. Could it be possible that she blames me for what's happened to him, the wreck he's made of his life?

'Didn't you know her once?' Verona asks, her brow wrinkled with curiosity. 'She mentioned a Faye before, and then something Michael said made me think –'

'Must be a different Faye,' I say quickly, my mouth dry, suddenly parched.

A beat and then she says: 'Okay. My mistake.' Brightening, she adds: 'We'd better go and join the others.'

Back in the auditorium, the lights are dimming as we take our seats.

'You okay?' Ed whispers, his eyes fixed on me with concern.

I nod, then add: 'A bit sore. Uncomfortable.'

He places a hand on my bump, gently rubs it. From

over his shoulder, I can feel Michael's gaze, sense the hunger in it.

'Actually, would you mind if I go home now?' I ask Ed. 'You don't have to come with me –'

'Are you not well?'

'I'm fine, it's just been one hell of a day and these seats are killing me. Seriously, you stay . . .'

Around us, there's applause as the conductor resumes his place at the podium. Ed glances at the stage before turning back to me, his features sharp and hassled.

'I'll come with you –'

'No, you don't have to –'

'It's fine.' He hurries me along, whispering something to Michael as we shuffle past. I don't hear it, refusing to look at him or Verona, not caring what either of them thinks as I hurry away.

We are both quiet on the drive home. A light rain begins to fall, and the windscreen wipers flick back and forth. Ed leans one elbow against the driver's window and sighs gently.

'You know you didn't have to come home with me,' I tell him.

'I know.'

'Honestly, I wouldn't have minded.' I feel guilty at cutting his night short, even more so because I can't explain it.

'I wouldn't have been able to relax and enjoy it,' he explains. 'I'd have been worried about you. And the little one.'

'I'm fine. We're fine.'

He nods and smiles, but the smile falls quickly from his

face as he turns his attention back to the road. There's a long silence, broken only when he turns the car into our driveway, switches off the engine, and says: 'You really don't like him, do you?'

I don't ask who he's referring to. We both know well who he means.

'No, I don't.'

'I don't understand – you've hardly even spoken two words to him. How can you judge him when you've barely tried to get to know him?'

'It's a feeling I get – an instinct.'

'Right,' he says, unimpressed.

I've been grappling with whether or not I should say something to Ed about what just happened. Part of me knows that it means opening a whole can of worms, but the other part just thinks, *fuck it* . . .

'You were wondering what happened to me during the interval, why I spent the whole time in the bathroom? Well, it's because just as you were heading off to the bar, as I was getting out of my seat, he sort of grabbed me –'

'He what?'

'He put his hand out on to my bump.'

Ed frowns, thinking about this. 'He touched your bump?'

'Yes, but not just like touching it. There was something aggressive in the way he did it.'

He props his elbow on the side of the door, rubs a finger over his mouth. I can see that he's turning it over in his head, trying to figure it out.

'Is there a chance this was a misunderstanding? I know how sensitive you are about people touching your bump.'

'Are you kidding? You think this is my being overly sensitive?'

'I don't know. Maybe.'

I stare at him, but he goes on: 'Remember what you were like when my mother tried to touch you? You jumped like a scalded cat.'

I shake my head. 'This is different. It's not just a case of his not asking first. He just lunged at me. I was frightened.'

He sits up straighter in his seat. 'Did you confront him about it?'

'Yes! I mean, I told him to stop, but he kept on pushing his hand there, like he wanted something . . . like he was leeching off me –'

'You make him sound like some kind of incubus! Come on, in the middle of the fucking Concert Hall?'

The argument is running away from me, but still the frustration is there, the swell of anxiety at how deeply and consistently Michael is infiltrating our lives.

'He gives me the creeps,' I say, shuddering a little.

'For God's sake . . .' he mutters. He thinks I'm being melodramatic, but he doesn't know what I know.

'Look, the other day, you said he was in the car with you, that you picked him up and gave him a lift back to our house.'

He eyes me warily. 'Yeah. So?'

'I found this today.' A quick rummage in my bag turns up the AirTag. I hand it to him, explaining: 'It was here in the passenger side, just underneath the seat.'

He turns the disk over, examining it, his mouth tense. He doesn't say anything and I can't tell what he's thinking.

Instead I go on, explaining to him about the device, its purpose.

'Don't you see? He planted it here in our car so he could keep track of our movements, see where we're going.'

'Are you serious?'

'Who else could it have been? All this time you've been spending with him – have you asked yourself why he's around so much? Every time you want to go for a pint, he's there. Or during the day, when you feel like popping out for a coffee, he's happy to come along. You didn't even know him a few months ago, and now he's suddenly your best friend? I think it's strange and, yes, sort of creepy, the way he's latched on to you. It scares me a little.'

He breathes deeply, exhaling through his nose. The AirTag is held between his thumb and index finger, and he holds it up to me. 'I bought this myself, Faye. Not for me but for my dad. He's getting old and forgetful, and he keeps losing his keys, which is driving Mum mad. I bought it to help them out but, ironically, it must have fallen off the keys when I brought him to the hospital the other day for his check-up.' His jaw clenches and I see just how angry he is. 'I can't believe you would jump to such a ridiculous conclusion. Do you have any idea how paranoid you sound?'

I don't answer. A well of shame rises inside me, pressing up against my earlier conviction of Michael's guilt and unsettling it.

'As for the way he's latched on to me, as you put it – I had thought that's because he actually might enjoy my company.'

'I just wish you didn't hang around with him so much. You have other friends –'

'Oh, yeah! There's a stampede of them wanting to hang out with me . . .'

There is real bitterness in his voice; it surprises me.

'You can't have it both ways,' he tells me. 'You can't push me to make new friends and then disapprove of them afterwards.'

'I don't push you –'

'Yes, you do! Jesus!' he cries, exasperated. 'You've no idea how controlling you can be. Trying to stage manage my whole life, dictating who I can and cannot be friends with.'

'He grabbed me –'

'Oh, please, just spare me the drama.'

I stare at him, a cool tide of panic rising within. 'You don't believe me, do you?'

He looks down at the AirTag still in his hands and says nothing.

'You're taking his side instead of mine.'

He makes a sharp grunt of annoyance, and snaps that it's not about taking sides. For a moment, he doesn't speak. Then he brings his eyes up to meet mine, his expression guarded, his tone careful. 'It was your idea to move back here, Faye, and I was happy enough to go along with it. But you've been difficult to live with lately. You're so focused on work, which is fine, but whenever we spend time together I get the sense that you're constantly trying to bolster me, boost my ego or something. I don't think you realize how much pressure that puts on me. It's like I have to constantly reassure you that I'm fine, that I'm happy, that I've no regrets. It's exhausting.'

He shakes his head, waiting for my reaction, but I say nothing, too shocked to utter a word.

'And your own behaviour,' he adds tentatively, 'well, it's been erratic. The day of my party, the way you disappeared like that –'

Instinctively, I squirm from the topic, and he continues: 'It was so out of character. At times you've seemed so distant, almost secretive. And then there's the baby –'

'What about the baby?'

'It feels sometimes that you're more frightened by this pregnancy than excited about it.'

'That's not fair, Ed. I'm just a bit nervous. It's perfectly normal.'

'I know, I know,' he says calmly, trying to be conciliatory. 'I just wish we could talk to each other more about this stuff. I've tried, but you push me away, and then I've ended up talking to other people instead – Martha, Will –'

'Jamesie?'

The set of his jaw hardens.

'I think you're wrong about him. He's a good guy. Isn't it possible that whatever happened between you two this evening was just a misunderstanding?'

I remember the incident, the letters, the footprint in the garden – the sense that's been building for months now that he's shadowing my life, seeking to destabilize my marriage, pulling me into his own orbit with a stubborn insistence that frightens me.

'I know what happened,' I whisper. 'I just can't get over the fact that you are wilfully choosing not to believe me.'

He holds up the AirTag, counters: 'Yeah, well, it's hard when you act so irrationally.'

My heart is thumping, frightened by how quickly this has escalated, and how Michael is winning, my own husband choosing to take his side over mine. And, worst of all, I have no idea of how to turn things around, how to get rid of Michael once and for all.

Ed puts a hand up to his face. Closing his eyes, he squeezes the bridge of his nose, a sure sign he has a headache.

'I'm tired,' he declares. 'Let's just leave it.'

We both get out of the car, he locks it, then follows me slowly to the house.

15

Faye

For the next week, Ed and I circle each other carefully. No more is said between us about what happened at the Concert Hall. Neither of us likes confrontation; we prefer to sit it out, allow the passage of time to work on clearing the air, the silent relinquishing of once entrenched positions. And the bad feeling does, somewhat, disperse over the course of the week as we focus on our work. The investor morning did not turn out to be the resounding success we'd hoped for. While there's been some funding secured, it's not as much as we'd hoped for, and none of the major investors – including Alan Wright – has chosen to come on board.

'I can't understand it,' Jess tells me. 'I was sure Alan was in the bag. What went wrong?'

'I don't know,' I answer. 'You know how tricky he can be.'

I don't tell her about the incident at the end of the meal – the perceived slight when I snapped at him. In a bid to make up for it, I put in extra hours, as if by staying late in the office I can alleviate my own guilt. My mind is busy, almost frantic, and all week I carry around with me the feeling that I have forgotten something. It lingers and nips like an annoying fruit fly buzzing about my ears, but at worst it's distracting. Work takes up all my attention, and when I return home in the evenings I am too tired for anything beyond the most basic conversation. Ed and I eat our dinner late in front of the TV, falling into bed to snatch a few hours of sleep. It feels like barely any time has passed before I'm shaken by the alarm and have to swing my legs wearily out of bed once more.

By Thursday evening, the tiredness has caught up with me, so I arrange to work from home the next day. That night I sleep heavily, and when I wake the sunlight is streaming through a gap in the curtains. From the quality of light, I can tell that it is well past mid-morning.

Ed comes into the room, carrying a tray, a large brown envelope under his arm.

'Morning, sleepy head,' he says, drawing back the curtains so that the room is flooded with light. He's already dressed and shaved, and as he puts the tray down on the bed next to me and leans in to kiss me, I catch a whiff of his aftershave, and the citrus notes of shampoo.

'Morning.' I haul myself up into a sitting position, and rub my eyes. 'God, what time is it?'

'Ten to eleven.'

'Seriously?'

'You were out for the count.'

'How long have you been up?'

'A couple of hours. I've been down to the village,' he adds, nodding to the tray, and I see fresh croissants, orange juice, coffee in a KeepCup. 'Decaf latte,' he points out. 'I picked it up for you at Bear Market.'

It's a sweet gesture. He knows how much I love their coffee, and it feels a little like a peace offering after the prickliness that's been there between us all week.

'Thanks, love,' I say with feeling, and he grins, then hands me the padded envelope.

'A courier dropped this off earlier,' he remarks, and I take it from him.

'It's from the office. Kelly told me she'd send some documents over.'

I rip open the envelope while Ed turns to his wardrobe, retrieving a navy wool sports jacket. I notice that he's smartly dressed, wearing his dark indigo jeans rather than the usual worn and faded ones he favours, and his shirt looks neatly pressed, his boots polished.

'You look fancy,' I remark, taking a bite of croissant. 'Where are you off to?'

He tells me about an event that's being held at the Irish Writers Centre that afternoon, adding that a bunch of them are going. He doesn't mention anyone by name, but I know it's his writers' group and that means Michael will be there. The pastry in my mouth suddenly feels cloying.

'Dan said he'd come along.' Dan, his publisher. 'He asked if we could grab a coffee beforehand.'

'Oh?'

'It'll be good to catch up. Sound him out about the paperback edition, discuss ideas for a new jacket cover.'

I empty the contents of the envelope on to the bed and a number of documents slip out. Among them is a blue envelope, floral motif.

Ed's got his coat on now, and, as he approaches the bed, he sees the letter and reaches for it.

'What's this?' he asks, turning it over in his hand. 'Doesn't look very corporate.'

I don't say anything. The pastry in my mouth has become a lumpen mass that I can't swallow.

'Faye Sadlier,' he reads, before handing it back to me. 'They used your maiden name?'

'Hmm,' I say lightly, even though my heart is beating wildly.

'Aren't you going to open it?' he asks.

My throat closes over. I put my hand to my mouth and spit the buttery pellet on to my palm.

'Are you okay?' Ed asks, concerned.

'My tummy feels funny. I don't know. It's the croissant — too fatty for this baby, perhaps.' I put my hand on my bump, force a smile.

'I can get you something else. Wholemeal toast?'

'Would you mind?'

He leans forward, kisses me again, 'Course not,' and takes away the plate.

Once I'm sure that he is downstairs, I rip open the envelope. No newspaper clipping this time, but a plain scrap of lined paper, a biro scrawl: *You will pay for what you've done.*

Is this it? Is this what it's all been about? Money? Blackmail? For the first time, my fear is replaced by a real anger. I am entirely sick of this, sick of being threatened, sick of being made to feel afraid. My work has suffered, and a wedge has been driven between me and my husband. I've had enough of being on the back foot with this thing. I snatch a quick glance at the note again – quavery writing, as if the hand that wielded the pen was shaky and weak. The same musty cigarette smell rises from the paper, and my conviction strengthens.

Min. That poisonous old crone, I think, anger making me venomous. I need to do something about this. I need to put a stop to it.

A rumble of footsteps on the stairs, and Ed's back with my toast. 'I'd better get going,' he tells me, breezy and rushed. 'So what was it?' he asks at the door. 'The letter?'

'Oh, nothing. Just a thank you note from my aunt Jean for a birthday gift I sent her,' I tell him, the note hidden beneath the blanket, balled up in my fist.

Once he has gone, I get out of bed and dress quickly, and within half an hour I am sitting in my car, moving steadily through the traffic towards Monkstown. A stream of invective runs through my head, all the anger and hurt of recent months coming to the surface. With no other thought beyond the conviction that this boil must be lanced, I pull the car up outside St Jude's, locking the door behind me, then I march up the driveway, past the mint-green Citroën and the garden choked with briars and bindweed, and press hard on the bell.

There are no kids playing outside today. The street feels curiously empty. The morning's sun has disappeared behind a bank of heavy cloud, and the house in shadow looks austere and dilapidated, half-dead ivy peeling away from the wall to reveal a network of cracks. The glossy black paint of the front door seems crackled with age, and, as I lean on the bell again, I hear it echoing deep inside the house, immediately chased by a catalogue of barking. *Foyle*, I think, with a strange twist of feeling – a tender shoot of nostalgia reaching out of the darkness. I take a step back and wait.

A shadow appears in the hallway behind the wavy glass, and I run a hand through my hair, draw in a long deep breath. I had been expecting Michael, but instead it's Verona, looking at me with puzzlement.

'What are you doing here?' she asks.

The sharpness of her tone gives me pause.

She looks different today: her red dress and headscarf have been swapped for workwear – a fleece cardigan, nurse's trousers. Her hair is pulled into a tight bun secured with a scrunchy, and there is tiredness around her eyes and in the dryness of the skin around her mouth.

'I need to speak to Michael,' I say in a loud voice.

'He's not here.'

'Then let me speak to Min.'

She blinks, her forehead creasing into a frown. 'Min?'

'I know I told you that I never met her,' I say, 'but I wasn't being truthful. I did know Min a long time ago, and I really need to speak to her now.'

The anger in my tone makes my voice shake, and her face changes. A softening about the mouth, and the unexpected trembling of a muscle in her chin.

'Min's dead,' she states quietly.

The news startles me. It takes a moment for it to sink in.

Then Verona takes a step backwards, holding the door open for me. Stunned, I follow her into the house.

'It happened two days ago,' she tells me, once the front door is closed. 'It was an accident. Another fall.'

'I'm so sorry.'

She shakes her head, and I can see how Min's death has affected her. Shocked, bewildered by her grief, she says:

'I don't even know why I'm here. I just wanted to do something.'

She shrugs and turns from me, stepping down the corridor. I follow her, taking in the familiarity of the varnished floorboards, the scattered Moroccan rugs. Plaster busts on plinths, urns sprouting spider plants, the same two antique geese still sitting on the console table – ugly things, they quake in the wake of Verona's footfall. A pair of toolboxes on the ground look out of place, along with a spirit level, a bucket of paintbrushes and scrapers, a giant tub of emulsion. Verona sees me looking and explains: 'Michael's things. He's been working on one of the rooms upstairs. Spending ages up there, sanding and scraping and painting.'

'One of the bedrooms?'

She shrugs. 'I suppose so. I haven't been up there in so long. Well, I've no reason to, do I? Min spent all her time downstairs. Besides, he gets a little cagey about it when asked. I guess he just wants his privacy.'

There's something different about the house since last I was here and I realize that it's the silence. In my memory, the rooms were always filled with music, the sweeping strains of Mahler or some smarmy Rat Pack crooner. But now there's only this funereal calm.

I think she's taking me to the kitchen, but I'm surprised when she pauses at the door on to the room Min liked to call the Parlour – a nod to her own grandiosity. Opening the door, Verona reaches for the dog's collar to restrain him, but he's too quick for her and she shouts in alarm: 'Foyle!' He launches himself at me. Thirty kilos of black-and-tan flesh and fur, his jaws grinning open to reveal a pink tongue and long gooey strands of saliva.

'Hey, old boy! You remember me? You remember me, Foyle?'

The dog's front paws return to the ground and I rub his flank vigorously, noting the grey hairs in his muzzle, the slowness of his gait.

'He recognizes you,' Verona observes, and I meet her eye.

'We're old friends.'

'Min told me that when Michael was in college, there was a girl who broke his heart. A girl called Faye.' Her gaze is steady, interrogative. 'I'm guessing that girl was you.'

Shamed by the memory of my previous denial, I lower my gaze and nod.

'Min said it made him go a little crazy.'

'It was a long time ago,' I admit, some steel re-entering my tone. Must I be blamed for everything that's happened to Michael? Can't he accept any of the blame himself?

Perhaps she reads the defensiveness in my voice, because she drops the subject and leads me into the room.

Immediately, I am struck by the smell – hospital disinfectant and, beneath it, the sweetly sickening odour of decay, as if death itself is in the room. The shelves that line the parlour walls are stuffed with books, just as I remember them, but much of the rest of the furniture has been stripped away. At the centre of the space, a lone hospital bed, empty now of its occupant. A neat pile of blankets folded over a clean sheet, crease marks on the pillow – I watch as Verona reaches to smooth out the wrinkles, tenderness in the gesture.

'She spent the last year or so down here. The stairs had become too much for her,' she remarks.

Queasily I think of Min's frail body, the snap of little bones, and wonder if she died in this room. The cloying feeling of the air in here seems to suggest it.

'Were you here when it happened?' I ask. 'Her fall?'

She shakes her head no. 'Michael was here with his mother. She'd come to see him. Things were tense – they always are whenever Nuala visits,' Verona explains, adding: 'They don't get on, you see. He calls it interference, but she's his mother – she only wants to help him.'

I think of her – Nuala, Michael's mother. A cool woman with frosted blonde hair and slightly bulging eyes. 'The golf club bores,' was how Min referred to Nuala and Jeff, her husband.

'Anyway,' Verona continues, 'things got heated between them. Min must have overheard and tried to get out of bed. That's when she fell.' Her voice breaks off, emotion threatening to overwhelm her. She shakes it off, regaining her composure. 'They called an ambulance, but the damage was done. She died in hospital a few hours later.'

'I'm so sorry, Verona. I can tell you were close to her.'

She smiles quickly. 'You're not supposed to get too close to your patients. But it can be hard to stay detached, especially with someone like Min, who just draws you in.' She laughs at some private memory that she doesn't share with me.

'What will you do now?' I ask.

'Look for another job, I suppose. I'll call the agency tomorrow,' she replies but sounds despondent about the prospect.

'It must be hard, starting over after you've been close to someone like that.'

'Yes. And I worry about Michael,' she tells me. 'Min kept him grounded, stable. I don't like to think of him here, alone, without her.'

Her words bring a chill to the air, the room echoing with a new and spiky presence.

Her eyes flicker towards me.

'What about Ed?' she asks. 'Does he know about you and Michael, your past history?'

I shake my head. 'It feels like the time when I could tell him has passed, and now it's this big thing.'

'Because you lied.'

The words sting, the hard truth of it. I try to explain.

'Ed and I, we've never been interested in talking about our past loves. It's never really mattered to us. I'm not claiming that what I've done is right, but it's more a question of what will make things easier. Simpler.'

'And has it? Made things simpler?'

'No. Not really.' My hands are sweating, and, when I look down, I see my fingers are swollen, my rings too tight, flesh ballooning around them. 'Did Min . . . did she ever talk to you about the ash cloud?'

Verona sounds sceptical. 'Ash cloud?'

At that moment, we're interrupted by a sudden eruption of music – 'Ode to Joy' bleating insistently through Verona's cardigan pocket. She retrieves her phone, glancing at the screen. She sucks in her breath, then says: 'It's Michael's mother. I should really take this.'

'Of course.'

'Nuala?' she says into the phone, already turning from

216

me and moving towards the door. I hear her voice as she disappears down the corridor, the murmur of it fading as she goes out into the garden to conduct her conversation.

Alone in the room, I look around me. The stiff-backed armchairs in creaking green leather, the small army of occasional tables that were once scattered around the room – all of it gone, but there, to one side, is the writing desk. An old mahogany bureau, with a drop front, I remembered its being stuffed full of letters and cards and old bills; part filing cabinet, part office, it was the site of much of Min's activity in the years I knew her, the place she replied to correspondence or paid bills. Now, as I tip the front open and look once more into the velvet-lined pockets, I see Quink pots of ink, a spill of paperclips, untidy bundles of cards and envelopes, along with other various bits and pieces of stationery.

From outside in the garden, Verona's voice rises. '*Of course! I'll gather up her clothes and any other bits and pieces. You know I'm happy to help in any way I can.*' There is not much time. My hands move quickly, searching among the pens for a red sharpie; then, pulling out drawers, I sift through files and folders, looking for newspapers, for blue stationery. I tell myself that it's here somewhere, the evidence that will prove my suspicions. And, even though I have no real idea what I will do with this evidence should I find it – the woman is dead now, after all – still I am impelled by the need to convince myself that my suspicions are real. That my tormentor has been identified, the knowledge of which will bring me peace.

I pull out drawer after drawer, my search becoming

more urgent. I grow sloppy. Papers drift to the floor, but I don't stoop to pick them up. I look beyond the desk and find a basket of newspapers, shaking out each one in the hope of finding a cutting, a tear, a gaping hole where a photograph should be. I can still hear Verona's voice from out in the garden, and cross the room to the shelves, where a mahogany box sits up high. I have it in my head that this box once contained writing paper, and, as I pull it out, the box slips from my hands, landing with a crash.

There's a cry behind me, and as I turn the door springs open. It all happens in a rush. He comes at me quickly – he seems to fly across the room. One minute he's at the door and the next he's upon me, pinning me back against the shelves with such force it knocks the wind from me – a sharp gasp. I can smell his breath, his skin, feel the hot rasp of his fingers as he grabs my wrists, slamming them against the shelves. His face is not five inches from my own; I see the flare of his eyes, the gleam of fury and glimpse the struggle within them, the wildness of his thoughts. I'm only mildly aware of the dog's barking – it exists only on the periphery. In that moment there is just me and him, locked in a wordless struggle, until Verona is there, plucking at his arms, pulling him away, looking from Michael to me and back again, her eyes wide, her voice aghast: 'What the *fuck* is going on?'

16

Faye

The change in him happens so quickly, it amazes me. I can see him marshalling his thoughts, making swift calculations. He lets go of my arms and takes a step back, instantly becoming calmer, reasonable, the hot anger inside him cooling to something unreliable and false.

'I heard a crash,' he explains for Verona's benefit. 'I was just coming in the front door when I heard it. I rushed into the room and saw a stranger standing over the bed. I didn't know who you were for a moment.' He addresses this last comment to me, his voice calmer now, but there's a note of remonstration in it, as if he's chastising me for the fright I've given him. He frowns, his voice dropping. 'What are you even doing here, Faye?'

'You know why I'm here,' I gasp, still shaking, still drawing in my breath. The deliberate blankness of his expression – the faux-innocence – infuriates me. 'Because I want it to stop!'

'You want what to stop?'

'This intimidation! This invasion of my life –'

'I honestly don't know what –'

'Don't give me that shit! You know exactly what I mean! This friendship with Ed. The insidious way you've crept into our lives when I made it expressly clear to you –'

'Whoa! Whoa!' He holds his hands up, backing off a little. 'Listen, Ed and I became friends before I realized what his relationship to you was –'

'Yeah, right!'

'It's true, Faye,' he continues in the same calm, measured tone. 'Call it a coincidence if you like, but, hey, this is Ireland, right? It's a small country. These things happen. And, as for Ed and me – we're just mates. Really. We're just hanging out. I don't see why you're making such a big deal out of it.'

'If it's so innocent, why didn't you tell him about us?'

'Why didn't you?' he counters – a swift punch that I should have expected. I bite my lip, unable to answer.

He relents. 'Look. I didn't want to embarrass you. And, besides, I like Ed – I genuinely do. He's a good guy and it seemed like we were both at a bit of a loose end. It suited him as much as me for us to meet up from time to time. You know – stave off the loneliness.'

'Even though I told you it upset me? I specifically asked you to stay away –'

'Oh, come on! You were serious about that?' he laughs, turning to Verona and gesturing as if to imply that what I'm suggesting is crazy.

Verona is standing by the bed, her arms crossed, frowning.

'That still doesn't explain what you're doing here, though,' Michael says, addressing me once more, his tone growing serious.

'I came . . . I came to try and get to the bottom of this –'

'But here, in Min's room?'

'It's my fault,' Verona interjects. 'I left her alone in here.

I didn't think she'd start poking around in Min's things.' Then, to me, she says: 'I trusted you.'

Her words bring a sweep of shame, and I look down, avoiding the heaviness of her gaze.

'I told you before,' I go on, but my voice has lost its power, 'that I want these threats to stop.'

'Threats?' he asks; then, making an exaggerated show of remembering, 'Oh, yes, these phantom notes you say you've been receiving – you're bringing that up again?'

'They're not phantom. They're real. Look. Here!' The note is still in my pocket, pressed into a ball, and I take it out and smooth the paper against the shelf behind me, then hand it to him. He scans it quickly.

'I had nothing to do with this. On my life, I didn't.' He looks me square in the face, and it's an expression I remember of old: calm, measured and deeply sincere. It knocks me off balance, makes me question myself again.

'Well, if it wasn't you, then I thought . . .' My eyes wander to the empty bed.

'Min?' Michael sounds aghast, and all at once I realize how inappropriate this is. The woman is dead, the pain of bereavement still raw.

'She couldn't even hold a pen,' he declares, his voice wrinkling with emotion. 'Why on earth would you think she'd threaten you?'

'Each time I opened the envelopes, I got this smell,' I try to explain, 'this really distinctive odour: smoke, dust, perfume – it smelled so familiar. It made me think of this house. And, because of what was contained in the notes, of what was so strongly implied . . . I thought that if it wasn't you who was sending them, it must be her.'

My voice has risen, grown desperate. Verona's eyes rest on my face and I feel the beam of her disbelieving stare. Whatever sympathy she might have had for me, I cannot find traces of it now.

Michael, on the other hand, is all sympathy. He has mastered his emotions, and now takes a step towards me, touches my arm. 'Are you sure you're all right? You don't seem yourself. Perhaps I should call Ed, have him come around here so we can talk all of this out.'

'No.'

'I've been thinking about it. All this hiding, all these secrets – it's not fair on him. I really think the best thing is to sit him down and to explain everything to him. About the past, how we were lovers once.'

My stomach turns over, revulsed by his words.

'I would have told him already,' he goes on, 'but I didn't want to embarrass you by contradicting what you'd already told him.'

'The only thing that embarrasses me is you,' I snarl, pulling my arm away, 'that I ever got involved with you. Look at you! Over thirty years old and still living with your old aunt. No home, no job, no friends – a sad, pathetic life. I look at you now and I cannot believe that I ever had any feelings for you. The thought of our being together makes me feel physically sick!'

He just stands there, listening to my tirade, the words seemingly bouncing off him.

'So what is it you want from me?' he asks quietly.

'I want you to leave me alone,' I insist, my voice choked with sudden tears. 'I want you to stop bothering me – to just stay away!'

He cocks his head to one side, his eyes warm and concerned. 'But, Faye, you're the one who keeps showing up here uninvited.'

I get out of there quickly. My hands are shaking as I start the car, my heart banging like it's trying to escape from its cage. A bank of clouds has filled the sky – gunmetal grey – and the air feels heavy, as if to signify a storm is coming. The engine roars and I pull out on to the road quickly, the way clear of traffic. I accelerate, needing to put distance between me and all that has gone on back in that house. A deep pain in my lower back travels through my pelvis, nerves screaming, the child inside me squirming in a way that suggests discomfort. My clothes, I realize, are drenched in sweat, and every time my mind wanders back to that room and what played out there, a fresh wave of mortification comes over me.

I feel ashamed of my suspicion and the sneaky way I went about exploring it. I keep thinking of Verona's expression – a mixture of judgement and disbelief, but there was also pity in her stare – and I realize how it must have looked to her: like Michael was the reasonable one and I'm the one who's unhinged and dangerous.

As I drive, I play it out in my head once more, all the things he'd said, and, as the scene unspools, I begin to doubt myself. Could it be possible that Michael's friendship with Ed was entirely innocent? Might the threat he poses to me in fact be a fabrication, some paranoid delusion scared up by hormones and guilt and too little sleep? *You're the one who keeps showing up here uninvited, Faye.* For the first time, I try to see it through his eyes. Could I, in fact, be the one at fault?

Tears – of confusion and self-pity – blur my vision, so that I don't see the pedestrian crossing ahead of me, I fail to notice the lights changing, the woman pushing a pram on to the road, a small child by her side clinging to the pram's handle. At the last minute I slam on the brakes, screeching to a stop. The woman screams and the child whips around to look at me – blue glasses, black hair in bunches: Amalia, giving me a wide-eyed stare.

The breath catches in my throat. I blink quickly.

The woman is shouting at me now. 'Slow down, you stupid cow! You might have killed us!' her face reddened with fury as she hurries across the road, the wheels of the pram squealing. The child, dragged along in the slipstream of her mother's anger, glances at me, and I see that her hair is brown not black. No glasses in sight. It is not Amalia, and, though I should feel a surge of relief, remnants of the image still cling to me, leaving me cold with shock, until the driver in the van behind me starts beeping his horn impatiently, and I release the brakes, the car creeping away.

I pull up outside my house, and the cloud that has been building overhead finally bursts. Rain comes sheeting down, and I have to dash across the driveway, my hair and clothes already soaked by the time I make it through the door. The silence of the house is broken by the noise of the downpour as it thunders on the flat roof above the kitchen. The house feels unusually dark and gloomy for this hour of the afternoon; a single pendant light that's been left on in the kitchen offers the only warmth. It draws me like a moth and I pause at the kitchen door, thrown by the sight of Ed sitting there at the island, his arms crossed, his face set as he stares at me.

'You're back already?' I ask. 'I thought you were going to an event –'

'I cancelled.'

His manner is cool, and I can tell at once that he is very angry.

'What happened? What's wrong?'

'I met with Dan for a chat.'

'Oh?'

'It turns out that he's not happy with the new direction I've taken. The book that I've been working on – he's had a read and he's not impressed.'

'He said that?'

'Not in so many words, but that was the general gist. Disappointment. He says he can't see how they'll publish it unless there's a serious change of tack.'

'Oh, sweetheart, I'm so –'

'Sorry? Are you?'

I'm taken aback by his curtness.

'Of course I am.'

He snorts with bitter amusement, and then he uncrosses his arms and reaches for the sheaf of pages bound loosely in a rubber band on the worktop in front of him. It's a copy of his manuscript – I can identify the title page from where I'm standing. He picks it up and flings it across the island towards me.

'It was found in a bag at the Concert Hall last weekend. Some Samaritan thought to hand it in to the publisher's office.'

'Oh, no.' I drop my weight on to a bar-stool, put my

hand out to touch the heavy wad of paper, the corners thumbed and curling. 'Ed, I'm so sorry.'

He sniffs, unmoved, and I tell him: 'Dan shouldn't have read it. Not without asking you first.'

'I agree, but he's only human, so he did. I gave this to you on the understanding that you would take care of it –'

'Wait a minute. Didn't you also give a copy to Michael?'

'Who?'

'I mean Jamesie,' I say quickly, correcting the slip.

He stares at me, something flashing behind his eyes. 'Yes, I did,' he answers carefully. 'But he gave it back to me.'

'Are you sure?'

'Of course I'm sure. The manuscript he gave back was covered in his written notes.'

'Perhaps he made another copy? For all we know, he might have handed it in to the publisher himself –'

Ed explodes. 'Christ, Faye! Can't you hear yourself? I am sick to death of this paranoia! This thing you have against him –'

'Why do you always take his side against mine?'

'I've had enough of this! You lost my manuscript and now you're trying to twist it into some reason to resent Jamesie, when he has nothing to do with it! Can't you just admit that you're to blame here?'

'I didn't mean to lose it –'

'Right, it just meant so little that you failed to take care of it.'

'It was an accident! Do you really think that I would do this on purpose?'

He shakes his head. 'I can't believe you would be so

careless. The old you wouldn't have been. The Faye I knew was careful and organized and meticulous. And you know the worst thing? We were at the Concert Hall over a week ago. A week since my manuscript went missing and yet you never said a word to me.'

'I didn't realize,' I admit.

'You didn't realize,' he repeats, hurt, aghast. 'God, was it that tedious?'

'No –'

'You didn't even think enough of my work to twig when it went missing.' Wounded, his anger intensifies.

'I am so sorry. Work's been crazy. I've been distracted.'

'Oh, I'm aware.' His voice is hard, and there's something deliberate about this response, as if he's been holding it back for some time, but, once released, it ricochets around the room. 'You've been distracted for months, but it's not just that. Your behaviour has become so erratic, your moods are all over the place. We have so much to be happy about, but a lot of the time you seem down. Depressed. Remote. Almost angry. Like you don't trust me enough to talk to me. I've seen it in you, Faye, the way you've cut yourself off from me, and I'm trying to understand why. Is it the pregnancy? Or is it something else?'

I shake my head, not trusting myself to speak, knowing that this response – my silence – only goes to prove his point. But if I open my mouth to speak, my voice will crack and the tears will come spilling out, and at this moment Ed is too angry for that.

He shoots me a look loaded with accusation. 'We were happy once. I felt I knew you intimately, but now' – and here his tone grows sorrowful – 'it's like living with a stranger.'

In the aftermath of our row, the house is quiet. A change comes over us. I feel it in the days that follow, as we go about the business of our lives as before, but now I feel the intensity of his scrutiny, as if my every move and mood is being noted. The row, rather than resolving our differences, has instead thrown a spotlight on our relationship, making us watchful of ourselves. Even the most normal of activities – making dinner, sitting in front of the TV together – feels unnatural. All our silences are loaded, and I find myself rushing to fill them, overcompensating for any dips in mood, as if that might prove him wrong, knowing that each show of affection, each display of joy or even satisfaction, might attract its own judgement. It's a cramped way to live, unnatural and exhausting to be so examined, and I feel the lack of privacy keenly.

In work, my mind wanders. I find myself conducting online searches for depression during pregnancy, mood and anxiety disorders, prenatal paranoia. I'm troubled by the doubts Ed has voiced about my own well-being – they compound my nagging insecurities. All the books I've read, the classes I've attended, tell me that I'm supposed to be feeling happy and content, floating along in my pregnancy bubble. The other expectant mums in my yoga class sit around on their mats swapping jokes about the size of their bumps, their changing bodies; afterwards, in a coffee shop around the corner from the yoga studio, I listen while they discuss varicose veins, pelvic discomfort, having to get up three or four times in the night just to pee, how sex has become a total turn-off for some, while others are as horny as hell. Nobody talks about anxiety or paranoia. No one mentions depression.

My work suffers. I forget about a meeting that's been on the calendar for months, only realizing when the diary alert chimes on my phone. I turn up late and unprepared, fluffing my lines, forgetting key facts. I can feel Jess fuming from across the table. Afterwards, she's curt with me as we walk back to the office.

'I don't know what's going on with you, Faye, but you just can't go into a meeting like that without being prepared.'

'I'm sorry,' I tell her, breathless as I try to keep up.

Her stride is longer than mine and powered by her anger. 'Just get your shit together, okay?'

The days run away from me in an autumnal flurry, like the leaves whipped off the trees. It's November now, the nights cold, wind howling around the house. The silver birches that line the back of our garden have all shed their leaves; their denuded branches and trunks are pale and ghostly against the grey concrete wall. Ed decides it's time to tackle the nursery. We drive out to Ikea and wander through the rooms, picking out a cot, a changing table, a rug for the floor. The car heaves with all the things we've bought, and I stare out of the passenger window at the buildings flicking past and try to picture all this new furniture assembled and put in place in the baby's room, and find that I can't. Ed clears the room of all remaining bags and boxes, dragging them downstairs, where they litter the sitting room. I am tasked with sifting through the contents, making decisions about what to keep and what to dump. It's slow methodical work that takes most of the afternoon but keeps my mind off other things. I keep going until Ed calls my name and I follow his voice upstairs, up to the top of the house.

The colour we have chosen is a pale apple green.

He's standing in the baby's room, the paint roller still in his hand.

'It's just a first coat,' he explains, watchful of my reaction. 'But what do you think?'

I look around at the freshness it gives to the walls, like the crisp bite of an apple, and I feel myself inexplicably on the brink of tears.

'It's lovely,' I manage to say.

'It's nice, isn't it? I'll give it a second coat tomorrow and then start putting the furniture together.'

'No, don't. Not yet,' I tell him, and now he looks at me quizzically.

'Why not?'

I can't articulate my reason, any more than I can describe for him the mixture of feelings set off inside me by his transformation of this room. Joy and hope, of course, but also an undercurrent of darker emotions: guilt, dread.

'You've done enough for now,' I say, trying to brighten my voice. 'Let's leave it for another day.'

Then I turn and go back downstairs to make a start on dinner, and all the while, in the back of my mind, the niggling voice of conscience is whispering that I don't deserve any of this. Not after what I've done.

17

Faye

At the end of November, Jess calls me into her office to tell me that we've lost one of our key contracts. It's a serious blow to our company, and I can read at once how deflated and worried she is.

'Oh, Jess, I'm so sorry, I really am. When did you find out?'

'Phil rang me last night.'

'And are you sure it's final? Is there no way we can renegotiate –'

'No. I persuaded him to meet me for breakfast this morning, tried to talk him around. But he was very clear. It's done.'

She swings slightly from side to side in her chair.

'This hasn't really worked out the way I thought it would,' she says quietly, and I feel the words heavy with blame.

'It's a setback, that's all,' I try. 'There are other options we can explore.'

'Yes,' she agrees, though without much enthusiasm. 'But I think a reset is in order. We don't have the funding to keep going as we are. Some decisions will need to be made about various roles.'

'You're talking about sacking people?' I ask, unable to keep the shock from my voice.

She winces. 'It's not that I want to. But we'll need to scale back a bit.' She meets my eye. 'I'm sorry, Faye, but once your maternity leave is over, we'll need to have a think about changing your role within the company. I don't mean letting you go,' she says quickly to reassure me, 'but it seems clear that you're just not cut out for the position you're in.'

She'd hired me because of my excellent management skills, she explains, my reputation for anticipating problems and my decisiveness when it came to resolving them. But instead I'd been hesitant and unsure instead of forthright and confident. My reports of late were often sloppy and inaccurate, and in recent months I'd turned up at meetings unprepared. Excruciatingly, she brings up the Investor Day we'd hosted, in particular my handling of Alan Wright and his subsequent failure to invest in our company.

'I heard a rumour,' she says with delicacy, 'that he decided against us because you were rude to him during the lunch.'

I close my eyes, remembering the moment I'd snapped. The fight has gone out of me, and when I try to marshal an argument, mumbling about Alan being overly sensitive, and how it was a split-second of weakness and I hadn't meant to cause offence, she takes it in sympathetically, but I know her decision has already been made. I'm to be demoted, my hours cut, my responsibilities reduced.

'I'm sorry, Faye. I really am.'

An awkward silence falls, and neither one of us is sure how to move this thing along. Eventually she breaks it, asking: 'Whatever happened about that letter? Those threats you were getting?'

I shift in my seat, my mouth dry. 'I sorted it out.'

'So they stopped?'

'Yes,' I lie. 'It's all over now. In the past.'

'Good. I'm glad to hear it.'

Our meeting has drawn to a close and, as I stand up from my chair, a sudden searing pain rips across my abdomen. I close my eyes and lean forward, bracing myself against the desk.

'Are you okay?' she asks. I feel her gaze, solicitous, concerned, and nod my head, trying to master my pain. It dips and then fades, and I open my eyes and release the breath I've been holding.

'I'm okay. Just a cramp.'

But I can feel the sweat on my forehead. The suddenness and depth of the pain have shocked me.

'Perhaps you should take the rest of the day off.'

'Honestly, I'm fine.'

But no sooner are the words out of my mouth than another jolt of pain pulses through me. I hold on to the table and groan.

Jess stands up and comes around her desk. 'On second thoughts, maybe we should get you to hospital.'

I shake my head. 'It's just Braxton Hicks. Practice contractions. I've had a few over the past week.'

She's unconvinced. 'You can't stay in the office like this. Even if you won't see a doctor, you should at least go home.'

She insists on calling a taxi for me and putting it on the company tab.

Alone in the back of the car, I cry a little. The humiliation of our conversation burns – it's the first time I've ever been demoted. For it to happen now, just before the baby comes and with Ed's career balanced so precariously, it's the worst possible timing. I think about the house, the mortgage we have taken on, the whole move out of London and how stupid it was – such folly when we were happy there. We were safe.

The house is quiet when I push through the front door. It's only when I've closed it behind me, dropped my bag and kicked off my shoes that I hear the sounds coming from high up in the house: music, a radio playing. I climb the stairs, following the tinny pop songs coming through the speakers. A sudden clatter overhead like a hammer dropped on bare floorboards, Ed's voice asking, 'You okay?', then another muffled voice in reply.

On the landing, here at the top of the stairs, are empty cardboard boxes – large, flat-shaped, stamped with Ikea logos; they lie leaning against one wall. The music on the radio is loud, drowning out the sounds of my approach, so it is not until I push open the door that they look up.

The changing table has been assembled and pushed back against one wall; the patterned mat sits atop. In front of it, Ed kneels, grappling with a screwdriver and the carcass of a cot, one slatted side resting on the floor beside him.

His eyes come up to meet mine. 'You're home? I didn't hear you come in!' His eyes are wide and startled and I hear him say something about how he wasn't expecting me, that I've come too early, how they had intended putting it all together and then surprising me with the finished nursery, but it's all just words – they skitter past like birds wheeling on a gust of wind. I hardly even look at him, my gaze fixed on the corner of the room.

Michael sits on the nursing chair zipping the cot mattress into a protective cover. I cannot believe it. The chair itself – upholstered in mustard-coloured velvet, on solid oak rocking legs, a splurge purchase but an important one, as it is here that I will spend hours nursing my baby, a private, intimate, loving act – has now been defiled by his occupation of it. That he would come into this room, a room that had been pure, the site of all my hopes, that he would sully it with his presence, dragging into this space the filthy reminders of our dark past, seems violently wrong. The sight of the cot mattress in his hands – the very bedding my unborn child will sleep on – brings with it a wave of revulsion so strong that, despite my exhaustion, my shock, I fly across the room and snatch the thing from his grasp.

'Get out of here!' I hiss into his face. 'Don't you understand? You're not wanted here!'

'Faye!' Ed cries, shocked.

Michael, his eyes cool and flat like pools of water, says: 'I was only trying to help.'

'I don't want your help! I don't want anything from you!'

'What the hell's the matter with you?' Ed asks, his grip on my elbow, pulling me around to face him. 'He dropped over his tools to me, and then said he'd just give me a hand putting it together. Why are you getting hysterical –'

'You know how I feel about him! What is he even doing here?'

'I asked him to come over,' he says, lowering his voice to add: 'His aunt died recently and he's been upset, okay? He reached out to me. What was I supposed to say?'

'How could you let him up here? Into the baby's room?' My voice quivers with emotion.

'You're overreacting –'

'Don't say that to me!' I shake off his arm and back away. Tears are rolling down my cheeks, and both men are staring at me like I'm crazy.

'Listen, I'm sorry,' Michael says, getting up slowly from the chair. 'The last thing I wanted was to upset you.'

'I don't believe one word you say. If you didn't want to upset me, you wouldn't be here.'

'Could one of you please tell me what the fuck is going on?' Ed demands.

'I'm sorry, mate,' Michael tells him, backing away to the door. 'I'll go and leave you guys alone. You can drop the tools back to me some other time.'

He's adopting the infuriating stance of a reasonable person who's trying to navigate carefully through the rocky waters of my mania. I can feel the pressure growing inside my head; a vein throbs in my neck. Pausing at the door, he casts a look in my direction that might be sympathy or pity. 'And I really am sorry, Faye, whether you believe it or not. I didn't come here to upset you and it worries me to see you so wound up. At this late stage of pregnancy, it's dangerous, and the last thing in the world I would want is to be responsible for you losing another baby.'

The word slips from his mouth so easily. That one single adjective injected into the room like a poison.

Ed stiffens. With shock in his voice, he asks: '*Another?*'

Congested with rage, I propel Michael from the room. 'Out!' I roar, and this time he goes, footfall rumbling on the stairs, followed by the firm sound of the front door closing, then silence.

I stand still for a moment and a wave of weary dread passes through me. It's as if some part deep inside of me has been holding its breath, waiting for this moment. Ed continues to stand where he was, his shoulders held high, but the blood has drained from his face, his features heavy and drawn, and his voice when he speaks is calm and very cold.

'*Another* baby?'

My heart is pumping too fast. I swallow hard, trying to bring it under control.

'It was a long time ago,' I croak.

'You were pregnant before?'

I nod, hardly able to bear the way he is looking at me.

'Was he . . . was Jamesie the father?'

'I never called him by that name. I always called him Michael.'

Ed explodes. 'Christ, Faye! What the fuck has his name got to do with anything?'

I try to moisten my lips, but my mouth is dry.

'Was it serious? It must have been,' he remarks, answering his own question. 'Why else would you keep it a secret?'

'We were just kids, barely in our twenties. It was a million years ago –'

'Wait,' he says, the penny dropping. 'That's the guy from university?'

I nod.

'So why didn't you tell me about him?'

'I don't know –'

'For God's sake, you expect me to believe that?'

'And you've told me about every single woman in your past?'

'I haven't lied about any of them! And I'm pretty sure I'd remember it if I'd gotten one of them pregnant. Christ! What were you thinking?'

I try to explain: 'When I saw him here – that first time, at your birthday – I was shocked. He was the last person I expected to see. And I should have told you then – I wish that I had – but I just panicked!'

'You deceived me. I never thought you would do that.'

'I am so sorry, Ed!'

He stares at me, genuinely perplexed. 'I just don't get it. Even to your own ears, this must sound nuts!'

'I know it makes no sense, but when I was put on the spot, confronted with him here in my own home, it was an instinct! To act like he was a stranger. And then he seemed to just go along with it . . . as if he accepted that we were strangers to each other now. So much time had passed – water under the bridge – it seemed too difficult to row back after the event. To say, "Oh, actually, I *do* know you." I was just flustered. Thrown.'

'And afterwards? You could have told me then.'

'I know –'

'On multiple occasions!' he snaps. 'All those times I spoke to you about him, and the night at the Concert Hall? Christ! I feel like a fucking fool! Have you two been talking about this behind my back?'

'No!'

'*Really?*'

'All right,' I admit, my hands going up to pat the air, trying to calm him. 'I rang him once –'

He shakes his head furiously.

'To tell him I didn't want him coming near me. That I wanted him to stay out of our lives –'

'But *why*?' His eyes bulge as he roars the word at me. 'All this secrecy, this lying, this deception – what's it all been for?'

'Please, Ed,' I say. His ferocity frightens me, and I'm desperately calculating how to explain this to him, the things I can say and the things I can't. 'This is difficult.'

His eyes flash with indignant rage, but he folds his arms and stands by the window, waiting and listening.

And so I tell him about how Michael and I first met. Young love, the two of us barely out of school, students, a time of innocence. That is until third year, when I discovered I was pregnant, and suddenly we both had to grow up, fast.

'He was away at the time – on Erasmus in Germany. We had arranged to meet in Barcelona for a weekend in April. I broke the news to him there and we tried to decide what to do, whether or not to keep the baby. But while we were there, a volcano in Iceland erupted – I don't know if you remember –'

'You were trapped,' he interrupts. I can see that the pieces are starting to fall into place in his mind.

'I was panicky. Michael wanted to keep the baby, but I wasn't sure. We were so young – I wasn't ready to be a mother. Time was of the essence, and the longer we were there, the more worried I became that by the time I got home it would be too late to do anything about it.'

'So what happened? What did you do?'

Now is the moment. Tell him. *Tell him.*

My heart leaps painfully in my chest, and I look at him and see the plain need in his expression. There is still love there, and I can still recall a time when he'd vowed that I could tell him anything and it wouldn't change his love for me. I want so badly to believe that. But there are some secrets too dangerous to tell, and when I think of how he would react were I to say the words aloud . . .

'Nothing,' I tell him, keeping my voice neutral. 'I did nothing. But I lost the baby anyway.'

His voice thaws a little as he asks me when and how, and I fill him in on the details, how within hours of landing in Dublin I began to bleed heavily. It was all over within a couple of days. And, once it was over, I ended it with Michael.

'I was a bit messed up afterwards,' I explain. 'Confused, stressed, sad. And I had my Finals to sit. I was all over the place. But I knew I needed to put it all behind me. A clean break. So I told him that I didn't want to see him again. He was very hurt. But I broke off all contact. By the time he returned to Dublin, I had finished my exams and had already left for London. I didn't see him again until –'

'Until he came here on the day of my birthday.'

Until I sat in my car outside his house.

But to tell Ed that would mean explaining about the threatening notes, and I cannot go anywhere near that.

'Right,' I whisper.

He has his arms crossed over his chest, and now he

puts a thumbnail to his teeth, his brow creased into a frown. I can see how difficult this is for him, but some of the anger has died away, and I sense a mellowing there – an opening – so I get to my feet, feeling a twinge of pain in my abdominal muscles. Taking a step towards him, I say: 'I'm so sorry, love. I really am.'

The distrust lingers on his face, but his tone is gentler now. 'You could have told me all this before, you know.'

'I know.'

'So why didn't you? Am I such an ogre? Were you afraid I'd judge you –'

'No! It's not that.'

'Then what?' he pleads.

'I was trying to deal with it myself. I'd told him repeatedly to stay away from me, that I didn't want him in our lives. But he just seemed to become so firmly entrenched, and any time I expressed my dislike of him, my distrust, you kept taking his side.'

'That's hardly fair. I didn't know the full picture.'

'I know. But he was part of the past and I just wanted to keep things that way. It's how I've always dealt with that whole episode. By just packing it all away – all those painful memories – putting them in a little box, locking it, and then shoving it down into the deepest, darkest corner in my mind.'

'You pretended it never happened.' He sounds unconvinced, but it is the truth.

'It's how I've always dealt with things that are hard. You know: ignore it, it will go away – aren't you always saying that it's the maxim I live by?'

I'm trying to lighten the mood, but it falls flat. This isn't funny. I have seriously injured the man I love more than anyone in the world.

'Ed? I'm sorry,' I whisper again, stepping closer to him.

His reluctance is still there, but he lets me lean into him, my head against his chest, and his arms go around me. My heart is still rocking painfully, but I feel the warmth and some of the familiar safety of his embrace. I want to stay here for as long as I can, like a bird inside a nest, a cold wind blowing around the tree.

'I'm not sure how to trust you,' he says softly into my ear. 'I want to, but . . . I can't help but wonder what else you might be hiding from me?'

Sudden pain rips through me. Since leaving the office, the muscle cramping has paused, but now it returns with a vengeance. My knees buckle and I fall against him. He catches me, saying, 'What is it? What's wrong?' and I can hear the spike of fear in his voice, but I cannot answer. The pain is rolling through me, cutting through all the layers of muscle and fat and tissue. My whole body is alive to this pain as it rises and rises. By the time it plateaus and then dips, I am doubled over and sucking in air like a fish pulled from the water.

'Jesus, what was that?' Ed asks, his arms supporting my waist, holding me up.

Through staggered breaths I explain about this morning's cramps, why I'd come home early, but this pain feels stronger, more frightening than my earlier experience. Within minutes, we're in the car, Ed hunched over the wheel, his face set in concentration. The pain comes in waves and he murmurs to me to hang on, we'll be there soon, but I can't stop thinking that it's too soon, that I'm just not ready yet. There's over a month to go until she's supposed to be born, and I will her to stay inside me.

There's heavy traffic around Holles Street, so Ed lets me out at the entrance to the hospital, and I go in alone while he finds a space to park the car. Because of this, we become separated, so that when I am swept up into the maternity procedures – the ultrasound, the examination, the blood tests, the monitoring – Ed is left outside, dealing with gatekeepers and bureaucracy, trying to argue his way in to find his wife. Later, when I reflect on this separation, I will realize that it was a good thing. It gave me space in which to think and to collect myself, and, for Ed, it gave him the time he needed to let go of his anger, to focus on all we share together, the future, this family we are trying to make.

When, finally, they let him through into the cubicle where I am resting, all the ugliness of the afternoon has been stripped away, so that what remains is love and worry and then relief when I tell him that it is all right. The baby is still safe inside me, and will be for a little while yet. Ed hugs me and we both cry and then a nurse comes to discharge me and Ed takes me home.

The lights are on in our house when we get back, and, as I step in the door and head straight for the stairs, I can hardly countenance all the events that have been rolled into this one day. Ed carries my bag up to the bedroom, helps me take off my shoes. He asks if he should run a bath for me, but I shake my head. I'm too exhausted. All I want now is to get into bed and fall asleep.

'You should eat something,' he tells me, sitting on the side of the bed after I've slipped under the duvet. 'If I heat up some soup, will you eat some?'

'That'd be lovely.'

He smiles, then lingers a moment and I can see that he wants to say something.

'You don't have to be afraid of telling me things,' he says. His voice is low, tender and serious. 'You can tell me anything, okay?'

I nod, too choked up to speak. And then I listen as he goes back downstairs.

The bedroom door is left open, and I can hear him in the kitchen, the sound of a pot landing on the hob, the cutlery drawer sliding open. After a minute, I hear the muffled sound of his voice, low and serious, and I wonder briefly whether he is calling his mother and father, recounting the drama of our scare.

But when he comes into the room a few minutes later, carrying the tray of soup and bread, there's a new clenched look about his face, his eyes glittery and hard, and when I ask him if everything's okay, he answers, 'Yep, fine,' but his voice is tight.

I realize at once that he has been on the phone to Michael. That he has warned him off. Told him to leave us alone. To stay away. Told him that he has lied to Ed and frightened me. And, as the door closes behind him and Ed drifts back downstairs, I think of Michael, alone in a room in that old house, the phone still held to his ear, absorbing this new rejection.

He'll leave us alone now, I tell myself. Bringing my spoon to my mouth, I realize I won't be able to swallow it. My throat has closed, plugged by all the things I cannot say.

I push the tray aside and lie back, try to sleep. But the curtains are open and in the sky beyond there is a full moon. It shines in through the window, silvery light finding me open-eyed and staring, as ghosts creep around the bed.

18

Michael

April 2010

It was Mateo who had the idea about the milk lake. Pointing behind him towards the eastern side of the mountain, he explained that there was a pool of water up there, hidden among the trees, that appeared white by moonlight.

'Like milk,' he added.

There was to be a full moon that night. 'Why don't we go up there?'

When Michael put the idea to Faye that she come with him and the others, she was dismissive. She was tired of the other girls, she said – their scrutiny, their unshared jokes – and, besides, she had to study.

'Really, I'll be fine,' she assured him, 'you go. Take pictures, and show them to me later.'

They set off late – later than they'd planned, as it had taken a while for Amaya to get the baby settled. Mateo led the way, the beam of his torch casting from side to side through the forest as the others fell in behind him. Efrain and Greg also had torches, but the moon was full and high overhead, lending a silvery light to the narrow path through the trees that was sufficient illumination for the rest of them.

'So what happened to Faye?' Sheena asked, falling back so that the two of them trailed along together at the end of the group.

'She wasn't feeling well,' Michael replied.

He wondered how much Sheena knew of their situation – the walls in the house were paper-thin. Since they'd arrived there, he and Faye hadn't made love once, which was partly on account of the spiky mood between them, but also because of their vigilance against listening ears. It seemed likely that Sheena had overheard Faye's concerns about money and about her exams, but it was unclear if she knew about the baby. Either way, he didn't want Sheena's derision aimed at Faye. He already felt guilty enough, leaving his girl-friend alone. The image kept coming to him – Faye, sitting forlorn with her head in her hands – and lingering over it was this strange sense of foreboding, which was baseless and stupid. Things had become intense over the past couple of days. In his own head, he reasoned that she would be fine taking a few hours alone to rest.

'That's too bad,' Sheena remarked, adding with a flash of a challenge: 'But her loss is my gain, right?'

They walked high into the mountain, tracking eastwards. Around them, they could hear the rustle and movement of nocturnal animals and birds in the trees, the click and murmur of insects in the undergrowth and on the forest floor. The air was cold and thin, and they could see the clouds of their breath before them, but their bodies were warmed by the exertion of the climb, and two hours later, when they arrived at the lake, Michael was sweating beneath his clothes.

It was as Mateo had promised: a pool of milky-white water that lay in a clearing, the surface still and unbroken, a perfect reflection of the lunar light. Around it, the trees rose tall and black, the spikes of conifers and spruces spearing the night sky. Someone passed a joint around, and for a few moments they just stared at the lake, savouring its perfection, unwilling to be the first to break the surface.

Amaya was the one that led them in. Michael didn't notice her shedding her clothes. He saw the water ripple and then there she was, striding in, assured, her black hair swinging down her back towards the twin globes of her buttocks, her thick strong thighs. She walked until she was waist deep, and then, without making a cry or a shout, she gave herself fully to the water, the surface briefly closing over her head, before she emerged triumphant, her hands aloft, her skin luminescent.

After that, they all piled in. The water was shockingly cold. So cold Michael thought he could feel the marrow in his bones shrinking from it. But it was exhilarating too. He whooped with delight and heard his voice echoed by the ring of trees. And then they were all hooting and shouting and calling to one another, a cacophony of voices disturbing the silence as their limbs churned the water, and each one of them felt completely and utterly alive and present.

When at last he pulled himself out of the water, he was shivering. They all were. He dried himself with quick abrasive movements of the towel, and was half dressed when Sheena approached.

'Hey,' she said, her voice close to his ear. 'Come over here. I wanna show you something.'

She'd put her shorts back on, but her torso was still exposed. Her bikini top was a shade of neon orange, which made her skin appear more deeply tanned, more luminous. In the water, he'd surreptitiously looked at her, and the other girls. He was twenty years old and pumped with youth, and observing their toned tummies and small breasts, the nipples sharp with cold beneath their bikinis, he'd felt himself turned on. Even Amaya with her milk-filled breasts and pelt of body hair had aroused something in him.

Now, shivering at the side of the water, Sheena took hold of his hand, and he allowed himself to be pulled away from the others, who remained by the shore, Efrain and Greg building a campfire, Adriana and Mateo sharing a joint.

'Where are we going?' he asked, but Sheena just laughed, and said: 'You'll see.'

She led him into the trees, giggling as she dragged him into the undergrowth, weeds and sharp grasses brushing against their calves and ankles in the darkness, looking back at him from time to time in a way that was deeply flirtatious. He felt a lurch in his stomach, realizing what this was. What she had in mind.

When they were far enough away from the others, she stopped and turned to him. Standing close enough so that he could smell the weed she'd smoked on her breath, she caught hold of his wrists and pulled him towards her, so that his hands were around her waist, her body pressed close to his.

'Sheena –'

'Kiss me.'

'I can't –'

'Come on! I've seen you looking. I know you want to.'

'No,' he laughed, pulling his hands away and attempting to step back, but she caught hold of him again and this time her hands went around him, so that he felt the press of her fingertips in the small of his back while she held him there. She had a wiry strength and a determined grin, and he wondered how best to disentangle himself while at the same time realizing he was aroused.

'I have a girlfriend,' he whispered.

Sheena laughed. 'So what? She's not here, is she? It's just us – you and me. Let's live in the moment. This night – this beautiful night. Come on – why not?' She bit her lower lip, angled her head to one side and looked up at him coyly. 'It's not like I'm going to make you marry me afterwards.'

It would be a lie to say that he wasn't tempted. She was fun, sexy, easy to be around. When she reached up and pressed her lips to his, he felt his mouth and body responding. They kissed for a few minutes, the kiss growing charged with a potency that felt beyond his control. She broke away briefly, only to draw him deeper into the trees, so that they were hidden from the others when they came together once more. He felt her cool nakedness beneath the bikini, her clear offer of herself, and his breathing quickened, his mind whooshing and throbbing until a flash of consequence moved across his brain and he pulled away quickly.

'No,' he said, breathless and shocked – at himself, at the distance he had already travelled into this thing.

'Come on!' she said, half laughing, but there was irritation there too.

She went towards him and he held his hands up and said, 'No, I'm sorry, but I just can't,' and this time his voice was firm, decisive. He saw the range of emotions crossing her face: disbelief, rage, hurt. Her eyes became small, her mouth straightening into a mean line.

'You're a tease, you know that, Michael?'

'Listen –'

'Fuck you!' she snapped, and shoved him so quickly he hadn't time to secure his footing.

Stones scrabbled beneath him as he staggered backwards, Sheena's eyes widening – neither of them had seen the drop, a sharp falling away of the rock behind the trees, a sheer cliff that stretched way down into a distant valley.

At the last second, he snatched hold of a branch and Sheena reached and grabbed a handful of his T-shirt. Hauling him back, she watched as he breathed quickly and heavily, his heart going like the clappers. But something had closed about her expression, like a hard varnish had come down over her face. 'Saved your life,' she said coolly, then turned on her heel and left him.

Alone, he waited a few seconds for his body to stop spurting adrenalin into his bloodstream. Then, glancing back, he made himself peer over the drop, to see for himself the distance he might have fallen.

The mood of the night – the feelings of exhilaration and vitality – had been punctured. He felt cold and tired – a deep-bone weariness had set in. He went back to the others to retrieve his towel and backpack, and, without saying a word to anyone, he turned to make his way back.

The moon shone on the path, and he followed it carefully, knowing that, once he'd circled back around to the other side of the mountain, he would see the house lit up from further down and it would guide him home.

It felt like he'd been absent for days, that's how removed from the world he seemed. He was dismayed at himself, at his easy faithlessness, and his spirits were very low as he rounded the mountain.

It was not until he saw the house that he recalled his earlier feeling of foreboding. But now, as he began the final descent towards it, he felt it again – a sense of doubt, a low whisper of fear. He began to hurry, charging quickly down the uneven path, even though his calves and knees screamed with pain. Fumbling in his backpack for a key, he reached the house, unlocked the door and pushed his way into the dim hallway.

Silence greeted him. He made his way down the corridor, padding softly, careful not to make a sound. The door to their bedroom was shut, and he took a step towards it, unsure of why it was he felt a clutch of nerves in his throat. His heart barely had time to quicken as he pushed through the door and took in the scene . . .

'Jesus!' he breathed, his legs buckling beneath him so fast that he had to grab on to the door frame to stop himself from falling. 'Jesus fuck!'

She looked up at him, her eyes wide with terror, but her voice when she spoke was surprisingly calm.

'You have to help me, Michael,' was all she said.

19

Faye

Finally, the last day of the year arrives – my due date.

For the first time in a long time, I sleep heavily. It's late when we wake; Ed turns to me, rubbing at one eye still crusty with sleep, and asks: 'Well?'

I have grown familiar with this question – this expectant query. The same one word has greeted me each waking morning for the past three days – ever since our last hospital check-up, when the doctor examined me and informed us that the baby's head was engaged and that it could be any time now.

I offer him a rueful smile. 'Nope. Don't think so,' and he lets out a small sigh that I can't be sure is disappointment or relief.

Then he kisses me and says: 'You stay here. I'll make tea.'

He pulls on his dressing gown and opens the curtains, and I sit myself up, arranging the pillows around me so I'm supported and comfortable, and then I relax, looking out our bedroom window at the sky burning blue, while Ed rattles around downstairs in the kitchen, preparing the breakfast tray. My bump sits heavily in my lap, the skin beneath my nightdress so stretched and thin that the network of tiny blood vessels is visible when I look, threading beneath the surface. The baby moves, and I put my hand to feel her, the scraping of a tiny heel or elbow along the wall of my abdomen. Her movements have felt slow and lugubrious these last couple of weeks. The flicks and sudden leaps of the second trimester have dwindled away, and I can feel how tight and cramped it has become in there for her. The hour of her arrival is approaching, but I don't sense it yet. Not today, I tell myself.

'Here we are,' Ed says brightly, returning with the tray.

He pours tea for us both, and drinks his by the window, a triangle of toast in one hand while he stares out at the day. Birds wheel past, a couple of magpies, the white plumage amid the black blazing in the sunlight.

'What a day,' Ed remarks. 'Looks more like April than December.'

He's right: the springlike freshness in the air, the gentle sway of the bare birch trees, the bright cast of blue to the sky.

'What are you going to do with yourself today?' I ask, and he shrugs.

'Try to write, I suppose. Try not to monitor your every movement, reading too much into every twinge.' He chuckles and I grin. It's become a joke between us, how twitchy with nervous excitement he's become. It doesn't annoy me, in fact I'm charmed by it. In the past month, a new harmony has come into our home. With the advent of our little one's arrival, our bond has strengthened. A tenderness has entered our dealings with one another. We are kinder to each other. I feel relaxed, happy.

'You should go out,' I tell him, enjoying the warmth of the tea, the delicious sweetness of marmalade, the cosiness of our bed. 'Make the most of this beautiful day.'

'Sure. Maybe we could go for a walk, if you're feeling up to it?'

'No, I mean you should take the bike out.'

'Yeah, right,' he laughs. 'And leave you here alone.'

'I'll be fine! And it's been a few days now since you've gone for a cycle. I thought it was going to be your regular exercise?'

'Yes, but what if it starts? What if you go into labour while I'm gone?'

'Then I'll call you.'

'But if I'm off in the Wicklow hills or –'

'Seriously! Stop worrying. Everything I've read says that with your first baby, the labour is long and slow. So, even if something happens, it will be hours before we need to head for the hospital.'

He looks at me sceptically, but I can tell that he's drawn to the idea.

'Go on,' I urge him gently. 'It'll be good for you to burn off some of that nervous energy. And besides – this will probably be your last opportunity before she arrives, so I really think you ought to grab it.'

He finishes his breakfast, leaving me the tray while he changes into his cycling gear. I'm downstairs by the time he's ready to go.

'Promise you'll call me,' he says, 'if you feel like something's happening – even the tiniest hint of a twinge.'

'I promise.'

He gets on his bike, and I wave him off at the front step in my dressing gown, one hand raised to shield my eyes from the sun.

*

In the calmness and quiet of the house, I take my time showering and getting dressed. Afterwards I drift from room to room, my earbuds in, listening to a podcast and admiring the orderly neatness of my home. I'd had a burst of energy in the days after Christmas, which brought on a flurry of tidying, but my movements have slowed now. I grow tired easily. It's nice having this time alone, the house to myself, without Ed hovering solicitously around me. For a little while, I sit in the baby's room, my head leaning back against the plush upholstery of the feeding chair, half listening to the voices of my podcast. The memory of that awful afternoon when I had found Michael up here has faded, and when I think of my heightened anxiety that day – the mixture of fear and fury that pulsed through my blood – I'm a little shocked by the strength of those feelings, almost ashamed of them. It seems like such a long time has passed since that day. All of it has receded now, a tide drawn back from the shore. There is peace in the waiting, hope streaming through my anticipation.

Midday comes, and I put on my shoes and a quilted puffer coat, the only coat that closes around my bump, and leave my house to walk the short distance to the Lazy Days Café. There is a small queue, but the girl behind the counter – Sally – sees me and raises her hand in greeting. They know me and Ed now, given the frequency of our visits, and she assures me she'll find a seat for me soon. An elderly couple vacate their table by the window, the old man catching my eye and gesturing to his seat; they have left their table a little earlier than they might have done in order to let me sit down. I'm grateful for their kindness and I tell them so.

'On your own today?' Sally asks, cleaning off the table with quick efficient swipes.

'That's right.'

I'm taking off my coat when she exclaims at the sight of my bump. 'You must be ready to pop now!'

'Yes, nearly fully cooked.'

She beams, and takes my order: apple juice and some pancakes with fruit. While I wait, I browse the news on my phone. Ed sends a WhatsApp – a panoramic photograph of the view from Enniskerry, where he has just reached. The vista takes in Dublin Bay from Howth all the way to Bray Head, the sea a deep azure, bookended with hills that are sparse and brown. 'Heading home shortly,' he writes, and I reply with a heart emoji.

My pancakes arrive, and I dig in, savouring their warmth and buttery sweetness, the pleasingly tart cut-through of raspberries. I'm taking my second or third bite, when I glance up at the window and see that beyond the glass, outside on the street, is a little girl wearing glasses, a plaster covering one eye. She is staring right at me.

My fork stops midway between my plate and my mouth. I am suddenly very cold.

The little girl is about four or five, her black hair in bunches. She puts her hands to the glass.

I know that it's not Amalia – that it can't be – but for a brief moment my mind trips past reason and logic, and I'm convinced that it's her. Staring at me through the window, stony-faced, her expression grave. Accusatory.

A sudden crash behind in the kitchen, a clatter of

cutlery falling on the tiled floor, jolts me from the memory. I look again and see that the glasses the little girl wears are red not blue, that her skin is fair, her face heart-shaped and delicate, not round and slightly flat like Amalia's had been.

I give myself a shake. A coincidence, that's all. My mind playing tricks. And, besides, years have passed. Amalia would be a teenager now. Ridiculous to make that mistake.

I address my pancakes once more but find that I am no longer hungry. The golden slide of melted butter oozing from them across my plate turns my stomach. I can feel the wet lumpen mass of carbohydrates sitting uncomfortably inside. I push the plate away, turning for my coat as I stand up.

'You're not going already?' Sally asks.

'Yes, sorry. I think I need to lie down.'

'Oh dear. Shall I wrap those up for you?' she offers. 'You can have them at home?' and I say yes to avoid offending her, even though I know I'll dump them in the bin as soon as I get back.

She parcels them up in tinfoil, and when she hands me the package, still warm, she frowns with concern and says: 'You know, you really don't look well. Why don't you let me run you home?'

I decline, saying I need some fresh air. I pay the bill but back away clumsily, my elbow meeting with a napkin dispenser balanced on a shelf by the door. It clatters to the ground and I'm all apologies, exiting quickly while Sally picks them up.

Outside, the little girl is gone. But my head is alive with thoughts now, a stream of them travelling like panic through me. Amaya with her swaying hips and bad teeth, Efrain with his easy laugh, his careless manner. And the children: Amalia with her one good eye blinking behind her glasses – 'My cycloptic friend,' Michael used to call her, teasingly – the way she would squeal with sudden laughter; and the baby – *bebito* – the whorl of black wispy hair on his crown, the soft pounding of his little fists against my chest . . .

I push them away, these dangerous, destructive thoughts. I had built a wall of steel around these memories, but it has been breached. One glance at a little girl with glasses and a patch over her eye and I am undone.

Back home, I try to calm myself. I make some fennel tea and sip it slowly, reminding myself that Ed will be back in another hour or so. I just need to hold on until then.

After a while, I go upstairs and lie down on my bed. I play a mindfulness meditation on my phone, thinking that I won't be able to sleep but it will at least help me to rest. But when I close my eyes, I do sleep. I go way down, into the very depth of sleep, and when I wake the sky outside my window has faded to grey. It confuses me, this darkness outside; I'm unsure how long I have been asleep. I glance at my phone, and see that it's almost four. The afternoon has drained away, evening seeping in. The house around me feels silent, empty. I check my phone again for a message from Ed, but there's been nothing since the panoramic photograph taken from Enniskerry. I pull myself up and look for evidence that he's come back. But everything is as it was in our bedroom, and it is as

I step out on to the landing that the banging on the front door begins.

I pause for a moment, uncertain. But then the banging comes again – three loud raps in quick succession – urgency there.

Ed, I think with sudden panic. I hurry down the stairs, encumbered by the heaviness of my bump. There is a deep ache in my lower back, and my heart pumps with the exertion. Worry runs through me like a prayer, and when I open the door and see Michael, my worry smacks up against surprise and fear.

'It's okay,' he tells me, holding up his hands, but his eyes are wide and there's a breathlessness about him. 'There's been an accident.'

A sharp intake of breath, my hand goes up to cover my mouth, and he hurries on: 'He's okay, he's okay. A fracture, maybe, but probably just a sprain. The paramedics were on their way when I left.'

There's a strain in his voice – shock, adrenalin – and a rushed jitteriness about him that brings with it something of the air of crisis, as if he's carried it from the scene of the accident itself.

'What happened?' I gasp, taking my hand away from my mouth. He's still standing on the front step, and I reach out now to grab hold of the door frame to steady myself.

An accident – a car turning on to the road had clipped the back wheel of the bike, sent Ed flying, he explains.

'But where was this?' I ask, confused. It doesn't add up – what was Michael doing in Wicklow? Why was he there?

'Dún Laoghaire,' he answers. 'York Road. Verona was driving past – she saw it –'

'Verona?'

'Yes, my friend. You met her, don't you remember?'

My thoughts skip and chase, rebounding, falling over each other. 'I don't understand. What was Verona doing there?'

'She was coming from work when she chanced upon the accident, moments after it happened. She stopped because she has some medical training, but when she saw that it was Ed, she phoned me. Naturally, I went straight there. It's not far from my home, so I was there within minutes.'

It starts to make sense, and I listen while he assures me that Ed was conscious, that he was sitting up, a little dazed, naturally. Shocked and sore.

'He was asking for you,' he tells me. 'I said I'd come and get you. Verona will stay with him until the ambulance comes. She's going to let me know what's going on, what hospital they're taking him to. Why don't you grab your coat? If we hurry, we might catch them before the ambulance leaves and then you can go in it with him.'

My coat and shoes are in the hall where I'd left them. Hurriedly, I put them on, then grab my bag and my keys, pulling the door shut behind me.

He drives quickly, hunched over the wheel, taking the corners sharply.

'Please slow down,' I ask, nerves quickening in my throat.

'Sorry,' he says, glancing across at me. There's something manic about his air, his manner. I have the strangest feeling that he is *excited* by this run of events. It grates on me, but I try to focus on the road, on Ed, on willing him to be all right.

'It's a good thing he was wearing his helmet,' Michael remarks, his phone beeping with an incoming message.

He glances at it as he drives, and I have to restrain myself from telling him to keep his eyes on the road. I look in my bag for my own phone, wanting to call Ed, to talk to him, needing the reassurance of his voice, but it is only now that I remember – it's still on my bed where I'd left it.

We have passed through Monkstown and now he drives along Upper Mounttown Road, but, instead of turning left on to York Road when we meet the junction, he veers right at the church. I sit up straighter in my seat.

'I thought you said the accident was on York Road?'

'That was Verona,' he says, nodding towards his phone in the well beneath our seats.

'Have they gone already? To the hospital?'

'No. She's taken him back to St Jude's.'

'To St Jude's? Your house?' The information jars, and I feel the warning shout inside.

'It's close by, and Verona still has a key.' He turns to me, his expression mild and inscrutable. 'I guess he can't have been that bad.'

The car turns off the road and pulls up outside the old red-brick. I stare up at the walls stained with damp, a crack running through the windowpane in the top-right-hand room.

'Michael. What's going on?'

He turns off the engine and unclips his belt. 'I've no idea. All I have is this text from Verona.'

He sees the look I'm giving him, loaded with suspicion, and, adopting a reasonable tone, says: 'Look, why don't you wait here? I'll pop inside and see if they're there, okay?'

So I sit in the car, and watch him stride up the path. He pushes open the door, stands in the threshold. I can see him talking to someone who remains out of view in the darkness of the hall. He turns briefly and gestures to the car, then resumes his conversation. It's Verona, I think. It must be. I remember her natural warmth, her earthy kindness, and the thought of her presence in the house puts me at ease a little. Leaving the front door open, Michael hurries back to me, and bends down to address me through the side window. He seems more relaxed, confident, at ease.

'Yeah, he's inside. He's fine. Verona says the paramedics checked him over. He's okay.'

He holds the car door open for me, and his hand goes beneath my elbow to help me out. I feel ungainly and huge. And annoyed. All this fuss, all this drama – the thought crosses my mind angrily that the paramedics should still have taken Ed to the hospital.

Inside the house, there's a radio playing in the back, and I move towards it, but he stops me, saying: 'He's upstairs – the back bedroom.' I hesitate, but he nods his head to reassure me, saying: 'It's okay, you can go on up.'

Foyle is barking out in the garden, and Michael tells me he'll follow me in a minute, after he's seen to the dog.

I climb the staircase, feeling the dragging weight of my bump. It seems lower than I remember, heavier. I'm listening out for voices, but I don't hear any, only the false jollity of voice-overs on the radio ads playing in the kit-chen. The carpet tread on the stairs is worn to the weave. It brings an unwelcome shiver of nostalgia – all those years ago climbing these stairs, the same framed mezzo-tints hanging on the walls, shadows of grime marking the wallpaper.

I reach the top of the stairs. The dog continues to bark outside. I cannot hear Verona, and it comes to me now as I cross the landing that her little car was not outside. Even before I push open the bedroom door, I know that Verona is not here. That there was no phone message, no ambu-lance, there was no accident at all.

I need to leave, but some strange force propels me through that door.

A baby mobile stirs in front of the window – stars and a moon – and there are more stars on the wall above the cot, decals that scatter in a broad arch that ends above the changing table. My hands tingle, and the sweat on my body cools, sending a shiver through me. Nappies are stacked neatly on a shelf beneath the changing table, an assortment of powders and creams inserted in the various slots and cubbyholes, stuffed toys lined up inside the cot, their black button eyes staring lifelessly at me. An arm-chair by the cot for nursing, and a pram, still folded and in its new plastic, sits just inside the door. I stare at all of this wordlessly, barely aware now of the fluid trickling out of me, or of the front door closing, the step upon the stairs. The alarm I'd felt has changed to something much colder as the realization comes to me that he has been planning this for some time.

'Remember what I told you?' he says, his voice in the

room behind me making me jump. 'All those years ago, in Barcelona? I told you that, whatever happens, I'd be there for you. You're not going to have to go through this alone.'

His voice is tender and the smile he offers is full of sympathy, of love. It sends a shudder through me of pure fear. I know it instinctively: he won't let me leave. I will not be able to escape.

PART THREE

20

Verona

Verona is in the bathroom, scouring the shower and sluicing the greyish suds down the drain, when she hears the crash. Reaching forward to turn off the tap, she feels an ache in her lower back and an unfamiliar feeling deep within her soul, a singular conviction: *I cannot do this any more.*

She gets to her feet and dries her hands slowly, before taking a deep calming breath and crossing the landing to Mrs Parke's bedroom. The tray is on the floor, toast lying face down alongside the plate it had been served on. Bits of scrambled egg are caught in the flokati rug, which now bears a spreading tea stain, the cup upturned beneath the bed. Mrs Parke, imperious beneath the blankets and supported by a panoply of pillows and cushions, folds her hands across her chest and tilts her chin up, triumphant.

'What happened here?' Verona asks, her voice calm and patient despite the weariness inside.

But Mrs Parke doesn't answer. In fact, since Verona began working here almost a month ago, the old woman has not spoken one word to her.

'Fine,' Verona says airily. 'If you don't want to eat, I'm not going to force you.'

She bends to pick up the tray but has to get down on

her hands and knees to load it up with the fallen crockery. Combing the long strands of the rug with her fingers, she scrapes up the bits of egg and drops them on to the plate. She's reaching forward to grasp the stray cup when the old woman leans down and pinches Verona hard on the nose. It happens so suddenly, and is such an odd form of aggression, she can hardly comprehend it. Sitting back on her heels, one hand rising instinctively to cover the injured part of her face, her mouth falls open with shock. Mrs Parke looks a little shocked herself, her eyes wide and enlivened, the corners of her puckered mouth quivering. It takes every ounce of Verona's self-control just to pull her gaze away and focus on the tray, the task. She does this without a word and carries the discarded breakfast from the room.

Back downstairs in the kitchen, she leans against the worktop and starts to cry. Hot tears of anger and hurt fall on to the worktop in large salty drops. Catching sight of her reflection in the kitchen window, she gives herself a shake.

'Pull yourself together,' she admonishes aloud, swiping at her wet cheeks with her fingers and elongating her neck. Verona imagines those words spoken in Min's wry scratchy voice and thinks again of how much she misses her.

It has taken Verona unawares, this grief. All the time she was working there, she'd told herself that Min was just a patient – a client. But the truth was their friendship had sneaked up on her. It had taken root without her ever noticing. 'Care for the patient, but stay detached,' was the mantra she thought she was adhering to. But Min had gotten under her skin with her dry pronouncements, her mischievous mind with its quicksilver thoughts, her gentle chiding, her humour. Nothing warm or cuddly about her, and yet when Verona had stood in the church and watched the coffin pass, she had wept just as she'd done at her own grandmother's funeral.

The next day, the agency fixed her up with a new job, and she'd found herself out here in this mock-Tudor mansion in Foxrock, Mrs Parke's querulous daughter outlining what she was to expect, while the old dowager lay upstairs in bed, silent and imperious. It had seemed like the smart thing to do – moving on with her life, burying herself in her work. But weeks have passed, and the weight in Verona's heart still hasn't lifted.

Before her shift ends, she makes sure that Mrs Parke is fed and clean and comfortable, the house tidy, then she packs up her bag and gets into the little mint-green Citroën and drives the shortish distance from Foxrock to Monkstown. The sky is completely dark at this hour, rain falling at a sharp angle. It feels strange but at the same time sort of comforting travelling this familiar route once more, and when she brings the car to a halt outside St Jude's her heart trips with giddy nerves.

His text message had come out of the blue that afternoon.

V, there are some things in the house belonging to Min that she wanted you to have. Could you swing by the house later today to pick them up?

Now, as she stares up at the house, she thinks of the last time they'd met. It had been after the funeral, outside in the churchyard. Throughout an awkward conversation, she'd been taken aback by his stiffness, his strangulated politeness. His lack of warmth towards her had compounded her grief, and Verona had slipped away as soon as she could.

But now she's back. The street is empty of kids, all fled indoors for the night. Her face feels the needle-sharp pricks of freezing droplets as she gets out of the car, pulls her hood up, and grips both lapels of her jacket tightly with one hand as she runs up the path towards the house. The first thing she notices is the sheet of plywood that covers the front window. Perhaps a pane of glass was broken, she thinks, before leaning on the doorbell. At once, there is a bark from deep inside the house, and then the slip and clatter of claws along the hall as Foyle dashes forward, the door shaking as he slams against it, yelping and growling. Verona pushes open the letter-box and calls to him: 'It's okay, Foyle. It's me.' Immediately, he grows calmer, his bark segueing into a low pitiful whine. She waits for Michael to appear as rainwater streams through a leak in the guttering, splattering off the concrete below, but, apart from the dog's claws scrabbling at the door, the hall beyond is silent.

Verona leans down, peers through the letter-box. She sees the plinths, the urns, the spider-plants – even the taxidermized geese remain – but there is no sign of Michael. The rain bears down on her back, her neck, and, disappointed, she releases the flap of the letter-box, straightens up and is turning away when she hears it: a high-pitched scream.

Immediately, she turns back, looks through the letter-box once more.

'Hello?' she calls. 'Is anyone there?'

But the dog is barking madly, unsettled by the cry – it drowns out her voice. She tries to see past him, angling herself to catch a glimpse of the stairs. Another cry rents the air, and this time Verona doesn't hesitate. She fishes in her bag for the keys to the house that she still has with her. Once inside, she drops her bag on the floor, pushes aside the dog and takes the stairs quickly. There's no time to deduce anything beyond the fact that there's a human being in pain. The cries are coming from the bathroom, and Verona crosses the landing lit by a single bulb dangling naked on a flex, and flings wide the bathroom door.

The woman is leaning on the sink, her back to Verona. Her shoulders are high and tense, and Verona can see the woman's body is shaking. Turning her head towards the sound of the door opening, Verona recognizes her at once and sees terror flash in the whites of her eyes.

'Faye? What are you doing here? What's going on?' Her words come out in a rush.

Faye lets out another strangled cry, her head dipping forward, legs shaking, and Verona's eyes travel to the spreading stain in the woman's trousers, liquid dripping on to her feet, which are bare against the linoleum floor.

'You've got to help me,' Faye says, and Verona instinctively goes to her, puts her arms around her, guides her to the edge of the bath, helps her lower her weight against the lip of it, her bump heavy and protruding, resting in the gap between her spread knees.

'All right, try to breathe,' Verona instructs, as much to herself as to Faye, whose reddish-brown hair is darkened with sweat and plastered to her pale forehead.

'You've got to get me out of here,' Faye gasps.

Verona shoots a glance at Michael, who's in the doorway now. His eyes are saucers, pupils like pinpricks, a dazed look about him that infuriates her.

Faye's body buckles as a new wave of pain goes through her, and Verona barks at Michael: 'Don't just stand there! Get an ambulance!'

He shakes his head slowly, mumbles: 'No. I can't.'

'What do you mean —'

'She has to stay here.'

'This woman is about to give birth! She needs medical attention!'

A deep moan comes from Faye's chest, her body tensing again as she leans into the pain, and Verona catches her by the shoulders, bracing her weight against her while the wave rolls through. 'That's it. Try to breathe,' she encourages, glancing over her shoulder at Michael.

'You'll see to her. You can take care of her,' he says, both hands in his hair, fingers raking over his scalp, a wild look in his eyes.

It's only now that Verona sees the stack of clean towels on the floor, the bottle of Savlon disinfectant, the scissors glinting under the bright bulb, awaiting the cord it will cut. A shiver of horror goes through her.

'For God's sake,' she utters. 'You can't be serious?'

Faye clutches for Verona's wrist, as the pain rises once more. And Michael backs away out of the room, pulling the door quickly shut behind him, and Verona feels the other woman's nails sink into her flesh as her cry becomes low and guttural. The lock on the door clicks. They are trapped.

21

Michael

He stands back from the door, frightened, exhilarated, nerves spritzing through the length of his body – he feels them tingling in his hands. The shouting, the pleading, Verona's voice gaining a shrillness he has not known in her before – it carries across the landing to where he stands, quivering with adrenalin. She pounds so hard the door bounces in the frame and he wonders if the locks will hold. And then a cry goes up in the background, a noise distinguished from all the others in that it holds a note of pure pain. The note goes through him, sets his nerves ringing, and he staggers away, down the stairs, almost losing his footing as he goes.

He needs to calm down, modulate his galloping heartbeat, get his thoughts in order. The police will be looking for him now, so he needs to be careful, to take steps that cover his tracks.

The van. It's still sitting outside in the driveway, and, as he opens the front door, he sees the mint-green Citroën parked across the entrance, blocking his exit.

Verona. He feels nudged by guilt at the manner in which he'd lured her here. But he'd needed her nursing skills, her womanly empathy. But now, looking at Verona's car blocking the driveway, and hearing her voice screaming at him from upstairs – 'For Christ's sake, Michael! Let us the fuck out!' – he begins to feel the burden of her presence, an unwelcome complication.

Her bag is on the floor in the hall where she'd dropped it and he picks it up and rummages through until he finds the car keys. Then, letting himself out into the night, he closes the door behind him, making sure he locks it first, then hurries down the driveway and gets into the car. It splutters to life, jolting forward awkwardly when his foot touches the pedal, and, jerkily, he manoeuvres it out on to the road before swinging sharply around to the little laneway that skirts the back of the house. It's a moonless night, the wind sharp and cutting, and, when he parks up against the wall and kills the lights, the depth of shadow from the wild overhang of ivy, the towering Sitka spruces behind the garden wall, makes the space surrounding the little car seem utterly black.

Next, he moves the van, watchful for any potential witnesses, but the street is empty tonight, the weather keeping people indoors. Once it's tucked neatly into the space behind the Citroën, he goes into the garden and pulls out the tarpaulin he's set aside for this purpose. The tarp is heavy, and, as he drags it through the overgrown garden, feeling the muscles in his back and shoulders ache, a memory is triggered of earlier that afternoon: hauling another weight through the undergrowth, struggling with it, his heart thundering, fear clotting in his throat. He thinks of the spot he had chosen deep in the forest – it had felt remote, far from anything, but he'd had to act quickly and, who knows, perhaps just beyond the trees lay a house he hadn't spotted. Maybe a dog, the owners letting it outside after dinner, the animal instantly picking up the scent and going straight to the spot. Perhaps, even now, the police were crawling all over that side of the mountain, cordoning off the woods, checking for CCTV, interviewing potential witnesses in the area, picking over the body with gloved hands, gathering evidence.

Michael pushes the thought away, gets the tarp out into the lane. It's not big enough to cover both vehicles, so he chooses the Citroën – the shade of it is too distinctive, he can't risk its being seen. Once it's covered, he goes back to the garden and looks around for something to hide the van. Earlier in the year, he'd made an effort to clear the wilderness out here. Back in the summer, when he'd still harboured a belief that he could bring Faye to reason, that there would be no need for force, he'd recalled a summer month in his youth, the two of them out here in the garden, sunbathing. A yellow bikini Faye had worn, red-framed sunglasses that she thought were funny. It seemed like a lifetime ago, and yet part of him has always believed he could recapture it, that one day she would return. He thinks of the woman upstairs in the bathroom stricken with labour pains. There's but a trace of the girl he remembers, a girl in a yellow bikini. Her cheekbones are visible now – two blades that cast a shadow – but he still remembers the warm curves of her face, soft and downy, dimpling when she smiled. Warm eyes and the heaviness of her hair – lying in bed at night, he can still feel the weight of it slung over his arm, can still catch the intimate smell of her flesh.

'Forget that girl, Michael,' Min had told him, again and again, her voice dropping almost to a whisper, a warning there in her eyes. And he'd sworn to do just that. But she's in his blood, so how, truly, could he ever let her go?

Instead, he'd laboured towards an imagined future, clearing away the overgrown shrubs, cutting back overhanging branches, pulling out weeds that were as large and settled as mature shrubs. The mound he'd piled high remains, and, as he picks branches from it and drags them out to the car, he smells the rot, the stench of organic matter stirring up nausea in his stomach.

Once the branches are in place, he tugs the ivy down further to cover the vehicle. The reg plates are already purposefully muddied, and he turns on the torch of his mobile phone and checks to make sure that the figures remain obscured. As the light passes over the van's fender, his eye is caught by a smear of blood. It catches the breath in his throat, brings him back to the instant when Ed turned and saw him – a clear widening of his eyes that was not just fear but recognition, and disbelief at the betrayal. The expression on his face has become imprinted on Michael's brain – he carries it in his body along with the crash, the thud made by the impact of the body against the van, the crunch of the bicycle beneath his wheels.

Walking back towards the house, he thinks of all the hours he'd put into their friendship, all the progress made – the slow investment of time and patience. The hardest part was first making the connection, and it wasn't that hard, in the end. It helped that the man was lonely, desperate for company – it almost made Michael pity him, how quickly he latched on to the friendship, how eager he was to talk. Michael is a good listener. Silently he received all the details that Ed revealed and packed them away into his memory, storing them up for a time he might need them. With the slow creep of friendship, he inched closer to the prize. It was steady, painstaking work which required vigilance and care. Foundational work – that's how he had come to think of it. And yet there were moments when he found himself forgetting his purpose, and relaxing into the conversation. In those moments, all thoughts of Faye disappeared, and Michael could almost believe that this friendship with Ed was genuine and real. And so there are feelings of guilt when he remembers his purpose earlier that day, how he had gone out in his little van, hunting, in the same way he had gone out every day for the past week, knowing that Faye's due date was approaching, and that time was running out. A lucky break, that's what he needed – to be there at the moment Ed left the house for his cycle – but, as the year ticked to its end and there was no sign of Ed, despair began to creep in, the sense that all of Michael's careful plans had been for nothing. He'd almost given up hope entirely when the Lycra-clad figure emerged from the estate, pedalling out on to the main road, and the sight of him had set Michael's nerves twanging. He'd pressed softly on the accelerator, the little van creeping along the roads as they left the city behind, following the bike up into the Wicklow hills.

A shadow of guilt remains over what he has done. Still. It had to happen. He remembers his *Macbeth*: *If it were done when 'tis done, then 'twere well it were done quickly.*

Satisfied that the vehicles are hidden, he wipes his hands on his trousers, turns and goes back into the house.

*

Silence greets him. There is only the slow tick of the clock in the hall, and the steady panting of breath from the dog, which sits staring up at him as if awaiting instruction. With a jolt of fright, he thinks: they've gone. Escaped into the night. But how could they? The bathroom door is locked and bolted from the outside. He had nailed all the windows down days ago. And, even were they to break the glass, the drop is too great a risk for Verona; impossible for Faye. He rushes up the stairs, puts his ear to the bathroom door and straight away fists pound from the other side, making his head ring.

'You have to let us out!' Verona shrieks, and he feels the flies crawling all over him, in his hair, beneath his clothes, thousands of them, the pads of their sticky feet trailing a silvery residue until his skin grows itchy with it.

'Michael! This is crazy! You must get an ambulance – quickly!'

He puts his hands over his ears, but still her voice penetrates. So he turns away and hurries downstairs, where he paces the hall, Foyle keeping step with him, the dog whinnying and complaining, confused by all this activity, the coming and going, the voices upstairs. When the air is rent by a scream, Foyle starts barking madly, his tail straight, the hair along the back of his neck bristling.

'Quiet, quiet!' Michael urges, but the scream has frightened him too.

He goes to the kitchen, trying to escape the women's voices, the thoughts that crowd his brain. A sudden thundering above him, the pipes clamouring, and he listens for a moment as the bath upstairs starts to fill.

'I have no choice,' he reminds himself. 'It has to

happen this way. There's no other option.' He slops whiskey into a glass and brings it to his mouth with a shaking hand.

You know you really shouldn't mix alcohol with your medication, Michael.

He hears his mother's voice in his head, surprised by her intrusion into his thoughts at this hour.

How long had it been since she'd said those words to him, he wonders? Six weeks? Two months? It was after the funeral, when he'd gone back to the house, the rooms filled with other mourners, but he'd found a quiet spot in the garden, his breath clouding out in front of him. He'd sat down on a wooden bench, the whiskey bottle at his feet, and felt the cold surround him, the sharp snap of winter in the air, his stepfather's meticulously tended lawns and flowerbeds all coated with frost. His mother, he knew, had come looking for him, as he'd known she would. They would have this conversation and then he could leave.

'How have you been, love?' she'd asked, tenderness mingling with the strain.

'All right.'

'You don't look all right. You look tired . . . distracted.'

'Given the circumstances.'

'You can't even look me in the eye.' A small mirthless laugh that betrayed her nerves. It was dangerous territory for both of them.

'I haven't heard from you in such a long time,' she continued carefully. 'You never call –'

'Are you surprised?' He turned on her. 'You had me sectioned!'

A bit of steel in her response: 'What was I supposed to do? You were violent towards Jeff. I was frightened.'

'It was an accident.'

She let that sit there for just a moment, and then said in a heavy voice, 'Oh, Michael, love. No, it wasn't.'

He stirred uncomfortably. The flies buzzed on his skin.

Tentatively, she asked: 'Have you seen Dr Chawke?'

'Nope.' He took a slug of whiskey, felt her bristling.

'You know you really shouldn't mix alcohol with your medication, Michael.'

'It's really not your concern any more.' He didn't tell her that he'd stopped taking the medication months ago.

'You will always be my concern,' she'd countered with sudden feeling, and to his horror she'd reached out a hand to his hair.

He can still remember it: the revulsion at the thought of her touching him; the way his eyes had flashed a warning and the little hand was hastily retracted.

It seems to go on for hours – the swish and slop of bathwater, the rising moans, the sudden shrieks that set every nerve in his body quivering. At one point, he hears the bathwater draining and rushes out into the hall, expectant of news. But then comes the drum of fresh water hitting enamel, and, as the bath refills, moans of pain filter through the air, and suddenly there is a shrill ringing that makes him jump.

Verona's bag, dumped on the bottom step, emits a jangly ringtone, and, instinctively, Michael moves to silence it. Fumbling in the bag, he finds the phone, struggling for a moment to turn the thing off. In the silence that follows, he feels his own quickened heartbeat, and then hears Verona's voice once more, subdued now, the urgency gone from it, replaced by a new seriousness.

'Michael?' she implores. 'I know you're there. I know you can hear me.'

He holds himself very still, listening to every word.

'This is very dangerous, what you're asking me to do. I'm not trained for this. You must know that there are huge risks.'

A cry comes up from the space behind her, followed by a low moan. He can tell that Faye is frightened, exhausted.

'Listen to me,' Verona tells him. 'I know you're upset. I know you're confused, but there's still time for you to do the right thing. Call an ambulance. Let us out. If you do that now, we can put all of this behind us. You panicked, you didn't know what you were doing – people will understand. But if anything happens to this child . . .' Her voice drops to an urgent whisper. 'Then you'll be in serious trouble. You do realize that, don't you, Michael?'

The phone is in his trembling hand. How easy it would be to simply climb the stairs, unlock the door and hand it to her.

There's a sick feeling in his stomach, a harsh acidic taste filling his mouth. If he lets Faye go, he knows that it will be over. Despite Verona's reassurance, he knows that if he makes that phone call, the police will come and he will be sent back to the hospital, returned to Dr Chawke's care, perhaps indefinitely. He will never see Faye again. He will never get to hold the baby, never get the chance to right the wrongs.

And, yet, that child's life ... To have it on his conscience.

The phone erupts once more, jangling and pulsing in his hand. Without thinking he drops it on the ground, raises his foot and sends his heel jamming straight through the screen. The iPhone shatters, the ringtone distorts, then dies. He lifts his foot and stares at the pieces of glass and plastic, the metal frame.

No going back, he tells himself, then steps away.

22

Verona

Verona sits back on her heels, her back and shoulders aching, and utters a silent prayer. *Thank God, thank God . . .*

Slick with blood and water and the last remnants of amniotic fluid, the baby's skin is darkly purple against the swollen pallor of her mother's flesh, but she has been safely delivered into the world, and for a brief few moments it is all that matters.

Faye cups her child's head, and cranes her neck to get a better view of the little girl's face, which is scrunched and creased as she wails, her tiny head covered with flattened curls.

'Is she okay?' she asks.

'She's perfect,' Verona replies.

There is wonder in the new mother's eyes as she runs her hand over the infant's head, then gently presses the pad of her thumb in the palm of her little hand. Tiny fingers flex like a flower opening, and Faye laughs. For just a moment, it all falls away – the horror of the last few hours, the fear that ricocheted around the tiled walls of this cramped space, their temporary prison.

'She's a beauty,' Verona remarks. 'Do you have a name?'

Faye shakes her head. 'We couldn't decide. Ed thought

it best to wait until she'd arrived before choosing. He wanted to get a look at her first before –' She breaks off, overcome by the well of emotion.

With trembling hands, Faye slides the baby closer so that she nestles into her neck. Faye's limbs are shivering uncontrollably despite the warm water, and, noticing this, her eyes flash with mild alarm.

'It's okay,' Verona calms her. 'It's just adrenalin. It will wear off.'

'Thank God you were here. I don't know what I would have done –'

'Hush. Let's not think about that. And besides,' Verona says, pulling herself up off her haunches, 'we're not quite done yet.'

She delivers the placenta quickly and easily, examines the liver-like organ to ascertain if it's still intact. The relief at the child's safe arrival is tempered by the return of self-doubt, the niggling fears that part of the placenta might still remain attached to the uterus, with its risk of internal haemorrhaging. Faye is nursing her baby now, her breasts veined and full. It is a shock for Verona to confront such ripeness in the human body. She is more accustomed to bathing the elderly and the sick. She is used to liver spots and papery skin, desiccated creases and folds, wasted muscles, collapsing skeletons. Not this flesh that is full and vital and burgeoning with life.

She drains the bath, then refills it with fresh warm water so mother and child can bathe, noticing with a nudge of worry the thin thread of blood that keeps running through the water. A tear in the birth canal, perhaps. She hopes it's not deep.

The baby is asleep now, her fists curled up like a boxer's shielding her face, and Faye is smiling down at her in amazement, when the lock turns and both women look up quickly in alarm. Immediately, the gentle intimacy within the room is broken. The stark reality of the situation intrudes upon them as Michael's pale face emerges from the shadows, and Verona feels a rush of anger so violent that it sweeps away every other feeling: her relief, her anxiety, her wonder at the baby's birth. She clambers to her feet and crosses the room quickly, pushing Michael forcefully out into the hall.

'What are you playing at? Locking us in like that. Such madness! What if something had happened? What if that baby had died?'

'It's all right, though, isn't it? I mean, it's safe. The baby. It's healthy?'

'No thanks to you.'

She smells alcohol on his breath, sees the sway in his body, eyelids heavy.

'Boy or girl?' he asks.

She wants to keep the knowledge from him, a punishment of sorts. But another part of her knows that she needs to go carefully with him. That their release will not come about through losing her temper, upbraiding him over his outrageous behaviour, pouring scorn on his concern.

'Girl,' she says. Then, dropping her voice, she tells him: 'There's some bleeding. I'm worried. We need to get her to a doctor.'

'How bad is it? Can't you –'

'No, I can't,' she snaps, then forces herself to stay calm.

'I've done as much as I can for her. Please, Michael. You must see the sense in this.'

From inside the bathroom, the child cries, and Verona turns her head to the sound. 'I need to take care of them,' she says. 'But Michael? You must do the right thing now. You must call an ambulance.' And she reaches out for his hand to drive home her message. It is so cold within her clasp. After the warmth of flesh and the vigour of new life that is happening just beyond them, the coolness of his flesh beneath her fingertips feels shocking and remote. Like touching something that is already dead.

After closing the bathroom door, Verona dries the baby and swaddles her in a clean soft towel. Then, with utmost care, she lies the little girl down on another towel on the floor, before helping Faye to rise on unsteady feet and clamber out of the bath. Verona pats down the damp flesh, noting the sagging belly, deflated after the birth; notes too the blood that stains the towel as she dries between her legs – red blood, still fresh and flowing. Verona frowns but says nothing as she wraps Faye in a bathrobe she recognizes as one of Min's. It barely fits, but Faye is too tired and distracted to notice. Her eyes never leave the baby.

'There,' Verona says when they're done. 'Let's get you settled while we wait.'

'Wait for what?'

'For the ambulance,' Verona says, forcing a brightness she does not feel.

Faye's eyes snap back towards her. 'Did he say? Will he let us go?' and Verona feels her confidence waver.

'He will realize soon enough that he has no choice. He can't hold us here forever,' she offers, trying to hide her own doubt, but Faye is not convinced.

'When I came into the bathroom, when I saw the towels on the chair, the scissors, the surgical gloves . . . all the careful preparations he'd made. And the room next door – all the baby equipment. Don't you see? This isn't some moment of madness. He's been planning this for months.'

Verona feels the truth in these words, but still it defies logic that he can keep them here. She picks the baby up carefully and returns her to her mother's arms.

'Eventually, someone will realize we are missing,' she reasons. 'And then the police will come. Once your husband discovers –'

'No! Something's happened to him. I don't know what.' Her voice rises in pitch, edging upwards with panic. 'He's been gone all day. And Michael . . . I think he might have hurt him.'

'Hush, Faye. I'm sure he's all right –'

'No, you don't understand. Michael wanted to hurt him.'

'Why would he want to hurt him? They're friends –'

'No, they're not! This was all just to get at me!'

Faye's voice has risen, become a little hysterical, and the child grumbles, her sleep disturbed. Verona puts an arm around the woman to steady her, but Faye continues on: 'He acts like this is all about love, but it's not. This isn't about love, it's about a reckoning. A debt that must be paid.'

'What kind of debt?'

'He thinks I stole from him.'

Verona's eyes narrow. 'What do you mean?'

Faye looks down at her child, the gentle creases of her eyelids, the delicate lashes. 'Not money – I don't mean anything like that. But a life. The life he should have had. A wife, children, a career . . . It might have been possible for him once.'

'But it's hardly your fault his life didn't turn out that way. Surely he can't blame you for his own choices, his own mistakes.'

'You don't understand,' Faye begins, her voice wavering.

There's a hesitancy about her, as if she is on the verge of blurting something out, as if she's barely keeping her emotions in check.

'What is it?' Verona asks. 'What happened between you?'

But then there's a creak of floorboards on the landing just beyond the door, and they realize he's out there listening. Faye's mouth closes; she holds the infant closer. 'Nothing,' she says. 'It was a long time ago.'

The bathroom door opens. Michael is standing out on the landing, open-mouthed and staring, his eyes feasting on the baby.

'She's here. At last. She's finally here,' he says, his face breaking into a smile full of wonder. 'After all this time. All these years, we've waited . . .'

Verona feels the effect of these words. The way Faye shrinks from him, shielding her child and stepping backward, as if seeking a return to the relative safety of the bathroom.

'You're drunk, Michael,' Verona says, her voice low and very cold.

But still he comes. 'If I could just hold her . . .' He puts his hands out, and Faye recoils with a snarl: 'Get away from us! Don't you touch her!'

Michael blinks with confusion, his face showing immediate hurt, but he backs away and allows the women to pass.

In the bedroom, Verona sees he has made up the bed with clean sheets. A bassinet has been set out on the floor, nappies and baby clothes stacked in neat order upon the bureau. She pulls back the covers and settles Faye against the pillows, the baby still wrapped in her towel and held against her mother's warm body. Michael hovers in the doorway, a jittery nervous presence, and Verona goes to him once more, whispering: 'Have you done it yet? Have you called an ambulance?'

'Not yet.'

'Why on earth not?' she hisses. 'What are you waiting for?'

'I need to think,' he stammers, rubbing his forehead. 'I need to work out what's best.'

'Listen to me now,' she says with urgency. 'There's a wound – a tear. It's bleeding. Unless she gets medical attention, it could become infected.'

'She'll be fine. You can help her, can't you?'

'No, I can't! She needs to see a doctor – she should be in hospital, not –'

'No hospitals, no doctors.'

'And what if it becomes septic? Do you understand what that means? Do you understand the seriousness of sepsis? She could die –'

He splutters with sudden laughter. 'Women don't die from childbirth any more.'

'That's because there are hospitals! Maternity wards,

trained staff, antibiotics! I'm not even a fully trained nurse, for God's sake!' Fury rumbles inside her. 'She could get seriously ill, and then what?'

'That won't happen. She'll be fine. The baby is here. They're both safe. They're both fine. The worst is over.'

'You can't know that – none of us can!'

'Just . . . okay, just hang on . . . I need to think.'

'Listen to me now, Michael. Have you thought this thing through? Don't you realize how much trouble you'll be in if anything happens to either of them?' She tempers her expression, her voice. 'If you do the right thing now, it will go easier for you. It's not too late to make amends. Please. Call an ambulance. You know that you must.'

He seems to consider her words, but gives no gesture of assent. Downstairs, the dog is barking at the back door to be let out. The noise reaches them, and Michael frowns.

'Just give me a minute,' he tells her, backing away towards the stairs.

She turns back into the bedroom. The baby is making snuffling noises, fuzzy little complaints, but Faye is staring at Verona, her eyes wide with a question.

'Where is he?' she asks.

'Downstairs. He's letting the dog out.'

Faye's glance moves to the door, the breath catches in her throat. 'He's left it open.'

The women look at each other, both of them realizing the opportunity.

'Go,' Faye whispers, 'quickly, before he comes back.'

'I can't leave you –'

'You must!' Faye hisses, taken by a new urgency. 'The stairs . . . I'd be too slow. You must go and get help!'

Torn between not wanting to abandon mother and child, and the burning conviction that this may be her only chance, Verona turns back to the landing, tiptoeing across to the bathroom, where she has left her shoes. After a brief survey of the chaos there – the discarded bundle of clothes, the soaked towels, the blood-drenched cloth containing the placenta – she grabs her shoes, but doesn't put them on yet for fear of the clatter they will make, instead hurrying barefoot downstairs.

Sounds of industry come from the kitchen – the clatter of crockery on a tray, the hum of the kettle beginning to boil. As she reaches the bottom step, the child upstairs lets out a shrill wail, and Verona freezes, terrified that she will be caught, now when she's so close. She waits for a few seconds, and when he doesn't come she steps down into the hallway and instantly something sharp slices through the sole of her foot. A small shard of broken glass, and she sees now that her phone has been shattered, deliberately so. But there's no time to dwell on it. She reaches for the door, turns the latch, but it doesn't give. In frustration, she runs her fingers over the Chubb and mortis locks, then remembers her bag. She turns around long enough to scoop it up, frantically conducts a search of its contents until she finds her keys. With trembling hands she unlocks the mortis, then slots the key in the Chubb . . .

She doesn't hear him come up behind her. All she hears is the liquid smack, a wild ringing in her ears, and the groaning rush of her own breath leaving her body as she slides down on to the ground.

*

She doesn't know how he gets her upstairs, drags her probably, like a sack of potatoes. But when her eyes open eventually, she finds herself on the floor, the side of her face matted with blood and pressed against the carpet. It's an effort to lift her head, and, when she does, she sees his trainers, his legs in jeans, and, briefly, as he leans down to her, a flash of his pale eyes when he twists down to stare at her.

'Don't even think about doing something that stupid again,' he snarls.

Then he dumps the tray on the floor beside her and retreats. She stares at its contents: a pot of tea with two mugs, a jug of milk, buttered toast. And, to one side, a box of Solpadeine and some steri-strips. She starts to laugh at the sheer absurdity of it, but the laughter wavers, then dies, overtaken by a wash of cold fear. She cranes her head and looks up at the bed, sees Faye's ash-pale face looking back at her, taking in her expression as they listen to the lock clicking on the door, and then the padlock; then there's silence.

23

Faye

Night falls. At least I think it does. It's hard to judge, given the lack of daylight in the room – a plywood sheet has been screwed over the window. Our prison is dark, lit only by a single bulb swinging from a flex overhead and a small desk lamp on the bureau. Michael's old bedroom – the same bed I had slept in as a student. I think of all the hours, the days and nights, I'd spent here as a teenager – it feels like a different life, as if it had happened to somebody else. The same bureau, the same creaking old wardrobe, the same threadbare Turkish carpet. Verona is curled up on this rug, a blanket drawn over her. She groans in her sleep, and I think of the injury she's received – a bump on her head the size of a marble: I'd run my fingers over it, trying to assess the damage done to her.

'Look at us,' she'd joked, a moment of black humour while I squinted at her scalp under the thin light. 'I don't know which one of us is in worse shape.'

'The bleeding has stopped,' I'd told her. 'Just swelling and bruising now. You'll need an ice pack on it. I'll ask Michael.'

She'd snorted at that. 'Like he cares. Like he gives a fuck,' her voice made harsh with a simmering fury. She'd looked at me – a hard stare – and asked: 'Why is he doing this?'

I'd shaken my head, then encouraged her to lie down on the bed, thinking she needed to rest, but she'd refused.

'It's better if I try and stay awake,' she'd argued. 'And besides, you need the bed more than I do.'

It's Michael's old bed – the site where many years ago I'd lost my virginity. But that thought brings with it a wave of revulsion. Whatever tender feelings I'd had for him once, I can find no trace of them now. My heart has grown cold. Instead, I try to push all thoughts of the past from my mind, concentrating instead on calculating how long I have been missing. Surely someone will have noticed by now? I think of Regina, her daily phone calls to me or Ed, trying to hide her anxiety as my due date approached. She will have tried both of us in the past twenty-four hours. Surely she will sound the alarm? But perhaps she will conclude that we're not answering our phones because we're at the hospital. Another twenty-four hours may pass before her suspicions become aroused.

The baby stirs in her bassinet, snuffling noises a prelude to her cries. I pick her up and go through the motions, still unfamiliar to me, of changing her nappy, encouraging her to feed. She is fussy and clumsy, her little body full of jerky movements, her head lashing blindly from side to side while I patiently try to get her to latch on. A floorboard on the landing alerts me to Michael's presence just beyond the door, and I shrink back against the pillows, pulling the baby in close to me. Does she sense the quickening of my heartbeat? Can she taste the fear on my skin? Her crying starts up again, and I try to shush her, Verona turning over on the rug.

After a moment, I hear a door close downstairs and the

tension in me unwinds a little. There's a pain deep inside me like a twisted knot being tugged at. I can feel bleeding still, a tightening around the wound, and, when I bend to settle the baby in her basket, I feel a whoosh across my brain and put a hand to the floor to steady myself.

The baby won't settle. Barely a minute after lying back on the pillows, I hear her cries starting again. I shush her, and then pick her up, pacing the room with her on my shoulder before trying to set her back on her mattress once more. This goes on for some time – I don't know for how long – but the hours of the night stretch like elastic, and I am so tired, my body aches. I hold her against my chest and sit on the edge of the bed, just for a moment. Just for a moment, I allow myself to close my eyes, let the darkness come . . .

'It's all right!' Verona says. 'You're okay!'

Distress in her voice and it is only then that I realize I was screaming. Sweat on my back and legs, the sheets bunched around me, my hands like claws gripping my child.

'I fell asleep,' I gasp, 'oh my God, oh my God . . .'

'It's okay –'

'The baby – if I'd hurt her –'

'Here, let me take her.'

I let her lift the child out of the stiff cage of my arms, feel my heart pound so hard it's like it's coming up my throat.

'I fell asleep . . .' I say again, my voice hushed but still aghast.

'It's all right,' she murmurs, her hand on my back, rubbing with reassurance. 'Close your eyes. Rest. I'll mind her while you sleep.'

I lean back against the pillows, watch as she gets up from the bed and begins to pace around the room, crooning softly to my child. I catch her glancing at me, though – the occasional side-eye – and I feel the question in her gaze. The flicker of suspicion.

Could she guess at what happened to me? Could anyone have guessed? Sometimes, it feels so unreal that I can almost make myself believe that it never happened. Or that it happened to somebody else but not me.

And yet some things are so vivid. Like the smell in the air that night when he left me sitting alone in our room in that house in the hills, and went off into the mountains to find a pool of moonlit water to bathe in.

April 2010

'You're sure you won't come?' Michael asked, but I shook my head, my mind made up. Outside waiting for us were Mateo, Sheena, Adriana and the others – but I just wanted to be alone.

'Really, I'll be fine,' I asserted, 'you go. Take pictures, and show them to me later.'

He was plainly disappointed, and reluctant to leave me, but I felt oppressed by his anxious hovering. All that week, I had felt it – a need within him that I could not fulfil. The air between us had become negatively charged – we were like two magnets that found themselves repelling each other. It would be good for him to get out into the hills, have his moonlit adventure, and I needed to be alone – to bathe and then to sleep – and then maybe, just maybe, things might seem clearer, and the tension and tetchiness that had tainted the previous couple of days might dissipate.

I listened to them leave, the crunch of boots over grit and stones, the lilt of their voices disappearing into the night, and then I got up, left our room and went to stand outside. The moon hung large and bright – a milky yellow – above the mountains; the sky around it seemed purple, the stars obscured by the brightness of the moon's light. A chill was in the air, but there was no breeze at all. Just stillness and silence. I breathed it in and felt myself grow calm.

For three weeks – ever since I had stared at that faint but positive line – I had been carrying around within me a nervy sense of dread. I had thought that once I'd shared the news with Michael that the feeling would lessen, even disperse entirely, but instead it lingered. Worse, it was compounded by a profound sense of disappointment in him. In us. The haze of love that we had existed in for almost three years had nurtured the belief in me that we could weather any storm once we were together. Now the haze had lifted and, with bitter clarity, I saw the truth: that we were two kids steeped in a hormone stew of first love. We were not just unprepared for this pregnancy; we were painfully ill equipped to deal with making the decision. We had prided ourselves on our relationship, thought our love was so strong and pure and unique. But I had realized what he did not yet see: that it was not tenacious. It could not withstand this pressure. And I saw something else: that, of the two of us, I was the stronger one. I had been foolish to think that I could lean on Michael, that I could rely on him to carry me through this. When I thought of the argument he'd used – that if Amaya and Efrain could bring up a child, then we could – I felt punched all over again with a furious incomprehension. What I had always thought of as his sunny optimism seemed like naivety. I understood now with painful certainty that I would have to get through this on my own.

There was an ache in the small of my back from the hours I'd spent sitting cross-legged on my sleeping mat while poring over my notes. The mat itself was very thin, and I awoke each morning feeling the whole frame of my body tired and sore from another poor night's sleep. I needed to make the most of this opportunity while I had the house to myself, so I went back inside, grabbed my towel and went to the bathroom for a shower. The water pressure was not much more than a weak stream, but the water was hot, and I was able to relax for once without someone knocking at the door, asking when I'd be finished. I washed my hair and soaped my skin. Already, the waistband on my jeans had become too tight – I was having to leave the top button open. But the sensitivity I'd felt recently in my breasts had eased. They also seemed less full and rounded. And, after I got out of the shower and towelled myself dry, I noticed a small show of blood. Not much, but it worried me a little. I'd had a bit of spotting a couple of weeks before which I'd put down to old blood being expelled from my body, but this was more than a spot, and the blood was red and vivid.

I cleaned and dressed myself, then combed my hair. The shower had drained the last bit of energy from my body. I needed to sleep. But no sooner had my head hit the mat than I heard it: the thin wail of the baby's cry. Carried on the air from where he lay in his room around the corner of the house, it found its way into my room, disturbing the brief peace that was there.

I turned over, tried to block it out. My mind moved busily over the twin anxieties I was nursing, but I forced myself to push away any thoughts about the pregnancy, and instead mulled over the problem of my studies, my exams. I recalled, once more, the email I had received from my lecturer that week. Earlier in the spring, I had applied for a place on the Master's programme he was running. I had received a tentative offer that was conditional upon my Final grades. In Barcelona, when we realized the situation, I had emailed him to relay my concerns. I was, I suppose, appealing for leniency. The reply from him was polite but terse: he sympathized with my predicament and conceded that it was unfortunate I'd gotten caught up in this, but it did make him question my commitment to my studies, taking off like that so close to my final exams. Reading his words, I was flushed with shame, and some of that feeling returned to me now.

From down the hall, the baby kept crying. It was growing louder, a note of fury entering his screams. I wondered irritably why no one was picking him up. I lay there for a while longer, trying to untangle the knot of my thoughts, but it was impossible.

Tired and cross, I hauled myself up and pulled the door open. The volume of his cries grew as I rounded the corner and entered the room. I didn't knock. Convinced I would find Amaya passed out on the bed and heedless of her infant's screams, I burst into that room ready to upbraid her about her carelessness with her children, her lack of consideration for the rest of us. But Amaya was not there.

It took a moment for me to register the full facts. I gazed through the gloom and saw the room in disarray, toys scattered on the floor, a mess of dirty dishes on the table, half-eaten food, a yellow glass ringed with milk. Clothes spilled from a black plastic bag like they had seeped through a split seam. And, at the centre of it all, in a mound of bedclothes on the small double bed, lay the two children: Amalia was turned on her side and had half burrowed into the blankets, her back to the baby boy, whose face was quite purple with rage, his fists bunched as he screamed himself hoarse.

I moved forward and scooped him up. He seemed to gulp with surprise, a brief pause in his rage, and when it started up again it had lost some of its power. I held him against my chest and rocked him quickly, nervously, whispering: 'Shh, it's okay. Shh now.' Amalia pushed herself up on to her elbows. She turned her head towards me, and I could see that she was no longer wearing her little blue glasses, and that the plaster patch that covered her left eye had been removed. She squinted up at me briefly, then slumped back down into the pillows, her black curls falling over her face, only one little ear visible as she sank into sleep.

I couldn't believe it. That Amaya's lax attitude towards her children would extend this far. That she had left them all alone without so much as a word to me to keep a watchful eye on them – it was either entirely presumptuous or a shocking dereliction of parental duty. The hot fury I had felt towards her on entering the room now cooled. It had changed, become something else – a deep and profound worry for these children, like a sharply indrawn breath.

The baby was hot against my chest. I couldn't tell if this was heat from his fury or whether his body still held the warmth of the bed. Perhaps he had some kind of fever? I wondered if I should make up a bottle to feed him, but then recalled I had never once seen him consume anything other than milk from his mother's breast. His nappy felt heavy, and I looked around for something to change him into – Amaya and Efrain were hippyish but made concessions for disposable nappies and wipes. I lay him down on the bed, his cries resuming their incensed note, and changed him quickly, glancing briefly at Amalia, who moaned but kept her eyes closed, too exhausted to observe. I dumped the soiled nappy in the bin, then picked him up once more. He was still crying, although his screams lacked the enraged quality of before. He was tiring of it. Looking around for something to pacify him, I grabbed a small toy – a blue cloth frog with long legs and beads sewn for the eyes – then carried him out of the room, shutting the door behind me.

I paced the corridor, the baby against my chest, softly cooing to him. The movement seemed to calm him. Whenever I stopped, his wails started up again. I don't know how long I walked that long hall, back and forth, back and forth. An hour, maybe. Or perhaps it was not that long, but it only felt long because I was so exhausted. I felt shaky with fatigue. When I thought he had fallen asleep in my arms, I returned to their bedroom and lay him back down on the bed, but no sooner had his little body touched the mattress than his eyes flew open and his lungs once again filled with rage. And so I picked him up again. This happened a few times. My nerves shredded, I was so tired now that I could hardly think straight.

A wave of anger came over me as I paced with him, and I shook him a little, snarling: 'Be quiet, would you!' Immediately, I felt ashamed of myself. He was a tiny baby whose mother had left him. He was defenceless – an innocent.

I took him then into my own room. His cries had weakened, flattened out with exhaustion, and I could tell he was very close to sleep. Keeping him in my arms, I lay down on the sleeping mat and pulled the blanket up over the two of us. As his crying ebbed and then ceased, his normal colour returned, and I looked at him. The light in the room was turned off, but it wasn't completely dark. Moonlight crept through the uncovered window, and under its pale bluish light I examined him. Eyelashes glued into spikes with tears, a small thin-lipped mouth, full cheeks so rounded and soft – I pressed my lips to them, inhaled his particular baby smell. All week, I had watched him being passed from person to person, while I myself had held back. I didn't want a baby in my arms – anyone's baby. I didn't like the thoughts that crossed my mind whenever I glanced at him, the cloud of guilt and doubt that settled over them. So I had avoided him, locked myself away in my room.

But now, in the privacy of darkness, I felt his warmth, the particular shape of him as he relaxed against me into sleep, and I felt relief and peace, a quietening of all the doubts inside me. It wasn't a question of changing my mind – it was more like letting go of the burden, just for a little while. I closed my eyes, felt the peace wash over me.

If you knew that once you closed your eyes you would slip into a nightmare – the worst nightmare you could imagine, one that would stay with you, haunt you for the rest of your life – would you keep your eyes open? Force yourself to stay awake? Sleep is so persuasive, it draws you in, seduces like a drug; you surrender to it helplessly without even realizing you are doing so. I did not know I had fallen asleep until the moment that I woke. Everything felt wrong – the bluish light in the room, the discomfort, the bulge in the sleeping mat beneath me. Then realization, understanding like an uprush of cold air – I sprang back and saw him lying there, his little body unmoving. I knew it straight away, felt it in the creep of nerves across the back of my neck. I put my hand to him, and he was warm but the warmth came not from within but from my own crushing body heat. I picked him up quickly, snatched him from the mat, my heart quivering with alarm at the way his body flopped heavily against me. I rocked and jiggled him, trying to wake him. 'Wake up, come on, wake up!' I urged, as if my words alone could call him back to life.

I put him down on the mat and rested my head against his chest, listening for a heartbeat that wasn't there. No breath entering his lungs. I tried to breathe it into him, the salt-and-milk taste of him as I blew air into his little mouth that was open like a fish's. Nothing happened. Nothing worked, but I kept trying for a few minutes before sitting back on my heels, staring at him, aghast.

I couldn't believe it. Even though I had gone through the motions, trying to resuscitate him, trying to reverse the deadly harm I had done, my brain could not keep pace with it. It was like I was watching all this from a remove. Floating up somewhere at the ceiling, observing the scene unfolding below, coldly from a height.

Did I hear a sound in the hall? I think I did. But I didn't panic. Shock had taken over, so that when the bedroom door opened, and Michael stood there, staring with unfolding horror at what lay on the mat beside me, I was barely able to speak. The voice that came from my mouth did not sound like my own. In that moment, I did not know myself. All I knew was that everything had changed. My life as I knew it was over. That the only way back, the only way out of this nightmare, was to hide what had happened. To pretend like it had never existed. I looked up at him in the doorway, fear fully occupying the void inside me.

'You have to help me, Michael,' I said.

24

Verona

The rain falls all night, lashing the side of the house, the wind whistling through the crack between the frame of the window and the plywood that's been screwed in place. Verona paces with the baby in her arms, glancing occasionally across at Faye, who sleeps fitfully in the bed.

Her head hurts. With her fingertips, she can feel the bump just behind her right ear. The bleeding has stopped but there's a zinging in her ears and in her brain that worries her. She blinks through the darkness, wondering if her vision is becoming cloudy, and relives the moment, again and again, when the blow came, the startling suddenness and pain.

Eventually, the quality of darkness changes – a grey granular light finds its way through the tiny space around the window and under the door. The rain dies away, and she can hear the distant sound of seagulls squawking on nearby roofs. The baby wakes with a hungry cry. Verona turns on the light and sits on the bed watching, while Faye struggles to get the baby to latch on. It takes a few minutes until the baby is suckling contentedly, and then Faye lies back, grey-faced with exhaustion.

'How do you feel?' Verona asks.

'Okay,' she replies, but there's a glazed look about her

eyes, and when Verona checks the woman's forehead with the back of her hand it feels hot and clammy.

After the baby has fed, Verona takes her and settles the child on her shoulder, patting her back gently. She watches Faye stir uncomfortably, lifting her hips, feeling beneath her, a frown of concern on her face.

'I've soaked through another towel,' she says. 'Is that normal?'

Verona nods, assuring her that it's perfectly normal, but, as she lays the baby down and changes her nappy, she feels the prickling of her anxiety. Faye needs medical attention, the baby too. The newborn's skin had been pink and healthy yesterday, but under the light cast from the bulb in the early morning there's a yellow tinge to it, and the scab around the belly-button has been bleeding again.

Footfall sounds on the stairs, and, when Michael opens the door to her, Verona is momentarily taken aback. His face has a wild look to it, the prickles of his beard sprouting thinly in patches. His eyes are reddened and watery; they shift around quickly in their sockets as if unable to settle. The shirt he's wearing is stained, and she can smell the musky odour of his body, like something raw and bestial.

They take it in turns to use the bathroom – first Verona, then Faye – Michael standing aside like a jailer, the door held wide for each woman to pass. When it's Faye's turn, she pushes herself away from the bed and the strength goes from her legs. Verona has to swoop in to catch her.

'Is she all right?' Michael asks, clutching and unclutching his hands in a nervous gesture as he hovers by the door.

'I feel dizzy.' Faye leans against Verona. She is trembling.

'Let's get you to the bathroom,' Verona says calmly, supporting the woman's weight.

But Faye is reluctant. 'The baby,' she murmurs. Fear pulses through the sudden grip of her hand on Verona's arm. But there is nothing for it.

'You can't make it alone. It will just be for a moment,' she reassures. 'Don't worry – I'll keep an eye on her.'

And so they shuffle across the landing, and Verona tries to hide her alarm at the run of blood down Faye's legs, at the shocking amount of it still flowing from her. The placenta has been placed in a plastic bag inside the bathroom door, and, once again, Verona worries that it has only partially come away; that, in the darkness of the uterus, shreds of it remain like an open wound that will not heal.

'A bath is what you need,' she declares in a brisk no-nonsense voice, but Faye hardly responds. She sits on the toilet, hunched over, her hair swinging forward in ratty strings matted with dried sweat.

Verona runs the taps, puts in the plug, then returns to the room, stopping short at the door. The child is in his arms. Michael sways from side to side, a slow-motion rocking.

'Michael?' Verona says carefully. 'Give her to me.'

He turns and looks back at her, and she notes with a start that there are tears in his eyes, an expression of pure joy on his face.

'She's so tiny,' he exclaims, and Verona feels the beat of alarm pounding in her chest.

'Michael,' she says again, stern this time.

'It's going to be all right now,' he murmurs. 'All the

mistakes we've made in the past – this changes everything.' He stares at the baby with wonder and awe. 'The past is clean now. All of it – washed away.'

Verona walks quickly to him, reaches for the baby. There's an instance of resistance before he relents and allows the child to be taken from his arms. He laughs with embarrassment, wiping at his eyes with the backs of his hands.

'I can't believe I'm getting this sentimental,' he says. 'What would Min think of me?'

'Min would be ashamed of you!' she hisses, and the smile falls from his face. 'Look at what you've done! What you've forced on that woman – the risks taken! You're not a fool, Michael, surely even you must realize that the longer this goes on, the more serious the consequences?'

'You don't understand –'

'No, you are the one who doesn't understand.' Her voice drops. 'She's sick – can't you see that? We need to get her to a hospital.'

'No.'

'She's still bleeding. I think it's infected.'

He shakes his head. 'She'll be fine in a day or two.'

'And if she should die? What then? This child will have lost her mother – do you want that on your conscience?'

He shakes his head, refusing to accept what she's saying. 'That's not going to happen.'

'And what about the baby?'

He frowns. 'What about her?'

'She should have had a Vitamin K injection by now. And there are vaccinations –'

'She can get them later.'

'Look at her. Look at the colour of her skin.'

He peers at the child. 'What is it? Jaundice?'

'Maybe. Or maybe it's a symptom of something else – something serious. I don't know, Michael – I'm not a paediatrician. We need to get them to a hospital –'

'Would you stop saying that!' he snarls, scratching quickly at his scalp, his jaw tightening.

She feels the simmering fury inside him and remembers once again the violence of his assault on her, the throbbing in her head a very real reminder.

She draws back but only a little. 'Even if it is jaundice, this child needs sunlight. If you're not going to let us out, then you'll have to take that plywood off the window – let the light come through the glass.'

He looks at her, eyes narrowed, thinks about that for a moment. But she stands her ground, and a few minutes later he unscrews the bolts and takes down the plywood. Thin sunlight falls on to the bed filtered through grimy panes.

Verona holds the baby close to her chest, watching him. From the bathroom comes the sound of water draining.

Michael pauses at the top of the stairs, looks back at her.

'You don't understand, V. You don't know all we've been through – Faye and me – the thing we did. This is the only way to make things right. Don't you see? This was meant to happen.'

And then he beams at her with that same calm and saintly look, and it frightens her more than his fury.

The hours pass slowly. He unlocks the door to bring them trays of food – beans on toast, soup, scrambled eggs;

nursery food, like they're invalids. Faye grows weaker as the day stretches, and by evening Verona has to half carry her across the landing. The bleeding continues, and when she examines the wound Verona is alarmed at how livid it appears: the tear is clearly infected. She treats it with an antiseptic gel that she finds in the bathroom cabinet, but knows it is not enough. And when she pleads with Michael to heed her warning and send for a doctor, he scowls at her, dumping the tray on the dresser, and withdrawing from the room without a word.

The baby cries for hours. Even when she's feeding, she bats at the breast with her little fists, her mouth emitting angry frustrated sounds.

'It's like there's nothing there,' Faye says, her voice containing an exhausted fretful note. 'I've no milk for her. I've nothing left.' And she gives in to a jagged weeping, her head sinking back into the pillows.

Verona paces the floor with the baby held against her, softly crooning songs from her childhood she thought she'd forgotten, but that have been dredged up from memory. After a while, the baby sleeps.

'You have to go to the pharmacy,' Verona tells Michael when he brings the morning tray. 'We need formula for the baby.' Her eyes flicker towards Faye, who lies heavy-lidded, wrung out, barely present. 'Her milk's drying up.'

He catches the note of deep concern in her voice, and, for the first time since this started, Verona glimpses real fear in his eyes. He takes a step towards the bed and reaches forward to touch Faye's brow, but her eyes fly open and she shrinks from him, back deeper into the pillows. He drops his hand and leaves the room.

Moments later, Verona hears the front door close, and her heart quickens, realizing that this is their chance.

She tries the door but it remains locked. Instead, she flies to the window and peers down; her view is of the back garden. The nearest house is a distance away, but there are voices on the street. She can hear them: the shouts and cries of the kids out there playing. She bangs hard on the window with the heel of her hand. The noise sets the baby off, but still she continues.

'Help! HELP! Somebody help us, please!'

For a good ten, twenty minutes, she keeps this up. Downstairs in the kitchen, the dog is barking madly, alarmed by their cries. But nobody comes into view, and soon the voices of the kids fade, then disappear altogether.

Faye looks up at her, pale faced and frightened. Her lips have grown dry and chapped, and there are purple daubs beneath her eyes. The very sight of her sets off a new alarm in Verona's chest.

'There must be a way out,' she says, determined, and, hastening to the bedroom door, she sinks to her knees and stares through the keyhole, darkened by the presence of the key itself. If she could just push it out! Her eyes sweep the room, landing on the chest of drawers. There's a notebook in the bottom drawer, and a pen. She grabs them both, then opens the journal to a blank page and rips it out, before sliding the page beneath the door, and carefully, carefully feeding the biro through the lock. It's difficult work, teasing the key out on the other side, requiring delicacy. There is the risk that the key will fall but miss the paper and she won't be able to reach it. Verona's knees ache, and she feels the blurring of her vision as she peers through the tiny hole, trying to calculate how much longer she has before he returns. The panic grows inside her, causing her to jab too hard with the pen. It snaps in her hand, and she stares at the broken biro, a cry of frustration rising from her throat, as she turns and sinks against the door.

She's bone-tired; her body aches and she needs to wash, to change her clothes. With her back to the door, she feels the sinking of all her hopes. It comes to her that she might never escape from here. And, in that moment, she hears voices. Faint at first, but, as she turns her head and focuses, they rise in pitch. Voices on the street outside. Adults talking. She can't hear what they are saying, but she knows that they are close. Perhaps on the doorstep. This is her chance.

'Make some noise,' she says urgently, clambering across the room to the window.

Faye stirs in the bed, and Verona snaps at her: 'Wake the baby up, quickly! We need her to start crying.'

Verona slams her fists against the window, banging so hard, she's sure the glass will break. Downstairs, the dog starts up again, and in the bedroom the baby bawls, frightened awake by the noise, by her mother pinching her. The house fills with clamour.

It must be enough, thinks Verona. Surely, someone will hear us. Surely now, someone will come.

25

Michael

'How bad is the infection?' the pharmacist asks. A tall narrow woman wearing glasses with thick purple frames, she has come out from behind the partition that separates the shop from the dispensary, and quizzes him with an air of deep scepticism.

'What are her symptoms?' she enquires, and he mumbles something about a temperature, a fever, loss of appetite, the drying up of her milk.

'And has she seen a doctor?'

'No. Not yet.'

'But why not? It sounds severe enough to warrant a visit.'

'She doesn't want the doctor. She just wants to rest.'

'But surely you could arrange a house call. What did the hospital say?'

'I haven't contacted them yet.'

Beside her, the girl behind the counter pauses in her work. She's been bagging the items she's found for him – milk formula, bottles, teats, sterilizing equipment – but now she stops, her interest caught by the sharp tone the conversation has taken.

'What about the district nurse?' the pharmacist persists.

'No.'

'No? But how old is the baby, did you say? Two days old? Three?'

'Umm, yes.'

'And the district nurse hasn't visited yet?' She sounds incredulous.

'What hospital was your child born in?' she barks, and he lies and says the Rotunda, then watches while she turns and steps back into the dispensary, begins tapping on the keyboard of her computer, lifts the receiver of the phone and punches in a number.

'Wait. What are you doing?' he asks.

The girl behind the counter stares at him with round eyes.

'What is your wife's name?' the pharmacist asks, then, alerted by a voice at the other end of the line, speaks into the receiver: 'Yes, hello? I'm calling from McAuliffe's Pharmacy in Monkstown. We have a customer here whose partner and newborn child were recently discharged from your care –'

'No, wait –' Michael protests.

'And they still haven't received a visit from the district nurse.'

'Please don't do this,' Michael says in a rising voice.

'What is your wife's name?' the pharmacist asks, addressing him with her stern gaze.

'No, look, I don't want this. I didn't ask you to do this.'

She frowns. 'If you tell me her name, I can get the nurse to call –'

'No! That's not what I want!' he cries, suddenly enraged. The girl takes a step back, exchanges a glance with the

316

pharmacist. 'If I wanted to call the hospital, I could do it myself. Jesus!'

'Sir, if you'd just calm down for a moment, we can –'

'Oh, forget it!' he shouts, then hurries out of the door, leaving the formula milk, the bottles and teats, all of it behind on the counter.

His hands are shaking as he marches back up the hill, furiously continuing the argument with the pharmacist in his head. He passes two older women walking a dog, sipping from KeepCups in gaps in the conversation, and, when he passes, one of them tugs the other one by the elbow, pulling her out of his path. He feels their glances at him and only then does he realize that he's been speaking aloud, cursing and swearing with spitting fury as he powers forward.

He shouldn't have listened to Verona. He shouldn't have left the house. It was all a ploy to try to trap him. She must have known there'd be questions asked at the pharmacy. She must have known they'd have poked their noses in, sniffing about for damning information. Even now, that pharmacist is probably on the phone to the guards, alerting them to his behaviour, voicing her suspicions, furnishing them with his description and the direction he'd gone in.

He hastens towards home, pulling his hood up over his head to avoid recognition. The feeling is back in his arms again – the weight of the infant, the chilling cast of stillness to his face. Michael had thought the feeling would be vanquished once the baby had arrived, once he had held her in his arms, but now he begins to understand that it will never truly go away. That some part of him will always have to carry that dead child around with him.

He turns on to the street and straight away sees a white patrol car marked with a fluorescent yellow band parked outside his house. He slows his step, but he's already been spotted. The driver's door opens and a female officer gets out. She's small for a guard, blonde hair scraped back into a ratty ponytail. The stab vest over her uniform lends her stature, makes her seem more authoritative somehow. Seeing him hesitating on the path, she addresses him: 'Are you the occupant of this house?' She inclines her head towards St Jude's, a curt flick of her chin.

His heart gallops. 'Yes?'

Quickly consulting her notebook, she says: 'Michael Jameson, is it?'

He nods, trying to quell the fear that comes with the uprush of thoughts: that the pharmacist has reported him, that Faye and Verona have somehow made their escape. And then another thought: high up in the Wicklow hills, the discovery of a bicycle thrown into a ditch, and, further in through the thicket, in a deeply quiet corner of the forest, another grim discovery . . .

She regards him with a humourless expression. 'You probably know why I'm here.'

His hands tingle, nerves stirring in his stomach, and he feels his body tense and grow still. Somewhere, in the back of his mind, these past couple of days, he's been waiting for this. The knock on the door. Behind all his busy preparations, his plans, his watchfulness, it has lingered in the background. The knowledge that eventually it would all unravel.

The guard's pale eyes regard him candidly, and he wonders how they found him? What clues had they discovered that traced back to him? Was it the little white van he drove behind Ed, following at a distance, his nerves jumping, as the road climbed and curled, waiting for the right moment? The wheel clipped at the turn, the bike flying into the hedgerow? By the time Michael had circled back and pulled to a halt, the front wheel of the bike was still spinning, Ed on his knees beside it, blinking in confusion. He'd barely had time to take off his helmet and look up before Michael was on him. There was a single split-second of recognition, and then came the clunk of the tyre iron across the side of his head, the dull weight of the body as he hauled it back into the forest, heaving until the sweat was pumping from his body, all his muscles screaming. A hasty effort made to hide the crime with leaves and branches, before returning to see to the bike.

The white van was parked at the side of the road for those minutes. What vehicles may have passed in the interim? Who knows whether someone spotted it there, the engine still humming, and wondered . . .

Michael's mouth feels tacky as he says: 'Sorry, I don't –'

'Your appointments?'

Confusion momentarily clouds his thoughts until she adds: 'With your psychiatrist?' sighing in a way that says she's got better things to do than go chasing down offenders like him who break court orders.

His heart soars. 'Oh, right!' He can't help it – a grin breaks out on his face.

'You are aware that attending your therapy sessions is a condition of your release?'

'No, of course. Yes.' Oh, the relief! The reprieve!

'It looks like you've missed a fair few, Michael. Says here, it's been months.'

'I've meant to go, it's just I've been feeling so much better lately. And things have been busy here . . . My aunt died recently –'

'These sessions are not optional. They're mandated by the court. And for your own benefit.'

'Of course. I'm so sorry. I'll make an appointment, I swear.'

'See that you do. Because next time we won't be having a cosy chat about it – we'll be taking you in. You do understand that, don't you, Michael?'

'Of course. Yes. Thank you, officer.'

He's still grinning like a fool while she looks up at the house behind him, frowning. 'What is that?'

He hears it now: the cry of the baby, the distant banging from deep within the house, the barking dog.

'Builders,' he explains, his voice so wooden it belies the effort this is taking out of him. 'They do make a racket.'

The flies are back again, crawling down his arms, swarming about his wrists. He can feel them flickering up his neck, buzzing in his ears. He forces a calmness he doesn't feel and says: 'Well, officer, I'd best be getting on. And I promise to follow up about my appointments.'

He watches the little swish of her ponytail as she gets back into the squad car and draws the safety belt across her chest. With fumbling hands, he gets the key in the lock, but he can't resist looking back. She's still sitting there, the mouthpiece of the radio held in her hand, her eyes fixed on him, her mouth moving – but the words she speaks he cannot fathom.

He closes the door behind him, his heart pounding, his skin prickling, and then takes the stairs two at a time, works the lock quickly, his blood pulsing with fear and rage. He bursts into the room, and gives Faye a blow that knocks her off her feet and sends her flying.

26

Faye

It feels like falling. A tumbling into darkness, down to the ocean floor. I drift in and out, surfacing only to feel the blow again, the memory of his violence rearing up and crashing over me like a wave, sending me to the bottom of the sea. I'm not sure how long I spend down there, but, when I wake, it's with a dizzying sense of dislocation, the certain feeling that something is wrong. My bones hurt and there's a tug deep inside me – the painful pull of muscles retracting. Through the darkness, I feel fingers flickering over me, plucking ineffectually at my clothes, someone's breath hot against my face.

'Get up,' the voice says. 'You must get up.'

The room is lit by an overhead light – a swinging bulb that hurts my eyes when I look at it. But then a face comes into view: Verona's eyes are wild as she leans over me.

'Get up,' she says again, urgency in her voice.

My heart is beating quickly now. Alive with panic, I haul myself up, stare frantically around the room – at the bedclothes that have fallen to the floor, the closed door, the empty bassinet. The breath catches in my throat.

The mounting anguish I have felt over the past couple

of days rises to a peak of terror as Verona's words shake me. 'He's taken her,' she says. 'She's gone.'

We hammer on the door, both of us shouting, screaming. I pull at the door handle, shaking and rattling the wood in the frame with a rising frustration.

'It's no use – it's locked fast,' Verona says.

'The window.'

She tries it, but it's been nailed shut. She bangs and shakes it in the frame. Outside, night has fallen, a cold wind whipping against the glass, rain lashing the pavements below. Distant sounds of traffic on the main road reach us but no voices; with the weather threatening to tip over into a storm, the street is deserted. No one hears us. No one comes.

'If he hurts her,' I begin, but Verona snaps back quickly: 'That's not going to happen.'

She elbows the window hard and a snaking crack appears in the glass, but, when she strikes it again, the glass holds.

The room is almost bare, stripped back – there's not even a chair or a plant pot to hurl at it. The bassinet is made of flimsy plastic wicker, the walls are void of pictures and mirrors, even the tray has been removed. The bed and the heavy bureau are the only solid pieces of furniture.

My eyes fall on the bureau.

I pull the top drawer out, dump the clothes on to the bed. The wood is old and porous with woodworm, but it has heft, which is what's required. Verona takes it from me – despite the fractious energy brought about by my panic, the effort of lifting the drawer has left me weak and shaking. It's as if my muscles have wasted.

She swings it once against the window and the crack lengthens across the pane. A second swing breaks it, a third pops the glass from the frame. A cold wind gusts through the room, and Verona leans from the window, her hands on the jagged edges of the frame, opens her mouth and bawls.

It seems to take forever, and Verona is almost hoarse when a light goes on in the house opposite, the pale oval of a face appearing in the window. Verona gestures madly, and moments later a man's voice reaches up to us from behind the fence of the garden down below.

'Are you all right up there?' he asks.

'Call the guards! Quickly!' Verona yells, panic sounding in her voice.

The man turns, and we hear him on the phone, the raised intonation – a jittery excitement in his voice – and I feel the panic of my own prayers running through me in a continuous stream: *Please keep her safe, please keep her safe* . . .

Verona turns and looks back at me, and I realize that I am groaning. There's a pain deep inside me that feels like a sharp emptiness, as if my innards have been scoured with the blade of a metal tool. I just want my baby back – a wanting so great it consumes me.

The minutes stretch, the wait agonizing.

'Hang on,' Verona tells me, her face puckering with concern. 'It won't be long now.'

Eventually, they come.

Blue lights flashing in the distance, the screech of

brakes, the loud crack and splinter of wood as the front door crashes open, footsteps thundering on the stairs, and then, at last, the door is open and we are free.

The silence that has gripped this house for all the long hours of our captivity is shattered, and the noise that fills it feels overwhelming: the clamour of voices, the sudden static from police radios, uniformed officers moving quickly through the rooms, boots pounding over the floorboards, and up and down the stairs. Initial statements are taken – our accounts laced with panic – and then one of the guards steps out on to the landing and I can hear the urgency in his voice as he speaks quickly into his radio.

More cars arrive, more voices, the rooms downstairs filling with movement, activity.

I feel slightly delirious as a female guard puts a mug of warm tea into my hands, tells me: 'Get that into you, love. It'll help with the shock.' Someone else has put a blanket around my shoulders. Through the open door of the bedroom, I can feel the sharp draught coming up the stairs and see the flash of blue lights reflected on the landing wall. And then a man appears in the doorway, tall and stocky, a brown leather jacket open to reveal a grey shirt, the buttons straining over his belly. He nods to the guard who's with us and then flashes his badge. 'Detective Inspector Derek Trimble. This is Garda Lisa Hanley.' She's small and thin with an angular face and dirty-blonde hair scraped back into a ponytail.

'Which one of you is the mother?' he asks, and I tell him I am, my voice emerging in a croak.

'Grand so. Verona? Would you mind going with Garda Hanley here and answering a few questions for her?'

Verona shoots me a glance loaded with concern, and Trimble sees it. 'Just to get a few details. It won't take long.'

Verona reaches out and squeezes my wrist, then gets to her feet and follows the female officer out of the room.

Trimble's jacket creaks as he sits down on the bed. There's a distance of a few feet between us, but I can still catch the muskiness of his aftershave mingling with other smells: coffee, cigarettes – an avuncular smell.

His voice softens. 'How're you doing there, Faye?' His kindness and concern almost have me falling into his arms.

'You have to find her,' I say. 'My baby – you have to find her.'

'All right,' he tells me, calm, assured, but with a gravity to his voice. 'We've put out a call to despatch, we're setting up roadblocks, and we've cars out looking for them now.'

'You've got to find her,' I say again, a tremble in my voice.

'We've issued a description,' he tells me, then nods to his colleague out in the hall. 'Garda Hanley spoke to Michael – she was here earlier today. We know who he is, what he looks like. We've got eyes on the roads now, checking for him. We'll find him.'

I can see across the hall to where Verona stands with her arms crossed, murmuring her answers to the questions put to her. Just behind her, the bathroom door lies open, and I watch as Garda Hanley peers inside.

DI Trimble adjusts his weight on the bed next to me, his leather jacket creaking.

'How long have you been here, Faye?' he asks. He has small eyes that are set close together, pock marks on his cheeks and along his jaw. His nose is bulbous and darker than the rest of his face. A drinker's nose.

'A couple of days, I think. Everything has been such a blur. There was a board up over the window – we couldn't tell what time of the day or night it was.' I think furiously, trying to remember. 'The 31st of December was my due date. I was at home in the afternoon, asleep, when Michael came to the house. He said there'd been an accident, that Ed was hurt.'

'Ed?'

'My husband. Michael said he'd take me to him. But then he brought me back here, and I realized it was all lies. Just a way to trap me here.'

'But why would he do that?'

For a fleeting moment, his air of avuncular bonhomie is clouded by a tightening of his features, his eyes sharpening in their gaze.

'Because he's sick, disturbed,' I tell him, taken by a new urgency. 'My husband, Ed – I think Michael did something to him. I think he hurt him.'

'All right, slow down –'

'No, you don't understand! Michael is dangerous! He wanted Ed out of the way, and when he never came home –'

'Hang on, just slow down and start at the beginning.'

His look is steady, even a little stern.

And so I retrace the last couple of days, starting with the moment I awoke to a pounding on my door. It is so strange, describing that moment, because it feels so distant. I can hardly imagine returning to my bedroom, my home, the life I had lived. Everything has changed. I explain how Michael tricked me into coming here, how he trapped me and then Verona in the house, but, when I reach the part about the birth, I have to stop, too traumatized to relive it.

Behind him, in the hall, I catch a glimpse of the other officer hunkered down on the bathroom floor. When she straightens up, I see her holding up a bag and sealing it – evidence, I think.

'When did you last speak to your husband?' Trimble asks, drawing my attention back into the room.

'It was that morning, before he went off for a cycle. Later that day, he sent me a photograph from up above Enniskerry – a view of Dublin Bay from the mountains. That was the last time I heard from him.'

'Have you tried calling him?'

I shake my head. 'I couldn't. I left my phone at home, and Michael broke Verona's.'

He takes out his own phone and I call out Ed's number. He puts the phone to his ear and listens, then shakes his head.

'Right. Just give me a moment, pet,' he says kindly, then gets up and lumbers out of the room.

I can see him, just beyond the doorway, exchanging words with Garda Hanley. She frowns and shakes her head, then offers DI Trimble the file she's been carrying under her arm. They speak some more, and she makes a hurried phone call; and there's urgency in it now as he opens the file, flicks through it, and then his eyes rise and meet mine.

My heart is beating hard in my chest now. When Trimble steps back into the room, I say: 'Your colleague in the hall . . . You said she came to see Michael earlier today. Why?'

He frowns slightly. 'Michael had broken some of the conditions of his release.'

'His release?' My voice shakes.

'Yes. He was released from detention a year ago but he was mandated to attend monthly meetings with a psychiatrist, which he has failed to do.' He sees the doubt in my eyes, and adds: 'You said it yourself – he's not well, disturbed.'

'What did he do?' I ask. 'To be put away like that?'

'He assaulted an elderly man. His stepfather.'

'Badly?'

'Bad enough. Put him in hospital for a spell.'

Something ugly has entered the space between us. The room is suddenly too clammy, too small.

My mind scrabbles over all this information.

'He wouldn't hurt the baby,' I say, quietly insistent. 'Whatever else he might do, I know he couldn't bring himself to do that.' Even as I say the words, I know it's not true. The injured stepfather, the librarian he attacked all those years ago – this history of violence creeps into the room with us, rubbing against the walls. Trimble's scepticism fills the silence. And then I remember how Michael had turned on me, how his blow had sent me crashing backwards – the suddenness of his aggression, his fury.

'He had some crazy idea that he could steal us,' I tell him, 'me and the baby. That he could steal us and make us a family of his own.'

Trimble exhales. 'Well,' he says, 'he does appear to feel a special affinity with you and the child.' I can tell he's saying this to be kind. Underneath these words, his doubt remains. 'How long has it been since he left with her?'

'I don't know. A couple of hours. Maybe more. I was asleep, you see. I didn't wake. She didn't cry out –'

'All right, that's okay,' he says gently. My voice has risen on a fresh arc of panic. 'And have you any idea where he might have gone?'

'No. I don't know. I can't think.'

'Any place he might regularly visit – a friend, perhaps? A family member.'

'There's his mother's house in Wexford. But I can't think he'd go there. They didn't get along.'

'In the past, might there have been somewhere special to him – somewhere he'd consider a safe place?'

'This was always his safe place. This house.'

'Try to think, Faye. If there's anywhere that might come to mind.'

I shake my head. 'I don't know. We really didn't know each other very well – not any more.'

'We found his van parked out the back,' Trimble tells me. 'Does he have access to any other vehicle?'

'Not that I know of.'

'It's likely he's on foot so. But I'm taking it that he hasn't just taken her out for a stroll around the neighbourhood to give you a bit of a break,' he says drily. He nods to the door, the padlock hanging off it.

'She'll be hungry,' I tell him. 'It's been hours since she's fed. And it's so cold outside. I don't even know if he's wrapped her in a blanket.'

A rush of sudden pain makes me lean forward. My breasts ache, swollen with milk.

He puts his arm around me, and I feel the firmness of his grip trying to hold me together.

'You need to see a doctor, pet,' he tells me. 'You're burning up.'

But I shake my head furiously. 'I can't. Not until I have her back. Not until I know she's safe.'

At the door, Garda Hanley appears, cold-eyed. She signals to Trimble, and once again he leaves the room. She speaks to him, her voice low, and he nods and brings a hand to his forehead, rubs it thoughtfully. When he comes back to me, his manner is grave and I steel myself for what's coming.

'A cyclist was found early yesterday, in the woods out past Enniskerry,' he tells me solemnly. 'He was taken to Vincent's. No ID on him, but we think there's a possibility he might be your husband.'

'Is he alive?' I ask, my throat made tight, constricted by the words, by the awful possibility.

'Yes,' Trimble says, but his frown semaphores the seriousness of his condition.

'How bad is he?'

'It's serious. He's unconscious, but that's about all I can tell you.'

'I want to see him.'

'All in good time —'

'I want to see my husband!'

'You'll need some medical assistance yourself first.' And, just as he says it, there's a commotion on the stairs, a flash of bright yellow on the landing, the high-vis jackets of the paramedics; one of them comes into the room, while the other turns into the bathroom to tend to Verona.

'Faye?' the paramedic, a man with a long kindly face, says, as he puts down his bag and hunkers down in front of me. 'My name's Ian. I'm going to examine you – is that okay?'

'Yes.'

Ian turns to Trimble and asks him to wait in the hall.

'One last thing,' Trimble says to me before he leaves. 'Cast your mind back and if there's anything you can remember – a place he might have mentioned he liked going, somewhere he felt safe, or somewhere that might have held a certain meaning for him. Somewhere nostalgic, somewhere special.'

'Let's give us some room to do my job, eh?' Ian says.

And, just as Trimble turns to go, a thought occurs to me. The blurred memory of a conversation. It's nothing more than a hunch, a fragment of intuition, and yet it pulls at me now with such power that there's a note of urgency in my voice as I call: 'Inspector?'

He looks back at me.

'I think I know where he might have gone.'

27

Michael

He holds her against his body in a tight grip. Not tight enough to provoke a burst of jagged wailing, but sufficient to keep her close, protected, safe. His jacket is zipped up over her, and he hopes that it's enough to stave off the elements, keep her dry and warm. If he'd had more time to think, he'd have bundled her up in a blanket, tried to fashion some sort of sling to hold her more securely against his chest. But there wasn't time. He just left the house, holding her, with nothing except his coat, his keys, the wallet in his pocket.

Trudging uphill with the wind in his face, he reaches York Road, the rain falling in sheets. Traffic is building, cars slowing before the junction where water is pooling over a blocked drain, buses queuing in a corridor, cyclists squeezing through the narrow gap. All around him, there is an air of impatience, a low hum of barely suppressed rage. A woman at a bus stop swears at a cyclist who skims too close to her. There is such aggression in the world. Michael can take no more of it.

He holds the baby tightly against him. Above the noise of the engines, the hooting of horns, the rain in his ears, he cannot hear her cry. Every few steps, he stops, opens his jacket to check on her, but she's sleeping soundly against him, the warmth of his body, the lulling move-ment, holding her fast in her dreams.

He thinks back to an October day many years ago – the surprise of an Indian summer. He had walked in the bright sunshine down to the coast and swum in the sea. Afterwards, he had lain in the grass above the West Pier, reading his book – *The Corrections* – until a shadow fell over him and he looked up and saw Faye, her hands gripping the handlebars of her bicycle, her distinctive lopsided grin. 'Hello there,' she said, and his heart had tipped towards her. That day, the sun had beat down upon them, the sea shimmering in the distance. How much younger he had felt then – how much more alive! It feels like a lifetime has passed since then, and he has grown weary, worn down, defeated. In these last few months, he has aged; the dark secret he's carried around inside him has accrued heft and weight. He knows that he can no longer carry it.

One last time, he goes over it in his mind.

April 2010

'You have to help me, Michael,' Faye had said.

He'd stood there, the whole scene hitting him hard in the solar plexus, leaving him gasping.

'Is he . . . is he dead?' Michael asked.

She didn't answer, but his heart stumbled and he took a step into the room, staring at the inert little body, the awful stillness on the floor.

'What the hell happened?'

'I didn't mean to – I just fell asleep,' Faye was saying, as he crept closer, reached out and touched the child.

'He was crying. Down the hall – I heard him crying. He wouldn't stop. She'd left him. Everyone had left. I was here on my own and he wouldn't stop crying. What was I supposed to do?'

A jag of hysteria had entered her voice, but he was too shocked to do anything about it, to tell her to calm down. His eyes were fixed on the baby, willing him to move, to make a sound, to take a breath.

'I just walked around with him in my arms,' she went on. 'I kept walking and walking, back and forth. You were gone for hours! I couldn't put him down – he just kept crying. I didn't know what to do. And I was so tired! I just thought . . . I thought that if I lie down with him for a minute, he'll calm down, he'll fall asleep. But I must have closed my eyes, I must have drifted off, and then when I woke –'

She stopped suddenly, a sharp intake of breath. Tenting her fingers over the bridge of her nose, she covered her mouth, but he heard the sob, saw the shine of tears filling her eyes.

'I must have rolled over on to him,' she gasped. 'I must have crushed him. Oh God . . .'

Her chest heaved as the emotion channelled through her body. He felt the crackle of panic in the air between them.

'I tried to get him to wake up,' she went on. 'I tried mouth-to-mouth, but nothing worked.'

'We should call an ambulance –'

'Wait!' she wailed. 'If we do that, they'll ask questions, make assumptions –'

'But if there's a chance –'

'There isn't!' Her eyes bulged and she shook her head adamantly. 'Look at him, Michael.'

She was right. It seemed like even in the few minutes Michael had been in the room, a change had come over the little body. There was a finality to his stillness now. The set of his face showed a vacancy, a void, and it occurred to Michael for the first time in his life that he understood what it was to be animated with the human spirit. Its absence in the little boy was tangible and stark.

His brain teemed with thoughts, myriad questions shooting off in all directions.

'We have to put him back,' Faye said.

He stared at her. '*What?*'

'If they come back and find him in here, they'll know I'm responsible. They'll think I killed him.'

'We have to tell them.'

She shook her head violently.

'Faye?'

'No.'

'We have to!'

'But they'll think I did it on purpose!' Her hand went to cover her mouth again, and he thought of how she'd railed against their parenting, how one of the others might have overheard, and a cool shiver of fear went through him.

He noticed that she had started quaking. Her limbs were trembling hard and her mouth was chattering noisily, something manic in her gaze. He watched as her hands – pale in the darkness – reached out for the child, but, when she lifted him, the shuddering in her body grew more violent and she put him down quickly, her hands recoiling in horror at the touch.

She backed away from the mat, scrambling backwards to the wall. There, she sat against it, as if the wall itself were holding her up, and she murmured: 'I can't do it.' Her eyes flicked up to meet his. 'You'll have to.'

'No.' He shook his head, tasted bile at the back of his throat, repulsed by her suggestion.

Her voice came at him, plaintively: 'If you love me, you'll do this.'

Outside, the night had darkened, clouds had formed in the sky, passing in front of the moon. The room had fallen into shadow. All the exertion of the hike, the spike of adrenalin from the swim, and now the horror that she had brought into their lives – he felt it as a terrible weight upon him. His energy drained away.

'Don't, Faye. Don't turn it into a test.'

'It's not a test. But I just can't do this. Don't you see? It *has* to be you.'

He looked at her. The shuddering continued, and in her small pale face her eyes looked enormous, watchful and scared. When she spoke, her voice was hoarse.

'Please, Michael.'

He put his hands to his head, massaged his temples, tried to think.

The others might be coming back from the lake now. At any moment, they could arrive, and the discovery would be made. He needed to think quickly but there was so much noise in his head.

'If you do this for me, I'll never ask anything of you again,' she told him. 'I'll do whatever it is you want.'

He looked at her.

'We'll never speak of it,' she continued. 'We'll put it out of our minds and act like it never happened. And when we get home, we'll go back to our normal lives, we'll go back to the way we were. We can have this baby together, if that is what you want. No one will ever know. No one need ever find out.'

'Do you really think we can keep something like this hidden?'

Her eyes gleamed with a sudden ferocity. 'We have to.'

All these years later, he can still feel the force of her desperation. And he remembers her promise to him: that they would have their baby together. The two things somehow conflated in his mind, so that it became a debt of atonement, a weird karmic exchange. One child substituted for another. Well, he had kept his side of the bargain, but she hadn't kept hers. It was only right he should exact his price, take what was his due. Faye owed it to him.

He hears the baby now, as the rain dashes his face. She's squirming against his chest, her little voice rising into wails of distress.

Overhead, the sodium lamps have come on, casting the rain in a murky orange light. He passes the Dart station, where commuters stream out on to the footpath, struggling with umbrellas, hunched in coats, dashing away towards homes, dinner, the evening soaps on the telly, the noise and bluster of family life, of love. Michael knows that these things will never be a part of his future. He had clung to the hope for a while, but it trickles away now like rainwater sluicing down the drains.

The baby's cries grow louder as he turns down on to the West Pier. He has always favoured this one over its sister to the east, where crowds and ice-cream trailers and coffee stands fill the promenade. It is always quieter here, especially tonight, with the weather keeping all but the most hardy dog-walkers away. Michael puts his face to the wind and walks steadily, purposefully, oblivious to the turned heads of people stopping to stare after a man singing Nina Simone numbers while a baby screams against his chest, getting drenched by the rain.

Another country, another infant. Years have passed, but the memory is fresh.

He had done as she'd asked. He had picked up the tiny body, held it close to his chest and stepped out into the corridor, checking first to make sure he was alone.

He went quickly, trying to keep his movements soft and measured, while his heart beat out of his chest, sweat leaking from every pore. The baby was a light dull weight against him. So tiny, so impossibly still. He smelled of bedsheets and milk, and the wisps of hair on his head brushed against Michael's neck in a way that was both tender and painful.

He was halfway down the corridor when he thought he heard a sound – a whoop of laughter from outside coming down from the hill. He faltered, feeling the fear creeping over his skin like flies gathering and swarming beneath his clothes. Then he was at the door, pushing it softly open: the little girl sleeping on the bed – Amalia, in white pyjamas with a sailboat motif – had one arm flung over her face. Gently he lay the baby down beside his sister. Amalia didn't move, didn't utter a sound beyond a sleepy murmur when he pulled the blanket up over the baby, covering them both.

And then he was out in the corridor, his heart skittering in his chest, rushing back inside his room, the thing done – the worst thing he had ever done in his life – the door closing shut behind him.

They didn't have to wait long. Within minutes, there were voices outside, still holding the giddiness of the mountains, the midnight swim. Golden laughter outside, and a swish of skirts along the corridor, the soft padding of feet going past their door. They held their breath for a moment, two . . . And then the screaming started.

Faye clapped her hands over her ears in a bid to shut it out, but Michael listened, transfixed, alert to every movement, every thundering footfall, every raised voice and rushed conversation. Within minutes, he was watching from the window as they clambered into Mateo's truck – Amaya clutching the baby, Efrain holding Amalia, still bundled in her blankets, Mateo behind the wheel. The others stood in the yard, staring in shock as the tyres screeched over the grit, red tail-lights flickering through the bushes, then disappearing as the truck sped off into the night.

'They must be going to the hospital,' Michael whispered.

Faye said nothing. Already, she was closing down, shutting herself off from him.

'We should go outside, talk to the others,' he went on. 'It will look odd, us staying in here like this.'

But she just curled into a ball and pulled the blanket over her. She had not stopped shivering.

So Michael went outside alone. Dumbly, he listened as the others explained in shocked voices what had happened. No one knew what to do next, how they ought to behave. For a while they just milled about, Bree and Greg washing dishes and tidying up the kitchen, trying to be useful; Adriana and Sheena sitting on picnic chairs under the parasol in the yard, talking quietly to each other, both wrapped in blankets against the chill of the night.

Michael returned to his room and lay down next to Faye, who had stopped shivering and seemed calmer now.

'We'll have to leave here,' he said quietly, sending his voice upwards towards the ceiling. They weren't touching. Neither one was able to face the other.

'Yes,' she answered, then turned over, putting her back to him.

He lay awake half the night, convinced he would not sleep. But he must have drifted off, because when he woke there was a spill of light through the window; and when he looked outside, he saw the blue truck parked under the eucalyptus tree. He hadn't heard it pull up. Mateo was out there next to Sheena, both of them smoking – she still had the blanket around her shoulders and Michael wondered if she'd been out there all night. He guessed she'd stayed up, waiting for Mateo's return.

Faye was still sleeping, so Michael slipped on his shoes, zipped up his sweatshirt and crept out of the room. The house was sombre with an unfamiliar silence. The doors to all the bedrooms were closed, and he could hear the shower running in the bathroom. The kitchen was empty, and when he went outside Mateo had disappeared and Sheena was sitting alone under the parasol. She looked up as he approached, and he saw her eyes were red-rimmed and swollen from crying. She sniffed loudly and offered him a cigarette, and he sat down opposite and lit first hers and then his.

'He died,' she said quietly, her eyes fixed on the carcass of an old car – one of the many bits of junk littering the yard.

'Jesus,' he breathed.

'Mateo got back a little while ago. He brought Amalia home. She's in bed now, poor little kid.'

Amaya and Efrain were still at the hospital, she explained. Mateo was going to go back for them later. There were procedures that needed to be followed – forms to fill in, an autopsy.

'An autopsy?' Nerves quivered in his stomach.

'To determine the cause of death,' she replied, putting the cigarette to her lips. The varnish on her nails had chipped, he noticed, and her hand shook a little. 'Although they already know, really,' she added.

'They do?' This came out sharply, and she looked at him then with an expression of regret or apology or pity, or maybe some combination of all three.

'Amalia,' she whispered.

The breath caught in his throat.

'It was a game she played sometimes with the baby,' Sheena went on. 'She'd hide him under the blankets. They'd caught her doing it a couple of times, and told her not to. But it looks like that's what happened. The blanket was over his head. He must have suffocated.'

Her voice cracked and her shoulders began working through silent sobs until she gave herself a shake, blinked back her tears and dragged deeply on her cigarette; through the silence, he heard the crackle of burning paper and tobacco.

'Of course, they're not going to say anything to her about it, poor kid,' she continued. 'But it's going to be hard. And once the police get involved –'

'Police?'

She glanced at him. 'Of course. Naturally, they'll have questions. They're going to find out that the kids had been left alone. Amaya and Efrain could get in trouble. Not that they'll care.' Her voice drifted. 'I can't imagine they'll care about much after this.'

It was still early morning, and the fog that sometimes circled the mountains had yet to lift. In that cold filtered light, all of Sheena's vitality – her golden Californian glow – had vanished. Her skin was ashen with shock and exhaustion, and for the first time he saw little lines radiating from the corners of her eyes, dark grooves running from the sides of her nose to the corners of her pale-lipped mouth. He caught a glimpse of the woman she would be in twenty, thirty years' time, and it made him tender towards her. He put out his hand to touch hers, but suddenly the sensation he'd experienced before came over him: the crawling of flies along his skin, moving beneath his clothes, probing with sticky antennae, opening and shutting their wings. He drew back his hand, clasped it with the other between his thighs, trying to get some warmth back into his fingers. He was terribly cold.

'Everything's ruined now,' Sheena said solemnly. She cast her eyes over the yard, over the house, the mountains beyond. 'Mateo says he'll drop us to the bus stop before he returns to the hospital later. There's a bus before noon that'll take us to the city.'

'He wants us to leave?'

'He says it's best if we're gone before they get back – Amaya and Efrain. They won't want us around, not now, not after this.'

Stubbing out her cigarette in the little saucer they used as an ashtray, she pulled the blanket tighter and stood up. 'Besides,' she added, looking around her now with a hardened glance, an expression that had changed to resentment, a dry disgust, as if she were sick of the place, 'we can get the hell out of this country now.'

Seeing his confusion, she added: 'Didn't you hear? The ash cloud has lifted. They've started flying again.' With an air of sad finality, she breathed: 'It's over.'

The lighthouse at the end of the opposite pier flashes through the sheeting rain. Boats in the harbour sway violently, the sea pitching against the old stone walls of the pier, high waves rising and crashing over the ends. The baby's tiny fists beat against his chest; her cries have risen to a pitch that he hasn't heard before – fury and exhaustion in a jagged wail. Nearing the end of the pier now, he stops and opens his jacket. Under the pale lamplight, he holds her up, sees the scrunched-up features, her tired red little face. Her nappy is full; its drenched weight sags in the bowl of his hand. The edge of the pier is so close. Sea spray hisses over the granite. He climbs up on to the wall, over the rocks and looks down. The sea is an angry churn, an infinite gloom. He steps towards the precipice.

*

When he told Faye that the ash cloud had dispersed, that the sky was clear, she had closed her eyes, squeezing them briefly shut, and he could tell she was feeling a wave of guilty relief. He watched her then, moving around the room, gathering up their things. There was something hasty and mechanical about her movements, a stiff jerkiness as she shoved her clothes into her backpack, folded the blanket and rolled up her mat.

'Doesn't it bother you?' he asked, before she left the room. 'About Amalia?'

He couldn't help thinking about the little girl, her whole life ahead of her, having to carry the burden of that dreadful death.

'They won't blame her,' Faye insisted. 'If anything, they'll surround her with love. You know they will.'

He wanted to believe it, but there was a bitter taste in his mouth, a nagging uncertainty. She saw it and came towards him. Putting down her bags, she put her two hands up and gently cupped his face. 'I'm sorry this has happened,' she admitted, her eyes beseeching him. 'I just want us to get away from here now, to pick up the pieces and put this whole nightmare behind us.'

'Do you think we can do that?' he asked, sceptical, for already he felt changed by it. Actually physically changed. He didn't feel right in his body, as if all his molecules were slightly out of kilter; his head hurt, and there was a whine in his ears like some kind of tinnitus.

'Yes, I'm sure of it.'

When she reached up and kissed him, he tried to feel the connection, but the same strangeness was in his lips, his mouth. He felt untethered from reality.

Faye went outside to wait with the others, while Michael gathered up his things. He was just straightening up, taking a last glance around the room, when the door opened behind him and he saw the little girl.

She was still wearing her pyjamas from the night before, white cotton spotted with sailboats. Her black hair was a corona of tangled curls, and she had put her little blue glasses back on. The plaster that customarily covered her left eye was missing. With both her parents at the hospital, no one had thought to fix a fresh plaster in place, and he saw now through her tired squint how the eye wandered out of true with the other eye. When she turned her face up to his, he couldn't be sure if she was looking at him or at some point beyond his shoulder.

'Hey there,' he said gently, hunkering down to her level.

She moved forward, and for a moment he thought she was going to go into his arms, that she had gone from room to room seeking out some kind of solace.

He wanted to hug her, to comfort her, but instead she walked past him to the window. His eyes followed and he watched her bend down and pick something up from the floor beneath the sill, hugging it quickly to her chest.

'*Mi rana*,' she said, in her husky little voice.

He saw that it was a frog made of blue cloth. Black beads for eyes. He hadn't realized it was in their room. Had no idea how it had gotten there.

She wrapped her fingers around one of its long back legs and put her thumb in her mouth, so that the toy dangled beneath her chin. Standing there, she watched him from across the room, her expression solemn, grave.

All his life, he would be haunted by that look on her face.

'Michael!'

Clutching the baby to his chest, he swings around. Looks down.

'Please, Michael. Please come down.'

They are both there, standing beneath him on the pier. Verona has one hand clutching the lapels of her jacket closed against the wind; the other arm is wrapped around Faye, supporting her, he sees now.

'Please,' Faye says, the word long and beseeching. There's so much in it, so many layers. The pale heart of her face stares up at him, and he remembers how much he once loved that face.

'She's crying, Michael. Can't you hear her? She's cold and hungry and frightened. She needs her mother. Please give her to me.'

Something had died inside him that day in the Catalan hills – not merely been broken but killed. Murdered. Everything he'd hoped his life could be collapsed. The thing inside him twisted and warped, strangling his potential, choking all his hopes.

'I know you're hurting, Michael. I know why you're upset. All these years you've carried this inside you. It's my fault. I should never have asked you to do that. And I'm sorry, I'm so sorry! But, please, don't punish me like this. Don't hurt her. Please, just give her back.'

He sees the police car, parked a little way off, an ambulance drawn up behind it. Several officers of the law stand by, some in uniform, some in plain clothes, poised to rush at him. A small clutch of people has gathered, despite the weather, the waves lashing the seawall, and he can hear the cloud of voices rising, the humming note of fear.

But there's only him and Faye now. The rest – even Verona – all fall away.

'Please, Michael,' she begs, and he hears the emotion in her voice, the tears on her face. 'She needs her mother. Don't do this. Punish me some other way, but not like this.'

The baby moves in his arms. And his arms are tired. His whole body cries out for rest. He's so tired of it all, these things he's been carrying that he can't put down.

'You made me a promise,' he tells her, his voice getting lost on the wind, but it's pointless anyway. Here, at the end of things, there are no promises left.

Faye climbs up towards him. She holds out her hands for the child. He thinks, if I could only just reach her, if I could only just take her hand. And he thinks of that night up by the milk lake, when he had stepped on to a precipice, not noticing until the last second, stones scrabbling beneath him, the sharp falling away of the rock and then Sheena grabbing hold of him and hauling him back. Her voice comes back to him now: *Saved your life.*

In the last minute before he falls, he gets a flash of clarity: the rain clears, the wind drops, and there's a little girl in pyjamas, squinting up at him through her blue glasses. As he plummets towards the waves, she raises her little hand, opening and closing it, like the blinking flash of a lighthouse, semaphoring a message of understanding, of forgiveness, waving him goodbye.

28

Faye

On an afternoon in late September, I kiss my husband goodbye and strike out for the coast.

It's colder now and autumn has clearly settled in, the hot days of summer swept into memory. I zip up my jacket and push my hands deep into the pockets for warmth, checking for the sharpness of the envelope against my palm, making sure that the letter is still there. It's early still, our meeting not for another couple of hours yet, but I need some time to think and some fresh air to clear my head. For the past week, I have been cooped up inside the house, filling bags and boxes, labelling everything, making inventories of items going into storage, separating out the things that are coming with us. The sign outside our house says SALE AGREED, and in less than a week we will have departed and someone else will be living there, another family making it their home. I feel no pull of nostalgia about that, no twinges of regret. If anything, I'm impatient to have it all behind me – I cannot wait to get out.

The moving vans will come on Monday, and, as I walk along the streets that have become familiar to me over the past couple of years, it occurs to me that I might be seeing them for the last time, for a while at least. The decision, taken in the early weeks of summer, was mutual and instinctive. A break from the violence of our recent past, a chance to try a simpler and quieter life away from anywhere that might spark bitter memories. We have taken a lease on a small house in Sligo, in the shade of Ben Bulben, a short drive from the coast. The nearest village is three kilometres away, and the house itself is flanked by fields and an old grove of hazel trees, their trunks and branches twisted and curved by the wind. Ed stumbled across it late one night when trawling online through property websites; we arranged to visit that weekend, and signed the lease the following day.

There are risks to such a move, I am well aware. And, if I wasn't, they have been spelled out to me by my mother-in-law.

'What if he gets sick again? What then?' She had taken me aside, after we'd broken the news, her face stricken and panicked. 'You'll be miles and miles from anywhere. It would take ages to get to the hospital!'

I had done my best to reassure her, although a certain anxiety still lingers.

In the early days, after Ed had been released from intensive care, so many questions about his health, about his future, remained unanswered. Back then, my main concern was keeping him alive. I recall the anxious conversations with various members of his medical team about whether his cognitive functions would ever fully recover – would he regain the memories he'd lost? In the months that have passed, the work he has done with physios and occupational therapists has helped to restore much of the range of movement in his left side, but there are still things we don't know. It remains unclear whether he'll ever be able to drive again. He gets headaches. Bad ones. And there have been times when the baby is screaming and I glance across at Ed and see his jaw tightened, his face grey with pain, and I rush to placate her, anything to hush the piercing noise of her cries.

So I do understand Regina's fear. Like me, she is haunted by dark imaginings of what might have happened had he remained concealed in the woods, had chance not brought a dog-walker through that grove of trees, the Labrador sniffing him out while he was still alive.

A move to the country: part of me is fearful of the solitude, all that time spent together alone. But there is also the overriding conviction that we need time and space to ourselves in order to heal. Not just the physical injuries but the deep emotional wounds. We need to rebuild our trust in each other, to become self-reliant once more. We need to learn how to be a family, just the three of us. And I think of Chloe, her delicate features and fair hair, her small catlike face. Nearly nine months old, she has started pulling herself up into a standing position, delighted with herself as she clings to the furniture and shuffles sideways, an awkward comical gait. It still thrills me whenever her lips draw back into a grin and she shouts with exuberant delight – like the sudden appearance of sunshine on a cold dark day. These things are to be savoured, to be treasured. I want to hold on to the memory of how special it feels whenever she beams at me out of the blue. I have learned too well how fleeting these things can be.

These past few days, I've been doing a lot of thinking about motherhood, about the lengths a mother will go to for her child. It's something that I've considered often since that night on the West Pier when I came so close to losing her, but what sparked this recent intensification of thoughts is the letter that arrived for me a week ago.

I suppose I had thought it was all behind me, that once Michael was gone it would all go away. Despite his protests to the contrary, and my own wavering suspicions, some part of me had always held him responsible for those poisonous notes that started this whole thing. So when I picked up our post and saw again the familiar blue envelope, the floral motif in one corner, I felt my heart seize with apprehension, as if Michael's cold hand was reaching out to me from the dead.

This time, there was no newspaper cutting, no garish red ink. Instead of the usual threat or attempt at intimidation, I found something quite different. A note of apology, and a request to meet. My secret correspondent of all these months wished to see me in person, so that an explanation could be offered, and forgiveness sought.

I'd sat on the bottom step of my stairs rereading the note, several times over, emotions roiling inside me as I tried to comprehend what it meant, tried to fathom the enormity of it.

'Just do it,' Ed had counselled me after I had shown him the letter, after I had explained it to him. 'No matter how painful it is. Otherwise, you'll always wonder, and this thing will never be put behind you.'

Verona had said the same when I rang her about it that night.

'What have you got to lose, Faye?'

'My sanity?' I'd half joked, and it was good to hear the warmth of her laughter coming down the line. I've missed her these past few weeks since she left for Edinburgh. A cousin living there had encouraged her to move. I understand that she too needed a change, and that she's excited to be starting again in a new city with new opportunities. A fresh start.

We talked a little on the phone about the course she was thinking of taking: 'Midwifery, of all things,' she had said wryly, and we'd joked about her baptism of fire and how I might provide a written endorsement of her skills. It felt good to be able to invoke humour when referring to what we'd been through together.

'Seriously, though,' she'd said, drawing me back to reality and the reason for my call. 'Ed is right. You should just go and meet this person. Time, once and for all, to face your demons.'

And so we have made the arrangement, my correspondent and I. We have agreed to meet in Vesey Park, but, before that, I have another place to visit.

I take the turn after Monkstown and head up York Road, and, as I wait to cross the road at Mounttown, two young clerics emerge from the church on the corner, black skirts flapping around their legs in the breeze. They nod at me in passing, and I have the thought that this day, for me, is a sort of pilgrimage. The chance to look upon the site of my pain, to confront what happened to me so that I might put it behind me. And I understand that it is both a test and a reminder: a test of my own strength and resilience, and a reminder of all that I might have lost. Ed's words come back to me. 'Face up to it,' he had advised, 'and then move on.'

And so I steel myself at the turnoff on to Fitzpatrick

Road, bracing myself, as if around the corner I might bump into the ghost of Michael himself, hunched forward, hands in his pockets, Foyle trotting loyally by his side. But there is no one there. The street is empty but for the cars parked in driveways or up along the kerb. The kids of the neighbourhood are all absent, cloistered away in school rooms, the sounds of their bikes and scooters replaced by the noise of construction. And there's another absence: St Jude's. It makes me stop in my tracks, a moment of confusion as if I have taken the wrong turnoff and arrived at a different place. But, no, I am not mistaken. The house, where so many pivotal moments of my life have happened, is gone.

Hoardings painted a dark shade of blue surround the site. There's signage nailed to it, advertising the different parties involved: architects and builders, the team of professionals supporting the project, as well as council notices and warning signs to keep out. Behind the boundary, machinery moves – the yellow arm of a digger lifts and turns. The earth reverberates with the rapid pounding of pneumatic drills. The house has gone, but the air is still full of dust, which leads me to think that the demolition happened recently. Perhaps, if I had come here a few days earlier, I might have had a chance to look one last time on the walls and windows, the patchy garden, the faded Victorian grandeur, like an old dame taking one last bow.

But what difference would it have made? I have invested such significance in returning to St Jude's, confronting it, when, really, what did I hope to achieve? For each time my thoughts have returned to this place over the past few months, I've found myself getting sucked into Michael's own dark vision of the future he'd dreamed up. I think of an alternative reality in which I might have remained locked inside that house with my baby girl, hostages to his twisted sense of family, living a life of fear while constantly plotting an escape. You hear about these things happening in the world, people disappearing, then turning up years later cloaked in some horror story of a cramped existence eked out under miserably punitive and frightening conditions. Always at the whim of some perverted madman. And, even though the thought of such a life makes me shudder with dread, I know that an even worse alternative could have been my fate.

In a way, it's cathartic, witnessing the aftermath of St Jude's' destruction. The memories of what happened to me in that house in those dark days of January bring only pain. The fear that those walls held for me, the terror they inspired – tear it down, I think with a shudder as I pull my coat tightly around me and turn away. Rip the whole thing apart. There are no ghosts here any more, no trailing regrets. No need for me to feel any kind of fear – Michael can't hurt us now. We're safe.

The leaves are falling in Vesey Park. They whisk along the path in front of me, swept over the grass by a gust of wind. At the base of the trees, a brown carpet of them is forming a mulch, while overhead a grey sky is visible between the denuded branches of trees, clouds scudding across. The park is quiet today, almost empty but for me and another woman pushing a pram slowly around the perimeter with a meditative tread. And, as I follow her, I see another figure sitting on a bench beneath the trees, ankles crossed, a point of stillness amid the flurries of leaves, the little eddying breezes. She is waiting for me.

A sudden dart of nerves makes me pause. Even though I am the one who's been invited here to receive an explanation and an apology, still I feel a hesitation, guilt trickling down my neck. But then our eyes meet, and it's too late to turn back.

The woman who rises from the bench is small and slight, wearing a neat suit made of heavy green tweed, a patterned scarf tied about her neck. Below the hem of her skirt are legs that are still shapely despite her age, her feet shod in sensible brown loafers, the leather matching that of the stout handbag by her side. Frosted blonde hair tending to grey is scraped back into a severe bun, giving her face a strained look and a slight bulge to her eyes, and as I approach she gingerly holds out her hand and I see at once the line of descent from mother to son. It's there in the crisp neatness of her attire, which calls to mind a boy I had once loved, the startling whiteness of his T-shirts, his ironed clothes. Her grip is weak and unsteady, and her eyes are made small and glazed with grief, but they still possess the same familiar pale shot of blue as they flicker uncertainly over me.

'Thank you for coming,' Nuala tells me.

I nod and release her hand. She lowers herself stiffly back down on to the bench, and I take my seat next to her.

'You must have been surprised to hear from me,' she begins nervously.

'It was a shock, to be honest. Those letters, the very sight of the envelope – I used to dread them. I still do.'

My voice is chilly, and she nods quickly, her breathing rapid. There is a skittish tension about her, and her eyes slide away from mine. They wander, taking in the grass, the low wall of the perimeter, the row of houses beyond that stands proudly above the park.

'I used to bring Michael here as a child,' she tells me. 'Whenever we were visiting Min, I'd buy him an ice cream afterwards and we'd come down here. He was such a happy little boy, scrambling around the bushes, running headlong down that path towards the green.' She points to where the ground falls away in a steep incline, a slight tremble in her hand. Just for a moment, I can see the memory that flits across her mind's eye – a blond boy whooping with delight, racing and skidding giddily over the asphalt.

'He came into the world happy,' she continues. 'The first few days when I had him in the hospital with me, he hardly cried at all. The nurses all remarked on it – the quietest baby in the ward! As he grew bigger, still he held on to that happy disposition. His first day at school, all the other little children crying or looking shy and uncertain. Not my Michael. He just skipped indoors, didn't even glance back at me. Nothing seemed to dint his optimism. Even after his father died and it was very difficult, he had his lows, but he wasn't defeated by them. His cheerfulness always bobbed back to the surface.'

There is a rehearsed quality to her speech, as if the words had been repeated over and over in her own head or perhaps spoken aloud for others. I have a glimpse of hours spent talking about the past, gallons of tea drunk while reminiscing about the son she has lost.

She smiles, but it dies quickly. 'But you never know how things will turn out, what the future will hold. Perhaps it's better that way.'

I think about my own child standing on unsteady legs, eyes widening with wonder, and feel that same snatch of fear, the reluctance to consider any pain that the future might hold for her.

'I remember the first time I heard your name,' she tells me. 'It wasn't from Michael. No, it was Min who told me all about you, this girl who had bewitched my son. That was the word she used: "bewitched".'

Down the long years, I can hear it: Min's dry, disapproving drawl, expressing her displeasure at her favourite's new girlfriend.

'It seems appropriate, for it was as if he had been cast under a spell.' Her eyes narrow, and I twitch uncomfortably beneath her stare. 'Michael had been living with Min for a few years by then, and I hardly saw him any more. He and Jeff, my husband, never really saw eye to eye. And he was always very close to Min – they were as thick as thieves. It was hard for me at times, seeing how close he was to her – closer than he was to me, his own mother! But he was happy, and that's what mattered.'

Above us, crows squawk and ruffle their feathers in the branches. A squirrel skitters across the grass – a flash of a tail before it disappears into the dense brush of the woods. And what has been a vague discomfort grows stronger and more defined as she goes on.

'I didn't see the change in him coming. Perhaps I was too distant, too removed. But, then, Min didn't see it either. Michael seemed content at university, and then happy while away on his Erasmus year – all his phone calls home were upbeat, full of his usual enthusiasm. And then he met you in Barcelona and something changed.'

The pointedness of her words, the sudden hardness in her tone, makes me look at her. Skin pink and chafed at the tip of her nose and around the edges of her nostrils suggests frequent rubbing, and there is a balled-up hankie in the curled fingers of her left hand resting in her lap. A stillness has come into her manner, though; her nerves have eased, whereas my apprehension has ratcheted up a notch.

'The ash cloud,' she says, enunciating the words with such clarity and deliberateness that it sends a warning shot across my bows.

I shift on the seat, feeling the cold of the bench travelling through my clothing to my skin. 'He told you, then? He told you what happened?'

But she gives a short bemused laugh. 'No! Not a word! Not then. Not even after he fell apart and assaulted that poor woman in the library. Not even after he was committed.' Her eyes sharpen, a certain sourness entering the tone of her voice, as if the words themselves carried a bitter taste. 'Do you know what it's like to see your child so changed – almost beyond recognition – and yet be completely bewildered as to why? I *knew* something had happened to him – I just knew it! The Michael I knew was not violent or dangerous. He would never assault anyone! Something had to have happened to throw him so wildly off balance. But of course he wouldn't tell me. Just shut me out. It was horrible, watching him close down like that, dropping out of university, retreating from the world, numbed with medication or else hopping with paranoia. He became a stranger to me.'

She describes for me, in agonizing detail, all the efforts they made over the years to reach him. The doomed attempts at getting him employment, the various induce-ments and encouragements to lead a 'normal' life, the pleadings and interventions, the research into various treatments, all the money spent on doctors and clinics, all of it with limited degrees of success but mostly failure. It had taken its toll on her, the pale oval of her face stretched with exhaustion and lined with pain.

'And then one night he showed up out of the blue, on my doorstep. I could see at once how on edge he was, completely wired. Ranting about all sorts of things, para-noid accusations – it was crazy, the things he was accusing us of. We tried to calm him down, but, when that didn't work, Jeff asked him to leave. Things got out of hand. The guards were called, and poor Jeff wound up in hospital, and Michael was sent back to the psych ward for treat-ment.' She lets out a long sigh of exhaustion. 'It was the last straw. I came up here to Dublin and I went over to Min's and demanded that she tell me what she knew. Because I knew he had told her. Whatever it was that had happened to him, she knew.' Bitterness there in her voice.

'Min told you what happened?'

She swallows hard, her lips thinning, clutching the hankie so hard her knuckles whiten in the otherwise pinkish hands. 'Yes, she told me.' Her voice quivers with emotion, and I have the sense that she's fighting to hold back tears. 'I couldn't believe it. A child dead – an infant? It was beyond belief. And that it had gone undiscovered, all these years. That my son had been so broken by the burden of it – it was too much to bear. And where were you in all of this, I wondered? Were you suffering the way he was?' She says this smoothly, almost speculatively, but beneath her tone there is vitriol.

'You might not believe this,' I tell her, struggling to keep my voice steady, 'but I never meant for any of this to happen. I thought at the time that the best way – the only way – was for us to bury it down deep. To never discuss it with anyone. To pretend that it never happened. I thought that the only way to handle it was to try to forget it. I thought that would be best for everyone.'

'For everyone, or just for you?'

I shy away from her stare, look instead at a dog circling the base of a tree, sniffing intently.

'Pretend it never happened,' she says, words laced with disgust. 'Only my son couldn't bear the guilt, whereas you were able to carry on as if your conscience were completely clear.' She lifts her hand, makes a gesture as if she's trying to bat away the emotion that threatens to overwhelm her. Shaking her head, she continues: 'I tried to just focus on Michael, on getting him better. That was the important thing. And, besides, what else could I do? It was not as if I could tell anyone what the two of you were covering up. Min had sworn me to secrecy; both of us knew that revealing the secret would only land Michael in more trouble than he was in already.' She lifts the hankie to her face, rubbing it swiftly across the raw-looking surface of her nose.

'For a while, I managed to put it from my mind. I was focused on Michael, on getting him better. But then one day, when I was feeling particularly low – Michael was seeing his psychiatrist a lot at this point – I was flitting despondently through some magazines in the waiting room, when I came across one of those social pages that feature photographs of various parties and gatherings. It's the kind of thing that normally doesn't interest me – I don't know why I flicked through it that day. But there you were, right there in the magazine, pictured with a group of your colleagues at some launch or other. You were beaming from the page, resplendent in a red dress, as if you hadn't a care in the world, while my son was grappling with his mental health, his whole life turned upside down. Something flipped inside me. My blood just boiled.'

I feel the heat of her fury, the incandescence of it as she describes how she struggled with the impotence of that rage.

'I tore the page from the magazine. Later, I tracked down an address for the company you were working for. I wanted to confront you. I even went so far as to get on a train to Dublin, thinking I would barge my way into your office and have it out with you, but somewhere along the journey I lost my nerve. I just couldn't go through with it.' She shakes her head, her fury momentarily pointed inward. 'I had put together a file of old clippings from newspapers, about the volcanic eruption and the ash cloud, all the economic damage done, the disruption it had caused. And I thought – yes! Why not! So I took one of the clippings and I scrawled that word in red marker and then I delivered it myself to your office, so that I could be sure that you got it.'

The venom in her voice, her flared eyes, is clear and

unmistakable. Her anger is barely in check. I have the sense that were it not for a lifetime of restraint, she would launch herself at me now and claw my eyes out.

'I thought that would be enough,' she admits. 'I thought that would get it out of my system. But it continued to rankle. And then, barely two days later, I opened the Sunday papers and there was another photograph of you, this time with your husband and his parents, all of you looking so smug, so bloody pleased with yourselves . . .'

The woman pushing the pram walks past, glancing in our direction. Michael's mother puts a hand to her forehead, pinches the skin at the bridge of her nose. Anger has exhausted her, and, when she speaks again, her voice has lost its power.

'I shouldn't have done it. I'm not entirely sure why I did or what I hoped to achieve. A desire to punish you, I suppose. Why should my son suffer when what you did was far, far worse? I wanted to make things even. Fair.' She shakes her head, and a tear leaks from the corner of her eye. She lets it run over her cheek, a wet track through the dusting of powdered make-up on her face. 'I dreaded the thought of him meeting you again. A class reunion, a chance meeting among friends . . . All these years, he was harbouring this wish, Min told me – this conviction – that if he could only reunite with you, it would somehow undo all the damage done. It was a fantasy, a dangerous one. I thought, somehow, if I could warn you off . . .' Her words fade, and she looks at me, fear entering her eye. 'I didn't know what would happen. You must believe me. I didn't realize that it would get so far out of hand. When I heard of what he'd done – holding you hostage, forcing you to have your baby there . . . I'm so ashamed –' She breaks off, the tears clouding her eyes, and for a few moments she gives in to them.

From overhead, a magpie swoops, gliding over the grass and landing on the low wall, where it pecks and scrapes as if trying to dislodge the mortar that glues the stones.

I think about those letters sent in anger, the fear they engendered, but, more than that, they were the spark that lit the fuse. Had I never received the note, I would not have ventured to his house that day. He may never have set eyes on me, and we might have lived our lives peacefully without ever straying across each other's paths. 'You're the one who came to me,' he'd told me. 'You're the one who came back.'

In trying to exact some kind of retribution for her son's collapse, she had unwittingly opened a Pandora's box of troubled obsession that descended into madness and ultimately claimed his life.

'So now you know the truth,' she admits, gesturing with her hands, turning them so her palms are shown – a gesture of surrender. 'Do you think you could ever forgive me?'

Tentatively, I reach out my own hand and take hers. Her fingers are cold to the touch, and I feel that coolness of their clasp as they tighten around mine. A desperate need there.

'I forgive you,' I tell her, surprised by the catch of emotion in my voice.

'I know you must hate him for what he did to you, but please try not to think badly of my son. He was in so much pain.' She repeats this last sentence, shaking her head as if she cannot really take it in. 'But he's at peace now. That's what he wanted. I realize that. He didn't want help; he just wanted to be beyond all the pain.'

We sit for a moment, wrapped in the stillness of the park. A gentle mist has sneaked up from the sea, wending its quiet way around the trees and dampening the grass, bringing a new chill to the bench. After the silence, we talk for a few moments – she asks tentatively about my baby, how she's doing, and I, in turn, ask politely after her own health, how she's coping in the aftermath of so much loss. But our conversation has become polite and subdued in its own way, with the fieriness of honesty replaced by something stilted, less compelling. And, soon enough, it peters out.

A second magpie comes in to land on the wall, and it brings a smile to her lips.

'Two for joy,' she remarks, then gathers her bag and gets to her feet. 'Seems like the cue to leave.'

After we have said our goodbyes, she heads back towards Dún Laoghaire, where she will catch the train home to Wexford. But the day is still young, and I'm not yet ready to go back to the house, to the packing. Instead I walk along De Vesci Terrace, tracking down Cumberland Street, until I am on the Old Dunleary Road. I take the footbridge over the railway tracks and descend once more on to the West Pier.

Today, the water appears calm, the greenish surface almost oily in its smoothness. Out near the Martello Tower, there are swimmers stroking through the brine. In

September, the sea still holds some of the summer's warmth. Not that I swim any more. I've had enough of water, of sea spray and foam, of the heart-stopping cold that grips as your body is submerged, the waters closing over your head.

It's never too far from my thoughts: that night on the pier, the waves crashing over the granite, the wind screaming around the harbour. DI Trimble had warned me not to make any sudden moves. 'He's jittery, so you don't want to alarm him. Easy does it, and, remember, we're right behind you.'

The sea boiled and thundered and battered at the pier, and, my God, he was edging so close to it! Wind whipped my face, rain plastering my clothes to my body. In his arms, my baby looked so tiny, so vulnerable. Even though I was weak and shaking and barely able to hold myself up, I crossed the distance towards him, powered by a more primal instinct than fear. I went forward and, with every last ounce of my strength, I hauled myself up until I reached the spot where he was standing. I could see that he was shaking, his eyes wide, even though the rain was slapping against his face. Something had broken in him – I could see that he had moved beyond fear to a different place. I put my arms out and stepped towards him. Our bodies trembled against one another's, and, between us, in a gesture that held a strange intimacy, he passed my baby back to me; and, with an instinct like a snapping synapse, I folded my body around her and turned quickly away.

That is what I tell people when they ask.

I explain how, on a different night, the sea might have been calmer, the lifeboat might had been able to brave the waves and reach him, and perhaps things might have turned out differently. In my telling, the fall is what he chose. I describe how he threw himself into the stormy sea to put an end to his mental torment, the long years of suffering.

It's almost the truth, isn't it?

When I am asked, I say that I didn't watch as he lost his footing; that I didn't witness his fall. Far easier to describe how I'd turned away, clambering back down over the rocks, Verona charging towards me. Easier to recount how I was unaware of everything else that was going on around me, all of my focus on my child's face, her breathing, her tiny beating heart.

This version of the truth is kinder. Less disconcerting. For sometimes the truth is too hard, it brings only pain. What is to be gained from knowing what really happened? How, when I put my arms out and took a step towards him, I felt him leaning into me, pressing the baby to me, and at the same time he whispered: 'Help me!' A detail omitted in every instance of my retelling. I have kept my story straight. I told no one about the terror there in his voice, terror at how far he had gone – and desperation too. A desperate desire to be saved. Through the rain and the howling wind, I saw him squinting against the elements, felt the drill of his stare, knew that he was pleading with me. 'Help me,' he said again, and reached for me.

The rocks were slippy. The sea roared behind him. I could so easily have held out my hand to him, pulled him towards me. It was in my gift to save him.

A split-second decision. A hardened impulse. One fluid movement, a lunge forward, a quick shove. He stumbled backwards, his arms flew out by his sides, a foot catching on a rock as he scuffled and slipped on the wet rocks. I caught the flash of terror in his eyes – terror and shock at my betrayal – but it lasted only a second. He plunged into the darkness and then there was just the wind blasting the pier, the sheeting rain against the seething mass of the black sea.

Sometimes I wake in the middle of the night and hear his voice hissing at me in the darkness, *Help me!*, and, blinking away the nightmare, I catch a glimpse of the whites of his eyes flashing. Straight away I'm back there on the pier that night, the elements swirling in fury around us, my whole world hanging in the balance. It takes me a minute or two to calm myself, to sip from a glass of water and wait for my heart to stop racing, to lie back under the covers and try to stop the memory from replaying over and over again. In those quiet moments before dawn, while my husband sleeps, I feel them all crowding into the room – all those faces from the past, all those ghosts. One by one, they glide past: Mateo, Efrain, the little girl with blue glasses, her one good eye staring at me blankly, Amaya with her swaying hips, the baby sleeping in her arms. And Michael as he had once been, light of heart, my blue-eyed youth. While I wait for sleep to come, or for the dawn to break, I breathe in the clean scent of him, like something fresh and newly laundered, pure. His ghost lingers in the corner of the room, and I tell myself that he can never hurt me again. That I am safe.

But, on a day like this one, when the sea mist clears and the water is a bluish green, it is easy to believe that there are no ghosts and that the past can be forgotten. With hardly any wind at all, the sea slaps gently against the pier, and the masts of the moored yachts clink, the sails folded away, redundant, hulls gently swaying. In the distance, the rocks are golden and benign in the sunlight. A seagull on the slip takes to the wing, and I follow its flight with my gaze, feeling my heart lift, as if my own hopes are soaring with the bird, up, up into a blue so bright it dazzles. There is not a cloud in the sky.

Acknowledgements

Heartfelt thanks to my agent, Jonathan Lloyd; my editors Joel Richardson and Grace Long; and the entire team at Michael Joseph. I'm incredibly grateful for all your support, careful steering and sage advice.

Unending thanks to my family and friends for your love and encouragement throughout the writing of this book, most particularly Conor, Rowan and Freya.

He just wanted a decent book to read ...

Not too much to ask, is it? It was in 1935 when Allen Lane, Managing Director of Bodley Head Publishers, stood on a platform at Exeter railway station looking for something good to read on his journey back to London. His choice was limited to popular magazines and poor-quality paperbacks – the same choice faced every day by the vast majority of readers, few of whom could afford hardbacks. Lane's disappointment and subsequent anger at the range of books generally available led him to found a company – and change the world.

'We believed in the existence in this country of a vast reading public for intelligent books at a low price, and staked everything on it'
Sir Allen Lane, 1902–1970, founder of Penguin Books

The quality paperback had arrived – and not just in bookshops. Lane was adamant that his Penguins should appear in chain stores and tobacconists, and should cost no more than a packet of cigarettes.

Reading habits (and cigarette prices) have changed since 1935, but Penguin still believes in publishing the best books for everybody to enjoy. We still believe that good design costs no more than bad design, and we still believe that quality books published passionately and responsibly make the world a better place.

So wherever you see the little bird – whether it's on a piece of prize-winning literary fiction or a celebrity autobiography, political tour de force or historical masterpiece, a serial-killer thriller, reference book, world classic or a piece of pure escapism – you can bet that it represents the very best that the genre has to offer.

Whatever you like to read – trust Penguin.